the
WARRIOR

the WARRIOR

KAY CAMDEN

THE WARRIOR
Copyright © 2017 Kay Camden

All rights reserved. No part of this book may be used, reproduced, or transmitted without written permission from the author.

This is a work of fiction. Any similarity to real people, places, or events is coincidental.

Editing by Debra Argosy and The Polished Pen
Cover art by Damonza
Book interior design & typesetting by Bookery

ISBN-10: 0-9910044-8-5 (paperback)
ISBN-13: 978-0-9910044-8-5 (paperback)
ISBN-10: 0-9910044-9-3 (eBook)
ISBN-13: 978-0-9910044-9-2 (eBook)

For more information about Kay Camden go to kaycamden.com

the ALIGNMENT SERIES

The Alignment
The Two
The Oak and the Moon
The Catalyst
The Warrior

VISIT KAYCAMDEN.COM FOR MORE

CHAPTER 1

SLOANE

MY GRANDMA TOLD me about this house. Gray-white castle stone on a green carpet of grass that goes on forever. Towers propping up the sky. The tall black fence surrounding it like a prison. And the menace infecting the air contained within that fence that settles deep in my bones as soon as I'm inside.

She and I share many things. Our name. Our magic. The secrets she's told me no one else knows. Now we share the same captivity in the same room of our enemy's house, only she was freed fifteen years ago and I'm here for the first time. Alone.

The symbol she carved in the wood floor is here like she said it would be. I take a risk and pull my amulet out of my boot to compare, side by side, the curved triangle inside the circle. My family's promise of protection. Smuggled inside this house, it's all I have here, all I had on that long drive from my mountain home to this hate-filled house in this heavy Southern heat. It's the biggest mansion I've ever seen but it's more stifling than Grandma Sloane described. She lived here so long, she must have become immune.

I slip the amulet back in my boot just in time—my captor has arrived. He crosses the room to lock the French doors that make up the wall to the outside. Grandma Sloane told me her husband removed those locks. These must be new, just for me. I hope they know to affect them with magic. I learned to break through locks when I was five.

Dillon settles on his feet in front of me, his lips moving even though he knows I can't hear. Hearing people always think the Deaf can read lips good enough to catch every word. I haven't yet figured out if I should pretend to read nothing or everything, so I do what I've done for the past few days: fake being stupid. He probably knows it's an act by now but that's his problem. He's the one who kidnapped a deaf girl.

He pulls out his phone, speaks into it, and shows it to me.

This room is the safest place for you tonight. Leave it, and I can't promise you won't be killed.

I struggle to give him the blandest look I can manage—I am my father's daughter after all, and he couldn't fake a mild expression to save all our lives. Luckily I'm my mother's too.

Dillon looks at me a long time. Deciding. Planning. Conjuring the memory of every member of my family he's killed. At least that's what I see. I don't break his gaze because I'm my brother's sister too, and he's a hard kid to beat in a stare-off. In my peripheral vision a shadow flutters underneath the closed door to the little sitting room that leads into the hall. Dillon turns his head to call out then the door opens to reveal another man coming toward us. He stops in front of me. I want to step back but I don't dare. He's uncomfortably close. He did it on purpose so I'd have to look up at him. And when I do, he smiles like I'm a piece of candy. The fist I've made has to go into my pocket so I don't ruin the 'stupid' act.

When he turns to speak to Dillon, the light plays on a scar on his cheek, from a many years' old cut running into his lip. He has a scar just like my dad's but I'm not sure why or how I know this confirms he's Jared, Dillon's brother and my dad's biggest enemy. I catch nothing of their conversation. My phone could help—two speakers would be confusing but easy enough to make sense of—but Dillon destroyed it, and I'm sure I won't be getting another anytime soon.

Then they're both facing me again. Jared is reaching for my own cheek but the look on my face must cause him to reconsider. He withdraws, makes some comment to Dillon containing the word *cat*, then he pantomimes a striking animal paw, claws bared.

If he's talking about me, he's right. As soon as I get my chance.

Jared moves to the desk to set down the notebooks and pens he's holding. I have room to breathe now that the attention's off me, and I try to control the air now freed from my lungs. That's my other act I've struggled to keep up during the long trip across the country in their car. Holding my breath keeps me from shuddering too much. Latching my arms across my chest keeps my trembling hands hidden. If they see how I'm rattled, they'll think I fear them. They don't know I've fought this my whole life. There's nothing special about them.

Dillon's speaking now, arguing maybe the way his eyes have narrowed and Jared is shaking his head. Then Jared says something that makes Dillon go, *Oh, right.* He says something else: *When ... tell her?*

Jared answers, *Tomorrow.* He steps close again—too close. My bangs are in my eyes when I look up, but I don't fix them. I don't move at all. He thinks his height is menacing, but he should know it's a disadvantage to be within range when I'm so much closer to the ground. There are so many ways I could use that height against him.

He grabs my hair so roughly I exhale, an unavoidable consequence of the counter I had to suppress. Stupid— that's me. I'm stupid, and slow, and all the things they want to believe. Not a threat at all. Knowing when to hold off is just as important as knowing when to fight.

I'm forced to turn my head as he twists the handful of my hair. It doesn't hurt like he thinks it should. Boys don't understand: if they want to pull hair and make it hurt, they need to grab just a few strands. The more they grab, the less it hurts. But the big handful does give him power over me. I'm just not ready to fight it yet.

After getting a good look at my now exposed neck, he releases me like an expectation has been cleared. He says something to Dillon who responds, *Already did.* They head to the door together, but Dillon hangs back, stalling, almost waiting for Jared to leave first. When we're alone together again, he types a message into his phone: *Food? I can send one of the staff up.*

What a hero, I sign, aware he won't understand.

He hands me his phone. I refuse like I have every time he offered. If he wanted to be able to communicate with me, he shouldn't have squashed mine. When it's clear I won't be speaking to him in any language he can understand, he gives me one last message, holding the screen in front of my face long after I've read it as if to drive it in.

You use any magic in here, we'll know.

I watch the door close behind him. Then I squat beside my grandma's carved symbol, fingering the time-smoothed edges. She survived this house. So did my dad. And so will I.

I do some stretching on the floor in front of the windows while the sun sets. The shadow from the giant oak on the lawn grows long, almost reaching the house. If only I could get through these doors I could leap onto its edge, let it carry me to its base and disappear into the night.

Now the room has become dark. Instead of turning on the main light, I flip on a lamp by the bed. With the lights still on in the hall, I'll notice the shadows under the door easier if someone comes to visit. I ransack the room for weapons, distracted by the things I find that must've belonged to Grandma Sloane. An old hairbrush with a silver handle. A box of assorted seed packets. Tons of books and antique vinyl records. In the bathroom vanity, I find an old shaving kit, which must've been her husband's. There's a razor—the flip-open kind, and still sharp. I pocket it, glad I don't have to scavenge something metal from inside the toilet tank and render the toilet unflushable.

Light shifts in the main room, so I peer around the doorframe to see I have another visitor, a woman wearing a cook's white uniform. When she sees me she beckons me over to the coffee table by the couch where she's laying out plates covered by metal lids like hotel room service. She's speaking but I can't understand a thing. Her lips move differently from what I'm used to.

I catch one question she aims right at me: *How old are you?*

I show her ten fingers, then five more.

Fifteen?

I nod.

Can you speak?

That's easy—I see that question often.

I'm deaf, I say. It's the one thing people always understand whether I speak it correctly or not. My brother Marcas says my deaf accent gives me away.

She produces a small notepad and short pencil from her pocket. *Can I get you anything else?* She gestures toward the food.

I shake my head without looking at it then reach for her notepad. *Thank you,* I write.

She gives me a smile and lets herself out of the room. I wonder if she knows about the scum she works for or what they've done to keep her from talking about what she sees in this house.

Eyeing the food, I take a seat on the couch. My mouth tingles enough to overcome my resistance. Plus, I'm not really stupid. I have no idea what's coming next for me but whatever it is will be better faced with a full belly. That's my excuse for digging in, anyway. I'm not sure what I'm eating but it certainly proves they're rich and I'm not. As if I care. Gourmet room service at home? Just weird.

It fits though, because the Moores are weird. Sick and weird. And badmouthing them in my head makes me feel not so tiny in this giant room while I try not to wonder what I'm supposed to be doing instead of sitting here idle, eating their fancy probably poisoned food.

My attention lingers on the bed where my grandma slept most of her life. After the long ride in the car, the plush cover and piled pillows tempt me worse than the food. If I could contact the wildlife outside, I could sleep. They'd warn me of any coming danger in time for me to wake and protect myself. I cross the room to check out the doors. The locks are old-fashioned and pickable—no magic required. With the right tool, I could get through it in minutes, prop open the door and call the animals for help.

That's when I notice the line of white dust on the balcony floor outside. I'm not sure the kind of magic, but I can guess: some type of boundary spell. The Moores might use different practices but our roots are the same. I'd use affected soil or ash. I don't want to know what they used.

I stack a tower of Grandma's books by the door that leads to the sitting room and hall, its corner just within range of door's swing. Beside it, I prop a hand mirror I found in the nightstand. If the physical thud of the falling tower doesn't provide enough vibration to alert me, hopefully the mirror will throw a reflection around the room for a visual alarm.

In the bathroom I wash my face. With Grandma Sloane's silver-handled brush, I work out the tangles then fasten the hair on the crown of my head in a high ponytail, leaving the rest loose against my shoulders. My lucky extra-long piece has frayed in its braid, so I untwist its silver fastener and start a new braid, trying not to think about my mom and how many times she's done this for me. I swallow hard because I can't cry. I don't want to cry. But my eyes already look red and puffy, and I'm choking and gasping and I can't stop. Something's shaking me from the inside. I have to sit down. The edge of the tub leaks cold through my leggings, which rises to meet the cold in my chest, and it's over. I can't help it.

Yes I can help it. I'm not crying in the Moore mansion. I'm going to lie down on their fluffy bed and take a nap. They won't kill me now if they need me for something tomorrow. So I lie down, trying to control the shivering and shuddering with the breathing my dad taught me. If I think about him, I won't cry. He's the one I can't fail.

It's the most comfy bed I've ever slept in and I hate them for it.

CHAPTER 2

REX

MY OPPONENT GOES limp on the mat, his hands up in surrender. I give him a few more jabs in his already bloodied nose because I can. Okay, maybe it's more like ten. The guys around us pull me off, but they don't say a thing. They know not to. Then I spot my father standing on the sidelines, and I inwardly groan.

"You know better than that," he says. "Are you trying to waste all your sparring partners?"

"Maybe I am."

He chucks a towel at me, too fast and hard to catch with anything but my face. "Clean up. We need to speak to you."

We. Well, great. That means another family meeting, more planning my every move. It'd be a lot easier if they'd just slip a set of instructions under my bedroom door each morning. Why involve me at all?

"Yes, *sir.*"

"Don't be a smartass. Dining room. Ten minutes."

I wipe down my neck and face while he crosses the training room toward the stairs. It's such a treat he's home so my life is back to the normal amount of people riding my ass. Usually I blame my family for the nonsense I deal with on a daily basis, but I remind myself they're not at fault. It's the Bevans who started all this, the Bevans who refuse to end it, and as soon as we can snuff them all out, my life will be my own.

My opponent passes beside me holding a towel against his wasted nose. The gash I opened on his forehead leaks blood down his face. He points at me. "Payback's a—"

"Unfulfilled fantasy of yours? Sorry to hear that."

My trainer clamps a hand on the guy's shoulder to steer him away. Most know not to cross me, some are still learning. It's not my problem if some guys only learn things the hard way.

After a shower I'm taking my seat at our meeting in the dining room—sixteen minutes late according to my watch but whatever. My only regret is my lukewarm plate, but I'm too hungry to tell one of the staff to heat it up. As usual everyone's watching me and as usual I ignore it. Uncle Jared shifts in his chair, impatient and starting to get pissed. But I keep on eating as if I'm the only one in the room. I'm too old to get smacked by him anymore. He had to give up that hobby when he figured out how hard I can hit back, and that I'm no longer afraid to.

"She's here," my father says.

I stop chewing my steak and look up at him. "You're so full of it."

"What'd I tell you about being a smartass?"

"Why am I eating dinner if she's here?"

He extends a hand to Uncle Jared, like he's too tired to give the orders tonight. He did just get back in town. Now that I'm paying attention, he's got some new lines in his forehead and a crabby look on his face. Probably needs a nap.

Which reminds me to take my pill that's now overdue—I check my watch—by nineteen minutes. No wonder I'm so foggy. I fish my pill case out of my pocket and pop one in my mouth, washing it down with water.

"Because you won't be seeing her until we're ready for you to," Jared says. "You're not to step foot on the second floor."

She's here and they're going to make me wait? I've waited my whole life for this. "Okay, so you've dropped her in a room so she can take her sweet time crafting some twisted Bevan escape? That's genius material there."

For the first time, I look around the table and notice how crowded it is. Some of these people must've wandered in while I was stuffing my face because I think I would've noticed the table this full when I came in. Silverware scrapes plates behind me too. A second table also full. What's that, forty people? Fifty?

"We need to get some information out of her first," my cousin Emily says. Her face is so hardcore with intensity

I nearly drop my fork. She's one of the few who's been a friend instead of a drill sergeant, and I get a nudge of warning that if I screw this up, that's going to change. "I'm going to talk to her tomorrow to try and get it out of her easily."

Of course they'd choose her to play the good cop. She's twenty-one, old enough to be an adult who should be minded but young enough to relate to Sloane Bevan. Plus, she's a girl. Girls like to talk to girls.

"So who gets to play bad cop?" I ask.

Charlie starts to raise his hand, but Emily swats it down while giving my father a pointed look.

"You let us handle those details," my father says.

But I'm too busy looking at the thrill of the hunt in Charlie's eyes. Another cousin—second, third, who knows? A cousin's a cousin in this family. My father thinks I don't practice good sportsmanship downstairs? He's never been down there when Charlie's just warming up. I've caught Charlie's attention though, and the severe look says he's wondering why the hell I care.

Sloane Bevan is mine to take down. Not his. And just as I'm about to enlighten him, Emily pushes out and comes to sit in the empty chair next to me. "Rex."

I used to wish she was my sister, mostly because I have a crap mom, a crap dad, and a brother who's fifteen years older than me and never here. Working on his master's, working on his PhD, blah, blah, blah. Reality to Aaron: who cares? We're rich. All that work is just a waste of time. But my big brother Aaron wants to earn his own money. How noble. And repulsive.

Emily messes my hair. I elbow her away. I know people see her sweet kindergarten-teacher looks and think she's some kind of angelic creature. She's as dangerous as we all are. Maybe more because you don't expect it out of a princess.

"Just chill until we get what we need from her," she says. "It won't take long. You've waited fifteen years, what's a few more days?"

Charlie cracks his knuckles and for some reason it makes me want to stab my fork in his throat. I would if he wasn't family. He's twice my age and my body weight, but I've put down guys bigger than him. I imagine how much force it would take to fully sink the tines, how long it would take for him to bleed out once I ripped it free. I look around the table at the twenty or so faces all locked in on me. Some of them don't even live here, probably drove down just to watch the Bevan blood run. And for the millionth time I wonder why they chose me. Why I'm the one they loaded all their hope on. Isn't something like this better handled by a team?

But no. They're a bunch of superstitious dorks, and what was decided by our ancestors a thousand years ago is what we're gonna continue to go on. Wait—why am I complaining? I ache for Sloane Bevan's death. I'm the one who was chosen, who's been working my whole life toward it. It's my job—all mine—and if Charlie even looks at her before I do, I'll go for more than popping his jugular with my fork. Then we'll burn him and Sloane Bevan on the same pyre. With all the Bevans we'll pile on after them, it will burn nonstop for a year.

"Fine. I'll stay off the second floor." I'm such a solid liar, sometimes I surprise myself. "But only if you tell me what info you want out of her."

Emily surveys the crowd, gets a nod from my father and Jared. Then she leans toward me to stage a secret, never mind everyone here is already in on it. "We're going to make her write down all her family's magic. Everything they know that we don't. As soon as we're sure we have it all, you can kill her."

I return to the training room after dinner because there's no decent way to sit still when I know Sloane Bevan is contained within these walls. It's my furlough; if I want to spend it on more training, that's my business. All I want is to see what she looks like. Taunt her a little. Give her a small test, see what she can do. Too many Moores are swarming every inch of this house for me to get anywhere near her room. The people at the meeting were only a fraction of who's here. If they're as restless as I am, they hide it well—behind another excuse for a mad kickback in the ballroom upstairs. Full of old people. So, not so much 'mad' as 'boring as fuck.'

Which is why I'm downstairs alone, buried under the muted sounds of partying above me. I only flip one row of overhead lights on so the darkness creates a box around me. While I warm up in front of the mirrors, I imagine Sloane Bevan has escaped her room and wound up down here. She's lurking in the shadow like the animal she is, waiting for an opportunity to spring. But she doesn't know I know she's out there, and when she makes her move, I'm on her faster than she can counter. I have no weapons so I pin her arms with my knees. Grasp her head. Start to twist. She's clawing at me, the training-room lights reflected in her big prey eyes.

Whoa—a human-shaped spot stained blacker than the dark behind me. I spin around, high on the adrenaline and the fantasy I've just created. But then I see the glint on the chain above it—it's the stupid heavy bag. I'm such a dumbass. But hey, if the bag wants it, the bag's gonna get it.

It's almost midnight when I've reached a modicum of chill, but I've got a gaping pit instead of a stomach, so I wipe down and head to the ballroom where I can eat at the bar. I'm hours past lights-out, but they've let me slide before on special occasions. The party's dwindling but there's still staff crawling around, so I tell the first one I see to hurry up and bring me some food. Then I settle at the bar and call the bartender to pour me a whiskey. He looks uncomfortable at having to tell Rex Moore 'no' long enough to grant me an ounce of pleasure, so I put him out of his misery and order ice water instead. With all the bodies and noise in the room, I disappear, a change I welcome during these get-togethers for how exotic it feels.

Some old guy who's probably related to me leans on the bar to order a drink before saying, "Take a shower, son. You stink."

"So do you, geezer."

After a delay he laughs, and I decide not to tell him to get out of my house. He's probably some descendent of my great-granduncle who used to run this house, and then I'd have to answer to shit from every still living Moore tomorrow. It'd be a lot, but not as much as it should be. When Sloane Bevan's rabid father went kill-crazy the year my brother was born, he shot so many holes in our family tree we had to forget the meaning of extended family. Second, third, and fourth cousins became cousins, and we had to pretend our family hadn't been massacred.

My great-granduncle and his son—the two and only Martin Moores—are legends in this family, but soon my name will be larger than theirs. I didn't find Sloane Bevan, but I will kill her. And then I'm going after her psycho father. They say he's indestructible, and I'm going to prove them wrong.

I push my empty plate away and spin on the stool to take in the room behind me. That's when I see my mother snuggled up to some creep on the couch by the windows. Some creep who's not my father. The twenty pounds of food I just ate feels like it's grown arms and fingers and learned how to climb. I reach for my water and catch sight of my father instead, leaning against the piano while chatting with my uncle. He glances quickly over at me like I called out to him.

In that moment I consider looking away, going upstairs to bed to save him from having to command it. My climb up the stairs would take me past the second floor, so close to the thing that's mine that they're holding from me. So I redirect my gaze hard at my mother and that creep. My father turns his head toward them. Takes it in. Stands up. His mistake is his glance back at me, and what I read in his face is not that there's a problem over there. There's a problem sitting on my stool. A judgment he doesn't want.

A witness he'd rather snuff out than bother himself with the unsolvable crime that is my dear mother.

The only thing to do is smirk. And it's not the one I give Emily when she's just lost a battle of insults against me—the pop-pop to the gut one. It's the one that's armed. The one that cuts people.

He crosses the room so fast I brace for a blow, hoping he doesn't notice. I stifle the urge to hop to the floor to better balance my weight. Then I go for my water again to show he's no threat to me. He can go to hell.

My father watches me raise the glass to my lips, and I see his next obvious move—I'm always a step ahead. He knocks the glass out of my hand. It crashes against the floor, the slap of water and crack of glass hushing the crowd like someone hit the mute button. I smile at him so he knows I allowed that to happen. He's such a fucking asshole, and right now the whole room can see.

"I've had enough of your mouth today."

"I didn't say anything."

He grabs the front of my shirt and yanks me off the stool. Even though I allowed that too, it surprises me. He hasn't touched me for a year and nine months. I'm jarred by vivid flashes of how these situations used to go down—when I was younger, smaller, less confident. Less dangerous. And what slips out is not my doing. "But you could call Trey Bevan. She'd love to snuggle with him."

Trey Bevan is a dirty word in this house, used sparingly to preserve its emphasis. And I have totally hit the mark.

He slaps me with an open hand, like I'm a little kid. The instant heat on my cheek that collapses to pin-and-needle cold feels so good I suck in a breath to relish it. The blood inside my mouth is like candy—I really shouldn't admit that. I stare at him and point to my other cheek. "But use a fist this time. Maybe then you'll make father of the year."

His hand goes over his mouth, rubs down over his chin. Wait—what's that … regret? That's gonna ruin the game. I scramble for something worse, a remark so biting it could only lead to him shoving me against the bar so I'll be forced to 'defend myself.' My mother rises behind him—attentive because of the drama, not to come to my aid. She never has.

This game they play—worship me one day, smack me around the next—it's a manipulation that might break a weaker mind. That's probably their goal, but it will never succeed on a person who figured it out long ago. And when I've killed Sloane Bevan and her father, no Bevans will touch me. I'll take over this house and reign as I was always meant to. Like Martin Moore but more powerful. I'll be untouchable.

My father mutters something I don't hear and retreats to the doorway, avoiding my mother but not the crystal lamp on the end table. The second crash of breaking glass undoes the silence in the room like a flipped switch. It's the Moore way—confrontations begin and end with objects being broken. Chatter fills the room again. For a stupid moment I think my mother might come talk to me because her normally tight face has gone soft near the eyes. Instead, she smooths her dress and goes back to the crowd by the windows, no doubt to her boyfriend of the week. When the bartender turns his back, I swipe a bottle of rum he was about to pour and head outside, sucking on my swelling lip.

The sky is a black pitch humming with an unspent storm. Webs of lightning pulse above the woods in the distance. I check my watch against the light coming from the house. I'm really violating my schedule now but there's no one out here to order me to bed. I descend the hill toward the lake while taking a sip from the bottle. The taste is syrupy and retch-worthy. It warms me from the tongue down. I check the label to make sure I'm drinking rum and not embalming fluid. After the third pull, I fling the bottle into the lake, watch it fly end over end and split the water. I sit on the bank while the clouds pull away, only the brightest stars now visible in a sky lit by a big round moon.

If Aaron was here I could pop the cap on the bottle of words inside me. Release some pressure, get a little relief. Option two is to go inside right now and look for Emily, but she'd only try to console me, tell me it's all in my mind, force me to let it go. I need someone to talk shit to. Someone like Aaron who knows how to properly vent. There's just no one else.

I'm going to pay for being out here this late if someone catches me, but the rum warming my stomach tells me not to care about my schedule. That it's bogus and meant for breaking. I feel my great-granduncle's old watch ticking against my wrist. Now that I've noticed it, tuning it out is nearly impossible. But there's something else out here, something calmly battling for my attention. I'm at once aware of the unsteady beat of lake water lapping against the bank. And the breeze, sneaking in the neck of my shirt, slipping down my back. The drone of some new awareness tempting me to do something different for once. To make a choice someone hasn't already decided for me.

Sitting beside this lake does this to me every time. It's calling to me in a language I don't know. I recognize the sounds but not the words. Shapes of a memory, but no specifics. Like knowledge that's been erased, or overwritten, leaving a residue just recognizable enough to drive me insane. There's a ready peace to it, a stillness that's such a contrast to my days of orders and training and the jarring on-and-off thanks to the pills in my pocket.

I get up and walk west, toward the moon. The side lawn is wide open and lit by its fat white light so I stick by the house, well aware of how close I am to the room where they've locked Sloane Bevan. She's directly above me, and if I cross the lawn toward the big oak, I could turn around and view her windows, check if I can see her. But the idea is cut short as the windows beside me illuminate. I hop silently up the steps of the side porch and flatten against the house. Voices sift through the open library windows.

"It should be in the safe, Dillon." My uncle Jared.

"That's the first place everyone would look," my father replies. "It's safer here. Even if someone decides to read this, they won't see it back there."

I risk a glance. My father is replacing a book on the shelves on the far wall. I memorize its position—up three shelves, over two.

I duck away just before my father turns around, saying, "Too many people have the code to that damn safe."

"Then we change the code," says Jared.

"And make everyone suspicious?"

The room goes dark. Across the lawn, a roiling gray haze rises from the woods and advances toward the house. It's a sinister looking shape in the moonlight, like a summoned demon stalking a target. I consider moving inside, but that might look like I'm afraid and there's no way. That thing doesn't know what I could do to it.

As it nears I see the flap of a thousand little wings all moving in different directions while the swarm advances as one being. The first thing I think is bees—but no, these things are too big. It's a swarm of something—not bats, not birds … moths? They reach the edge of the porch but instead of coming toward me, the whole formation bends up the side of the house above me.

It's weird but it doesn't matter. What's hidden in that bookshelf is more important right now. I head toward the front of the house, passing the train of parked cars snaking along the front circle drive and all the way down the drive-way as far as I can see. Our house is full of this many people, and not one of them wants to hang out with me. I let myself in the front door. The foyer is dead except for the sound of the party coming from the east side of the house. The west side is dark and quiet. I slip through to the library, my eyes now adjusted so the moonlight pouring through the windows is enough to see which shelf I need. I pull the book out and slide my hand into its spot, finding a small object against the wall. It's sunk into a nook behind the shelf so I have to pull up to extract it.

In the dim light of the room it's a small glass apothecary bottle, opaque with something corked inside it. I replace the book and take the bottle to the window for better light. And that opaque substance comes alive like that swarm of insects outside. Purple rolling into black then back to purple, a slow churn of magic held captive. This is the bottle my father scored from that black witch. This is the black magic primed to destroy all Bevans.

If this bottle is uncorked, the magic will steal my chance. It will do my work and claim the destruction of the Bevans for itself, and whoever releases it will take all the credit and power that comes with it. I can't trust my family to preserve what they've promised is mine, what I've trained my whole life for. It's up to me to take it before someone else does.

I sneak up to my room and change into my multi-pocketed military pants. The bottle of black magic goes in one pocket, wrapped in a cloth for protection. In the bathroom I study myself in the mirror to the tick on my great-granduncle's watch. I smooth the shaggy hair that Emily messed at dinner. I'm not their tool anymore. Now I do things my way.

A rummage of my drawers rewards me with an electric hair clipper I use to shave my hair army-short. Clumps fall into the sink like some kind of metamorphosis is taking place. The reflection that greets me when I straighten is a person I don't know. A person no one knows. Someone once bound who's just been freed. Things are about to change in this household, things no one saw coming.

They raised me to be their soldier. Soon I will be their king.

CHAPTER 3

SLOANE

I CAN'T SLEEP IN this room. It was Grandma's room but it's too far from the trees; it doesn't breathe with them like my house in the mountains. The air is stagnant and still with a quiet I can feel in my core. It's as empty and spacious as an old European tomb, like the one where Romeo and Juliet die in that final scene.

A new awareness trickles toward me, filling in the pieces of an unused sense like a slow stream filling a pool. I know it's not the same as normal human hearing because there's a translation I must do, as I do to communicate with any animal. It gains intensity, so I get up from the bed to place my hand on the wall. They're in the walls, seeking me out.

Sent by my grandma, maybe, or I guess it's possible they came to my aid on their own.

One of them crawls from the vent in the floor and takes flight—a greater wax moth. No land animal has better hearing. People used to think that award went to the bats, but the greater wax moth has evolved to hear better than its own predator. I open my hand for it to land. Sticky legs tickle my palm as it settles in, closing its wings. It's hard not to admire prey that overcame its predator by using its predator's best weapon against it. I stroke its silky body and it opens its wings and flies toward the bed, landing on the floor to crawl under the bed skirt. I see my grandma signing, *Where's the best hiding place? Under the bed, inside the floor. Remember that, Sloane.*

I drop to my belly beside the bed and wiggle underneath, testing floor boards for movement as I push toward the middle of the bed. I find not one board but a whole section that slides away, revealing a collection of dusty jars containing ingredients for magic. If Grandma left this for me, she didn't foresee I'd be banned from using it. Or is this her way of telling me I should ignore Dillon's threat?

It's not something I can answer now with the little I know, but it can't hurt to be prepared. Sifting through the jars, I can't decide which ones would be most useful in my limited pocket space until the rosemary settles in my hand like it should be there. It has many uses to my family, but the one that springs to mind is its help in identifying an unknown threat. Since I still don't really know what I'm supposed to do here, maybe the rosemary can point me in the right direction. Along with rosemary I take mint, for its ability to steady an unsettled mind.

I take the candles and matches out of the stash as well and slide the floor back into place. With the four candles in position—north, south, east, and west—I light them and sit in the middle. Then I dump the rosemary out on the floor and divide it four ways with a finger. *No magic*, I remind myself. This solitude is too precious after all those days on the road with those men, my constantly sweating palms, my prickly anxiety. I hate how it betrays me, how it makes me look to them. I'm not afraid, not in my conscious mind. Something deeper is on freak-out, and it's completely irrational and uncontrollable and has nothing to do with me.

My moth lands on my knee and folds its wings. Through it, I sense a movement below us. Through the floor? A sound, translated into something I can understand, and from what I can tell there's a person moving around on the floor below us. There's no immediacy though, no sense of threat. The candlelight dances, throwing tall shadows on the walls. I return to the four piles of rosemary. There has to be something I can do that technically isn't magic, something that won't alert the Moores. My moth flaps away, joining two more on the glass of the French doors.

All four candles blow out as if by an imaginary wind I feel inside my skin instead of across it. Strange, since my four piles of rosemary have also scattered. I peer around the room looking for something I missed, a falling object that could've created a gust of air. But I felt no movement of air, nothing against me. I actively calm my heart. There's no reason to panic. I reach for the matches to relight my candles when a small spot in the floor bursts into flame. Not just any spot, but Grandma Sloane's carved symbol. The flame dies to a smolder, the outline of the bent triangle consumed by a different symbol glowing orange inside its circle: a symmetrical cross, intersecting in the exact center.

Before I can recall this symbol from everything my dad taught me, I get a prod that powers the magic inside me—but it's wrong, it's not the magic I know. It's flipped somehow, unrecognizable yet still strangely accessible. I have to shut it down or the Moores will know. Dillon will return, Jared too, and do … what? I turn away from the glowing symbol and wait for my eyes to adjust to the shadow of the room. The shadow that's now animated. Alive.

I crouch—instinct when faced with a surprise attack. Is that what this is? I glance upward but the ceiling has disappeared, replaced with heavy hanging smoke—no, a cloud, seething and rolling with anger and hate so palpable its presence is almost human. It dawns on me then: what I've felt in this house isn't the lack of breath from the trees. It isn't the hollow, stagnant air of an old mansion. It's an accumulation of so much hatred it's become a power source for a certain kind of magic I hope never to use. This house stores a pocket of fuel for black magic like none I could ever imagine. It seems to be collecting here as if drawn to me.

Are the Moores sensitive to my use of any magic or just our native magic? Will they sense my use of black magic? Do they even know I've been trained in it?

I scoot on my knees toward Grandma Sloane's smoldering symbol a run a finger over its design to douse the glow. When I look up I'm captured by the image through the window: the full moon hanging high in the sky and the oak directly below it, its straight thick trunk in perfect alignment.

With my palms against the floor strewn with rosemary, I bow my head and remember what Grandma Sloane told me so many times. *When the moon aligns with the oak, a danger will come for you.* I feel a miniscule vibration in the floor that mimics human footsteps. Unhurried but determined and growing more pronounced with each beat. There's a pause, as if there were a door to be opened. I feel someone shut it then, near enough to be my door to the hall.

I spin on my knees to face the sitting room door, my finger in my boot to loop my amulet's chain and yank it free. One hand still against the floor, I feel another pause in the footsteps. The door to the room opens, sending the tower of books to the floor and the mirror spinning. Light from the sitting room spills toward me. In silhouette is a man—broad shoulders, shaved head. He regards the mess of books before he steps inside and closes the door behind him.

As I stand I raise the amulet over my head and meet his gaze. Now with the moon's light on him, I find he's not quite a man. Maybe in height and muscle but not in the face. He's young like me.

He takes another step like he owns this room, like this whole mansion is his domain. His eyes don't stray from me. Above him, the black cloud churns, gaining strength by the sick, hateful pleasure this meeting has lit in his face. My name forms on his lips, spoken so slowly I almost can't make it out.

Rex Moore, I want to say back, to name him like he's named me, like an object put in its place. I could try but I don't, not with the way he's smiling at me now. He knows what I want to do, what I can't do. I refuse to offer my deaf voice and give that gross smile any more power.

With his forward step, I move to the right, forcing him left. I want the unlocked door to my back so it's a possible escape I won't have to get through him to reach. He's in the full light of the moon now, and I see his nose has a dark line across the bridge like it's been recently broken. With his build, he'd fit perfectly into the wrestling team at my school. His battle stance is hunkering and heavy, unlike the balance I strive to achieve on my feet. Where he needs to use his weight as a weapon, I need to move—and use his weight as a weapon against him.

Another sideways step puts him into shadow, me in the moonlight. I catch a flash of teeth while he sizes me up. Along with the driving gaze it's almost animalistic, but I know better. Only humans are capable of such dark personal hate. I'm tempted to smile back at him, but I know it would appear forced. I'm not letting him force me to do anything but kill him.

His lips are moving but I can't catch a thing until he points to my amulet, and I recognize one word: *cheat*. I realize I'm glowering at him too late to smooth my face so I just let it be. And he's laughing, shaking his head, disgusted. The next words are obvious for how perfectly he directs them at me: *Bevans can't win without cheating.*

I rip the amulet over my head and toss it away. He straightens, taken aback, like his comment wasn't meant to coerce me to get rid of the amulet. He actually believes that crap, and he's surprised I took it off. Apparently he's had some misinformation about Bevans.

He strikes with snakelike speed and grizzly power. My defense is automatic, processed by the muscle-memory of a lifetime of training. I don't think it; it just happens. A higher part of me sees the dance that it is, scrutinizing every move to make them faster, more powerful, more precise. My elbow smacks cheekbone—he's not as tall as I thought he was if his face is that easy to reach. My own cheek erupts hot then cold—his retaliation I can't believe I missed coming. I duck a second blow and rise fast to crack my skull against his chin. He deflects, using my off-balance to twist my arm and spin me against his solid plank of a body.

I'm in a constrictor's grip, both arms pinned, breathing in the musk of his soap and sweat as he tightens even more. And now he's sliding a leg around one of mine, disabling all appendages but one. Struggling would only wear me out, so I wait. He'll mess up. They always claim victory too soon, and that's when I'll get him. And all the energy he's using to hold me is energy draining from him when mine is allowed a moment of rest. He tightens again, impossibly tight, but with that tiny motion his bicep has moved dangerously close to my mouth. All I need is a fraction of an inch. So I release all air from my lungs, giving him more grip and me an arm right where I want it.

I turn my head and bite with everything I have, then I rip, tasting the hot metal of blood, feeling his bellow vibrate against my back. Nearly retching from the human flesh clamped between my teeth, I release him. I've gained enough room to drive an elbow into his ribs, and I fall to the floor and scramble out of his reach.

A mutilated arm doesn't slow his pursuit. He makes no notice of the gush of blood darkening his whole arm. I get the couch between us, stopping when he does. He's panting hard now, not due to exertion but rage. I make a show of wiping his blood off my mouth. This smile isn't forced at all. He punches the arm of the couch so hard it shifts against me. A tickle runs down my cheek; I resist the urge to wipe away blood. My brow tingles with swelling setting in even though I don't remember taking a hit there. He shoves the couch, sending me a step back. Then he hunkers down and pushes it until I'm forced to move aside or be slammed into the wall.

I opt to leap on the bed instead of skirt by him; he follows me up and over. It's a game of chase now, and I'm keeping my footfalls light to not attract attention. He's not so thoughtful—I can feel the whole room quaking in reaction to his thudding. This has to stop before someone hears and comes to help. It won't be me they're helping.

In the middle of the room I switch to offense. He grazes my jaw, which would've been a knockout had I not moved in time. He adds a blow to my knee and I'm down, but I use my other leg to sweep one of his. My knee rings with pain that's hard to shut off. I shove away but not fast enough because he's got a fistful of my shirt and he's dragging me back. I let him pull me close and send an elbow into his gut and a knee between his legs.

We're both on the ground now. He's snorting from that last blow, but he hasn't released my shirt. I kick at his other arm but miss, and he somehow ends up on top of me, turning me over so my back's against the floor. The mess of blood from his arm has made everything slippery. He's too strong, and in this position I can't use his weight against him. I have no range of motion for anything. Above him, the dark hateful cloud seethes, dipping down as if trying to taste us, to join us.

I can't control the reaction to squirm. My breath is being rolled out of me. He's snaked both his legs around mine, pinned my left arm under me and the other above my head. If he moves his face closer, I can break that nose again with my forehead. He knows that and he's staying far away.

My arm underneath me goes cold, robbed of blood flow. The urge to cry out is hard to contain. He's brought it just to the snapping point, one slight move and it will break. Why bother when he wants to kill me? Maybe he wants to separate me a piece at a time.

Because I refuse to look into his eyes, I look past him into the dark cloud. Its sentience scares me as it acknowledges me and offers a test to see what I'm made of. To see how far I'll take this. It's hungry for more. It can't just be happy with the hate he has for me, it wants me to hate him back.

Well, I have a different idea.

Rex presses his body even harder against mine to keep my arm underneath me without the aid of his own hand. Now with a free arm, he produces a short blade and turns his face toward me. His teeth are stained red. *Can the deaf girl read lips?*

My response is to remain still, keep my eyes trained on his. He knows the answer is yes.

Good. Then read this: find your voice. I want to hear you scream when I kill you.

I close my eyes and reach far into the dark cloud. My connection with its power is instantaneous and true. A kinship so unexpected I'm gasping and choking for the force it awakens inside me. I'm trained in black magic but never has it felt so integrated, such a complement to my native magic. I'm split down the middle: one half Bevan, one half something else.

Rex has freed my arm to take a handful of my hair and pull my head back. His blade rests against my throat. I drag my finger into the blood spilling from the bite wound on his arm and draw an encircled symmetrical cross on his forehead. He tries to pull back, but I've got my other arm now, and I'm holding him with the power I've drawn from the dark cloud, a fuel to my black magic. An enemy he's not trained to fight.

I dip my finger in his blood again and draw the same symbol on my forehead. His knife hand has gone to the floor to push away. I latch my hands behind his head and draw his forehead against mine.

The collision is a white-hot discharge, sending an electric burst from my teeth to my toes—and through him, too, for how rigid he goes. In my mind everything is blinding white, but I keep my grip as he fights me. I'm like a stone cemented into the ground, my hands a vise. He's spitting words, his breath hot on my lips. It must be curses for the power packed in them.

Everything around me fades into something new. I'm enveloped by so many unfamiliar sensations I want to retreat, but I push further, reaching for something I can grasp. That scent of his musky soap isn't just a random unnamed fragrance in my nose anymore. I know it like it's part of my life because I'm inside his head. And I see what's here—that same cloud hovering above us resides in him, only more compact. Coiled and tightly packed into a space not large enough to contain it. I feel his hate, his anger. I push further and find torment. Loneliness. Despair. Emotions I've felt in my life that are easy to recognize but hard to accept in this space for how concentrated they are. My loneliness has never been so bottomless, my despair never so profound. I can't be in here and not do something about this mess. It's not right. It's not even human.

So I pick at the mess like it's a tangible thing. It breaks off in pieces I start to gather. They overflow my hands, so I fill my shirt like I used to with pebbles on the shore of the Black River as a little girl at home. So many pebbles. So many pieces. Different shapes and sizes, but I take them all in as a weight lies upon me. When I finally have them all, I pack them together and hold them close, a dark, tarry clump compacting in my hands. I can't just drop it, so I draw it near me, into me, swallowing it down. Away.

That weight lifts off, and I open my eyes. From inches away Rex looks back, the bloody symbol on his forehead smeared, his eyes so wide I can see the blue in them in the dim light.

What did you do?

It plays in my head as it forms on his lips as if tendrils of our mental connection are still in place. He slams a palm against the floor beside my head. I don't flinch because I expected it. I reach for his face for a tactile sensation, hoping it will overwrite the mental and end this spell that holds us. He jerks back before I make contact because *he* expected that. Then he's on his feet, crouching over me.

What the fuck did you do?! Yelled with so much force his breath stirs my bangs.

I shrug. I don't know what I did.

He makes a motion to grab me by the throat, but I don't bother to move because I know he won't go through with it. Realizing this himself, he punches the floor, and I do flinch for that—not for fear of being hit but a reflex from the busted knuckles he's just experienced.

I raise to my elbows and propel myself backward. I have to get away from him. This mental link is more than I bargained for and I want it gone. He sucks his knuckles, watching me. All that savage rage now gone, replaced by unmistakable confusion that has me wanting to explain what I don't understand myself. I took something from him. It's a hot coal in my throat, slowly slipping down. I place a hand against my chest where it is, just under my breastbone. And he continues to watch me, awaiting an explanation I can't give.

He turns quickly toward the door, mumbling words I can't make out. Then he's on his feet. For a moment I think he's going to offer me a hand up, but that's crazy, and he must think so too because he takes a step back to prevent it. He makes one last glance between me and the door to the hall then picks up the desk chair and hurls it through one of the French doors. Old glass rains every-where. After using his boot to kick remaining shards free from the frame, he launches himself through and over the balcony, dropping out of sight.

With the boundary spell already breached, and an oncoming threat he's made apparent by his glance toward the hall and hasty escape, I snatch my amulet off the floor and follow. On the balcony, I pause to pull the straight razor out of my boot so it won't get in the way of a hard sprint.

I tug my elastic silver armband from my upper arm to my forearm, stretching it to its full width so I can tuck the razor inside. Then I hop the railing, drop to the ground, and run. It's a struggle to ignore my wounded knee, but I focus ahead of me. Rex reaches the woods and fades away. What I don't understand is what he could possibly be running from.

CHAPTER 4

REX

I DON'T STOP RUNNING until I'm deep in the forest. They'll send a search party as soon as they can gather enough guys, and I need to gain enough of a lead to figure out what the hell to do. One part of me thinks maybe they won't find out, maybe their boundary spell was junk. Maybe they didn't hear the breaking glass. They'll stay inside, thinking Sloane Bevan and I are in our rooms asleep.

I tell that part of me to shut the fuck up.

As I catch my breath, ribbons of gray clouds lit sideways by the moon cruise across the sky. A breeze swells, swaying the creaky tree branches above me. When the air settles, I catch a far off sound: barking dogs. Okay, so not a human search party. They released the dogs. And I don't know who they're hunting—Sloane Bevan, or me.

Underbrush stirs in front of me and there she is, materializing like she knew I was here. I take a step back and bump into a tree trunk—real smooth, genius. Bevans *must* be animals if they can move through the forest with such stealth. That's an advantage she'll have when the dogs get nearer, so I take off, hoping to get far ahead so when they bust her they'll be satisfied and give up on me. I've always hated those dogs and they've always hated me. As soon as they catch my scent, they're going to be fighting each other for the opportunity to dismember me.

Passing an outcropping of rock, I snatch a fist-sized stone off the ground. Sloane Bevan caused all this. The next time she and I meet, I'm bashing in her skull.

I alter my direction to head away from the dogs. Thirst haunts me. So does my paranoia. There's no reason my family needs me to kill her. With her captive on our land, they can do it themselves. As soon as they figure out I jumped the gun, defied orders, thought for myself for one damn second of my life, they'll not only see me unfit for my mission but also as a direct obstruction. Disloyal. Defiant. I know what happens to the ones who defy them. I've seen it firsthand.

Now that I've left an erratic path of my scent to hopefully buy me some time with the dogs, I pocket the rock and hoist myself into the nearest climbable tree, ignoring the sight of my wrecked arm. It's a risk to crawl out on the branch, but I have no choice. There's a thick vine I need to reach that will help me move to an adjacent tree. The branch creaks under my weight as I extend my arm and lean. Then I'm grasping vine and swinging over, latching onto a new branch that won't hold my weight either but that's okay. It lessens the force of my fall enough so I don't break my legs. As soon as my boots hit the ground, I cover my head against the falling limb.

It comes down hard on top of me, gouging me good in the lower back. I twist to check the damage but can only see the top of the rip in my shirt. No time for first aid now. I get a shoulder under the limb and lift—not enough to leave the forest floor undisturbed but it's the best I can do. About a hundred feet away I drop it and stomp it apart, flinging pieces in every direction. They'll probably figure it out, but I can do no more here. I need to move.

Crossing water would be the best strategy, but I'm too far from the stream on our land. So I cut north toward the site of the old stone buildings. If the dogs do catch me, it will be nice to have a wall to my back.

In their clearing, the buildings sit in a natural spotlight from the moon, peaceful upon first glance, sinister if you look closer. Or know what went on here. I do, and the peace I find is what comes of wrongs made right. People earning what's due them. Justified consequences. But as soon as I think it, there's a clash of dread for what I've done and what consequences may await me.

That's if I'm caught. Or if I don't kill her and claim the power that's mine.

I walk to the closest building and toe a loose piece of stone, half expecting the whole structure to crumble to the ground. I wonder what this spot looked like before the buildings burned. Without their roofs, the rain has decayed them. Young trees sprout against the walls, leaning away as if they didn't mean to root so close. Vines climb up about half a foot before turning direction like the ground is a better bet. And nothing grows inside. It's just a fight between mud and debris. The mud is winning.

A figure in my peripheral vision has me spinning around to find Sloane Bevan emerging from a doorway. I feel the rock in my pocket—no, Rex, don't go for it, not yet. Her black eye makeup has smeared, turning her eyes smoky in the moonlight. And those dark clothes? No one told me she's a stupid goth. The blood from her split brow has dried along with that screwed-up symbol she drew on her forehead. And probably mine too. I need to find out what kind of shit that was, but I'm not talking to her. She studies me, hugging herself, frowning so intently I get a jolt of memory when she was in my head and I could sense things—

She'll pay for that. I don't even care how she beat me here, how she knew I'd be coming here, or why she didn't attack me when my back was turned. She's stupid like the rest of them, a dumb animal to be put out of its misery. I extract my rock. Unconcerned, she watches me. Still that frown. Like I've done something to disappoint her. It makes me laugh, and I do, fully aware I'm the cackling villain in her story. Because how could she expect anything but disappointment from the guy whose job it is to kill her?

I advance on her but she puts up a hand, distracted, like she's so through with us and there's a bigger issue at hand. She's not even looking at me—she's tilting her head, eyes intent on the trail that dropped me into this clearing. A swarm of insects bursts upward from the stone building behind her, clouding the sky with their number. It's those moths again, and a perfect distraction for me to attack, to smash her head with this rock and go home to bed. I don't know why I'm not doing it.

As the moths disperse in the sky, I hear a disturbance in the woods. A range of it, not from one direction but many. It's obvious now she's tuned into this somehow, and I want to ask her what it is but remember she's deaf and voiceless—how she's surviving all this is a real trip. A bark splits the summer night, provoking more from all around, and I back into the wall as she comes forward, passing me as if unafraid of what I'm about to deal her.

The anger I've been taught to use as fuel rises from the pit of my gut. She's got her full back to me now. It would be so easy and so due; dismissing me like that is a lesson she needs to learn but won't because she'll be dead. The kill needs to be slower than a brain bashing so she can fully process the mistake.

I start toward her and she drops to a squat, not in reaction to me but to the pack of dogs that's now shooting from the trees. She turns around to face me, one hand pushing down toward the ground, eyes big and reassuring.

Reassuring? What the—

I squat, my body taking control over my brain because it doesn't want to be torn apart by a pack of Dobermans. And apparently it trusts Sloane Bevan over me. Seriously?

She points two fingers into her eyes then points to the ground. I follow her lead, my gaze on the ground along with hers. The Dobermans reach us and swarm, bumping me with their shoulders and muzzles, but I feel no teeth. No claws. Out of the corner of my eye, I see her extending a hand level with the ground, palm down. I raise my eyes just enough to see one of the dogs sniff her hand then nudge it with its head. She shuffles forward; the dog growls but she goes in closer, unalarmed because she can't hear it. I restrain myself from shouting at her because she wouldn't hear that either. Is she stupid? If she provokes an attack, these dogs will steal her slow death away from me.

I stand. The dogs who were watching her wheel on me raise their lips, snapping, barking. She motions *get down* again to me as if I'm going to take orders from Bevan trash. I take a step; a dog latches onto my thigh. Piercing teeth bad, hefty clamp of jaw worse. The fist I'm swinging toward its ribcage is derailed, and I find Sloane Bevan clinging onto my arm.

I'm at once aware the dog has let go, but she hasn't. It's an invasion almost as bad as what she did to me in her room, but this time I don't fight it for the shock it lays upon me, the realization that bursts so painfully in my head. The reason it's brought that mind connection up again is because of how similar it feels. It doesn't feel like I'm being fought by Sloane Bevan at all. It's more like I'm being saved.

I grab her arm and twist, forcing her to release me. She has no chance against my strength. She spins and ducks, breaking my grasp too fast for me to counter. Dogs gather beside her, looking primed to leap at my throat should I make one more false move.

"Okay," I say, hands raised. Temporary truce because I'm not stupid enough to fight her *and* a pack of attack dogs she's somehow tamed and recruited before my eyes. "Back the fuck away from me, then."

She has the nerve to stand her ground and smile at me. And I'm in no position to backhand her without getting torn to pieces. The fantasy of it is awesome … until it turns my stomach in a way I've never experienced.

I need to find out what the hell she did to me in her room and make her undo it. I can't go back to my family like this. If I sense something has changed, so will they. And even if I try to hide it, they'll find out. They always find out.

She points to the bite mark she left on my arm, but I simply stare at her. She leans to the side, pointing around me at the wound on my back from the falling limb. I have no idea how she noticed it or why she'd be pointing it out.

"What is wrong with you?"

Of course I don't expect an answer because the girl is surely mental on top of deaf. Or has some sick fascination with other people's wounds. She did cause one of them. Maybe she's rubbing it in. But there's no perceptible gloating—it's something else, another emotion I refuse to name. She drops to a squat and writes in the dirt: *Infection*. Raises her face back to me.

This is too much.

I turn around and barge through the throng of dogs. They've lost all threat. Because even if they rip off my limbs and eat my face, it would be easier to deal with than this.

After putting some distance between me and her, I locate the stream. I quench my thirst then take off my shirt and wash my arm and back wounds with handfuls of cool water, careful to avoid the watch I should probably be taking off. I scrub the dried blood of her evil symbol off my forehead, wondering if I just introduced some flesh-eating bacteria into my open wounds. But who cares. Let it kill me.

I'll probably get some hellish diarrhea from drinking the water too.

I need to go back home and get a rifle with a scope. I could kill her from a distance like a first-person shooter game. I'll admit to myself, it's so I wouldn't have to watch her die. Hard to believe I'd go out of my way to avoid something I've anticipated my whole life. This change in me must be a result of some hardcore exhaustion—something to explain my hesitation for completing what I need to do. I'll need to tell them to adjust my pills again, or I need a different mix. Something stronger? Less strong? Anything that will return me to normal.

Forget it though. I need to focus. I'll get the rifle. Return to the woods and hunt her down. Then I'll go home, find my father and tell him she escaped and I caught her before she made it to the road. Yeah, we didn't get her Bevan magic, but we won't need it after we eliminate all her kind. We can let it die with them. And by the way, now that I've completed my mission and killed Sloane Bevan, this house and all of you belong to me.

One small problem: The eastern horizon has a morning glow to it and birds are getting loud and restless. I check my watch—not good. It's a long hike back to the house and by that time the sun will be up and the house will be awake. Sneaking in wouldn't be hard on a normal day, but today they'll be watching. It's strange I haven't encountered a search party but it's no coincidence the dogs were loose last night. They know we're gone. They might be waiting for me to take care of it. A bit unusual they'd leave such a decision to me, but really, it's about time. It is my mission after all.

Shit, I'm starving. I didn't bring a snack but at least I have my pill case. I swallow one with stream water and wait for it to kick in and clear the sleepy fog from my brain. Not much later I'm overcome by a rush of energy that leaves me shaky from so much activity and not enough calories. And a missed night of sleep. I can't go home without killing her. I can't sneak in to retrieve the rifle in the daylight. And the longer I stay out here, the thirstier and hungrier I'll get. So that settles it. Screw the rifle. It's time to kill.

I hike toward the old stone buildings because that's where I left her, and I can track her from there. I half expect her to be hiding in one of the buildings, but they're all vacant. My combat boot footprints are easy to spot mingling with dog prints. Hers, not so much. I try to recover the image of what she had on—yeah, soft fabric ankle boots, flat sole. She's small, her feet must be too. I poke around where she tamed that first Doberman and find the arc of a heel, then another, following them around the largest building to a pile of sticks stripped of their leaves. Not ripped off, but shaved off by a knife. She's armed. And making more weapons. Good to know.

Now that I've identified that heel print, it's easy enough to track. She took a deer trail I follow northeast, losing her path a few times so I have to double back. I can't think about my stomach. It's well past breakfast now. I probably won't be getting lunch either. A grasshopper lands on my shoulder as I plow through a clearing. Yeah, not yet hungry enough to take advantage of that. Try me again in a few hours.

Almost at the opposite edge of the clearing her prints disappear. There's nothing she could have jumped up on. No trees to climb, no running water. I backtrack and try again. I scour the whole clearing. The sun's overhead now and beating me down, boiling my nerves. The sunburn I earn today is going to be brutal. I slap another mosquito. And the insect bites? Not gonna be pleasant. Damn the elements, they're no help to me now. How could I let her get away from me? I had her how many times—three? And I walked away? Since there's nothing to hit, I reach into my hair to pull and find it buzzed off.

Now that I'm admitting all these things are pissing me off, I should probably call attention to the human bite mark on my arm that's weeping blood and pus-looking crap. Serious bad news. Nothing to do about it. The tree branch wound on my back is killing me too, more bruised than raw, though. I use the bottom of my T-shirt to wipe the sweat off my face. I need to find that stream before I get dehydrated. Or *more* dehydrated. My lips are dry enough to split.

The stream. That's the key. Of course she knows to stay near water, unlike my dumb ass who's hiked far away. Once I find it, I'll follow its length and will no doubt find her too. If she's smart, she'll take it to the northern boundary fence and use that Bevan magic to escape. I have to catch her before then.

I up my pace, ignoring all complaints from the deep tissue bruise on my back, my damn human bite wound— oh yeah, and my sore leg thanks to the Doberman's latch. The canopy above keeps the sun off my shorn head and bare neck. The relief of the shade convinces me to increase my jog even more.

Catching sight of the stream, I just about make a dive for it. I guzzle water knowing full well the intestinal upset I bought earlier just leveled up. After washing my face and neck, I get dizzy so bad I almost can't get my pill case out. I swallow one down, taking note of the time. The doses are too close together, but I'm not sure how to help it.

I lean back on my heels. A moth flutters past, then two more. Following them with my eyes, I catch sight of Sloane Bevan upstream, wading into the water with her pant legs pulled up to her knees. All her focus is on the water. I stay in a squat and slowly back toward cover—one step, two, three. She looks up, right into my eyes from a hundred feet away.

Okay, no ambush then. I'll play friendly. I stand and stare at her a moment. Can't appear too chummy, she'll be suspicious of that. She was concerned about my arm—I actually cringe at my own thought, at that emotion I refused to name before. Concern is such a disgusting concept I pack it away. But wait, Rex, you can use that. Maybe I'm here because I need her help. So I raise my wounded arm, point to it.

She straightens all the way up, rubbing her palms on the front of her pants. Gives me a nod. I approach. Her shoes and socks sit on the shore. I notice the stretchy band on her forearm isn't just for decoration. There's a slender object stashed in there that must be the knife she used to strip those tree branches. She remains in the water, watching me with her head cocked like an animal angling its ears for a better listen. Which would make sense if she could hear, because the birds have started wigging out above us.

I could attack her now, press her face under the water, and end her quickly. There's something so unsatisfying about not seeing the blood run, though. I raise my arm again and point to it. "Infection."

She nods knowingly but stays put. Her face is clean and totally healed. As expected, but it annoys me more than it should.

I half turn, pointing to my back. She leans to get a better view, but I don't move to make it easier. She'll have to come out of the water to see it. No one ever taught me how to lure an opponent, but no one ever predicted I'd be such a dumbass to let one get away three times. She takes one step forward but stops there. I'm under such scrutiny I'm overthinking every breath. There's no way to know what's the best look for me right now, what would sell it so she'll draw near. If I should hide my shaky exhaustion or let it show. Showing weakness is so against my training, but will she trust me if I look normal? Will she want to help me if I look weak?

Weak is less threat. I let my shoulders slump, relax my stance. Pretending to look at the wound, I twist, stretch my neck, and can't see a damn thing. At least it's not a lie. "I can't see it at all."

She comes out of the water and drips for a moment as if still trying to decide if I'm safe. *Yes. I'm very safe. I promise.* I rotate my torn arm to pretend to give that a look. She comes closer. Walks around me. As soon as her eyes move from my face to my back, I lunge.

The first thing I go for is that amulet she's put back around her neck. She either doesn't predict it or lets me get it, and I yank hard, snapping it off her neck as the metal burns through my palm. I fling it into the stream. For a moment I think she's going to go after it, but when my head jerks to the side, I realize that was a distraction and she's popped me in the jaw instead.

Every move I expect to drive home meets a block or open air. Fighting her is like catching a mouse. So much speed and power packed into a little body that slips through my fingers every time. If I can get ahold of her, though, it's over. She knows that too. I need to get her on the ground. Soon. I'm fighting two opponents right now: her and my exhaustion.

I take a risk to sweep her leg—she jabs me straight in the wound in my back I just exposed. As I fall I make a blind reach that rewards me with fabric I clamp onto with my tightest grip. She falls with me, landing close enough for me to wrap a leg around her waist and an arm around her throat. Something really bad is going on with my torn arm but right now I don't care. I tighten on her neck. She chokes a little before slamming her head back. I take it in the mouth and feel the blood well onto my tongue. It's a slippery mess leaking into her hair. She's working a shoulder under my arm. Then she heaves all her weight, rolling us, sending a deadly foot into my knee and a hit to the jaw that turns my vision black for one sick second. *No.*

I reach deep into my stash of Bevan hate. The knowledge of what they've done to my family, what we've lost because of them. Instead of it flowing hot into my bloodstream, I hit a dry bottom. There's nothing there.

Sloane Bevan did something to me, and she's going to pay.

Powered by the injustice of it, I flip us so her back is against the ground, held by my knee on her stomach and my forearm across her shoulders. She goes limp like she knows it's futile, it's over. With my free hand, I slip a finger under the band on her arm, slide out her weapon: a straight razor. I open it with my teeth. Press the blade against her neck where her pulse beats strong.

"This is how I end your kind." Blood and drool string from my mouth onto her cheek. "Your father is next."

She's watching me, breathing hard, but serene like that damn lake behind my house. No anger, no fear. Resolute in knowing she's about to die. Or pretending she's not.

"Scream," I say. I need something, anything, to prompt me to dig this blade in.

I feel the pull of that lake sweeping against me. The perfect rhythm of its unsteady beat. Like the gradual slowing of her pulse under the razor in firm opposition to the precise tick of my watch. That tick feels wrong against my own wrist's pulse. Like if I had something new to sync to, things would be right again. I see the canopy above us reflected in her eyes. I see my own face, my bloodied mouth, my shorn hair that makes me a stranger. I see how she sees me. Angry. Misguided. Broken. Used.

I want to let her go, get up, get away, but I'm glued. I can't not kill her.

I can't kill her.

"Finish this!" I yell, an order to myself. I hear it echo through the woods then it's gone, like the part of me that wants to end this the way it's meant to end.

A tear swells in the corner of her eye until it spills down her temple. She's not crying for herself. She's crying for me.

Instead of seeing all her family has done to mine, I see all my family has done to me. There's a thickness in my throat I have to swallow down. She's moving underneath me. My strength over her has been compromised by something out of my control. Then the straight razor is in her hand, not mine, and she's closing it and tucking it back in her armband.

"You're wrong about me," I say, knowing it's a lie, wishing it wasn't.

She raises two fingers, presses them against my chest right over my heart as I involuntarily recoil. The prod reaches something primitive, something so long untouched I shove away from her and jump to my feet. The knee she kicked buckles. Dislocated. I put space between us even though my knee is trashed. She gets up from the ground where I had her pinned. Brushes herself off. Gathers up her tangled hair and twists it, leaving that extra-long braid hanging loose. Then she squats to write something in the dirt I don't look at until she turns her back to me.

I can fix your knee.

The glare on my face must be nuclear. She goes to the water, hoisting her pants up past her knees before wading in. I watch her search the bed of the stream until she plucks out her amulet and returns to where she left her boots on the shore. I've swallowed so much of my own blood I could consider it my missed breakfast and lunch. I feel around for missing teeth, find it's not just my mouth bleeding but also my nose, so I take off my shirt and wad it against it. Over the black fabric, I see her bend and puke into the weeds, studying it for a long time before she wipes her mouth. Then she's straightening her clothes, pulling on socks and boots, and standing up to appraise me.

I give her the finger.

She gives it back.

Several yards upstream she stops to admire a tree trunk, picks something off it, and pops it in her mouth. If she knows what to eat out here, damn it all, I need her. Hunger is the one thing that will sell me back to that house. If I get some calories into my system, maybe I can find it in me to finish this.

"Hey!" I holler. Of course she doesn't hear. To be so oblivious of the demands of others? Must be nice. And I'm going to ignore how hoarse and spent my voice sounds.

She moves farther away, silent in those soft elf boots, the chaos of birds and insects and the gurgling stream covering her every sound. I hobble to the water and rinse my mouth. Wash my face. Drink. Cold water fills the chasm of my stomach. I glance at my torn arm and have to sit down. It looks like it's been maimed by a rabid dog. Lacerated skin, ribbons of muscle—is that bone? Oh shit. I shake out my shirt and wrap the wound, tying it with the help of my teeth. Shadows gather at the edges of my vision, and I pat down my pockets for my pill case, knowing it's too soon to take another but I can't fight this exhaustion on my own. I'm more in need of a pill to sleep but I can't leave myself vulnerable like that. I'm vaguely aware of leaning onto my good arm, then I'm on my back glimpsing blue sky through tree branches.

I wake up cursing. Tree branches above me stand out dark and featureless against a muted purple sky. I dig knuckles against my eyelids and open them again. Around me the forest is dim. I check my watch—after eight at night? I sit up fast and get punished by a nauseating spin in my head that takes way too long to subside. And guess what. There's Sloane Bevan across the stream watching me.

The note she wrote in the dirt earlier about fixing my knee has been amended: *and your arm.* Which means she was that close to me while I was out cold, and she didn't kill me. This is bad.

I was prepared to lose against her, to die. A disaster, yeah, for both me and my family. But a possible and acceptable outcome. I never imagined there could be anything worse, but somehow I've found it.

CHAPTER 5

SLOANE

Rainclouds gather slowly enough that when Rex collapses again to sleep I'm not concerned he'll die from overexposure just yet. Not that I care. But maybe I should, since I'm the one who's supposed to be killing him. Does it count if I do nothing when the rain comes down? Soaking wet might do a guy in who already has a hideous wound. Crippled by that dislocated knee, he can hardly help himself. Am I his killer if I watch him die from infection or hypothermia?

My moths fled when the bats moved in to feast on the mosquitoes trying to feast on me. So I appeal to the bats to act as my ears and alert me when Rex stirs. They seem to know me, or my kind at least. I wonder if they've inherited knowledge of my grandma from their parents and grandparents. I don't remember her telling me about bats in her time here, but she sure has a comradery with them at home. I curl up on my bed of ferns and return to sleep, content in knowing the bats have my back.

It's hours later when I'm roused by the tickle of bat wings on my face. I sit up and check Rex but he's still flat against the ground. Maybe he's dead—no, the bats wouldn't bother waking me if he was. He stirs and I thank the bats. They take to the sky, leaving me alone with him.

First I notice the power building behind each gust of wind. Then I sense the chill riding on it. I squint up at the sky and see the rain clouds have grown. The moon still fights to shine beyond them but it will soon be obscured. Temperature is dropping. All my battle wounds from Rex have already healed, but even I'm at a risk for overexposure once that rain hits.

It takes a few minutes for Rex to fully wake and sit up. Now here we are, staring at each other across the stream. The current still plays in the moonlight as if unaware how dark this forest will soon be once those clouds roll all the way in. I need to build a shelter now. I just don't know if I should build it for one or for two. On my side of the stream or on his.

Saving him would be crazy, right?

I can't stop seeing him as a scared, injured animal I need to tame so I can help it heal. That he's this vicious only because he's afraid and not listening to me. If not a wild animal, he's an animal at the pound—neglected, abused, trust wholly broken. He's never seen a compassionate soul, never encountered a helping hand. And all I have to do is lure him with patience and sympathy and a bowl of good food.

He's looking up at the sky now. Probably feels the same sinking feeling I do. If our positions were reversed, he'd have already killed me. I should get up and hike away. Find the breach in the fence my dad told me about and get myself home. I'll have days on the road to decide if I should take credit for his death because if I leave him now, he will die. His arm is overdue for treatment. His knee needs to be fixed so he can start home and get inside before the rain comes.

I should leave him, but I can't do that. I'm not a Moore; I'm a Bevan. The least I can do is fix his knee.

He makes no move when I take off my boots and wade across the stream. I don't trust him after he tricked me last time but it's pretty much irrelevant now. He's in such bad shape he's not a threat to me anymore. I go to where I wrote in the dirt, circle the part about fixing his knee, and look to him for an answer.

For a long moment he simply regards me. He's trying to decipher my motive. He doesn't understand why I'd offer to help. *It's called being human*, I sign to him before realizing he won't understand it. Not enough sleep has left me groggy.

He swivels his disabled leg toward me and nods. I get a rush—it's not that I didn't expect him to accept my help, I just didn't think that far ahead. Now I'll have to get close to him. I give him a hard look that vows pain if he tries any stunts. His eyes are cold but carry a note of resignation that looks so out of place on a buzz-cut sadist wearing military surplus. Now's my chance.

I straddle his leg and pop the knee back in before he can resist. Back on my feet, I turn to see if he survived it. He's dropped his head back to scream at the sky. Cursing, for sure. I know it when I see it. Each word looks like it's being hacked off by the next one pushing in.

Because I'm not sure how much survival training he's had while living in his Disney palace, I write a new message in the dirt for him: *Overexposure can happen at 70 degrees.* There's no room to add all the things that make it true—dehydration, fatigue, wet clothes, neglected wounds. He pretty much has it all.

Fuck you, he says. Emphasis on the *you*.

It bothers me more than it should. I stare at his face, the mottling of bruises, the split, gored-up lip, the eyes narrowed to slits. I see what my help looks like from his side. Pity from a Bevan must sting. We're well aware of their skewed view of us but it's only been unfounded up until now. It's never caused my pulse to quicken like this. It's never made me want to really hurt one of them.

I step back because I want to step forward, and I know that would be wrong. The raw flush that made me vomit earlier rises in me again. I swallow it down. It nestles next to that tarry lump I took from Rex, doubling its presence. If I gave in, I'd be throwing up again right now. It's a bad move. I can't let myself get dehydrated out here.

Keeping an eye on Rex, I return to my side of the stream. He tries out his knee while I'm gathering my bed of fern fronds. Then he stalks off. I head in the direction the bats flew. Not much later they swoop down from above, so I follow them to their cave and find a clean spot to make a bed and a fire tiny enough to not disturb them too much.

With my back against the cool cave wall, I feed twigs to my fire and revisit that last encounter. It left such a strange vibe over me. His hatred seemed almost falsely overdone, like a show that had been performed so many times it was losing its mojo.

He's in pretty bad shape, though, so I'll give him a pass on his sorry level of Moore sadism. Tomorrow I expect him back to normal. A little prodding will probably help, and if he detests my help as much as he appears to, he'll have a perfect reason to get more cranky. Tomorrow I'll be fixing his arm.

When the storm hits I lie down, lulled by the pulse of thunder in the earth. For the first time I invoke the memory of my family. Marcas' little round head and big gap-toothed grin. Dad's crushing hugs. Mom's gentle fingers rebraiding my braid even when it's already perfect. Nicky's velvety hound dog ears. Buzz's wild wagging tail and chin on my lap. Dillon promised the Moores wouldn't hurt them if I cooperated. I believed it to be true because I couldn't allow thoughts of anything else. Those thoughts are here now. I'm no longer cooperating.

I close my eyes and build a mental bridge home. I conjure the highway that brought me here. The imagery out my window. The soft roll of the Appalachians. The flat farmland of the Midwest. The even flatter Great Plains. Back to my craggy mountains and my home nestled between them. Across my river to Aunt Tara's house, to Winnie, who can tell me everyone's safe and take my message back to them saying I'm okay.

I wake up being cooked in the sun. Its morning angle shines right into the mouth of the cave, and I must've slept in the beam for a while because I'm sticky with sweat and glued to the cave floor. I shuffle into the shade, feeling hunger and thirst like a sharp pain. A dip in the stream would be nice too. Then I need to work on figuring out what I'm supposed to be doing here to call the Moores off my family—

Winnie. I plop onto the ground, our conversation dropping on me fast and hard. She's okay—they're all okay. She wanted to know if I'd killed Rex yet, and I couldn't tell her how badly I failed. *I'm working on it*, I told her. She wanted to know how, but I had nothing to add. Dislocating then fixing his knee? Healing his arm? They wouldn't understand. So I told her I'd befriended the Moores' pack of attack dogs, and she laughed—how I miss her laugh. The way her eyes tear up, how she holds her side and smacks at Will if he starts laughing because it only makes her laugh harder.

Marcas sits in the driveway waiting for me to come home every day. She didn't want to tell me, but she slipped and I saw it. She said he's okay, he's a big kid. And I know he's a big kid. But he's also so little, and he cares too much about things he can't control. He takes it all on when he has no business to. *Like his dad*, Mom always says. I wipe my face on my shirt. I miss him so much.

Where are you, Rex Moore? I have an arm to heal.

On my path back to the stream I eat a breakfast of mushrooms, grateful for my awesome luck at being stranded here in the middle of summer when the forest is a smorgasbord. The heat, though, I'm not cut out for. Just walking drains my energy; I'm melting in this jungle air and longing for my mountain breeze. A serious thirst builds with every step. I wish there was a way I could carry water. I wish I could have a veggie omelet and my favorite organic chocolate milk Dad always buys for me. I wish some wise, ancient Bevan—or Farrelly, really, since that was our previous name—would materialize between the tree trunks and tell me what I'm supposed to be doing here. Why they chose me.

Scratch all that because it's stupid to daydream right now. What I *really* wish for is some way Uncle Christian could come here, but he hasn't been back to this house in so long they probably wouldn't trust him to let him in the door. Aaron, though, he could come. I know he's here a few times a year to visit his mother and Rex. How in the world are he and Rex brothers? Half brothers, really, and it's that dissimilar half that made one normal and the other a sadist.

My moths join me. I'll take their company any day. I raise a hand to be a perch, and one flutters down, sticking easily to my open palm and folding her furry tree-trunk wings. I shouldn't tell her I spent the night in her predator's lair. I'm bouncing between two enemy camps, but I doubt either would think I'm a traitor. Nature doesn't play those games. Maybe if the Moores hadn't stepped so far away from nature, they wouldn't be playing their games and I'd be home with my family.

Around a bend I walk right into a huckleberry jackpot. I transfer my moth to my shoulder so I can load my shirt and take some back with me to enjoy by the stream. Then I find the largest tree nearby and make note: fifty feet due north of the towering sycamore is the highlight of my lunch and dinner. I'll gather more mushrooms near the cave, and I can also hike back to those old stone buildings. I saw chicory and a million dandelions there. While there I can search the rest of the buildings for tools or something to cook in. If I could get some water over a fire, I could boil some chicory root and eat like a queen.

Okay, not really. A queen would be eating a veggie omelet, but I can pretend queens eat chicory root as a delicacy and it might taste better—actually no. It will still taste like crap.

I pick some honeysuckle flourishing in the sun at the edge of a small glade and gather yarrow and dandelions from the middle. The honeysuckle and yarrow will be perfect for Rex's arm, and the dandelions … well, they're edible but they taste heinous. So if Rex is hungry I'll offer those to him. Who knows? He might like them. He is a Moore. Heinous is their brand. It's what they're built on and powered by.

When I reach the shore of the stream, I lay out some oak leaves for my berries and dandelion greens and make a pile of the honeysuckle and yarrow. I glance around, seeing no sign of Rex or anyone else. What I'm picking up from the moths seems like normal forest life on a steamy sunny day. There's more of a buzz of activity after last night's storm, but other than that it's all routine. A hawk circles overhead. I could sure use his eye, but I'm afraid calling him would frighten my moths, and they're much more loyal than he would be. I have nothing to give them in return. Although this weighs on me, I need them now, and if they're willing to help I'll gratefully take it.

A bath in the stream was a great idea before I was here facing the openness around me and the glare of sun from uncovered sky. The moths must pick up on my discomfort because they split into two groups, one heading upstream, the other heading down. Now alone, I'm more vulnerable than I want to be. It doesn't last long. As the moths flutter back unconcerned, I strip to my underwear and bare feet, wade in, and dip down. It's heaven to wash off the caked-on sweat and dust from the cave floor. I use the current to untangle and comb my hair. I'd swim for hours but now that I'm half-naked, Rex's return feels imminent and threatening. I wade to the shore and wring out my hair, taking an eagle-eye glance in all directions. Then I race out of my underwear and back into my long tee. My leggings are filthy. Now that I'm clean, the thought of squeezing into them in this wet heat? Gross. My T-shirt is long enough, so I'm good. I rinse the leggings in the stream and hang them and my underwear in a tree to dry. The moths swarm close, diving down. I gather some fern fronds to make a seat on the ground so I can keep my state of cleanliness as long as I can. The moths turn frantic. I spin around.

Rex is standing across the stream, glaring at me. His buzzed hair blazes gold in a beam of light angling through the trees. I shouldn't be so relieved to see him alive. He looks the same although more angry—impossible, I know, but there you go. That dirty T-shirt is still wrapped around his wounded arm. His cargo pants hang lower on his waist so I can see the tops of his underwear. Which makes us almost equal—he can see mine swinging in the breeze. He probably eats like a king at home. A couple days of starvation in the woods and he's withering away and about to lose his pants.

I break eye contact first because I'm not a creepy serial killer like him. I lay a pallet of fern fronds beside my huckleberries and start a hunt for a set of stones I can use for grinding. I find a nice flat one, slightly concave as if weathered just for me. It takes longer to find a perfect pestle. By that time, my underwear are dry enough to slip on behind a tree. My leggings are still soaking wet so I leave them. I reemerge. Rex has finished washing up and has resumed his psycho killer stare from a spot on the ground at the water's edge. I sit on my fern seat, facing him, and eat a handful of berries. The key to surviving in the forest is to eat nonstop, a lesson he's obviously never learned. As soon as my eyes meet his, my amulet heats against my chest. The rest of me goes cold.

My amulet knows it's not just anger he's shooting across the river at me. Being deaf has taught me to read faces and what I see isn't good. He's finally decided there's no hope for his arm wound. His arm is collateral damage. He *is* withering away, and the longer he waits to kill me the harder it will be. He leaps up, my recognition of his intention like a spark at his feet. Shirtless, he's more threatening than when we first met. His muscle tone alone makes our fight unfair. His added height and weight, his hearing—all features that didn't matter before but now that I've spent so much time alone I'm losing my connection to my family. *I'm faster than him,* I remind myself. *Smaller, more balanced, more nimble. Impossible to catch.* A choke builds in my throat because does any of that matter against a hate-fueled rage beast? I'm second-guessing everything Bevans stand for, everything my family taught me. Their confidence in me. They selected me to fight Rex and end the Moores, but no one ever mentioned whether I'd be going back home.

What did they see in me? What do I do here that stops the Moores from killing my people? They've taught me how to do so many things, but they never told me what to do.

Rex starts pacing along the water, talking to me, or himself, or whatever forest creatures are still on their side or under their power. He's moving too much for me to catch any words at all, but if it's spell words I'm running out of time. I scramble on hands and knees toward a puddle of mud by the water and smear my arms and chest. Then I close my eyes and pass a palm down each arm, inscribing the design my dad taught me. I do the same to my chest. With the mud on my fingers, I paint lines across my cheeks and chin. If this battle goes to the woods I will blend, and he won't just have to catch me—he'll have to find me first. An awareness scatters through the design, uniting me with the elements and awakening my ancestors within my blood. It reminds me who I am and why I'm here. I'm found again. I'm home.

He's stopped pacing to stare at me again. Instead of firing anger, now he's released a fierce curiosity. And clear offense to what my family knows, what his has lost. I curl a finger at him. *Come over.*

He eyes the mud at my feet, lingering a few breaths before shifting his attention to the wildflowers I've gathered, then to my makeshift mortar and pestle. I'm not sure I want to fix his arm anymore. He takes a step toward me but one knee collapses—the sore one. He drops, catching himself with his good arm. Oh? A weak moment I can take advantage of. I take a step; water laps at my toes. I see it all in my head: my rush toward him, my leap knocking him facedown. My arm around his head, clutching it tight against my chest. Then the twist. I'm strong enough to snap his neck. My dad and I practiced the move repeatedly for years with dummies he constructed of wood and soccer balls, with bungee cords to level up the strength of the "neck" until I could snap the wooden braces on the tightest one he could build.

If my fantasy plays out in real life would that be the end? Would the Moores surrender a millennia-old war?

He's back on his feet, clearly angered by the exhaustion and sickness he's fighting, along with battling me. My amulet pulses once, a warning, any more and it would burn me. I don't know what magic he's using but it's sensing something.

He sways. Staggers. I see the whites of his eyes, and then he's crumpled to the ground. Not getting up.

Decision time. I see my dad sign, *Warrior,* the day Dillon Moore took me away. My dad taught me to fight. To fight or defend myself? I see what my mom has told me many times: *Do what you feel is right.* My Grandma Sloane: *Bevans are warriors, but not all battles are fought with fists.*

What do I feel is right? To kill Rex Moore and add another casualty to a war when there's no guarantee this will be the end? Or to fix a problem I see, a problem I caused, a problem I set off this morning to solve?

I go to my mortar and pestle and grind the honeysuckle and yarrow, struggling to focus and locate the spell words in my head. Which text? The cobalt one. I see the page and the words recalled perfectly from memory. Now I understand why my dad was so dedicated to making me memorize every last word.

With my ground ingredients still contained on my concave stone, I cross the stream, watching Rex for any movement. I kneel beside him, setting the stone on the ground carefully so the fine particles don't spill.

He's fallen in the most uncomfortable way, legs twisted, neck bent, but his wounded arm rests right on top. His brain is trying to protect it even when falling into a black-out. I unwrap the T-shirt he's using as a bandage, holding his arm away from his body and watching his face for the slightest tic. When the shirt falls away, his wound—oh stars. The infection has eaten through healthy tissue and it's crawling … there's something inside … little white worms—

I shove backward, dropping his arm. Several worms sprinkle from the wriggling cluster onto the ground. Not worms—he's neglected the wound so badly it's become infested with maggots. I scoot farther away, my hand on my throat gripping hard so I don't retch up all the food I need to stay inside me. Good elements, please help me. I'm in so far over my head.

Deep breaths steady me, so I glance at him again. It triggers a gag so forceful I bend out of reflex and stagger to the nearest tree for support but no, no, no, I can't throw up. I need the nutrition I consumed. I can't get dehydrated. I'll get through this. I've sutured many wounds at home. I can handle maggots. I just need to calm down and think because even though they're repulsive, they aren't hurting him. They're eating the dead tissue, which is a good thing. But they have to come out, they just have to. Now, right now. I could sharpen sticks to use as tweezers, but they wouldn't be sterile. Who cares? The wound is already infected. Is it bad to introduce more germs to a wound that's already so bad? Probably, but what choice do I have? My worry is getting them all out with such a crude tool. Because I have to get them all.

I turn to face the stream, take in the trees all around, the insects like glitter in the sunlight over the water. This forest is alive with so many things I can use, all I need to do is figure it out.

Poison them. Easy. I mentally flip through my family's texts for a suitable recipe for poison—but wait. I'd have to pour it into the wound and that would poison him too. There must be a way to draw the maggots out, to charm them somehow. Above me, the hawk circles like he wants to weigh in. If he has any ideas, he needs to tell me because I need help here—

Birds! A beak is better tool than any set of crude tweezers and to certain birds, a maggot is a tasty and nutritious snack. What's going on in Rex's arm is a free buffet.

I drop down, planting my palms against earth and calling to the whole forest for the aid of any willing birds. Two crows immediately swoop down from a half-dead evergreen. They're pleased to help me, but not the slightest bit interested in Rex. I swallow down all revulsion for the maggots. They're creatures just like any, filling a role in the elements as meaningful as the crows' and mine. I straighten Rex's arm and beckon my helpers, turning my face away, so very grateful but unable to watch.

The smell of sickly flesh hovers in the swampy heat. I press my nose against my upper arm to mask it. I'm afraid if I release Rex's arm and move away, the crows will be startled and leave. They don't trust him any more than I do, and they're doing this for me, not him. A breeze builds, twisting leaves on branches, stirring my hair against my shoulders. I glance at my concave stone holding the crushed flowers for my healing spell, hoping it provides enough shelter for the feather-light ingredients. Air pushes against me and I reach, a second too late. My crushed flowers scatter in the wind.

That was everything I gathered. I know where to find them again but is there time? Rex's skin radiates heat, his cheeks are reddened with fever. The sweat has darkened his pants from waist to mid-thigh; his face and chest are wet with it. I doubt these symptoms are new. If they're bad enough to bring a rage beast to the ground, I don't think he has long to live like this.

Rex's legs twitch. I lean to look at his face, catch a flutter of eyelid. No, he can't come around now. I ease his arm into a position I can hold with one hand and clamp my other hand over his mouth. Eyelids flip open then narrow to a squint like he's lost and trying to make sense of things. He notices me, too groggy to do anything but stare.

Stay down, shut up. I should say it, but I won't speak, not to him. Never to him. As if figuring it all out at once, he jerks. The crows flap their wings but hold on, and he sees them for the first time. I see a battle light his eyes. I shake my head fiercely, sure he can see the panic in mine, and by some miracle he settles, his eyes going tame. All his breath releases. Surrender. The moment the scared and wounded animal finally takes the piece of food from my hand. The relief of the breakthrough pops the tension inside me. I become aware of the feel of his dry lips against my palm, his clammy hot cheeks against my fingertips. I can't be helping Rex Moore. What am I doing?

One crow hops onto my shoulder and tilts a cocoa bean eye toward me as if to say, *Anything else?*

I stroke her neck and she flaps away, her friend following. Rex closes his eyes. Now that his shouting is no longer a threat, I remove my hand from his mouth. He's as still as a swell in the earth, and I sit and watch him so long I feel the urge to take his pulse but I don't. I can't touch him again.

The wound is much easier to look at without the maggots, but holy oak, it's bad. I've never seen rotten raw meat, but I'm sure this is what it looks like. Red streaks in the skin around it are a bad sign. Without the swelling taking up all extra space, I'm sure there's actual missing tissue and that's just—I turn my face away, choking down my meager breakfast, trying to breathe—that's not something I should think about right now.

I try to imagine what my mom would do but first aid requires supplies I don't have and Rex needs a hospital. I know what my dad would do, but he'd have done it long ago, and I'd be on the road home right now. Aunt Tara— same as my dad but by a more humane method. Uncle Christian—he'd be cracking jokes, unconcerned about the noxious flesh wound. Wait—

I'm suddenly on my feet. Uncle Christian told me something when I was twelve years old I swore to him I'd never repeat. *Your dad can't know I've told you this*, he said with the agonizing slowness of fingerspelling because he was too lazy to learn good ASL. I decided it had to be a secret from his family that no one else knew. Something he should've told my dad but never did.

Your blood heals.

Heals me, I fingerspelled back. My dad had already told me that.

No, I read on his lips. *Not only you.*

He watched me to make sure I understood. Then he zipped my lips and kissed my forehead, and I never thought of it again.

I stand in the elements, my ancestors' war paint alive on my skin, syncing to more than just the forest so present around me. Under my feet the earth is cool. Sun warms the crown of my head above. Beyond our day-lit sky spreads the immensity of space, the same stars my ancestors lived and died by. A deeper union stretches back through time and awakens a song in my blood. This is the moment I choose, the moment they predicted. This is why they selected me.

Rex lies corpselike at my feet. Another casualty in a war that's had so many. His death means nothing but another win for our side, another life to avenge for the other. If no one ends this, it never ends. It continues as long as the stars shine, in as many generations forward as it spans backward, filled with people I sense with me now, so alive in my blood.

If my ancestors appointed me to make this choice, then I've already decided. I choose peace.

I slide the straight razor from my armband, open the blade, and slash my palm. Blood oozes free, seeking the easiest path back to the earth. I kneel beside Rex. Blood trickles from my palm to my elbow. Unhurried, its confident flow calms me when all I want to do is scream from the fire of split skin. I aim my palm down, watch the red drips find a home inside his wound. His eyes open at once, but he remains utterly still. I see the surprise register on his face. He's too feeble to be angry now, and for the first time since I was in his head I see the real Rex Moore. I get a glimpse of how he sees me: a witch like he's never seen. Earth witch and something else. Something I don't recognize myself.

His eyes are drawn to the open blade in my hand. I snap it closed and tuck it back in my armband. Threat now gone, he closes his eyes. His head rolls to one side, and just like that he's out again. And I look up from my work and find a spread of wild geraniums have bloomed around us like they were here all along.

I wait until his breathing slows. Then I check his pockets for weapons. I find a pill case full of two types of homemade pills that I put back. Another pocket contains his phone. This might be an invasion of privacy, but I have to see if he's been communicating with them, if they know where I am. They'd have to know—no one's come out here to find him, and surely they're worried about him.

Careful not to wake him, I press his fingerprint against the sensor and the screen unlocks. Missed calendar entries pop up: reminders to take his pill, for training, Latin class, history class, more pills, more training. His most recent text is from Aaron one week ago. A promise to visit, with no response from Rex. I check recent phone calls—nothing. I hover over his pictures, decide not to snoop because pictures you'd rather not see are very hard to unsee.

What I do see that I wish I could unsee are his contacts. Aaron, Dad, Emily, Jared, Mom. Five contacts. That's it.

Enough searching for me. I tuck his phone back in his pocket. There are many more to search, but I've lost the urge. His face is tipped into the light, revealing a white scar interrupting the stubble on his chin like he's been chipped there. I wonder if he'll have a scar on his arm after my work, if he'll ask me about it … if I'll have to explain. There's a strange patch of skin on his good arm—not another infection but an old wound, discolored and textured like a large burn. I suppose it could be a birthmark, but its shape is too precise and it wraps all around his forearm like a cuff.

I retrieve my leggings from my side of the stream. Now dry and cut into pieces with my straight razor they make a perfect compression bandage for his arm. After washing his T-shirt in the stream and hanging it in a tree, I return to my pallet of fern fronds and my huckleberries nearly ruined from the heat. Rex sleeps as his arm heals, and I nurse a leaden heart, imagining reasons why that contact list would be so short, why his text and phone logs would be so sparse, and wishing I could undo the pocket search and erase this new knowledge about Rex Moore.

CHAPTER 6

REX

THE GURGLE OF the stream is in my ears, so close it sounds inserted. Playing through an earbud so it drowns everything else out. My skin is no longer mine. It's too hot, too cold. I shiver, but I'm boiling alive. There's no way to move my legs. My thoughts don't complete. Nerves have been severed. A shaft of sunlight comes through the trees, too bright. Something's going on nearby. I work to roll my eyes in that direction. There's a roar in my head as tear ducts release but there's nothing there. It's too dry.

I see Sloane Bevan beside me but it's a dream, a hallucination. She's an ancient Celtic warrior, painted face and arms, wild hair, ripped tunic and bare legs and feet. I've had this dream before. Soon, an army will come over the hill, their feet pounding earth, javelins raised. I'm always alone though. She has an army behind her, and I'm a lone warrior, facing a solitary death no one will remember. Okay, whole truth: it's not a dream. It's a nightmare. Graphic, gutting, and recurring.

She stabs my arm. Wait—what? This is new. Awareness crashes down around me. I feel the hard ground underneath, hear the wind in the trees, the call of birds across the forest. I try to move my legs to get up but they're unconnected. My eyes burn in the light, trying to focus but they're too dry to move. A hand comes toward me, goes over my mouth. I blink to wet my damn dry eyes and there's Sloane Bevan for real and much too close. Smothering me. I curse inside, fighting to get up. Glossy black wings flap inches from my face. Two crows are perched on my arm, staring almost human brown eyes at me. Everything comes back in a rush. My totally wrecked arm. Acid hunger. Fever so bad I'm hallucinating. I need to get a grip because I have to kill Sloane Bevan before this shit gets worse.

The hand tightens on my mouth. A glance at her face tells me my silence is a life or death situation for some reason, and even though she is who she is, I've got a screaming sense telling me to listen to her. And the pain in my arm—it's a hell I've never known. I clamp my teeth and bite down because someone please get me a chainsaw. It would hurt less to just cut the whole thing off. And those birds. What the *hell* is she letting them do to my arm?

She's shaking her head at me now, pleading with eyes so hypnotizing I see how pointless it is to struggle. It's Bevan magic, too powerful to fight. This is why we want them all gone. Our knowledge died, theirs survived, and they're so dangerous they're unstoppable. This is the end of it all. I've failed. My people have lost. And if she and those birds are killing me, it's a mercy I'd ask for if I could.

I try to wet my lips but my tongue is too dry and glued in my mouth. Somehow I still taste the chalky dirt from her palm. And something bitter like she's been picking weeds. It's the last thing I'll taste before I return to the earth, and I'll take it.

I'm jarred loose, painfully aware and alive. But dreaming for sure because I'm back in the nightmare again. Sloane Bevan stands above me, her hair waving in the breeze except for that one long braid hanging against her chest like a grounding wire. Her face paint is a harsh set of slashes against her skin. And that painted arm runs red with blood dribbling down, cooling a part of me I lost sensation to until now. It's dripping right into the heart of the too-hot-too-cold that's overtaken my whole body, and this crawly liquid heat of her blood is deadening that mess of nerves one drop at a time. I catch sight of a blade in her hand. She's about to end me, and if I could speak I would say, "*Le do thoil*, do it." It'd be the first sincere 'please' I've ever said.

The gurgling stream is back. Faster now, in real time, not slowed and echoing like it was before. Other sounds begin to register—birds calling mid-flight so the sound bends around me, the *wee-ooo* of cicadas, the soundtrack of summer. I sit up, my empty stomach a new pain that's gone off the chart. I scratch at the dried blood splattered on my chest and stomach. There's a black elastic cotton bandage around my arm. I peek underneath it but can't see a damn thing so rather than disturb it I leave it alone. My strength will be better used getting something wet to soothe the death that is my throat.

I'm not alone. I drag my wrist across my eyes to clear them and look around. Sloane Bevan watches me from her side of the water. Something about her gaze makes me uncomfortable. She's newly clean, her wet hair combed away from her face so it hangs straight down her back. Without bangs she looks like a different girl. One notch down on the goth scale, one notch up on Girl Scout. And there's no sign of the Celtic warrior paint I saw in my dream. All she's wearing is her long gray T-shirt, sleeves ripped lengthwise at the shoulders but not from our combat. It's a fashion statement. Her amulet is back but her tight pants are missing. I eye the black bandage on my arm and suddenly hate it.

I get up like a stiff old man, my knees popping. Let's take care of the thirst so I can think straight. I guzzle water that hasn't yet given me the shits, so points for that. Thank you, water.

"Don't fucking look at me," I say to her when I straighten. I can't believe how rotten it makes me feel. Damn her and her eyes. She goes back to whatever she's doing—building something out of leaves in her lap.

More water. It's too good. I splash my face, my whole head, my neck. A shaved head dries instantly in the heat so I do it again, carefully avoiding my bad arm and bandage that needs to stay dry. I'd love to lose the pants and get completely in the water but with her right there—ah, screw her. I drop the pants and wade in, my bandaged arm held high. The current curls around me like a friendly pet. This stream is the fountain of youth. No one ever told me we had this on our land. I don't stay in long because it's too annoying to hold my arm up. When I emerge, my underwear clings all over my junk. I risk a glance across the stream. It's true that I'm out here to kill her, but I'm no pervert. She's busy with something on the ground, her side to me. I have nothing to change into and don't want to put the pants back on in this heat so I simply sit down.

It's weird. The hunger is brutal but everything else … I feel I've been made new. Across the stream she stands. As if convinced of my attention, she does something in sign language, stopping abruptly like she just realized it's not real talking and I'm not a freak like her and can't understand it. I have a sign I could give her back, but it's already been used. And when she so easily returned it, it lost all its fun.

She goes to the water and walks upstream. Then she catches my eye, releasing the green leaf thing she built in her lap. It finds a current and sails right to me, beaching itself beside a large rock. Because I'm stupid, I get up and look inside. It's a salad. Or something. What looks like blueberries, leafy greens, and mushrooms. "Where's the dressing?"

She fucking smiles.

I catch myself before I smile back. The shock of my near slipup travels my nervous system in the grossest way. What's going on here isn't friendly. She's not Emily. She's Sloane Needs-To-Die Bevan. And she's smiling because I'm about to eat a poisonous salad. Her face looks so pure though. So … honest. As I'm trying to figure her out, her smile has gone all shy, and I don't know what caused the change. I don't care either. I get an automatic urge to bloody her nose but the image of it turns my empty stomach sour.

She points to me, then to her bicep. I shrug. What am I going to say? *Yes, your evil Bevan magic healed my rotting flesh wound. Go ahead and gloat. We Moores are oh so helpless in your presence.*

Screw *that*. This isn't over. Compassion is a weakness, and she's about to learn this in the hardest way. I find a stick and a rock and start sharpening. It'll be me with the javelin this time and it won't be a dream. I feel great. I don't need food. She sits on a spread of fern leaves and starts eating from a pile of the same stuff she sent over to me. My stomach actually moves inside me, like it knows I'm not giving in and it's going to jump ship and go eat the food for me.

My phone dings. A text from my father: *Report*

I have to close my eyes and reconstruct what's happened since I last saw him. They would've found her missing the night I busted out of her room. They should know I've been gone since then too. I assume the dogs returned to the house with nothing, but my family won't know it was because they'd been charmed by the girl they were hunting. She must've told them not to report me either. I have no idea where my family redirected their search, but I can't let them know we're out here. I also can't be stupid enough to think they don't know. It's suspicious this is the first contact they've tried to make with me. It's also strange they haven't sent a team of men to sweep the woods after the dogs. I wouldn't expect them to be so easily fooled.

The only answer is they're letting the prophecy play itself out like they should. Leaving it all up to me. That's the angle I need to play. I reply: *Can't say. Don't try to find us. Everything is under control.*

I have a million missed reminders about classes and pills—shit, my pills. I pat down my pockets and find the case. If I don't stay on schedule, I'll pay. I swallow one dry. It practically ricochets around my empty stomach.

When I look up, Sloane Bevan is watching me. Her bangs are back. For the first time I notice how uneven they are, cut that way on purpose to make a statement like her shirt. What it does to her face—damn it all. I go back to sharpening my stick. Not much later I get up to take a leak and go dizzy from the upward motion. I've never gone this long without food. So what if I eat something she's provided? Maybe she should be gathering food for me. Maybe I should demand more. We should've made the Bevans our slaves long ago. Then we could have all their magic we wanted, and we wouldn't be in this mess. She's missing when I return, and the leaf boat full of forest salad is still waiting for me.

I eat it all. Even the mushrooms that taste like moldy dirt. I consider eating the leaf boat but don't—it's too perfect, and I can't understand how she could weave something to be waterproof long enough to sail the width of a stream without sinking. I turn it over in my hands, trying to make sense of the construction.

She's gone so long I start on a second javelin. It's not as long or straight as the first but it doesn't matter. It gives me something to do. The weeds and fungus I ate are hitting my bloodstream, making the hunger worse. If anything was poisonous, I'm sure I'd know by now. I should've saved one of each thing she gathered to have something to compare and find my own. My underwear has dried so I unwillingly struggle sticky sweat-soaked skin back into my pants, socks, and boots. I find my shirt in a tree and put it on. It's hotter than hell but makes me feel like myself again. It makes me feel ready.

It's time to end this and go home. I wish I had an ax so I could bring back her head. Put it on a pike on the front lawn. And then go get her father's and mount it right beside her.

I lose the grip of myself I just regained when she returns. She's found a metal pail that's loaded with leafy greens. Clamped under her arm are two dry pieces of a dead tree. What I'm most interested in is the load in her shirt that looks like more food. She has a moth on her shoulder and a little fox on her heels. None of this is weird at all.

She lifts her arm, dropping the wood to the ground. Sets down her pail. *My* pail, really, since she pillaged it from my land. I'm tempted to remind her of that, but she takes a step toward me with that food in her shirt, her face so expectant I'm cursing, and I don't know why. This is not a truce. We're not getting along here. She's thinks she's going to feed me, but she's wrong. I'm going to kill her.

Then I'm going to return home, demanding that everyone acknowledge the power I've gained from killing the Bevan destined to end us all.

Because I don't respond, she dumps the load in her shirt onto the leaves she lined up on the ground earlier. It's everything I ate before, multiplied in volume. I need to follow her next time to see where she's getting all this.

No. I need to cross the stream right now and kill her. Why is it so hard to convince myself of that? This paralyzing hesitation must mean the timing is wrong, but how could it be?

She starts building a fire. I rub down my face, harder than I should be able to after taking all those hits to my face. Nothing's swollen or tender. No split skin. I get out my phone and open the camera to selfie mode. What I see isn't right. No bruising, no scars. Face is untouched. Even the line on my nose from that psycho heavyweight I fought last week—gone.

I tug the bandage on my arm down, exposing what should be a sick-ass wound. The skin is pink and new. Sealed with the faintest scar. No sign of the rot and decay that was eating me to the bone.

"What did you do?" I holler across the water at her because I can't stop it. She looks at her fox then looks at me, dropping some kindling and standing fast. The leafy green things she had in the pail lie on the ground at her feet, their giant taproots clean and white.

I rip the bandage all the way off my arm and turn my bicep so she can see.

She squats down, returning to her task. Totally uninterested.

This is so daily to her. She has the inherited immortal blood from her father. Does she not know mortal people don't heal this fast?

All at once I realize what's been stewing in my head since the bouts of unconsciousness and near-death experience. My family wanted her magic, but they never got it. But right now, I have her and all the magic that comes with her. Killing her would be a waste of power that could so easily be mine. The trick is convincing her to teach me. A threat on a family member would surely do it, but her family is too far away to make it convenient. But that fox … I wonder how attached she is to that fox.

Flames dance in her kindling. She's started a fire the vanilla way. Probably afraid my family will sense if she uses magic out here. She builds firewood around it then goes to the stream to fill the pail. She pauses to look at me; it strips me bare. I know what regret is, but I've never felt it like this, never wanted to come clean to a person about some sick thing I've thought.

She did something to me in that room that night that warped me. It's time to be real to myself and admit why I'm not waiting for her back to turn so I can jab this javelin through her spine. Whole truth is I just can't imagine killing her anymore. And I'm so ruined that I can't even find it in me to get vengeance for what she took. It's like she grabbed a loose string and pulled a whole web of things out of me, all connected, one dependent on the other.

But guess what, Rex? What you think has never mattered.

My job is to kill Sloane Bevan so that's what I'm going to do. It doesn't matter that what's made the idea so easy for fifteen years is now missing. Soldiers don't think about their jobs, they just do them. I take another pill, knowing it will keep me alert until night hits, and that's when I'll finish this.

The sun dips low through the trees while she works on her side of the stream. Evening frogs start up their noise—it's so annoying I wish *I* was deaf. I sit on the ground and watch her like the creep I am. She cuts the leafy tops off the taproots with her straight razor. Her silver armband has relocated to her hair as a holder for her ponytail which means no more sheath for that blade. I need to watch where she stashes it. The heat of the day is dying, but I'm still sweating like hell and she's over there barefoot and cool. Moores are supposed to be the smart ones, not Bevans. I take off my boots and socks and roll my pant legs up to my knees. Her fox follows her to the shore where she washes the taproots and cuts them up on a flat rock. The pieces go into the pail she's put over the fire. Her moth flies away; minutes later the sky fills with bats.

No, this is definitely not weird at all.

Okay, so she's the first girl I've ever met in real life who wasn't family. But I've seen enough TV and movies to know most girls don't put bats on security and cook meals with crap collected from the woods. I need to get closer if I'm going to do this. I need to earn some trust from not just her, but from the whole forest.

CHAPTER 7

SLOANE

I'VE JUST ABOUT mastered the task of ignoring Rex's gaze when he stands. Stalker boy didn't unsettle me, so he's changing his play. He throws his boots with the laces tied together over his shoulder, grabs his spear, and wades across the stream. Just like that? He's coming over?

I walk around the fire to situate it between us. He dumps his boots and stabs his spear into the ground like he's claiming land. I can't decide if he's talking to himself or talking to me until he turns around with a question on his face. He speaks again as if answering it himself. I don't catch any of it. The forest is too dim and the firelight too erratic. I'm tempted to suggest he use his phone, but I'd have to get close enough to view the screen. And I'm not so sure I want to be able to talk to him anyway.

He circles the fire. I stand my ground. My companion fox releases whatever he was chewing on at the shore of the stream and watches us, ears pointed high. He looks simply like a pet dog in this light. Friendly, curious, helpful. Only part of that is true, but he's a good actor for our guest. After Rex determines wrongly that the fox is no immediate threat, he offers me a handshake. I feel a laugh released on my vocal chords and cut it off fast. His smile is an unsheathed blade—fast, deadly, determined. I shift to the balls of my feet just in case because it feels so much like I'm about to be attacked. Before the next round, there is something I'd like to know, so I point to the smoke from the fire then point in the direction of the house. If they're looking for us, this fire is a bad idea, and I need to put it out.

It's okay, he says, now close enough for me to read.

But does he understand? Hard to know from his deadpan expression. I point to the house again then point to the two of us.

He swats a hand toward the house. *They're not coming.*

That's good news. He absorbs my expression like it's a common ground we've reached. That we're alone out here pleases him too, although not for the same reason. The sadist is glad to know I'm all his. People like him can't change. What am I trying to do here? This is crazy and a waste of everyone's time.

I sign, *You're Moore scum and I should really be killing you right now.*

He points to my pile of berries and mushrooms, his face asking, *May I?*

If that will get him sitting, yes. So I nod and hold a finger up then point it to the ground.

He says, *What?*

Time for some charades. I pantomime holding a handful of food. Then I sit on the ground and pretend to eat. He looks confused. Really? The Moores' chosen king is this slow? I point to him, point to the ground.

Sit? he says.

I nod. He helps himself and sits. Every time he gets up for more, I stand with him. I don't like the looks he's throwing toward the fox. He gobbles my whole hoard then goes to the stream to drink and wash the berry stain from his hands, trusting me enough to turn his back. Saving his life has upset our roles. Now he knows I won't actively kill him. I hope he knows I'll kill him in self-defense because that part is still very true.

Upon his return, he relocates his spear closer to the fire and sits beside it. The fox wanders close, engaging Rex in a stare-off that gives me a tingle at the top of my spine. Sharp teeth and crushing jaw are useful in combat, but Rex is bigger, meaner, and armed with a human-made weapon. This fight would not be fair. I send the fox into the woods, promising him I'll be fine. I poke the chicory root in the pail of boiling water, trying my best to judge if it's ready to eat. A meal of something other than berries and mushrooms sounds better than a solstice feast.

All color has drained from the sky now, stars sneaking out one by one. So close to the stream we have no branches above us, but with the fire as our only light we'll be swimming in shadow until moonrise; even then, the darkness under the canopy will be difficult to navigate. It won't be easy to find my cave.

Rex fidgets. His face carries new angles with the firelight and few days' worth of stubble. He starts tapping out a fast beat with fingers against his leg. I study him over the flames, trying to ignore his father's square jaw and squinched eyes. His head is shaved to match his military surplus wardrobe, but his faint eyebrows suggest he's as blond. Just because he looks like Dillon doesn't mean he can't find a different road. Uncle Christian is a Moore. So is Aaron. They've broken from the evil clutch of this place and this family.

I skewer some chicory root from the boiling water with a sharp stick and hand it to him. His fingers brush mine during the transfer. I feel his eyes snap toward my face, but I don't meet them. His body has made contact with mine in so many ways—there's no reason the slightest skim of skin should be such a thing. He's making it more than it needs to be. But then, he doesn't know I bled myself into his open wound. It's kind of hard to top that.

He starts talking, exaggerating the words like people always do when they want me to read their lips. They don't realize that makes it harder. No one can ever stand sitting with someone in the quiet. Except my dad. He and I have shared much companionable silence. The thought gives me sympathetic pain for the next piece of chicory root I stab. I blow on it, watching him talk like I'm trying to decipher the words because I know people find comfort in knowing they're being heard in some way even when they're not. And comfortable people hassle me less.

There's no immediate reaction when he takes his first bite. As he chews I see the downturn of lip and brow furrow that signals his taste buds going on full alert.

Don't think about it, I want to tell him. *It's not gross. You're just not used to it. Just eat it.*

He gets it down and thumps his chest with a fist. *Got any …*

The last word isn't recognizable. He must see my confusion because he repeats it until I get it.

Ketchup?

If only our ancestors could see us now. It's a Bevan-Moore peace meal, complete with jokes. The menu stinks but it could be worse. We could have winter to contend with. Summer in the South is a witch's feast, and I'm only getting started. In the morning I'm going on a hunt for a sweet birch so I can make tea.

I'm fishing another piece out of the pail when an unwanted idea smudges my mood. This is nice and all, but where is it going? Curing Rex Moore—really? It's a stab in the back to every Bevan. A gasoline fire set to the prophecy itself. Spit on the grave of every one of my family who's died in this war. They chose me, believing I was born to end the next great leader of the Moores before he can rise to power and exterminate us all. And here I am working so hard to give him a new beginning. He's not an animal I can release back in the wild for a second chance at life. He'll go straight back to that house, into that black cloud of corruption, his new scars from me tacking on more reason to kill. And once again my family will be hunted, and I'll be to blame.

Rex leans forward to write something in the dirt. It's too far from the glow of the fire to read with the uneven dips and shadows on the ground. When he sees me struggling, he passes a hand across the letters and sets them to an orange smolder. They light up against the earth. *How did you fix my arm?*

I pass a hand over to extinguish them. Either from the act of it or from the way I look at him he easily concludes I'm not talking.

He smears the ashy dirt and writes something new, each letter glowing orange as soon as his finger creates it. *There were birds. Crows? And your blade.* He scans our little camp as if searching for the straight razor. It's secure in the elastic bottom of my bralette, but he doesn't need to know that.

Magic, I write below it in a short blue flame.

He blows it out and writes, *Witchcraft.*

I shrug like it's the same thing. He shrugs back in agreement. I look at the discolored band of skin on his forearm. There's something so shocking about it, but I'm not sure what.

Bats emerge from the trees, dipping and diving all around us. They flutter against my arms and legs. *Danger,* they tell me. *Predator.* I send them away to safety and look at Rex who's leapt to his feet.

Someone's coming, I sign stupidly.

The way his face has changed forces me several paces back. I can't unsee the Moore in him now. Distrust burns as bright as our letters in the dirt. Beneath the distrust crouches the hate, now uncovered and unhinged. He's become his dad. His uncle. Every evil Moore from Winnie's mind, collected from the memories locked up in Aunt

Tara and Grandma Sloane. They guard those images with an iron will, but Winnie's picked up enough bits and pieces to build whole monsters to keep me and her and Will awake at night.

Danger. Predator. That's not someone coming. It's Rex the bats are warning me about.

He picks up his spear, and I push power into the fire until it blazes higher than the trees. The heat is ferocious, pushing into the sticky night like my personal brigade. It's moved him back but not enough—that spear can cover distance all the way into the trees. My Bevan immortality won't protect me from a spear through the heart. I could run, but with bare legs and arms, I'm like a running light in these woods. I should've left my war paint on. I could douse the fire and use ash but there's not enough time.

There is time for something else though. I stick a finger in the blackened ground around the fire and draw the encircled cross again on my forehead. Rex starts as if hit. My view goes clear, and I realize that hate and distrust I saw before isn't really there. It was an expectation, a memory, painted on him by something inside me. He raises a hand to his forehead, coming away with evidence of the mirrored symbol automatically drawn on his. He mutters curses— *that* I can read—but instead of looking up at me, his focus lands behind me. My back crawls but I'm not going to be fooled like that. Still, I have to see. I reorient myself away from the fire so I can keep an eye on him while turning to see behind me.

It wasn't a trick. Someone's there. A woman, older than us but not *old* old—college age, maybe—taking careful steps into our camp. She's talking to Rex like she's expected here. No greeting, no "*Hey, there you are.*" Rex fires words back, clearly agitated. The woman starts talking over him. From the way Rex raises his chin, it's apparent that doesn't happen often and when it does, it's someone's bad move. She's repeated something now, a question he's answering by not answering. She repeats it again with an added sharp look my way. Rex seems to have forgotten all about me. His words back to her are impossible to read for how they're squeezed out through a tight jaw and almost immobile lips. As he speaks, the fighter in him unconsciously prepares: feet shift ever so slightly, hand slides down the spear to a better position.

The woman reaches behind her back. Something glints in the darkness, its shape harsh and otherworldly in these gentle summer woods. She says one last thing to him before aiming that gun at me. It's an impossible shot—too dark, too far away. She also knows this because she's moving forward as I'm moving backward. With each step I draw power from the earth with no idea how I'll use it. I was primed for physical combat, not magic, and the mental flip isn't sticking its landing.

My amulet sings against me. I close my fist around it, the connection to the earth's power like a spark in my hand. An unseen force shifts, curling around me. Ahead, the pistol flashes in the night. The bullet scorches the wind beside me; my amulet turns lightning hot, searing my hand. She's lining up another shot.

Rex's spear shoots through the flames. The ground it covers between exiting the fire and entering its target is a blur of time. My head roars, vision zooming in as if physically covering the same ground, and I see the sharpened point meet the exact corner of an eye, clearing a path through tissue as the conical end gains width. The burst of blood as the eye bulges. Skin torn from bone.

This view is not mine! I frantically scrub the ash symbol off my forehead. At once I'm yanked out of Rex's head, back to my position, the fire to my left, the intruder to my right. On her back, face skewered like a piece of chicory root. The spear stands proud and heroic, a monument of death. Rex has already crossed the camp to snatch the pistol out of the woman's hand, but I don't know why. She's not getting up, ever again.

Rex bends at the waist, hands on knees, gun dangling down. *Oh my god,* he's saying. *Oh my god, oh my god, oh my god.* Over and over until he collapses to his knees, pitching forward, fists against ground, head bowed. Before him, the woman's body releases one last shudder before going still. Rex lifts himself up to grasp his spear with both hands, his muscles tightening to prepare for the pull but at the last second he opens his hands, releasing the spear like it's infected with a frightful contagion he doesn't want to contract. Slowly, he turns his head toward me. His expression is a hastily constructed homemade bomb. Panic is the fertilizer, fury is the kerosene, anguish is the nails. And the distance between him and me is the wick.

Instead of running for the trees I rush toward my boots. They're too essential to leave behind. A mistake—Rex plows into me, his shoulder digging into my waist as we slam against the ground. My amulet smacks against my neck, cold and quiet, drained of juice. I twist and contort, but Rex meets every move with a better one until I'm so tangled there's no hole to slip out. I pant against his cruel weight and he only presses with more. His stubble scrapes my cheek as he tries to orient his face without giving an inch for me to move. He knows that's all it will take.

We're sharing breath then, his eyes an inch from mine. If I had any ability to move my neck, I could break his nose with my forehead. He knows that too. My sweat congeals with his. We'll be brazed together if he doesn't release me soon. He shifts his chest so it's flat against mine. My hidden blade digs into my ribs, a reminder of its useless presence. He shifts again, testing the feel of it until recognition crosses his face. We stare at each other, both knowing the other one knows that blade is there. He wants it, but he'll have to release me to get it. And if he even tries to get a hand in there—just the thought gives me a burst of adrenaline so ripe I get my knee under his hip and my elbow into his throat. His palm slams against the ground beside my head—the same move he made in that bedroom when he wanted to hit me but couldn't. Then I sense the power draw from the earth under me. Before I can brace against an onslaught of magic, my vision goes white. A sharp point of pain between my eyes builds so much pressure I feel my body go limp in his grasp. Words drive into my head but they're not mine: *You invaded me, now I invade you. You saved my life, I saved yours. We're even. Now leave my land before I make it uneven.*

Cool air rushes between us. He's released me and stood, but I'm paralyzed by his magic. *Our* magic. Earth magic used like a weapon against me. The betrayal cuts so deep tears collect in my eyes. Our families weren't meant to be enemies, but here we are using shared magic against each other. He scrubs blood off his lip with the back of his hand. Straightens his twisted shirt. Looks down at me.

Leave, he says. Wiped so brutally clear of all emotion, his face is a plastic mask. Eyes machinelike and constricted, mouth a featureless line. All versions of Rex Moore I've seen and heard about have never been as terrifying as this.

I push power to my arms and legs but still can't move. I feel the tear escape down my temple. His eyes follow it but his face remains in its harsh mold. He could kill me right now. He could make it uneven so easily. From the way his eyes roll before he shakes his head to force away exhaustion, I can tell the magic he just used against me has depleted his resources, natural and supernatural. Standing above me is sucking strength he doesn't have.

He shuffles his feet to gain balance but not soon enough. One stumble back gives me space enough to view the pinpoints of light beyond the trees. Stars I'm alive to see. Stars to lead me home. I don't know who that was he killed but it had to be an accident. I know enough about him to know he wouldn't give a damn otherwise. Whatever he and I were doing before has been zeroed out. The cycle has restarted with one slight change: instead of me being captive, he's letting me go.

My family made a mistake. As hard as that is to admit, it's true. I'm not weathered enough to handle the Moores. Every bit of truth and advice my dad fed me has been a waste on me. *Because I know them,* was his answer for all my questions on why they couldn't be trusted, why they couldn't change, why we had to fight this war. A statement like that should be the baseline for every thought I have about them, but somehow these last few days I allowed a new one to grow: hope. And another—dare I admit it?

My blazing fire reflects on Rex's face as he stands above me, one hand over his bandaged arm, the deadly wound I gave him then decided to cure.

Yes, I'll admit it because I've already lost. I sowed trust. I saw it sprout and I let it grow. I should've pulled it like a nutrient-sucking weed. Instead, I let it overtake my dad's words, choking them out so they could no longer see the sun.

I traded my trust of my dad for an untested seedling of trust for Rex Moore.

If this failure is what's left me paralyzed on the ground, then I'm done for. I'm buried in imaginary sand, muscles restrained, burdened by a weight too great to overcome.

Rex has recovered some strength. He has the gun now. His shaved head is glazed with sweat. Blood and dirt from our tussle streak his face, their lines blurring with perspiration. He aims the gun at my face with two hands and a wide stance fully prepped to fire. *Go home.*

I can't go home. Not knowing how badly I've failed.

My amulet's power has drifted away, impotent against another bullet until enough time has lapsed for recharge. He readjusts his aim for my heart. The breeze strokes me, scattering the imaginary sand, waking muscles and nerves from slumber—a gentle poke here, a nudge there. I get my elbows under me, then my legs. He watches as I tip, landing hard on my knee. I don't see him waver, his quick intake of breath. I don't see the muzzle of the gun lower by half an inch before he can recover it. If I did, there would be a tiny drop of possibility here. There's nothing. There never was. I let it all go.

On my way past the woman's corpse, I rip the spear free. It comes loose in a slick of blood. He doesn't shoot me for taking it, and I don't turn around to see if he's grateful or angry that I removed it. I force my gaze anywhere but her face. My dad trained me to be strong in the face of violence; my mom raised me with a stomach of steel. I wouldn't want to disappoint them.

Once out of his sight, I climb a pine snuggled under the thick limb of an oak, trading the sappy branches for the height and better view from the oak. There I watch Rex. He stares at where I disappeared into the trees for so long I'm about to get down and find my cave. Suddenly he spins, heaving the pistol into the water. He returns to the woman's corpse, dropping weakly into a bow, his forehead against the ground beside her. He stays there motionless as the stars blink and shift. If he's calling to the elements, it's a lonely, prolonged call, and I'm a jerk for invading his privacy.

His bones finally give, leaving him flat on the ground. He slowly turns to his back to face the sky. A fist pounds the earth once, twice. With the third, anger has surrendered to something else, making that final tap against the earth slower, more deliberate. Pained. Defeated.

I want to return to him, to sit with him. To help him cover her body with the fern fronds I'd laid on the shore. I call the bats instead and ask them to lead me to the cave. I won't be sleeping tonight but at least I'll have company. The moon sneaks into the sky as I walk, lighting up white clouds rippled like windblown snow. It reminds me of my riverbank at home when winter blows in like an overnight surprise. I'll never see that again. Everything from now on will be tarnished with that woman's violent death, with Rex's face as he used our magic against me. With the knowledge of my failure, my betrayal of my dad's teachings. Even if I make it home, it will never be the same.

CHAPTER 8

REX

IT'S EASY TO sneak into a fortress when you no longer care if you live or die. I spider up the side of the house and enter the way I left: through Sloane Bevan's broken window. The house hibernates. Not a living soul roams the halls. All the non-security staff has gone home. Should I care my mother's beauty sleep hasn't been compromised by the disappearance of her youngest son? No, Rex, you shouldn't.

Up in my room I shove clothes into my gym bag. Then toothpaste, toothbrush, deodorant, phone charger. A few sheathed knives from my drawer. My whole stash of pills. Down three flights of stairs for some snacks and sports drinks from the kitchen. Down another flight for some guns and ammo.

Stealing among shadows, I avoid two patrolling guards outside to reach the garage, catching the night attendant by surprise. He opens his mouth but can't quite decide what to say.

"Load three of those water jugs into the back of my car."

"Master Rex—"

"Do it and don't talk to me."

He does. They're the five gallon ones used in the garage's old-school water dispenser and he's sweating after the first one. I'd help the old man if I didn't have to keep watch for those guards. It's not easy wrangling the jugs around my ride's roll cage, and it wastes precious time.

A real-deal rally car promises a fast getaway but sucks for luggage. For my next birthday maybe I'll ask for something more practical. Everyone knows the sixteenth birthday demands you go big, bigger than a ŠKODA Fabia R5 that owns the European rally scene and looks sweet doing it. Too bad I got that for my fifteenth. Mine's been weighed down by a custom luxury sport interior but it can still haul a-dollar-dollar. The ruts in the southeast corner of our land can speak to that. I'm going to need to do some thinking about what I'll ask for when I turn sixteen. I don't have much time left to choose.

The night attendant finds a spot for the last jug but the hatch won't close. Damn that roll cage. Maybe the sleek Audi sedan parked beside it would've been a better choice, but the R5 is the only car I know how to drive. Plus, nothing can beat it off road.

I take my eyes off surveillance to help him shove the jug farther in and finally, all jugs are in and the hatch is closed.

"Now get in the driver's seat." I squeeze my bag into the back and take the passenger side. I could do this myself if I had a code to the gate. For the first time I see how balls it is that I don't have access through the front gate of my own fucking house. Once there I get out, pointing a gun at him in full view of the camera as he peels himself out of the deep bucket seat. Here's the proof so they don't kill him for helping me escape. It puts me in a bind for my getaway because whoever's monitoring the cameras probably has my father on the phone right now. So be it. This guy doesn't deserve a bullet in the brain because I'm the shitbag who can't kill Sloane Bevan. The dirty traitor who kills Emily instead.

Who *kills* Emily! I can't believe it—can't unsee it—can't deal—have to get out of here. Have to go somewhere—any-where—*oh shit*, Rex, you killed Emily. Oh *shit*.

The night attendant's saying my name, shaking my shoulder. I raise the gun again and tell him to go back and tell them not to look for me. As if they'll listen. I get behind the wheel and screw the takeoff from first and grind second and it dawns on me I just fail at life. I fail at every-thing I try to do. I fail so hard it's unsalvageable.

What Sloane Bevan did to me is worse than death. She let me live so I had to face my family as their failed savior. She baited me to her side of the stream knowing Emily would show and I'd react to that gun like I've been trained to react. Don't think. Follow through. My training is my guide, never my brain. Muscle memory. Shoot to kill.

That's exactly what throwing that spear felt like. My hand guided by some invisible force. By the wind itself. Easy for me to say and an excuse used by many murderers: I plead insanity. As if that's an option in this family. Insanity is our family trademark.

No, it's gotten very real. Body count is now at one for the Moores due to my own hand, and no kill points for Sloane Bevan. Bevans are leading thanks to me. I can never return home.

I swerve to a stop on the shoulder and dig the box of granola bars from my bag, inhaling three of them while texting Aaron. Sometimes he responds in the dead of night, sometimes not. Sometimes all I get is a crabby lecture about how *some* people work for a living, *some* people have a schedule, *some* people value their sleep. I plug my phone in to the R5 to recharge. While I'm waiting for him to respond, I grab a Gatorade and fire up the navigation in the car. The screen paints with street names and points of interest that mean nothing to a kid who's never passed through the iron fence surrounding his family's property. After poking around the screen for a few minutes I give up, lower the windows, and power off the engine. The sudden lack of engine hum and exhaust drone is almost painful.

The thick summer night presses into the car. It'd be nice to hear approaching tires on the road but the shrieking insects have ruined that plan. They won't be using the headlights if they're looking for me. Which leads me outside to the water jugs in the trunk, to apply one of the few nonviolent Moore effects I know by heart: a cloaking spell that can be easily applied using water. I feed the spell into those jugs so I'll be prepared if they come for me.

Back in the car my phone's screen is empty of all texts. Because of course. The one night I really need him, and he feels no need to lecture me. I open all my social media apps and scroll through messages from my online friends. Any plea to them for help would pretty much be pathetic. *I've never left my house. Can you tell me how streets work?* There's no proof any of them are real human beings, anyway. They could all be bots programmed to help me advance through the game levels so I buy more games.

Okay, Rex, pick a city. Any city, any point of interest. Set the nav and start driving. Easy.

I start the car. The initial roar and persistent noise of it is like a beacon to anyone searching for me. I open the nav and zoom the map out. There's a puddle of green I zoom in to called Pocahontas State Park. That sounds like an ideal place to chill while I figure all this out. I set it as the destination and see the calculated time and miles—it just doesn't seem far enough. My family can track Bevans in the remotest corners of the U.K. and Europe. A blood relative? They'll nail me before I can find a place to park. I zoom the map out and look again, but nearby states cause new problems as I try to remember where all my extended family members live. There are estates all over the eastern part of this country. Not to mention all the people my family hires in big cities to do their work.

I'm looking at the whole map of the U.S. and it's impossibly huge. So many cities. So many highways. I don't even know how to get a hotel room or how to buy food. At least I know how to drive—kind of—thanks to Aaron. And I have a credit card for emergencies, also thanks to him. He never told me how to use it. Only: *Don't use this, don't speak of it, always keep it with you.* Way to be vague, Aaron. But I'm used to it. Vague is the language my family speaks to me, him included.

After grabbing some clean clothes from my bag, I get out of the car to change, moving my mostly empty wallet to my new pants. Before I toss the dirty ones behind the seat, I check all the pockets and find a small vial.

The bottle of magic to end all Bevans.

How could I forget I had this? Somehow this will be my salvation. I just need to figure out how. Now in clean clothes, I get back in the driver's seat. Phone check: still no texts. I take out the bottle, noting how the magic churns and slithers against the inside of the glass like it's coaxing me to release it. There's one person who can help me escape because she's working on her own escape. She's familiar with the world outside my family's estate. She could be my Pocahontas in this new frontier. She's already saved my life—didn't the real Pocahontas save some dude? Too bad teaming up with her is out of the question.

Right?

I rest my forehead on the vibrating steering wheel and close my eyes. It rattles my brain as if shaking out all the thoughts I don't need right now. Through the sieve goes Emily's ruined eye. Her lifeless limbs. My uncaring mother. This loud car, probably audible from the house. My inadequacy in surviving outside that iron fence. What's left is a blinding clarity: I saved Sloane Bevan's life after she saved mine, but then I freed her. We're not even; she owes me. Full of all that magic my family thirsts for, she's a treasure trove I should've never let go. She's the gold nugget left in that sieve. Possession of Sloane Bevan plus the bottle of

Bevan-killer means I'm not just king of the Moores. I'm king of the Bevans too. Rich in magic and power.

The hardest part? Finding her on my land with this car. I can't go back in. I have to go around, navigating roads I've never seen in the loudest car a boy racer could dream of. That's assuming she hasn't already reached and escaped through the fence. Would she leave tonight, or would she wait for sunrise?

Movement in my side mirror catches my eye—a small group of deer leaping across the road. I peer past them, down the gray strip of road disappearing into the dark made hazy by swarming insects and humidity. An unnamable sensation nudges me until I turn around in the seat to squint through the back window. All my family's time and effort went into training me for combat, not passing down their knowledge of magic. What little I do know was casually passed, dwelling in places rarely touched in my head. This strain seems to belong to that buried perception.

I kill the engine, shove out of the car and drop to one knee, fingertips against the pavement, eyes closed. The insects are surely violating noise ordinances, but I choke them out of my brain, sending all sense through my fingers against the road. There—a rumble. A hum. Not of the woods. Something mechanical. I scramble for the R5's hatch release and haul out a water jug, its unexpected weight knocking it against the roll cage with my fingers acting as a bumper but it has to be ignored. Brace my legs, heave the jug onto my shoulder, slam the hatch. Dump the water over the entire car. Run.

I've barely made it behind the tree line when a herd of roaring engines and hissing rubber blows past. I count three black fleet cars used by our security guys followed by my father's BMW and my uncle's Aston. Thanks to that water spell, my car's gone invisible on the shoulder to them, but not to me. I watch it drip water, trying not to piss myself.

If I'm doing this, I need to do it now. My car is coated in magic that will linger after the water evaporates but not for long. Only two more jugs in my trunk mean two more times I can hide. The hunt for Sloane Bevan must be pure stealth and efficiency. As I wipe the tickle of sweat on my face against my shirt sleeve, I'm reminded of the symbol she drew, the one she used to invade my head and steal a part of me. We're undeniably linked now, whether I like it or not. No doubt there's a range limitation on that thing, but what if—

What if I reverse her attack? Use it back on her.

The moon's light settles on me when I emerge from the trees. The obnoxious insects take a break from their noise, like the hush of a stadium crowd before some epic play. The dirt beside the road is mush from the last rain and unending brutal humidity. I scoop up a handful, mud mixed with road grit, wondering how to do this to myself. All tricks must be employed to find her. All convictions abandoned. Self-preservation? Screw it. I've already been tainted by the Bevans. Nothing can get worse.

I smear my forehead, blinded by the power of it all. My eyes no longer belong to just me. I've joined a multiplayer RPG. And I realize then, the reason this connection feels so tainted isn't because it's Bevan-created. We're followers of the same damn magic. This, though, swarms with something different and wrong. Black magic? No way. She's not that bad-ass.

Boots and socks come off for a better connection to earth. I raise my hands to study them, trying to ground myself. Both palms on the cool wet fender of the R5 send a familiar signal to my brain. Good. Now to make sense of that other input. Breathing myself into my core, as my trainers always tell me, I reach for the unfamiliar. There's a dizzying shift in my perception. I swallow down the nausea.

Who ... Rex?

I focus a thought: *Tell me where you are.* It echoes back to me, reflecting a moonlit vision of my family's border fence, the broken portion they fixed a million times only for it to go back to being broken. As a bored little kid I'd follow the workers there to watch each time they tried to fix it. I know exactly where that is.

Stay there, I think. The connection rings in my ears, breaking up like harsh feedback. I breathe back into it, but I sense blocks, hastily constructed, like someone flipping furniture as I pursue them through a room. That's her doing, for sure. It doesn't matter though. She won't make it far on foot from that spot. I draw a mental map of our property to see the relation of that broken fence section to the front gate I just exited. Straight back to the northern border, then a little west. Now to find it in a car.

The roar of the exhaust is too sweet for this life. It's a kick in my blood so perverse it should be illegal. The road ahead is my victim pleading for its life. I rev to just under redline and dump the clutch, sending rubber particulate into my nose and joy into my heart. Holy oak, this *car*.

Guilt spirals in like a lethal projectile. Not because I've killed one of my own. There are too many Moores I'd love to use as target practice. But Emily? My only friend? They'll find her body and blame Sloane Bevan, but I know how these things work. The truth is always waiting outside. Whether they find it or it sneaks in doesn't matter—they don't trust me. That's why I've been kept inside the fence, why they've planned every hour of my every day, why it's such a surprise they left me alone for so long in the woods while I dealt with the Bevan trash. So if I'm tied to Emily's murder, they'll believe it, and when they reconstruct the scene and find I did it to protect Sloane Bevan, I'll pay in unimaginable ways.

Enough. I've already decided I can't ever go home. It's time for a new plan. I need to capture Sloane Bevan, lock her in a room, and make her write down every spell she knows. Once I have that, it won't matter who I've killed.

A side road appears ahead at my left. This would have to be the east border of our property. I downshift and engine brake to take the turn. Ahead, I see nothing but the stripe of road and bordering trees, the moon high ahead like a spotlight. This could be the route my father and crew took, but it's also the one I need. My water spell has surely evaporated by now—a stupid point since there's no stealth mode while driving this car. The slightest tap on the throttle loads the air with the turbo's screech and the roaring, popping exhaust. I grip the wheel and slam the pedal, eating road. We scream ahead into the night, stealth out the window, speed my new best friend. At least Sloane Bevan won't hear me coming.

CHAPTER 9
SLOANE

THE DOE NUDGES me in my side. She's led me to the broken part of the fence and now she's shooing me out as if she knows I must hurry. I turn to look into her eyes, still trying to dissect the mystery about her. She reads differently than every other animal in the woods. Her mind is older somehow, as old as some of these one-hundred-year-old oaks. And I can't understand why she's pushing me to get on the move now, in the middle of the night, instead of waiting for the sun. I want to tell her my vision isn't as good as hers, but she probably already knows that.

She moves forward to head-butt me gently in the stomach, forcing me to take a step back. The power in her restraint is a bit humbling—she could kill me with such simple grace if she wanted to. I'm aware of the hustle she's trying to inspire, but I can't leave before I figure her out.

At a loss, I sign, *Who are you?*

She tosses her head and comes in for another nudge, but I sidestep it this time, placing a hand on her muscular neck. Maybe she's been with me this whole time, waiting in camouflage until I lost Rex. Now she's trying to scoot me to safety before he comes back. It's a motherly gesture that pokes me in a tender spot. I'm too slow to raise a shield against that last memory of my mom. Her face full of pride, her eyes full of tears. Her grip on Marcas, full of fear.

Ears high and open, the doe has raised her head to peer stiffly ahead. Her rigid posture appears cautious but in this forest she's not the prey. She reigns. For how long? And why? A heartbeat later she's dancing around me, and I have to move for fear of getting trampled. She nudges me again—hard. Okay, time to mind. I step through the break in the fence, and she follows me out, ready to nudge me again should I even think of slowing down.

There's a faint light through the underwood ahead, almost like we're about to reach a clearing painted by the moon. It must be high by now but it's hard to spot through this thick canopy. Twin lights blink through the trees, streaking low. A car? Can't be. If we've already reached a road, that's insane. This can't be that easy.

Unless it's someone looking for me.

The lights pass by and the doe presses me on. A road ahead would explain this light already permeating the forest around us, seeping in from a reflection off what must be pavement. One dimmer white light appears to my right, creeping left until it slows to a stop directly in front of me and blinks off.

That makes me stop in my tracks. Which makes the deer go in for another shove. I brush her away, suddenly sick with a new fear: she might actually be working for them. They could've affected her, forced her … or she could simply be their companion like the creatures in my woods are to me. It would be easier to catch me by car and drive me back than hike all the way out here for me.

I raise an arm to make a call for the moths. They burrowed into the Moore castle to help me so they must be on my side. My plea is disrupted by another mental stampede. Rex, snapping through my carefully built barricade to plant himself front and center. I can't decide whether it's bad manners or ego that makes him think this is okay. Yes, I did it to him. When he was killing me. That's the difference, moron.

This time I pinch my inner arm, close my eyes, and do the alphabet backward. The pain and mental work consume enough brain power to degrade his connection. My closed eyes prevent him from seeing anything through me. Then I take the input I just received from him and jumble it up. A car's muddy tire? Make that a Ferris wheel. His bare feet against earth? Chicken feet. I send the images back to him and resume the backwards alphabet. Winnie deserves a thank-you for teaching me this trick. Only the best mind invader herself can teach such a righteous defense.

I have to lean on a sycamore trunk to collect my breath, not because of his invasion or the defense, but what it all woke up. That pit of dark hate I stole from him flexes in my chest again, stronger this time. There's probably something I should do to disable it or better contain it. My family's black magic texts were incomplete. My dad always said he could only teach me enough black magic to be dangerous. And that practice of non-native magic is always a risk, that we should learn it but never use it. I promised I'd only use the exact spells he taught me, and only in an emergency. And I'd never improvise, no matter what. Well, I lied, because that's exactly what I did in that room.

The symbol I drew in Rex's blood stands for unity in black magic. Remembering that only proves the truth of what my dad said. Using it did save my life, but right now it's enabling a danger that's about to kill me. Rex is using the connection I opened to find me, and I don't know how to turn it off.

Never do unless you can undo. It's an important rule of magic. Is it okay to break this rule in a life or death situation? Yes, but everything in magic has consequences. Knowing how to deal with this one would be convenient right about now.

Ahead, the doe is flipping her white tail at me. No animal has ever betrayed me. Trust is a given, even when it's a pack of attack Dobermans trained in service to the Moores. Calling upon my moths would only prove my distrust of the doe, and maybe I'm stupid, but I can't do it. It's a path I don't want to take.

I'm sorry, Dad. I'm here on the Moores' land, and I still can't stop being 'so damn optimistic.'

I catch up. She passes through the final line of trees and turns to wait for me. Beyond her sits a road, banked a few feet off the ground. A car perched on top. Rex leaning against it, hands tucked casually under opposite biceps. Waiting.

He ducks down to peer into the darkness of the woods where the doe exited. Her eyes glimmer at me as she turns, reassuring. But I'm already crouching, then backing away, slow as a sneaky cat. One step. Now two. How far do I need to get away before I can run? How deeply into the woods does his sight penetrate? I ease branches aside so their leaves don't catch any moonlight. As soon as I can't see him anymore he won't be able to see me. One more step and—

He straightens, his eyes locking right onto me. I freeze. He leaps off the embankment and runs straight for me as lithe and swift as a deer.

I dart to the side, shoving through the branches of a young pine that scratch my face and arms. Coming through blind I stumble over a fallen log, banging a shin before I catch myself and launch over it. He had to have heard that. I risk a glance over my shoulder and see nothing but the silvery needles of the pine jiggling from my passage, the dark streak of a fallen log like a tear in the landscape.

I turn and run. I don't get far.

He comes in from the side, first just a blur of human-shaped gray, then a lighter gray arm whipping out. I can do nothing but brace for the landing as we smack together and roll. He's turned into a wrapper around me, absorbing so much impact the only collision I feel is my frame against his. Followed by more detail—my hip against his pelvis, my cheek against his arm.

And a couple additions once we find rest: my knuckles smashing into his sternum, my elbow crashing into his chin.

He's choking for air, so I clock him again in the sternum and twist away, all at once realizing he's got a fist tangled in my hair and he isn't letting go. I wind up to rabbit-kick him in the previously dislocated knee, decide that would be mean, and aim for the groin instead.

I'm glad I don't have balls because the position he's contorted into is painful to watch. The way he's gone into the fetal position but still hasn't released my hair shows real grit for a rich, spoiled jerk. I find his hand and start prying fingers but they're locked like a seized muscle, so I enclose his hand in both of mine and perform an alligator death roll, twisting his arm until he's forced to let go.

One last minute grab and he's got me by the wrist, a yank and I'm against him. Arm around my throat, legs constricting mine. Interesting he'd expose the groin again so quickly. I need to kick harder next time.

This is all going totally déjà vu now. All I need to do is bite him again and we can repeat the whole performance. We need to stop doing this. Or maybe continue until one of us wins and can go home. His breath is hot on my ear, words released like jabs he can't deliver with a fist due to how he's holding me. He must be telling me off. Such a shame I can't hear it.

A different kind of language alights over me. My moths are here in the branches above. They're calling me off. Telling me to relax, there's no danger here.

Do you not see this? I shoot back.

My head is going light. I'm panting too hard, and Rex is holding too tight on lungs that need to fill. I feel my blood rushing but it's pained, struggling. My pulse goes into my head, slow and thick. Flecks of black float upon my vision of the gray forest, swimming too close to be outside of me. I struggle against him—a primitive urge I can't control.

I need to breathe. The flecks of black are turning purple. Plum. Red. I choke.

Rex loosens an inch. Instead of fighting back, I breathe. I drag air in, gulp it down. He loosens more. Without my fight it feels like an embrace. He unwinds his legs from mine. His arms remain. The breath on my ear is hot once more but the words have lost their percussive vulgarity. They're soft now, almost conversational.

I try to pull away and he allows it, one arm fully releasing, tentative. A test.

We untangle and sit up together. His chest heaves in rhythm with mine. All that joins us are his remaining fingers clamping down on my forearm. Not even hard. I raise a hand to his face. In his night-darkened eyes, I see he wants to flinch, but he doesn't. I relish that for a second because it proves I didn't lose here. He knows I could attack him right now. This is only over because I say it is. I smear away the part of the symbol recreated on his forehead not already washed away by his sweat. He watches my face as I do it, aware I know what he did because of how he lifts his chin as if to say, *yeah, what of it*? Caught, yet unashamed.

So I see co-opting black magic from a Bevan isn't beneath him. Good to know. I can't decide if it's a step in the right direction or seriously twisted.

I give a pointed look at his hand still clamping my arm.

He shakes his head. *Don't even think about it*, is what that head shake says. His eyes say, *I wish I could let you go.*

What he actually says is, *Stop.*

Three completely different meanings, all seemingly genuine, all at battle with one another. He says it again: *Stop.*

Really? I fingerspell. *You chase me, then tackle me, and you want me to stop?* It takes forever to spell out but the action of it brings release to the coiled fight mechanism and buildup of tension that comes from not being able to sign with any human being for days.

I twist my arm and pull. He releases it, grabbing the other one with his empty hand. He's changed his clothes. Soldier boy is actually wearing camo now—digital camo, and only the pants but still. The black T-shirt is clean too. Boots look the same. So he either had extra clothes in that car or he went back to the house. Probably got the car from the house anyway, so either way he went back. He's talked to his family and they sent him back out here to retrieve me.

He's produced a phone he's talking into. Then he puts the screen up to my face.

I'm getting out of here and you're coming with.

I laugh, out loud this time, unrestrained. He startles, fumbling the phone, and in his effort to catch it before it hits the ground my arm is freed. I push off, making it half a step before my ankle sticks in the trap of his grasp. We're both stretched on the ground now, neither one of us making any move because the fatigue must've just hit him as it hit me. All adrenaline and endorphins depleted. Too many calories missed. And tired, so tired. Tired of all of this.

Rolling onto my back on the ground, I let him keep my ankle. The moon has reached its pinnacle, suffusing the tree branches with silver set off by inky black shadow. There's a perfect tunnel in the canopy above me, revealing the edge of moon and purple-gray wisps of clouds. An object shifts over my view, so close I have to blink to focus.

His phone again. *They're hunting both of us right now. It only makes sense to stay together. And if we don't move now, we're dead. Ask your stupid deer if you don't believe me.*

As if on cue, the doe dips her head next to me, snorting a breath that stirs my bangs. I reach for a stroke on her velvet nose, but I pull back at the last second. She betrayed me. She *is* on their side. And just as I think it, her spirit brushes against my mind, beckoning, reassuring, pushing me to move, to go. I've never had my trust broken by an animal. That's a human game, or has been up until now. Something is crumbling inside me and there's no way to brace against it. Yes, it's stupid to lay a blanket of trust over all woodland creatures including those I've never met. Yes, I'm that naïve to be so bothered to find out some aren't on my side.

All the things my ancestors have done to ensure this moment and I can't even follow through with it. I bang my head on the ground, hoping for some idea to spring loose. For some moment of unhinged instinct to rise and help me kill the leader of my enemies, to bring the end to the ones who murdered so many of my people. All I come away with is a damning truth: they made a mistake in choosing me.

Rex has released my ankle and now stands above me, one hand offered to help me up. He's eaten the wrong mushrooms. There's no way I'm going anywhere with a Moore sociopath. So I get up on my own and brush myself off, hoping he can read that in my face because I'm in no mood to play charades. The doe stands beside him in visible proof of the side she's chosen. I ache to call my moths, the bats, birds, or the fox, just to confirm I still have allies here. There's a chance they won't come. Or they will come, but line up next to him. I can't bear it, not when I'm so tired already and the tears lurk so close behind my eyes.

Being safe in the woods was the one thing I could always count on. Well, no more. And for once I truly feel like I've stepped foot on foreign ground. Inside the Moores' car and in their house was enemy territory, but as soon as my boots landed on earth outside it I was home, and there was hope for survival. If the animals aren't on my side here, then I'm truly on my own.

Rex hooks a finger in the direction he wants me to walk. I give him my best eat-dirt glower. He jumps in front of me as I step away. With another step I brush past him; he gives me a shove backward. I sense the suppression of power in it—he knew I was off balance and could've knocked me flat on my butt. Only he didn't.

He says something I miss until I see the end: *with me.*

I sign, *I'm going nowhere with you, so back off.* I know he won't get it but it feels good to be signing again.

With how he drops his chin and takes a deep breath in, it's almost like he understood me. Another slow breath— he's coming to terms with something. Then his eyes are back on mine and something in them is turning corrupt. It's so easy to forget the first Rex Moore I saw, the one who fed that dark cloud with hate so heated it rose off him like a toxic gas. He's back now, and that new, other magic jerks awake inside me. As a natural defense? Or because it's being powered? Could it be both?

Rex pulls a pistol and aims it at me.

Five different moves to disarm an opponent light up in my brain. I act on none of them. The doe is too close, too much at risk if the trigger gets pulled in the scuffle.

Rex twirls his finger: *turn around*. I do, feeling the muzzle against my spine, its slight pressure turning my whole back creepy-crawly.

He steers me back to that car on the road and opens the passenger door while the gun is still jabbed into my back. I start to get inside, but he catches my arm instead, turning to stare down the strip of pavement where it disappears around a bend. I see a curse on his lips. Then he's tossing the pistol into the car and slamming the door with me still on the outside. Such a rapid change in plan leaves me stuck with a hard decision—I know I could run and get away with him so preoccupied, but is that a good idea?

Now he's wrenched a huge jug of water from the trunk. He pops the cap and dumps it over the car. The force of water drawing out of the small neck rocks the jug on his shoulder with such force he has to hold tight. Then it's empty and he's dragging me down the embankment to the woods. We go flat on the ground together, him of his own volition, me under the weight of his heavy arm. For some reason I resent it more than that pistol jabbed into my back.

Light sweeps the weeds around us, and we both duck. I swivel my head to check his expression and find him turning his face toward me at the same time. All I read is vigilance—furrowed brow, alert eyes, and that cocked-ear, distracted look hearing people get when they're intent on listening. Rex Moore has entered soldier mode. I raise my head to peek through my bangs and see two cars speed past on an empty road. Wait—empty? His car—

His phone pops in front of my face. *See? That was them. Get it now?*

I snatch the phone and write back: *And your car?*

He trades soldier mode for a grin so evil I scoot back a few inches. Taking the phone, he responds, *Water effect. Child's play.*

I follow his lead when he stands, wishing I had my leggings. The heat has eased enough to allow the breeze to actually do something, and now my shirt-dress is damp from our dive into hiding. And my legs itch, scratched up by the grass. It doesn't matter though. Wherever Rex got his change of clothes isn't somewhere I'm interested in going. The opposite direction though? Yes, please.

And I'm free to go wherever I want now that he's unarmed. Oh wait, spoke too soon. Pretty sure that's a boot knife he's going for right now. He doesn't unsheathe it though, he only lifts his pant leg so I can see the threat.

How do you know I haven't decided to go with you? I sign. His car will be a bit faster than my legs if the Moores catch my scent. Plus, invisible. Hard to beat that.

My poise turns inside out when I realize how long he's been watching me. In the flash of that realization, I'm too hot in my skin even though I've cooled in the breeze. I try to rub my suddenly sweaty palms on my pants but find the damp bottom of my shirt instead. Stuck in a car with a Moore was a nightmare the first time. Any enclosed space with any new person is enough of a trial. Coping with social anxiety seems so stupidly easy out of the moment, but when this tension rises from nowhere, I forget how to think. All strategies are drowned. Steady ground is out of reach. I flap and flail and try to breathe. Yes, breathe. That's all there is to do. Focus on that, not the prickly heat of my skin. Not the spotlight of his gaze. Turn away. Fill my lungs. Feel the ground beneath my boots.

I gather the hair on the crown of my head and fasten it with the band. Distraction helps. Anything to get the attention off me even if it's still on me due to something I'm doing. Movement is good. Doing anything is good. The rest of my hair blows against my shoulders in a harsher gust of wind. The elements sense my unease and are trying to help. Prickles have turned into gooseflesh, and I'm starting to feel normal again, which always brings a pang of self-disgust. I'm fifteen years old and I've got the stage fright of a child.

Cast it away. It serves no good. If only I could obey Aunt Tara's words like she does. I could say them a million times, and even though I believe them, the disgust is still there like anxiety's sidekick. They work together to empower one another. Knowing this doesn't help me fight it. It just builds on more disgust each time I fail to defeat such an obvious and predictable team.

When I turn back around, Rex doesn't seem at all changed by my crisis. He's rotating his shoulder and wincing until he spots me looking at him. Then he's just rotating, face cleared of the wince. I gloat anyway because that's what he was trying to prevent. That sore shoulder is my doing, and he needs to be reminded of that.

Rex extends a hand that says, *after you*, and I visualize my options. Banking on his desire to escape his family as truth, I could go with him and deal with my anxiety and the unknown destination of his choosing, safe from all Moores but him. Or I could flee now, on foot, with no change of clothes and a chill building in the air, surviving for who knows how many more days in the forest, scavenging food, water, and shelter while the Moores hunt me.

Option one keeps me close to the one I'm supposed to kill, option two strands me far away.

A decision so easy it answers itself.

I walk to his car. Its cloak has started to show—where the magic has worn off it shimmers, part white car body, part shadow. As we near it Rex taps my shoulder, and I see Irish on his lips. The true image of the car blinks in front of my eyes. Soap-bar-white with electric-green racecar stripes outlined in black, it looks like one of Marcas' toys. Giant spoiler, big wheels in that same wild green, *R5* splashed diagonally across the hood. A small car with a huge ego.

The visual mutes into real life, all colors turned to varying grays in the light of the moon. Now that he's given me its true image, I can see it to get inside it. I stop in the open door to enjoy one last moment of calm before I enter my cell. With cellmate Rex Moore. Don't think. Just get in.

Thick metal bars intersect in the door opening. I step over and in—this isn't a car, it's an amusement ride. The seat is more like a cup than a seat. We're packed so close his arm brushes mine as he buckles himself into the racecar seat harness. The surprise contact makes him jerk away. I manage to get my harness going the right way but can't figure out how it all clicks together. He looks over like he's about to help, and I figure it out real fast. He starts the car and my seat turns into a massage chair. The vibration is so thick I can feel a quiver in the air. It's not the muscular chugging of my dad's car but a different type of power. Higher, more hyper. We're not sitting in a car, we're strapped to the back of a hummingbird. I can't decide if it's the type of motor that's powered by gasoline, electricity, or rocket fuel, but from the way we launch from a stop, we're going to fly, not drive.

Then we're rolling down the road, but not quite. It's more like a boxing match. Our tires are beating the road and the road is beating back. And even though I'm cradled by a cushioned seat, it feels more like I'm bolted to the frame of the car, taking each bump along with it. The gearshift sticks up high, a fitting setup for the quick shifts that don't seem to have a pattern like my dad's car does. I elbow Rex hard. This car is virtually unsafe, and the way he's driving it makes it unfit for human passengers.

My elbow makes no dent in his heavy foot. I guess he's busy with more important things, like keeping the tires of this wild thing on the road. He shifts a gear before reaching behind my seat. I look at the helmet he drops in my lap. I look at him. I didn't think it was possible to hate him more.

At the first stoplight he talks into his phone and hands it to me. *It's a rally car. It can't be helped. Get over it.*

I elbow him again just because. I want to ask him where he's heading but at this point it doesn't matter. My goal is to get far away, and from the speed he's going, he agrees. Headlights appear in my side mirror, far behind on the road but closing in fast. He's tilted his gaze toward his mirror too before turning it on me. The intensity of it puts a tumble in my belly. Not long ago that same look of brewing war was directed at me, and for a second I wonder if he's had a change of heart. But there's something else in his eyes—a question I must decipher. Every battle starts with a deci- sion, a first move, a first reaction. It's what sets the rules, what draws a line in the earth. It only takes a beat for me to figure out our options, and all at once I see what he's asking.

Hide or flee?

I sign, *Both,* because freedom is so close and we have to pull out all the stops to get there. He can only spare a quick glance away from the road, and from the crease in his forehead I know he doesn't understand. The car lurches under a gas pedal stomped so hard I'm jerked backward with the force. The speedometer advances at a glorious rate. He looks at me again, so I quickly fingerspell the letters hoping he can figure out the word. His eyes pinch at the corners, then he's jerking the wheel to send us off the road, bouncing into a ditch then out again as I feel a lift in my stomach like we've caught air. Our headlights catch on barbed wire, and Rex jerks the wheel again, pivoting the car in a new direction as if it's on a spindle.

We're in the grass beside the road going the opposite direction, tall weeds smacking the front and sides of the car as we speed through it. He turns off the headlights. No car should go this fast off road. And I need a mouthguard because my teeth are about to knock each other out of my head.

He turns toward me and says something. *Help me? Help it?* Oh—*helmet.*

Leaning down to fish the helmet off the floorboard where it landed after that last stunt gives my head a few knocks against the dashboard. I hand it to him but he shoves it back at me and says, *You.* It's nearly impossible to strap on the helmet in this off road bumping hell but somehow I manage, pleased that when we crash and roll and this toy car crumples, my skull will be intact and Rex's will be in pieces. Job complete, prophecy fulfilled, I can go home. A thought like that days ago would've lightened my mood.

But now, sitting beside him while he pilots our insane escape pod, the thought gets gobbled up by others. What's left is a vibe too complicated to dwell on when my stomach is busy being tumbled by outside sources. I don't want to barf in Rex's car. At least not while he's trying to save us.

CHAPTER 10

REX

THE CAR THAT was behind us makes a U-turn in the road to pursue us now that we've been spotted, and I can't decide if I should keep going or turn around myself. I look at Sloane, but she's as clueless about these roads as I am. Even if she wasn't, she couldn't tell me a thing. Note to self: If I ever do a real rally, don't pick a deaf girl for a co-driver.

I flip the headlights back on because we're apparently not fooling anyone. That car gains on us fast. They look like Jag headlights, but I have no idea who'd be driving the Jag. Even though my car is quicker, they have the advantage of flat pavement. I punch the navigation screen, hoping my worthless co-driver will take the hint and find us an escape on the map. Her intake of breath has me hitting the brakes hard. We hit the embankment anyway. Instead of trashing the front end of the car, I manage to get us safely over it. Second note to self: Real rally or fake rally, never take my eyes off the road.

She points across me—through my window a pale dirt road bends away from us. I back up, turn, and floor it onto this lucky path, kicking up so much dust I can taste it. Behind us, our pursuer follows, but he can't keep up. He's all over this loose road when my loyal R5 is owning it. All that practice drifting in the southeastern field has paid off. This car has seen as little pavement as I have, and we're a perfect team because of it.

The dust cloud behind us has completely obscured the other car's lights with the increasing distance between us, which means my dimmer taillights aren't going to be visible to him at all. Pull off the road and hide? Or keep going? I want to ask her, but I can't tempt a second crash by taking my eyes off the road. She's also gone all weird again. Rigid, closed off, quiet. Ridiculous to call a deaf girl quiet but that's what it feels like. Her normal quiet is unnoticeable. This quiet is a *thing*.

I downshift, tapping her arm by accident. She jumps so hard it makes *me* jump, which causes enough of a jerk in the wheel to catch a tire on the edge of the road. I wrestle it back on course. "The fuck is wrong with you?"

Besides being locked in an idiotic car with her sworn enemy, chased by a car full of guys hired to kill her. Or something.

Out of the corner of my eye, she lays a hand against the base of her neck like she's trying to keep herself in the seat. Well, that's understandable. I let off the throttle and downshift again, careful to avoid her arm this time. Not sure why. It wasn't but a few days ago I lived to terrorize her. Now that she's making it so easy, it's lost all its appeal. But it's not just that. It really has nothing to do with how she's acting right now and everything to do with what she did to me in that bedroom in the house. That symbol she drew. That odd magic she invoked. And whatever she took away from me.

As soon as we can find somewhere safe to hide, I'm going to force her to tell me what she did. I'm going to make her undo it. Then I'm going to kill her.

The dirt road straightens out before dumping onto a paved one. A lone streetlight marks the intersection next to a row of mailboxes leaning in the weeds. Right or left is a complete toss-up. I open the nav for a clue. With no idea where my family's land is or which road we took that led us to this dirt road, it all just looks like a mess to me. I look at Sloane. She leans closer to the map as if trying to figure out where we started, where we want to go. I'm not sure I want her calling the shots though, so I make a right turn and floor it.

We have lines on the road now, and the middle one keeps changing from dots to lines and I have no idea why. Aaron was supposed to teach me how to drive on real roads, but we never got around to it. Little houses on small parcels of cleared land keep popping up on either side of us. I have to stop in the road to digest that people actually live in something so small. Movies and TV haven't even prepared me for this. Cheap cars sitting beside them, trash cans lined up, porch lights swarming with night insects. Now a face in the window looking out at us, and Sloane's poking me in the arm and gesturing for me to go.

I should probably let her drive. I'm about to go into culture shock.

At the next intersection I make another right like I know what the hell I'm doing. Up ahead there's an object in the road. A car, tilted to the side like it skidded and found rest across both driving lanes. Headlights blaze in my rearview mirror. Okay, this is all wrong, so very wrong. I hit the brakes to slide but find we've been flanked on both sides. I go for reverse, find a car barricade behind us.

Sloane has both hands braced on the dashboard. No point to even trying to get out of this. We're surrounded.

A man exits the car that's sitting across the lanes in front of us. I don't recognize him but it doesn't matter. He's one of my family's trained men, here to collect their property. I twist in my seat—five cars. Five guys minimum. More likely ten.

I unbuckle my harness and reach for my bag in the back. Sloane grabs a fistful of my shirt, forcing a look into her eyes. I hear my name being called outside. "They won't kill us," I say, grateful for the noise of the R5 exhaust drowning me out. She doesn't need the spoken words and neither do they. All she needs is the form of them, and I don't think whispering is the same thing. "But we have to kill them."

She jiggles her fistful of my shirt, demanding more. She doesn't understand. I can't tell if she wants more info about what I said or didn't catch it at all. If we don't kill every one of them, they'll take us both back to the house. My uncle

Jared—or even worse, Charlie—will get to kill her instead of me. I'll be punished. I'll lose my standing, my place, my chance to reign. I'll be nothing.

"Kill them," I say to Sloane.

Eyes sober with understanding. She lets go of my shirt. I press the release on her harness, make a motion that shows taking it off. I'm not doing this alone.

One gun from my bag goes into my waistband. The other? No idea where it is. I root around in the floorboard but they're calling my name with less patience now, so I poke her hard in the arm and point to the floor. "Gun."

She nods. I get out of the car. The guys in the cars flanking me get out too. Three in one, two in another, plus the guy from the car ahead. I turn around—at least two in the car behind.

"Master Rex, I'll drive you back. The girl will go with Thompson there. Moretti will drive your car back."

I take out my phone and dial my father. He picks right up.

"Call these assholes off."

"You've pushed too far, Rex. We'll talk when you get here."

"Don't make me do something stupid."

"It's a bit late for that, don't you think?"

I pull the gun and aim at the closest guy's head. "Count of three."

"Rex."

I fire. It wasn't three but sometimes I lie. Pistols draw all around me. Everywhere I look there's a hollow barrel. "One down. I know the amount of training you put in all these guys. How many more do you want to lose?"

"The more damage you do the worse it will be for you."

"Bullshit. It can't get worse. But if you'd back down and let me finish this my way, you'll see …" I can't even come up with a decent lie. What will they see? What the hell am I even doing?

"See what, Rex? Your disregard for orders? Your abandonment of duty? Is she with you right now?"

I aim at a second guy. Through the ringing in my ears, I hear safeties going off all around me, rounds being chambered. They won't kill me. There's no way they've been given that order, and they're too afraid of what their employers will do to someone who harms their prince. They'd rather die than have to face that terrifying unknown. And so would I. "Number two. Should I actually count to three this time?"

My father sighs sharply into the phone as Sloane pops up on the other side of the R5's hood. Her eyes are so much like the barrels that surround me. Fierce, deadly, pleading. She's supposed to be backing me up, not talking me down. I glance at the dead body on the ground, the dark circle of blood surrounding his head. Life bled out, a life I took. It's not the first, but it's the first I took while under my own command and not theirs. They trained me well, because the second body goes down without a thought. Sloane covers her mouth with her hands and draws a breath. Coming from her it's more like a shout, packed with too much for me to think about right now. She probably knows some perfect Bevan magic that could put all these guys to sleep. Well I don't have that. This is all I can do on short notice. This is the only way.

"Last chance," I say into the phone. "Or I'm hanging up and finishing them off."

"You think we can't find you?"

With Sloane Bevan on my team? "Yep."

I hang up, but I don't finish them off because Sloane has walked into my aim. Guys shuffle closer around us. I shift my back against the car, jerking her around beside me but it's not quick enough—one of the guys makes a grab and she dodges, another comes out of nowhere and spins her against him, arm around her throat, gun against her temple.

Something happens to me. It feels like a massively unexpected bass drop. A lurch in my chest. A double heartbeat. A heart attack. I adjust my aim for his face because there's no one in the world I've wanted to kill like this. I need more hands, more guns. I need to blow off every one of his appendages. I need my knife so I can butcher him. I want to kill him and eat him and shit him out.

I'm laughing instead, a sick release to ease the crazy. How it's finding a way past my clenched jaw is some kind of miracle. I'm drawn into Sloane's gaze—it's like being caught in a colossal lie and actually giving a shit. Humbled, but I'm not sure why. It's shut me up though, and then I see something else. She's passing something to me, a wordless message. She's about to do something and she wants me to be ready so—

She bends, flipping her captor to the side and twirling away from him. His arm whips out; she captures it and twists her whole body around it, snapping it at the shoulder. Bodies erupt around me. Bullets zing by and pelt the ground. Aiming for her, no doubt. They won't kill me. But in this commotion maybe they will because no one would know who's responsible.

I've managed to get between my car and another. My hearing has gone fuzzy now because of all the gunshots and I can't tell what direction the sounds are coming from. I aim around the bumper, take down two more guys. Without a visual on Sloane I have no idea which way to go. Calling out to her would do no good. She can't hear me, and right now, I'm not sure I could hear her response even if she could speak.

A body drops onto the car's hood and slides to the ground beside me. Injured, not dead. Looks like his knee is blown out. And there's something not right about the angle of his wrist. When his eyes lock onto mine, I see his recognition. I also see the hilt of a blade at his waist and the hand creeping toward it. I don't want to risk popping one of the R5's tires with a bullet, so I snatch his knife before he can and drive it into his chest. It's messy but I've done this before and it's never bothered me. And right now I'm not bothered. Definitely not bothered.

I stand and back away, bumping into a body I spin to face—Sloane. She grabs my shirt and yanks me toward the R5, everything about her saying, *Get in, get in.* The car that had been blocking us at the front bumper has been moved. She hops into the passenger side as I hop in mine, and I'm pulling away before she's even shut her door. I watch the mirror as we bail. In it is a jumble of cars and bodies, some immobile, some upright giving chase, some bent over. One lone square of light from a phone. Someone on the phone to my father. *They got away, sir. We've lost men. We need to regroup.*

Let them. They can't defeat me. Their only option now is to wait for me to come back.

Hands come at me. Not just one or two, but a hundred. Pulling, jostling, restraining. I knock them away, but I'm not fast enough. There are too many. A vicious squealing fills my ears, giving perfect meaning to the smell of burning rubber. All at once I come to, realize the blackness I'm seeing isn't right. What's right is the silver strip of road, the brilliant moon, the frame of dark woods on either side. Then I see the real hands. There are only two and they belong to Sloane. She's now holding them up and away, but I remember where they were: helping me into my safety harness.

Now that we've come to a screeching sideways stop, I can buckle in myself. I should thank her for trying but no way. She needs to keep her hands off me. I should also apologize for the freak-out but no to that too. For the same reason.

I check my watch as she buckles up beside me. Then we're off. No trying to consult the map this time, no attempt for any sense of reason. I just drive. The sun will be lighting the horizon in a few hours, and we need to get far enough away that the search radius is too great for the amount of guys my family can round up. Then Sloane Bevan needs to whip out some tricks and make us untraceable.

She hasn't moved a muscle since she withdrew her hands. The only movement from her side of the car is the jostle from the bumps in the road. Her chin stays tipped high, her hands flat on her thighs with fingers fanned out like she's afraid to touch anything. Then I see how bloody they are, and the posture doesn't look so much haughty as uncomfortable. It's a bit prissy for a girl who can fight like that to be bothered by blood.

I pull to the shoulder and get out my phone. *We need somewhere to lie low. Any ideas?*

She looks at the screen for a long time, contemplating. Thinking of a spot? Or knowing a spot, but deciding whether she should tell me? Both options could explain what's on her face. For the first time I see how easy she is to read. She puts everything out in the open with no filter.

After wiping her hands on the only clean part of her shirt, she writes, *Ask Aaron for the address to the cottage he was born in. If he doesn't know, his dad will.*

I shoot off a text to Aaron and toss the phone in her lap so she can monitor it while I drive. We need more distance. We need somewhere to rest. We need food—damn how I need food. I poke her in the arm and point to my bag behind us. "Food."

She shakes her head, pointing instead through the windshield toward some lights in the distance. Above the glow hovers an illuminated sign. She does something in sign language that looks very much like it could mean 'food.' Holy balls, if she can lead us toward something hot and salty, I think I might have to be her best friend.

Okay, that's a lie. But it sounds good.

Tacos. So many tacos. Burritos too. And a flimsy box bending under the weight of loaded nachos. All washed down by a coke as big as the water jug in my hatch. We had to go inside to order because I had no idea how to use the drive-through and she can't do it deaf. So we stood just outside the ring from the streetlight in the parking lot behind the R5 and used the remaining water jug to wash the blood off our hands and faces. My clothes were splattered but it wasn't noticeable on camo or black. Her dress was fitting attire for the undead. But she waved her hand like she had it covered then poked my wallet pocket and opened her hand. Curious, I handed it over.

She removed some cash and held it straight between two praying hands, eyes closed, bangs falling over her fingers. The magic took affect with a static charge that skimmed across my skin. When she handed the cash back I wasn't just salivating over the food it would buy, but the promise of all the magic I would force her to teach me.

Inside she took a paper menu from the counter, and we took turns circling items with a borrowed pen. From the cashier's raised eyebrow it didn't seem like the normal way to do things. Sloane didn't bother explaining she's deaf, and I didn't bother explaining I've never left my house, have only eaten meals cooked by a gourmet chef, and only know about fast food from TV commercials and internet ads. It'd probably be easier for me to pretend I'm deaf too. It's not as hard to accept. I simply handed over the Bevan-blessed cash, guessing it would smooth over the cashier's memory of this strange encounter and Sloane's slasher-movie getup. Then I stood there and tried not to gawk at the uniformed people behind the counter, the little plastic benches in the dining area, the food ads plastered to the windows. Every inch of space lit by so much terrible artificial light it was hard to believe anyone ever used those plastic benches for anything but open heart surgery.

Then we brought the bags back to the car and here we are, stuffing our faces with the weirdest junk food I've ever had. If anyone shows up looking for us, we can speed away. Not that we'll be able to stop eating, but it's a nice thought. I'll need to remember there's a separate entrance and exit to this parking lot, and to take the correct one this time so Sloane doesn't throw another hissy fit in the seat. As if it matters—we're the only people out at this hour. Yeah, I ran over a few curbs, but this car is built for that kind of abuse. Okay, when day hits maybe I should just let her drive.

I say into my phone, *You don't eat meat?* and show her the screen. Her answer is the blankest of stares, and I can see she thinks she's being judged and definitely not going to answer. I don't know why I asked, because of course it would be awkward to eat furry creatures after sharing brain space with them all day.

"Hey, your loss." I really wonder how much she can read from lips. Probably not much when I'm chewing like a slob. "Hope you're enjoying that veggie burrito."

She's totally being judged. Bevans are animals because they've commingled with them so long. It's not my fault they chose to be savage instead of civilized. When she starts rewrapping the remainder of her last burrito like she can't handle one more bite, I steal it and finish it for her, Bevan corruption and all. Hey, hunger calls. Thankfully mine has no morals.

I'm slurping the last of my coke when the text from Aaron comes in with the cottage's address he got from his dad along with a warning: *Trey Bevan still owns that place. He lived there with Mom. It was and still is Bevan territory. Be careful.*

I return a thumbs-up emoticon and enter the address into my car's navigation. Sloane's gotten out to toss our trash, and now she's standing under the parking lot light straight-up hanging out with the moths. Girl's definitely cracked.

Another text comes in from Aaron. *You know what you're doing, right?*

I type back, *Nope!* then I delete it. He's a deadbeat brother, but he did deliver on that address. Making him worry would be funny but the fallout might be inconvenient. *Totally,* I say instead. Then I add, *Now go work on your thesis or something.*

He won't reply again, but I watch the screen anyway. His obligatory once-a-month contact with me has been met, and now he can return to his life with a clear conscience. I reread my answer, feeling so disgusted by my wuss-out that I have to remind myself why I changed it. The first answer would've raised doubt, and who knows what he'd do to try to save me. But me pondering consequences of my actions is such a new thing, I'm not sure how I feel about it.

The food high reminds me of a different high, its absence proven by how blurry my eyesight is, how heavy my limbs are. How easy it would be to succumb to sleep right now. I find my pills and pop one as Sloane takes her seat, eyeing me like she has some nugget of wisdom for me. The moths must have explained the meaning of life. I start the nav and we pull away, destination: Trey Bevan's abandoned cottage in the Virginia wild. As suggested by his very kidnapped daughter. I'm being lured onto Bevan land with no plan and no backup. I so totally don't know what I'm doing.

CHAPTER 11

SLOANE

Rex can't drive. I thought maybe the dark of night was the problem, but now the morning sunlight spreads from the horizon to turn the sky a wild pink and he still can't drive. No, correction: He can drive. Just not between the lines. Or correctly use turning lanes. Or properly use clearly marked entrances and exits to parking lots. More cars are out now, carrying angry-faced drivers cutting around us, middle fingers stabbing out windows. He's going to get us killed in a road rage incident.

So when we arrive at what should be the entrance to the driveway but instead looks like an overgrown hole in the woods and Rex stops in the middle of a 55 mile-per-hour road to scrutinize it, I yank his sleeve, hoping to encourage him to take the plunge before we get rear-ended. He shifts gears and turns in. At least it's paved. If it wasn't, we'd have never found it. The pavement has preserved enough of the path so the woods haven't completely reclaimed the driveway.

The tunnel of trees and underbrush thins; I spot a swatch of white through the green. Unbuckling my harness, I lean forward, heart thumping hard to see this forbidden place, the cottage my dad built for his ex-wife who's also Rex's mom. My dad, living here with Rex's *mom*. It's so freaky and disturbing.

It appears like an apparition ahead. Gray roof, stained with age. Ivy-covered stone chimney rising from one side. The shutters are a green so faded they almost match the dirty white body of the house. One shutter sags, swaying in the breeze. If houses have souls, this one is broken. It's more sad and neglected than I expected, and I wonder what happened here and why my dad abandoned it. Feeling the sadness in the air, it's very hard to blame him.

Rex seems unaffected by the heartbreaking vibe because he's gone to his phone. I lean and see him writing a text to Aaron: *Wrong address. Nothing's here. Or maybe it burned down?*

I poke him in the arm and point ahead, giving him my best *it's right there, dumbass* expression. He shifts forward to peer out the windshield, looking completely through the house and all around like it's hiding far in the distance.

Again I point, pumping my finger twice toward the house as if to say, *right there*. He looks at me like I've lost my marbles. *You don't see it?* I sign, proving I've lost my marbles by signing to someone who doesn't know ASL. I take his phone, swiping into the writing app we've been using to talk and typing it out.

See what? he types back.

The house right in front of us!

He lowers the phone to look again, still focusing completely through it. He really can't see it.

I type: *Drive. I'll tell you when to stop.*

He puts the car in gear, and we crawl forward. As the tires bump across something in the road, he jumps in his seat, head jutting backward like the house just sprang into view. One second I'm ready to say "told you so" and in the next I'm overcome by a pounding alarm—something wrong, something about to be wrong, something we would've been prepped for if we'd have just picked up on the clues—

My head snaps as he slams the brakes. He's curled forward, released the wheel, released the brakes because we're now rolling back. I scramble to remember which one's the gearshift and which one's the brake—they both extend high—find it and set it. Veins bulge in his neck. He's strangling himself in his seat harness. I burst from mine and wedge my hand under his seized arm to release his but all it does is give him more slack to hang himself in. I see he can't help it though, his back is curling forward with such force he can't possibly be doing it himself. Muscles contract in his arms and thighs. He's fighting against some imaginary force and losing.

I push out of the car, run around to his side, and yank the door open. Pressing him back in the car is a wasted effort—he's curling too hard out of it. His face is quickly going from deep red to purple. Next will be blue and then he'll be dead. I shove his head back with all I have, awarding me with a few inches of slack in the seat harness to get it released and off him, only for him to fall out of the car like a corpse frozen stiff in the fetal position. I kneel beside him, trying to find his hand. Maybe somehow I can pass strength. I need to gather my calm and think. That's when I see the smooth stones running in a line under the car, behind both tires. Marked with my family's symbol, the same as the one on my amulet.

Boundary spell. Of course! I kick the closest stones out of line, breaking the circle that will be surrounding the house. Rex uncurls, rolling to his back. His fists open, palms facing the sky as his chest rises and falls in the short hurried breaths of someone deprived of oxygen for too long.

I'm sorry, I sign, his eyes sliding slowly over to me. *That was my fault. I should have known. I'm so sorry.*

He wets his lips, closing his eyes. Thinking about what I'm trying to say must be too taxing for him until he can catch his breath. This was another opportunity to easily kill him, and this time it's my dad's magic, most likely designed to protect against—and attack—Rex's own Moore blood. Almost like this moment was foreseen and my dad knew I needed help, needed someone else to pull the trigger after I'd lined up the shot. It doesn't surprise me that I reversed it. What surprises me is this new war I'm fighting, these battles to save Rex Moore when I've been taught my whole life I was born to kill him.

But maybe there's a different interpretation to that destiny. To destroy does not necessarily mean to kill. Maybe my job is to disable and disarm him. Not to end his life, but end what makes him a threat to my people. When I gathered those foul pieces, bundled them up, and yanked them out of him, that's exactly what I did. He's not a threat to me anymore. He had his chance to kill me, and he didn't do it. Saving his life each of these times hasn't been a betrayal of my duty but a preservation of the work I've done.

He opens his eyes. They're a strike of blue, a rainforest-bright lizard eye on an otherwise camouflaged body. In them I see gratitude and a biting curiosity that gets more intense as he holds my gaze. Again he's wondering why I saved him. He must be flashing back to our first encounter and every one after that, and I see the one-eighty of our lives is as jarring and stomach-stealing for him as it is for me. His next step is missing; if he takes it he might fall off a cliff.

Well, my next step was just rebuilt. I see where it leads me. And I can't take it without him.

Rex hangs back on our walk to the front door of the cottage, not afraid but cautious. After he got to his feet, he dug through his car for a sheathed military knife that's now attached to his belt. That kind of weapon won't help him against my dad's magic. I should explain my dad would never double up boundary spells. He'd just overpower the one spell to the extreme, making a second spell unnecessary. As we just witnessed.

The door is unlocked, because why bother locking it when a circle of stones renders the whole place invisible? I wave Rex forward; he stalks in warily, not wanting a repeat of what just happened anytime soon. I can't blame him. My dad's spells aren't pretty things.

Then we're inside and I'm consumed again by this house's broken soul. He heads farther in and to the right, out of sight, when all I can do is stay planted in the little entry hall and try not to let the sadness press too hard on my chest.

A small table hugs the wall beside me, a perfect spot for dropping keys. What's on it now are picture frames lying facedown in the dust. Hanging above them is a clutter of dark violence so similar to the cloud I plugged into for power in that bedroom in the Moore mansion. It's the residue of some long-ago action that never found peace. I raise one picture. A younger version of my dad stares back, intent, his arm hooked around the neck of a tall, gorgeous woman. Uncle Christian stands beside them with his hands in his pockets and that hotshot smile I know so well. I set the picture up so Christian's smile will warm the room like it always does.

I lift the second frame and find another photo: that gorgeous woman holding a newborn baby. The picture is too old to be Rex. But that's got to be his mom Kate, so who's the baby? I flush like I've unearthed some frightening secret I was never meant to see. I slam the picture back to its facedown position, horrors filling my head. My dad had a baby with her? I have a half sibling?

Rex bumps my arm and I look up at him, still only seeing that photo. I watch him set it up next to the other one. He does a double take before picking it up for a better look. Recognition settles in. *Oh,* he says, setting it back down.

I point to the baby.

I don't get his spoken answer, partially because it's hard to read, partially because I'm freaking out. He shows me his phone: *My brother.*

But that doesn't make sense. His brother's dad is Christian. This is *my* dad's house. We both look at the other picture, the one with the three of them. *Oh,* I form on my lips.

Oh, he says back, nodding, his eyes going averted and tight. I can't decide which person in the picture is the target of his resentment.

I take his phone and type: *Weird.*

He types back: *Fucked-up.*

I type back: *Your mom and my dad. Also weird.*

He types back: *Also fucked-up.*

I type back: *Your dad and my mom.*

He wrinkles his forehead, shifting his eyes away to ponder that. I wonder if they even told him. Then I see *Oh my god, yeah, you're right,* on his lips, and he absentmindedly straightens both pictures, aligning them with the edge of the table.

We look at each other then, mutually grossed out, trying to figure out if there's any way we could be related. If either of our sets of parents were still a couple, we'd be step brother and sister. But if that were the case with either set, Rex and I wouldn't exist. We seem to arrive at the same conclusion because we both shrug at the same time.

He types into his phone: *There's no food.*

Well that's good, because it would be decades old and only be an inedible temptation. He checks his watch—a strange thing to do after looking at a screen that displays time, but maybe he prefers seeing time in analog. I leave him to go on a hunt for the bedroom to scrounge for a change of clothes.

The closet and dresser are both filled like people left this house and didn't bother bringing anything with them. Kate's clothes are dated, and it would be too weird to wear them around Rex, so I go after my dad's stuff which is pretty much what he wears now: jeans and T-shirts. There's a suit and a couple button-down dress shirts I could easily cut the sleeves off to make a cool summer dress. With a few mods to his shirts and some of Kate's reluctantly scavenged tights, I can make some of them work. His white undershirts fit the best but ugh, white? Maybe I can find a black marker or something to smudge them up. A black marker that isn't dried up after sitting in a house for a hundred years.

At the back of the closet I even find a gym bag, so I load it up and drag it out to the living area. I get a pair of scissors from the kitchen and get to work, cutting and tying in the right places to turn a man's shirt into a girl's sheath dress. After I have a few ready to wear, I pick the best one, grab a cobweb-covered bar of soap and an old bottle of shampoo—oh, elements! Shampoo!—from the bathroom, and find Rex in the backyard, staring at a twisted tangle of overgrown rose garden.

I hold up the soap and point out past the yard. I know he has the water jug in his car but I'd rather find a stream. He doesn't appear to like the idea, but he seems anxious to get back to his vacant staring. He tilts his head like *go ahead,* so I set off through the waist-high weeds. Deer paths are easy to find when the land is this untouched, and soon I find a sluggish rocky stream that's cool, clear, and just perfect.

Soap is an amazing invention. Shampoo is witchcraft more hardcore than Grandma Sloane's. I was worried about the modded clothes being too dusty, but after being shaken out they smell way cleaner than the dirty rag I took off.

Rex is missing from the house when I return, so I explore the bathroom drawers and find a set of sharp scissors perfect for trimming my bangs. I go uneven again, the up and down pattern different than last time. Straight is boring. And too hard to achieve anyway. *Did you butcher your bangs on purpose?* my dad always asks, fully knowing I did. If Dad's not there, Marcas will be sure to do the line. He loves to play Dad's backup. Then comes Mom's line: *A rule-breaker just like her dad.* After this it becomes some private joke between the two of them. My dad says, "State trooper?" without signing, and my mom gives him a look of death. Marcas told me the 'state trooper' part. We both decided we probably don't want to know what it means.

I miss them so much. The stupid jokes, the predictable lines. They're the only ones who completely understand me. It's not fair I'm here and not with them. But it's not about fairness. Fairness doesn't fit into destiny. I can't argue with centuries of planning. I can't argue with prophecy. I can't question the stars.

Now there's trimmed hair in the sink and no water to help gather it up. I clean it the best I can and continue my search of the drawers, finding everything else I could possibly need: toothpaste, bobby pins, razors, and gold in the form of a new-in-box first aid kit. What a grand find for two kids on the run from serial murderers. I pack the stuff in the gym bag and go out front to look for Rex.

The hatch of his car is open. And there's Rex but the black tee and camo pants are gone and all I see is skin. Too much skin. He's taking his own bath from the water jug in his trunk. Tipping the jug for a handful to splash his face. And even after I've figured this out, I stare longer than any Bevan should ever stare at any Moore like that. I know what trained muscles look like on a boy. I've seen the boys on the wrestling team at school. Never like this though. It's never been so …

Interesting.

He runs the heel of his palm over both eyes to clear the water, and I know the next step is to open his eyes so I back through the doorway and close the door, praying he doesn't see the movement, doesn't notice the sound I feel of it clicking back into place. Doesn't hear the savage and confused beat of my heart.

I rummage through the kitchen cupboards to give myself something to do far away from the windows facing his car. If I spotted him spying on me like that, I'd make him pay for it in blood. I owe him the same privacy even though he doesn't seem to demand it—he did strip shamelessly to his underwear in front of me on his family's land. Not an excuse though. I shouldn't have looked. I shouldn't still be thinking about it.

I need to be thinking about what we're going to do for food. We have pots and pans now, and utensils, which makes everything easier. I climb onto the counter to check the top shelves and find a dry box of matches and two votive candles. Not that Rex or I need the matches, but it's still a sweet find. The candles will be useful when the sun goes down.

I'm hopping off the counter when Rex returns. Clothed, of course, but it's still a relief to see the return of those camo pants. Moores love to make us miserable and prancing around naked would sure do the trick. He gives my new outfit an extended glance, drops a box on the table, and tosses me his phone, a text on the screen.

Aaron: I'm sending you some stuff via my drone. Tell me when you get it so I know.

I type back: *Got it. Thanks!* But I show him before I send it. He deletes *Thanks!* and hits Send. I scowl at him. He scowls back. Then he unsheathes his belt knife and slits the tape on the box.

Inside we find gourmet deli sandwiches packed in dry ice. One meat, one veggie. That makes him laugh. Under the sandwiches is a bushel of bananas, two giant blueberry muffins, tortilla chips, fancy homemade salsa, and two large bottles of expensive looking mineral water. He digs to the bottom of the box, mouth crooked and disappointed. Seriously? He can't really be this spoiled and ungrateful.

I take his phone off the table and type a text back to Aaron: *Sloane says thanks* but Rex grabs my arm before I can send it. I swivel and twist, breaking his grasp. He snakes an arm around me and snatches it from the other side. I let him do it because if I didn't we'd be grappling forever and I've got a sandwich to eat. I'll give Aaron my thanks later. Rex probably doesn't know Aaron and I know each other. Just like Christian is my uncle, Aaron is my cousin, and even if we share no blood we certainly share hatred of the Moores. Maybe that's as weird as Christian being Aaron's dad and the partner swap between Rex's parents and mine. Maybe it's weird that my dad was once a Moore. That he was adopted by them and lived among them long enough to accept Uncle Christian as a brother. Everything is weird, set up by my ancestors so I'd be born exactly when I was.

All this history made me who I am. But there's also a part of me that's *me*, something they didn't craft. That part of me has failed them. I'm doing the opposite of what they predicted. And my plan to salvage it all is an undertaking every one of my family members would try to talk me out of. I don't need their blessing even if I could get it. My way is a risk but it's the only way. I won't kill Rex Moore. I'm going to use him to save them all.

CHAPTER 12

REX

I'M HALFWAY THROUGH my sandwich by the time she sits at the table with me. Then she unwraps hers carefully like she's not dying of hunger. I guess this is lunch, but we didn't sleep last night so maybe this is yesterday's dinner?

She's taking thoughtful little bites while staring a hole through my face. There's no way she can detect any interest in her new dress. Yeah, she's handy with some scissors and an old oxford shirt. That was noticed, accepted, and quickly cleared from my expression. So I have no idea what her deal is right now.

"For you to not be deaf would make things a lot easier." I twist the cap off my water and chug. When I put it down she's still staring. "What?"

Her bangs are different. Shorter? But still cut in that irregular line like a two-year-old did it. Somehow it doesn't look like a screwup, though, in fact, it's kind of awesome. Rebellious. Something goes loose inside me, and I shift in my seat so I'm not directly facing her anymore. I can't look at how it's changed her face.

Now that I'm looking at the safety of the wall, I try the word again in my head. *Rebellious.* Such a crime to even name it. At home, rebellion is forbidden and unthinkable. An illicit thought to be purged by whatever means and never think again. But now? It's come alive in there, and I have no idea how. Did I rebel before I thought it possible? Or did I think it first and it dirtied my actions?

She gets up from the table, returns with a piece of paper and pencil. She writes a big letter A. Points at it. Holds up her right fist with the fingers facing me.

I don't know what she wants me to do so I do nothing. The heat in the room has suddenly gained several degrees. Inside with no air-conditioning on a summer day in Virginia is just stupid. We need to be bunking somewhere that isn't a dump, somewhere with cool air and running water and a live outlet to charge my phone. And now I'm looking at her face again under those bangs and thinking: rebellion. A crime as repulsive and disgusting as the Bevans themselves. Why the hell does it feel so right?

On the paper she's written a letter B. Now her fingers are straight up in the air, thumb crossed over her palm. She writes a C. Her hand curls, forming the letter itself, the opening a mouth coming to bite me. She points to the letters on the paper in succession: A, B, C. She makes that fist, then the straight fingers, then the hand curling into a C.

I stand up fast, lit by adrenaline. She writes new letters on the page: R, E, X. She's not stopping. She powers right into spelling my name with her hand. It's like a faraway call, my name transmitted through the air, crossing boundaries and borders and settling between us. Spoken, but not voiced. Shared.

Sweat trickles down my back. I need to get the hell out of here. But I'm not fast enough because she's reaching—bridging the space—and her eyes, green like summer—those fucking rebellious bangs—

She spells my name again with her non-reaching hand, and I don't only see it this time, I hear it in my head, understood like a real spoken word, like input received. I see what she's doing now, she's appealing to me like she tamed those Dobermans. That's how she sees me: instead of her being the primitive animal, I am. She thinks she's trying to befriend me, but we aren't friends. We can't be friends. I had one friend named Emily, and she's dead because of this nonsense the Bevans started generations ago. They may as well have killed her themselves. And I'm holding them accountable.

My chair crashes into the table. I see my boot on its bottom rung, but I don't remember putting it there. Sloane has jumped to her feet, knocking her own chair aside in the process.

This isn't a reach for friendship. It's domestication. Her way of conquering animals is now being used on me. I rip the bundle of bananas apart and throw half at her. How she braces herself for the catch shows how hard I threw it and how much I've lost my cool. As if the blood pounding in my ears isn't enough.

I toss my half of all the food in the box and leave. Settle down, Rex. Mistakes are made when cool is lost, and I've used up my quota of mistakes. Only correct decisions can be made from now on. I'm crossing through the weeds then I'm in my car, slamming the door, hands on the steering wheel. Trey Bevan's junky house leers at me in its classless Bevan way. The silence is thorough and cavernous. Damning, if I let it be, of all the things I've done wrong and will be punished for as soon as I step foot on my family's land. I finger the dent in my skull behind my ear—that was for disrespect. I tongue the spot between my lip and my front teeth that's never been right since they got knocked out—that was for talking back. The list continues a mile beyond those two, each incident blurring with the next. They didn't teach me good behavior. They taught me obedience—but only when they were looking. They also taught me hate. And oh, I'm good at that.

I'm baking in the heat, so I start the car and crank up the air. Adding a/c to this car stole some of its rally cred, but I'm sure thankful for it now. My heartbeat slows with the tick of my great-granduncle's watch against my wrist. The schedule I've lived by for my entire life has been put on hold, and I want it back. Wake, train, eat, train, class, eat, class, train, sleep. It's the only thing that keeps the rebellion at bay. This isn't just homesickness, it's loss. I want my life back.

I look at the house again. I've brought Sloane Bevan here. That's more than I should've done. She's on her own now.

I have my cousin to bury, a long list of mistakes to own up to, and a punishment to survive. I shift into reverse, turn to check the back window.

She's right behind me.

I give the car some gas to scare her into moving away before I realize she won't hear it. So I release the clutch a little, making the car lurch back. She stands her ground, so I do it again until I'm close enough to bump her knees. The resistance isn't a hindrance but an incentive. This car could flatten her and it would feel just like a bump in the road. I look ahead—there's not enough room to pull forward and spin around. It appears this is a stand-off. Well, I don't do stand-offs.

Setting the brake, I get out of the car. My eyes are wet and I don't care if she sees. It's not despair but anger. Failure. The sin of rebellion. Grief for my disregard for the teachings of my family, the victors in this war. I'm being drawn to the losing side by manipulative Bevan trash. And even as I'm trying to get the hell away, she's trying to stop me and pull me back in.

"Move." It comes out gritty and doesn't sound a thing like me.

She only stands there, her top lip curled in and her eyes tight like she's making assumptions about me.

"Move!"

Her lips relax. Her eyes thaw. She's shaking her head. Not at me, but at the assumption she arrived at but doesn't accept.

I step forward to move her myself, but she comes against me too fast, her arms latched around my torso. It's an unpredictable move only for how uncombative it is. Its violence is her softness against me, the steadiness of her cheek against my chest. Not a grapple, but an embrace. My natural recoil does nothing to stop it.

Bringing my elbows down only makes her cling harder. Softer? Somehow both. I've never been hugged so I don't know what's normal or how to combat it. I twist but she comes with me. This subdual is too good a move because I have no strategy to counter, and there's something happening inside me now, a melting of muscle, a breaking of will I'm going to give in to if I don't get her off me.

My eyes are newly wet—how? Why? I don't know, but I'd pay in blood for this emotional fail at home. I grind my palms against them to make it stop. She releases me, putting a few inches between us but her hand goes over my heart and some madness in me doesn't stop her. I become aware of the tick of my watch now grossly out of sync with my pulse. She places the fingers of her other hand on its beat in my neck, turning her head away as if to listen.

Hugs? Taking vitals? She's cracked. But I can't move away, or stop feeling the ghost of pressure left by her arms around my torso, the contact of her face against my chest. She smells like the forest—earthy, wild, and alive. Like purity and independence and rebellion, and a magic I never learned but feel hidden inside me. I'm taken back to waking up beside the stream on my property, newly healed, the air clean and free moving, my body reborn. Standing beside her is like being near the lake at home with its magnetic pulse, its perfectly irregular tempo. She's choices and freedom. She's life and unshackled will.

Birds chatter at me from all around. I look up. They've collected in every nearby tree, branches bobbing as they hop back and forth. She hasn't broken from me to call them, but I know they're here for her. She's of the forest just as they are. I've been taught how gross that is. It's the secret though, isn't it? The secret to the Bevans' power.

She places a hand against my cheek. I flinch—again, never been touched like that. It's a strange, unwelcome yet so painfully welcome invasion. A guilty pleasure. And I'm not moving away. She trails her index and middle fingers down my cheek to my chin where I know that scar is. Not a childhood scrape but another punishment. Another mark of their power over me, of my obedient hate.

Rebellion. I hear it whispered in my head, a secret like her fingers on my face. The sense attached to the word has gone from guilty to warranted. If it wasn't in my own mind's voice, I'd think she was breaching my head like she did before. I straight-up jump then, surprised by fingers weaving into mine. She raises our joined hands between us. Friends? Partners? More than all that. Once enemies, now—

"*Comhghuaillithe.*"

No idea why I spoke it aloud. I should say it in English: *Allies.* So maybe she can read it. But no, Rex, that'd be crazy.

She places her other hand over mine, sandwiching my hand between hers. The intimacy is such a shock, I have to swallow to clear a lump in my throat before I place my free hand on hers. We could be cuffed together for how permanent it feels. As hot as the day is, I'm rolled over by a fierce wave of heat unconnected to the weather.

I shut it down fast. God, Rex, you're such a virgin. Our allegiance is purely practical. I need her for her magic. She needs me to get home. We need to stick together to survive my family. That's it.

My hands are on fire against hers. I pull them away. There's honey in her hair where the sunlight's hitting it. It's hard to accept that color resides anywhere in that dark mass, and makes me wonder what else is hiding inside her. In the right kind of light maybe I'll see even more. She stands there looking up at me, and I'm shot through by the image of that prick holding a gun to her head. They know she's valuable; they know she's mine now. They're not getting her back.

Now I just need to figure out what to do. And how to stop staring at her. And how to slow my heart rate. And stop this disturbing thing, this me-and-her, from feeling so good.

Return to your people. It comes from nowhere, so distinct and perverted I turn around expecting someone to be there. Then I feel the feather-light tick against my wrist. I check my watch, a habit I'm usually aware of on some distant level but today that distance has been overcome. The moving hand is in my face, not ticking but pounding, the watch's antique luxury offensive and brazen and tumorous. I unbuckle it from my wrist and hurl it into the woods so far I don't hear where it hits.

Rebellion isn't just a forbidden thought anymore. It's a storm I'm driving into. Rain muddying the earth, my foot pressing pedal in complete commitment of the slippery grass I'm about to hit, the loose dirt that could send me spinning into a tree. And the destroyed turf I'll have to answer to.

Sloane's fingers enclose my wrist. She brings it forward to scrutinize the lighter band of skin now exposed by the missing watch. My pulse it hot, hard, and untethered. For once it feels in line with my breath, like it's not such a struggle to keep everything together. It all just syncs now, unaided. She moves her fingers to my neck, taking vitals again. But this time she doesn't appear to be working something out. The curve of her mouth is pleased. Relieved, maybe. And a little bit awed. Then she's raising my own hand to her neck—and that's just too damn much.

I break away. Get my box of food out of the car and shut off the engine. Back in the house I sit at the table and scoot in like I'm at a formal dinner at home, closed off, minding my food and nothing else so no one thinks they should talk to me. She takes up that piece of paper and leans over it, writing like a crazy girl. She shoves the paper across the table at me.

That watch!

I knew there was something off about your pulse.

It was messed-up.

It was … controlled?

Her eyes are huge when I look at her. The green leaves of a lavender plant—that's the color they are. Not in summer but fall, when they take on that frosty tone. A color so perfect it's nearly undefinable. There are so many things I want to bark back, mainly *fucking butt out* and *leave me the fuck alone* but there's no satisfaction in scribbling them out with a pencil. By then I'll want to take them back. So I send her a look to shut her down, to shut her up, hopefully make her go away. Give me a minute to find the fragments of my head after I just blew it off by vowing allegiance to Sloane Bevan because damn it all, I have no idea what to do with that.

Instead, I get another note shoved in front of me.

Okay, but you know I'm right. You don't have to be such a jerk.

I give her another look. She takes hold of her long braid, and I see a tremble in her arm. Scaring her doesn't seem to have the appeal it used to. In fact, it makes me think her last comment is dead-on. But jerks don't ever feel their stomach sink like this when they do something shitty, right?

She wads the paper up and pelts it at my face, proving that tremble to be something other than fear. Okay, she just swore allegiance to a Moore, so she's probably got the dump of horror flushing through her too.

I point to her half-eaten sandwich. "Shut up and eat."

She does something in sign language that looks like a rude gesture. I see now every sign has a facial expression to go along with it, and even though I don't know sign language, a face alone can communicate a lot. Especially hers. And right now it's telling me this isn't over.

I finish up and go outside in the sun because I'm not sweating nearly enough inside. A somber drone of a single cricket rises from the brush by the mutant rose garden. The scent of roses thickens the air, turning it sickly sweet and nauseating, and I wonder if my mother planted them. No, of course not. With what time? She was too busy making babies with her husband's cousin. Good ol' mom. So glad to know she hasn't changed.

I'm the one who's changed. Even though my sweat goes cold for a heartbeat, I have no regret. For once I've made my own decision. I make the calls now. I design the strategy, I carry it all out my way. The bottle of Bevan-killing black magic sits in my pocket at the ready.

A gust of wind hits me in the back, flapping my clothes like this sticky heat is about to implode into something wet and loud. So much for the sun—it's about to tap out. Storm clouds bulge down from above, a rolling mixture of grays hanging so low they're almost touching the treetops. The storm isn't just building around me. It's reached inside, the elements alive inside me, no longer a distant call.

My phone rings. I take it out and check it—Aaron. I pretty much have to answer it, right? Yes, Rex, you do. I clear my throat to make sure my voice sounds normal. "Bro. *Aon scéal?*"

"I talked to my dad," he says. "He's going to help you out of this mess."

"Your dad's a Bevan sympathizer." My accent is so glaring whenever I talk to him, mostly because his has never been as strong. Not that I've spent more time with our mother than him—she ignored us both equally. The difference is his father actually had conversations with him, so he's picked up more speech from him. My father has only ever given commands.

He sighs because he knew I'd say that. "He's your dad's cousin. Your cousin. He can help."

"At this point, anyone related to my dad is more of a prob for me than a help."

"Why's that?"

I walk to the edge of the old stone patio to watch the grasshoppers going ape in the tall grass. One lands on my shoulder, and I flick it off. I wonder if they're here to hang with Sloane. God, she's so weird. And so fucking off limits.

"Rex?"

"My dad pretty much wants to kick my ass right now."

"Doesn't your dad always want to kick your ass?"

I let that question sit. Aaron knows what jacked-up punishments my father and crew come up with. A kick in the ass is not accurate. At all.

"Point is, they're going to send a shitload of guys after you and you won't walk away from it. My dad's willing to help you, but only if you'll meet in person. He wants to see Sloane, make sure she's okay. How fast can you get to Roanoke?"

"Couple hours, I guess." Who says I need help? Or that I want out of this? I know exactly what I'm doing. But I don't dare tell him that. He'd send a helicopter for my retrieval.

"I'll text you an address and meet time as soon as he calls back to confirm. He and I will be waiting for you. You *and* Sloane. Got it?"

Thunder grumbles far away. A few random raindrops splatter the patio around me. Big brothers are supposed to be overbearing and stupid helpful so there's no reason for me to yell at him. "Got it. I'll be there."

"And she better not have a scratch on her."

"Can't promise that."

His voice gets low and slow. "Why not?"

"We had a few scuffles. She's all grins though. I think she likes it."

"Don't be a creep."

I hope he doesn't go to too much trouble getting himself to Roanoke because I'm so not going to be there. "Born and bred by the best," I say and hang up. I'm not sure I can pull off any more lies with all the other crap on my mind.

Crap like Sloane Bevan crushed against me.

And how I want her to do it again.

CHAPTER 13

SLOANE

LIGHT DRAINS FROM the kitchen as the clouds sweep in. Rex's phone call ended long ago, but he's still out there watching lightning zigzag across the sky. His hand goes to his head, pausing abruptly like he expected something else to be there. A nervous tic, now broken for some reason.

Because he's the creepy stalker, not me, I stop watching and go out the front door to the porch. The scent of rain rides the breeze, damp and cool, charged by the combative masses of air. I hope the cold front wins. My Montana blood is begging for relief from this heat.

Thunder vibrates the porch below my feet and the sky unloads. It's more a dump of water than a rain shower, hitting the ground so hard it's kicking up mist on the paved driveway and bouncing off the porch so I have to step back to avoid being sprayed. Rex's car is instantly clean, the thoroughly mudded wheels and fenders now glistening green and white like a piece of candy. We should probably cloak that car. If the Moores come looking, he and I can easily hide in the woods, but not if that car is here.

I go back inside expecting Rex to have come in, but he's still out back in the same spot, standing in the pouring rain. Either he's more desperate for a cool-down than I am, or he's having a psychotic break. My fault, probably. The bearhug, the whole let's-be-a-team thing—that was all crazy enough. But casting away that watch? I can't decide whose fault that was. He was tied to that thing, affected somehow. Ripping it off was probably like tearing off a limb. His face showed nothing, but retreating back to the house and refusing to talk to me about it gave away more than he knows.

Boys acting tough to cover how sensitive and confused they are. They're the only ones who don't see through it, and they're the ones doing it.

The house has gotten yet even hotter inside with the contrast of cool rain outside. I let myself onto the screened porch. A few steps off the ground, it's out of the path of the splashing rain so it's nicely dry with just a bit of mist sneaking through the open three sides. Rex should notice me, but he doesn't. His back is unguarded, not because he trusts me—even if that's true now. It's more like he's chosen to be oblivious. When I pound on the porch framing and he doesn't turn around, I know I went too far. I broke his brain. Why did I hug him like that? And why didn't he shove me away?

I leave the porch and stand beside him, instantly soaked. The rain is so thick it's hard to keep my eyes open; I turn to him and find his closed. I elbow him. He elbows me back, unstartled, almost as if he expected it.

You're getting wet, I sign, barely getting it out before he's taken hold of my hands, silencing me. I'd be very annoyed if not for the gentle way he did it, for how he held them a little longer than necessary. But gosh, he's going to ruin his phone, and we kind of need it. So I poke him in the pocket where I know he keeps it and that sparks some reality back into his eyes.

I follow him onto the screened porch. He drops his phone where it's dry and grabs my hand, hauling me back into the same spot in the rain. And we stand there until we're cooled to the bones, massaged and sleepy and much too companionable for two people raised to hate each other.

We've made beds on the screened porch as far away from each other as the encroaching wetness from the storm will allow. The blankets and pillows we found in the house were full of dust and spiders, but we shook them out and now they've soaked up the humidity and smell like rain. The storm has calmed, falling now like a fine mist.

Rex lent me a T-shirt to sleep in, which was weird, but nice, and fits me better than my dad's. We found an old paraffin lamp and raised the wick high so it lights the whole porch. We just finished off the muffins and bananas and now we're working on the salsa. He's double-dipping even after I complained. On paper. He's such a selfish jerk.

I scratch out my complaint and write below it: *We need to cloak the car in case they come.*

He takes the pencil. *They won't. Aaron doesn't think they know this place exists.*

How not? Your mom used to live here.

He shrugs, yawning. It is hard to care, surrounded by this curtain of rain that's stirred up the scent of the roses and untouched land. He leans back on his elbows to watch me, partially in shadow. I watch him right back. Wimp can't take what he dishes out though, so he gets up and goes into the house. I spot his phone on his bed, the screen still lit and active. So I snatch it and search for the speaking app I use to talk to hearing people with my phone at home. By the time he returns it's installed and ready to go.

There's a heavy pause when he sees me holding his phone, but he's chosen to play it cool. What's more interesting is what he's brought back: a stack of books, and a curve of the lips that could be an actual human smile if he'd let it loose.

I type into the phone. *Moores read?*

He stiffens at the point the voice must be reading it back. I chose the same voice Marcas set as default in my phone, the one he said sounds the most like me, without my Deaf accent.

Rex reaches for his phone, but I hold it away, pointing to his mouth then the screen in the hope he knows how these apps work.

He speaks, and I check the screen. *Your dad's actually literate? Who'd have thought. Because these sure aren't my mom's.*

I type: *Because your mom's not literate?*

Probably not. She has servants for that. His smile rises to a full-on grin. Spontaneous and real and friendly, peaked higher on one side.

With a dimple.

For once, it's not a weapon or a power play. A wild quiver in my belly interrupts current to my brain, stealing my last rational thought. I hand his phone back because I don't want it anymore. I drop to sit on my bed. Disturbing. That's what that smile is. A little bit delicious and a whole lot disturbing.

A book goes in front of my face. Then another. He's showing me his finds only I can't see anything but that last unleashed smile. Because let's be real. It's not a little bit delicious, it's a whole heck of a lot. It's a calamity, really, how cute an evil person can be when he puts his mind to it.

Now he's sitting cross-legged on his bed, bent over a book open in his lap, pensively running a knuckle over his lips, and I don't know how he thinks it's okay to rifle my dad's stuff and then insult his intelligence. I don't care if Rex's mom lived here. My dad owns this property and always has. So hey, maybe ask if he can go through my dad's books. Act a little respectful in another person's house. Be humble, not so grabby, not so entitled. But that's the Moores. Taking what they want. Screw everyone else.

We're both standing then, because I've snatched the book away from him and he got up, affronted, as anyone would be when blindsided like that. I'm hot and prickly all over; my heart beats in my throat like it so wishes I could yell at him. There's a much more rational organ wondering what I'm so upset about, telling me this is stupid, calm down, stop being a child. My heart slows as my brain wrangles it in, and I start to grasp the situation. Rex is a Moore and it doesn't matter how attractive he is. He's both evil and an enemy. Let him smile nonstop until he dies. It doesn't change a thing.

But there is a changed thing. It shouldn't be changed, but it is. Not our new allegiance. That's business—mostly. It's survival and common sense. But there's this other thing—

He jerks the book out of my hand. I gasp I'm so startled—the rapid intake of breath gets my heart pounding again. No one makes me gasp, and the fact that *he* did strikes a match in me. I shouldn't be mad at him for doing the same thing I did to him. I couldn't help it though; my action may have been childish but it was in no way premeditated. But him—he's done it on purpose, vindictively.

You're an entitled, spoiled jerk, I sign.

He shoves his phone at me but I ignore it.

Evil. Unlikeable, unlovable, so don't try to change my mind with a cute smile. I remember those measly five contacts in his phone and flush cold. I'm terrible, so terrible. *Stay away from me,* I finish. Without looking at him, I snatch up my bedding and drag it into the house, kicking the door closed behind me. I'm aware of my overreaction but unable to stop it.

The darkness inside is complete. I feel around for the table where I left those votive candles, lighting one with a pinch when I find it. Because I don't want anything to do with the room where Dad and Rex's mom slept, I clear the cobwebs from the doorway of the tiny second bedroom still decorated for a baby. The last person to have slept in this room was probably Aaron, and I'm cool with that. His percentage of evil is trivial and much diluted. He grew up rich and spoiled, but he doesn't hold it over people. He doesn't take and expect and use.

One problem though: There's a separate layer of darkness my candle isn't breaking away. It's hanging above, murky and looming, more desperate than when I first entered this cottage. Either due to my recognition of it or my mood, I'm more connected now, and it's reaching, touching upon that same nerve that possessed me to inscribe Rex's forehead with that symbol in his blood. It's appealing to that other magic in me, the one that knows how to take power from this residue formed by sadness and anger.

This room is a bad idea, but I'm stubborn and not leaving. I roll out my bed and lie down, drawing the sheet over me. I should apologize to him. I would, if he hadn't reacted the way he did. That tucked chin and leveled, enraged gaze—forget him. If he can so easily step back into that role, then so can I. We can be allies and still hate each other.

Blowing out the candle covers me in such darkness I command it to relight. A whole team could ambush me in dark like that and I'd never know until it was too late. I don't like the idea of sleeping in such a void either, my body lying alone in this tank of nothingness. It's been too rainy to befriend any animals. With Rex on my side, I didn't need to. Clearly that's the stupidest mistake I've made yet. All my trust in Rex Moore? No backup plan? My dad would kill me.

My throat constricts. I take a shuddering breath in, but the awareness of the shudder hollows out the strength I've piled inside. The quake in my chest overcomes me so completely I don't even have time to turn my face against the pillow. I'm crying so hard my effort to subdue it cramps my stomach. I bend, getting no relief. I've gone instantly snotty and congested and it's even harder to catch my breath.

I called him sensitive and confused, but I'm the one falling apart over a smile.

I have no idea what sounds I'm making, and I don't want Rex to hear any of it. I turn to my stomach and smother myself against the pillow. Can't think about my dad. Not my mom or Marcas, my dogs or my house. The glitter of sunlight in the river when it's rushing hard in the spring-time. Coyotes smiling at me from the opposite bank. The smell of the pines, of lavender and rosemary drying under the eaves in the summer sun.

Can't think about all the things that my dad has taught me, all the things that have gone to waste. Instead, I think about my plan I'll need to break to Rex tomorrow, the words I'll use. The tears roll but let them. They're silent, and I'm cool with silent.

Winnie stands in my dream in her ironic WITCH sleeping tee and a severe case of bedhead. The room is full of flickering light from four votive candles at her feet—north, south, east, west. Behind her, a rumpled bed and some guy raising up on an elbow, blinking sleepy eyes at her. *Whatcha doin', babe?*

She turns around. *Sleep,* she commands, and he drops back onto the pillow.

Her image fades so I reach, latching onto the edge of her mindspace and dragging myself in. *Winnie, how are you with me while awake?*

Her image doubles for a second before straightening back out, and I see she's facing a mirror. I'm in her mind but don't have access to her thoughts, which is why she's using the mirror. She signs, *I can't sleep so I had to try something different. We're worried about you.*

Guilt sweeps in. I should be checking in with her every night. I have to sleep to do it though, and it doesn't seem like I've gotten much of that. Exhaustion plagues the little sleep I've found lately. Now that she's with me, the comfort of her presence is something I can't let go of, not when I'm so lonely, so confused, so desperate for help. *Winnie, I'm doing everything wrong. We're going to lose.*

She signs into the mirror. *Follow your heart. Your way is the only way to win this, even if it seems so wrong.*

You're just saying that to make me feel better.

She turns around to check the sleeping guy. Something about how he's rolled makes her go to her knees in front of the mirror, probably to save him from catching a glimpse of his girlfriend signing to herself in the mirror in the middle of the night like a weirdo. And that sleeping tee isn't helping her keep any secrets. *No. I'm saying it because I've seen it.*

My dad's going to hate me.

Without pause, she signs, *Yes, but my mom and Grandma and I will make him understand.* She's probably already accounted for this.

Our connection falters and I grasp at the remaining strings, trying to tie it back together. I'm reconnected with her, but she's gone into a withdrawn stare. She abruptly puts a hand on the mirror and yells, *Sloane! Wake up!*

I sit up fast, my eyes adjusting to my own votive candle and a cluster of moths dive-bombing me. They must've snuck into the house while I was asleep. Now they're here to warn me of a sound they don't recognize but insist must be danger. And they're right because my amulet has gone hot against me, its magic bright in my head.

Getting up. Touching nothing. Only my bare feet against wood floor like it's made of air. I'm an osprey gliding on the wind. A fish in a stream. As I open the door I blow out a slow breath, scattering any sound of a moving hinge so no human mind can reassemble it. A burst of light explodes beyond the hall, a simultaneous jolt in the floor. That can be one of two things: firecrackers or gunshots, and I'm pretty sure I know which it is.

Crouching down, I scurry forward because there's no way I want to be trapped in a bedroom for a gunfight. The forest is my safety and that's where I need to go. Another flash lights the room ahead, giving me a split-second view: Rex ducked behind the toppled couch, firing at the closed front door. The paraffin lamp sits beside him, the wick turned as low as it will go. He had time to get the lamp, the gun, and turn the couch, yet didn't wake me?

He spots me then and holds up a hand. *Stay there*, it says.

I point to the floor beside him. That's where I'd rather be. He pulls a second handgun out of his waistband and slides it across the floor toward me. I snatch it up, retreat to the bedroom, and part the window shade to get a view of the front yard, expecting a cluster of shiny black cars with bright headlights and men returning fire.

But there's nothing—just a darkness so black the only way to see the sky is to imagine the gray clouds from earlier in the day are still there. I blow out the candle, hoping to see better out the window but it's a pit of nothingness. Cracking the window gives me a strong scent of rain. Then I see the faintest shade of gray above—clouds doing their best to steal the light of the night sky. If there were men out there, they'd be as blind as me. I relight the candle and set it in the window, gathering power to send its flame high. It casts light across the yard, illuminating a slow rain. I see shadows moving in the waving grass. The pointy ears. The bushy tails.

I take off down the hall before Rex starts firing again. If he thinks coyotes are a threat to us, he's either gone crazy or he's never learned a thing about our magic. He's missing from his post. The oil lamp lights up bullet holes in the front door, and I resist the urge to rush outside for any hurt coyotes. I have to stop Rex first, before he shoots more.

Something strikes my ankle from the shadows. I go down, rolling to avoid a broken bone. Kicking away rewards me with a few inches of distance from the assaulter—just enough to see the body attached to the arm and the face that goes along with it. Rex?

He grabs both my ankles, yanking me toward where he kneels on the floor. I should be fighting back, but I'm paralyzed by the crazed, distracted look in his eyes that seems even more sinister in the low light. Recognition unfurrows his brow, and he releases me to hunker down and dart into the kitchen. He waves me toward him, as mechanical as a cop directing traffic.

If mistaking me for an enemy is that easy, then I need to relieve him of that gun. Disarming him turns out harder than I thought—he's in fight mode and slippery with sweat. Two effective counters by him allow the weapon to remain firmly in his hands, and judging from the words he's spitting, he's a little angry that I'm suddenly against and not with. So I change my strategy: I aim the gun he gave me at his forehead.

He leaps under the table, knocking down chairs around him. So much for that. No pants means nowhere to stash a gun so I toss it in the sink and chase him out the other side, tackling him in the middle of the living room. He goes down easily, one robotic hunk of muscle just switching off. Even though he's limp on his back on the floor, I jab an elbow into his forearm so he releases the gun. A kick slides it out of reach. His eyes lock onto the ceiling; I grab the front of his shirt with both fists and give him a hard shake. It's the only way to communicate *What the hell is wrong with you?!*

A panic attack, that's what, by the rapid panting and running sweat that don't seem to want to quit. I pat around his pockets for his phone, but he grabs my wrist, frantic, almost like he has something in there he doesn't want me to see. With no phone, there's no way to ask, *What's your problem?*

I sign it anyway. He makes a circling motion with his finger all around the house, and I catch one word: *Surrounded.*

Coyotes won't kill us you idiot. More ASL he won't understand. Where's his stupid phone?

He tenses like he heard something. Then he's halfway up, eyes on that gun on the floor. I tackle him before he's made it upright but his strength is supernatural, and I have nothing to overcome it. Exhaustion stretches across me. What sleep have I had? Not enough for this. He drags me across the room, swiveling the overturned couch as we pass by. Behind it, he squats, holding my arm to keep me down with him. He's gone so intense I don't fight him. Whatever he hears has him breathing harder than during any of our brawls. He's also got the shakes—either his muscles are too tense and exhausted like mine, or it's nerves and fear. But from what?

When I turn to get a better look at his face, he puts a finger to his lips like he's forgotten I don't speak.

I close my eyes and find my moths. They've retreated because of him, but they're still close enough to reach. I need their sense of hearing to tell me what's gotten him so scared. They arrive, claiming no humans nearby, no predators. Nothing but nighttime and rain. Rex has me shielded behind a couch because of something he hears, when all the moths hear is a normal rainy night. I think I'll go with the ones who have the best hearing of any earthbound creature.

Shaking Rex's arm, I put an imaginary phone to my ear.

He unpockets his phone and shows me the black, dead screen. Great—I'll have to figure out how to tell him everything's okay the hard way. Some earth to write on in flame would be helpful right now, but all I have is a wooden floor, a couch, my body, and his.

Marcas and I used to play a game where we'd write invisible words on each other's arms and try to guess what they were. Before Rex can stop me, I reach around the couch for the lamp and drag it between us. I grab his hand. He jerks so violently I almost lose grip. I extend his arm, and lose my train of thought for a moment at the vision of that strange patch of skin on his arm. He catches me looking at it and tries to pull away, but I hold on. With my finger I write, *Rex*.

His eyes flick to mine. *Rex*, I write again, tilting my head so he'll look at his arm and not me.

What? his eyes say.

Moths, I write as he watches. He nods once, so I continue. *Say all is OK.*

He lifts the shoulder of his T-shirt and wipes sweat off his brow. A muscle is trembling in his jaw.

I write, *What are you afraid of?*

I extend my arm in front of him. He takes hold of my wrist, hesitating. His breathing has slowed to a more normal level but that jaw muscle is still going nuts. He writes, *Them.*

I take his arm and write, *They are not here.*

He writes, *Here.* And points to his temple.

My heart loses a beat. He means they're in his head? The whole thing was in his head, an imaginary attack, some kind of PTSD hallucination. For real? I take his arm to write something else but there's nothing simple enough to be written in the space on his arm. So instead I write, *Are you OK?*

There's a change in the way he's looking at me then, a depth to how he's taking me in. Instead of losing just one heartbeat, I lose them all.

He takes my arm. The warmth of his hand against my wrist is a new, unexpected thing. Not just a hand anymore but skin and heat and pulse I'm painfully aware of as if it's my own. He writes, *I am now.*

But he doesn't release me. Not that I'd have a response if he did. I should pull away, but I don't because his thumb has traveled from my wrist into my palm. It's an exploration, a forbidden move I'm not stopping because the solid pressure of that thumb has found a nerve and reached all the way up my arm in a way that's left me unable to move. He's watching it happen like he has no control over it, lips parted, fascinated.

Somehow I manage to pull my hand away. He starts a little, still looking at the air where my hand used to be. I get up and move around the couch, tripping over its edge on legs that have lost their ability to hold me up. Now I'm the one breathing hard, though I've done nothing to cause it. I'm the one with the fatal pulse.

He flips the couch so it lands back on its feet and stands up behind it. Then he presses his fingers against his temples and gazes at me. I shrug because, what? He rubs a hand across his mouth, looking at me as if I have something to say.

Stop being weird, I sign. But "weird" isn't the right word. Unless I'm a fan of weird. And if this is weird, I could totally be a fan.

He gives me a half grin, like I've done something cute.

I cover my mouth so I don't smile because I'm so about to smile. Smiling would be bad right now. This territory we're about to enter is super inescapable and a million times wrong. He comes around the corner of the couch and steps toward me as I'm stepping back until he's backed me against the wall. I don't know how he's gotten closer because my hands are against his chest to keep him away but the rest of my body doesn't seem to want to obey that or put any strength behind it. And now he's flattened his own hands against the wall above me—some attempt to hold himself back that's clearly not working for him either because we're close now, very close, and my stupid hands have slid around him. His eyes have gone squinty with the effort of trying to figure something out. He's not going to kiss me, no way, that would be a nuclear bomb of crazy I can't allow. I can't *not* allow it either, because if he doesn't kiss me, I'm afraid I might kiss him, or die, or both.

He licks his bottom lip. It sets a fire at my feet, flames climbing my legs and urging me to do something. I can't stand here like this. It would be suicide.

Don't, I read on his lips.

Don't what? Think? Breathe? I'm already not doing that.

Stop, he says. As if I'm the one who started this. The jerk's way off.

Don't stop, he says, and I'm pretty sure the world implodes.

Because I'm the sane one, I peel my arms from around him and flatten my body against the wall. It's such a tearing, brutal gouge all over me that I raise to my toes and kiss him. For survival. I'd die otherwise.

It's a rushing river of sensation in the smallest physical touch. I press my arms against the wall—to reach for him now would be too much; it would short the circuit we've just made. I sink down, breaking the connection. His hands have turned to fists on the wall. His eyes are untamed.

Don't stop, I mouth.

Now it's his turn to kiss me. It's not just lips this time, it's a singular bond, his whole body crushing against mine, every masculine part of him joined to me like an unbreakable chemical connection. We'll have to split atoms to get ourselves apart.

He pushes away then, cursing and pressing fists against his temples. F-bombs all over. Looking at me while dropping them as if I'm to blame.

I point at him. *Your fault. Not mine.*

He points to himself, says, *Me?*

I nod. For some reason I'm trembling—way too hot and trembling. We need to open more windows, get some air in here.

He's saying something I can't read, something a lot gentler than what he was saying before. I unglue myself from the wall and step closer to better see his lips. I sign, *What?*

I need sleep. He digs in his pocket, extracts his pill case. Takes out a pill and swallows it dry. It happens too fast for me to react, but I wish I'd had a warning because I'd wrestle that case away from him and ask what they're for. I have a feeling whatever they are can't be good. Before I can do anything, he's backed up to the couch and fallen onto it, arms crossed over his eyes.

I drag my bedding from the other room to the floor beside the couch. His arms have fallen away; he's sleeping hard. Repositioning the oil lamp focuses light on the bullet holes in the front door. How could I be so distracted? I rush onto the porch, calling for the coyotes. They're nearby and unharmed, only here to offer aid in case I need it. Turns out he probably wasn't firing at them but imaginary Moores. It's hard to decide if that's going to help or hurt my case when I tell him my plan, but either way, I tell him. As soon as he wakes up.

He sleeps slack and unmoving for twelve hours. The pulse in his neck is the only proof he's even alive. I feast from the woods and another food box that arrives by drone. Aaron sent a lot of packaged snacks this time, perfect for a road trip. Rex must've told him we're heading out soon, which works for me. The sooner we get started on ending the Moores, the sooner I can go home.

I can't stop thinking about what I did. What *we* did. That thing that's wrong but feels so right. No way Winnie was referring to that, just no way. We can't do it again. In fact, I'm going to deny it. He was probably in such a state his memory will be foggy, and if he brings it up—which he won't, because come *on*—I'm going to plead the fifth. That's another wrong thing that feels right. Deny making out with Rex Moore. I'm so very in.

I'm cross-legged on the floor, gobbling snack mix and flipping through an old magazine, when he sits up so fast I skirt quickly out of range, spilling snack mix across the floor. Then he's up and pacing, stepping all over the mess and squishing it into finer bits. And asking me something. Yelling, it looks like. Showing me his dead phone, pointing to his wrist.

Well if he wants the time he's going to have to stop freaking out and charge up that phone. I stand to peer out the windows for the sun—it's not a perfect gauge of time but it's close enough for two kids with no schedule whatsoever. I hold up two fingers and shrug because it's not that precise.

He checks out every window and clears the hall and bedrooms before plunking down beside me. Apparently I'm stupid enough to sit here and snack while the house crawls with enemy Moores. I can't decide what would be more suspicious: looking at him or not looking at him. Staying in place or getting up. There's a new form of matter filling the space between his body and mine. It's not simply empty air anymore. It's active and alive and moving, liquid and fire. A raw awareness, a draw.

After sifting through the food box, he finds a bottle of water and twists the cap off. He closes his eyes to drink and that's my chance to get a good look: the tight bulge of his trap muscle, the buzzed blond hair turned darker and spiky with sweat at the nape of his neck. I'm not quick enough to look away though; he's lowered the bottle and paused, cheeks round with water still in his mouth, eyes on mine. Lowering to my mouth. My chest. He swallows, that bottle still held halfway to his mouth, stuck in place. He remembers. And his awareness of the element between us powers his side on, leveling everything up to unbearable.

I stand but he's faster, up and out the door, food box in hand. The door closes fast, thumping in the floor, an inferior degree of thump compared to what's going on with my heart.

Stewing in the heat of the air and my excited blood, I sit. We need to move, to get on the road, but how do I bring any of that up with the definitely-not-a-dream kiss that feels like a dream and I wish was a dream hanging between us? Unacknowledged it's only going to grow, like a mistake caught early but not fixed, or a lie uncovered but allowed to remain without an apology to diffuse it.

Because I'm not leaving a food mess in my dad's house, I get the broom from the kitchen and sweep up. Rex hasn't returned so I head out front and see him sitting in the car, doors closed, windows up. A distortion in the air by the back bumper tells me the car is running. I wouldn't mind sitting in some cool air-conditioning either. The day is a smothering blanket of hot. The rain did nothing but add more steam to a rainforest.

When I get in the passenger side, he keeps his focus on his phone that's plugged in and charging. But that focus is strained. I can tell he wants to look at me. I poke him in the arm and with an open hand ask for his phone. He brings up the talking app and speaks before handing it over.

The screen says: *Your fault. Don't do it again.*

He's still hung up on blame? Elements help me. I type, *Okay, I started it. But you did it back, and yours was …*

I pause, undecided between words. I want to say 'better' but I shouldn't say that.

Worse.

He shifts his jaw sideways. That's a mechanism, I see, to subdue a smile. Once it's under control, he speaks. *Next time will be worse. So don't push me. I know pushing is in your Bevan blood—*

I take my eyes off the screen to glare at him hard enough he stops talking. There are so many things wrong with what he just said, and the way he turns in his seat to face me squarely and unashamed tells me he knows that, and right now *he's* the one pushing *me* because he wants to see my reaction. And this sleaze-ball act is a game, a grasp for power. Well, try again, bro, because I could totally kill you.

I type, *That's only a threat if it's not consensual.*

He's an escape artist for how fast he can leave a car. Heat billows into the open door as he paces, both hands on top of his head. Nothing about him is my type: muscular and brutish, rich and spoiled, blond and evil. At some point in the night he changed from the camo pants to shiny athletic shorts, turning him from army boy to jock. The geeky shaggy-haired artist boys I crush on at home must live in an alternate dimension. Rex Moore is nothing like them and nothing like me. Which makes him not just a challenge, but a thrill.

How disgusting.

I swipe out of the talking app because he's obviously got a fit to throw in place of talking to me. Behind it is an ASL learning app. It looks like an alphabet lesson stopped on the letter S. Bombarded by questions of *why* and *when*, I glance out the window. He's gone to a squat, fingers laced over the back of his bowed head. Right then the phone vibrates in my hand. A new text.

Dad: Last chance.

Resisting the urge to open his texts and see what it's referring to, I lean over and tap on the window. A text from his dad is the perfect thing for him right now. If only I had some popcorn to go along with it.

CHAPTER 14

REX

OUR EYES MEET through the glass. She holds up the phone like it's something urgent. I can't be in that car with her right now, but I can barely breathe out here it's so muggy. Come on, Rex. Grow the hell up. She's Sloane Bevan. She's not cute and she doesn't feel like heaven against you. She has magic you need and then you're going to uncork that bottle and kill her.

Control—I have it somewhere. It'll be easier to find in the air-conditioned car and out of this heat, so I get behind the wheel and slam the door.

"It's fucking hot out there." I don't know if her Deaf person app picked that up but it doesn't matter. I'm not really talking to her anyway.

I take the phone and see the text. Last chance? Right. Let them try to find me.

Piss off, I type back. Sloane looks quickly away like it's a thing she didn't want to see. Princess is shocked by the disrespect I show my own father? Maybe I should tell her he's the one I learned it from. No—that would require looking at her, and I just can't do that right now. The memory of last night has me wound so tight I can't trust myself not to do it all over again. Being confined inside this car with her is not helping.

"Get out of my car." She probably can't read my lips if I'm facing the steering wheel. I open the Deaf person app, repeat it, and hand the phone to her.

Do you feel that? she asks through the phone.

She's going to have to be more specific. I feel a lot of things right now.

I think someone's coming.

I hear it then—a car with a loud exhaust. She's twisted in her seat to look out the back window down the driveway, and I'm watching my side mirror. At the same time we look at each other—we need to go. Convenient we happen to already be in the car. I release the brake and find the gear, but she lays a steady hand on my forearm and leaves it there long enough to refresh that memory of last night and the feel of her mouth on mine. It was for sure real, right? Had to be—I saw the way she looked at me when I woke up. Her face hides nothing. And it couldn't have been one of my nightmares because it was too damn good.

Get a grip, Rex. Just handle it already. Stop being such a little boy.

That's not a car exhaust, that's a motorcycle. I kill the R5's engine and reach into my bag in the back, wrestling free the .45. No one in my family rides a motorcycle, but there is one Bevan who does. And if he's here to claim his daughter, I'm going to blow his head off.

Unfortunately the rider is definitely not male. She doesn't look like any Moore I know. Sloane has joined my side behind the R5. I chamber a round and aim as the motorcycle approaches. The rider stops several yards away, turns off the engine, takes off her helmet.

"Take that away from him," she says to Sloane, who jumps as if poked.

Sloane reaches for the .45, and I'm handing it to her without wanting to, my hands having gone weak and grown their own brain and free will. Weird magic hangs heavy around us, powerful, overtaking, unfamiliar—shit. Black magic. A black witch. Shit. Shit. Shit.

"*Dúile daoibh*," she says, taking off her gloves. The greeting is obviously aimed at us, but I'm not greeting her back. She'll have to make me say it just like she made me release the .45. Just as I think it I wish I hadn't. She looks as old as my father and has had a whole lifetime to collect power. She can probably read minds.

Sloane takes a step forward, and I have to check myself. Don't reach for her, Rex. Lighten the hell up. And even as the black witch steps forward, my arm wants to shoot out and grab Sloane. Yeah, she can probably fight her off better than I can. Brain, please get that message to my idiotic arms.

The black witch presses her index finger against Sloane's forehead. "Daughter of Liv, son of Dillon," she says, glancing at me.

Sloane covers her ears, which is pretty weird for a deaf girl.

"What an unlikely couple you make. Do your families know?"

I choke and laugh. There's nothing happy about it though, unless you count the joy I get from the image of kicking her in the throat. "Let's not jump to conclusions, old lady."

"Rubbish choice of word? Okay, how about 'team?'"

Sloane nods like she's following along completely. I hand her my phone. Total dumbass for not doing it sooner. If we really are a team, then I need her to follow the conversation so she knows when to attack. But she doesn't even look at the screen.

The woman reaches into her jacket and removes a pouch. From it she pulls a bright green leaf she tucks in her mouth and chews. I shift my weight so I'm closer to the .45 in Sloane's hand. She's too observant though, because she switches the gun to the opposite hand. I'll have to reach around her body to get it now. It'll add time to my offense but that's no prob. I'm much faster than an old lady even if the old lady's a black witch.

"Sloane. You're a gatherer of darkness. Collect it, harness it, use it, and let it use you. The stronger you are, the more it will bend to your rules." Now the woman holds that pouch out to Sloane, and Sloane is taking it. "This will relieve your eyes from the daylight."

Sloane types into my phone and it says, *My dad said—*

She pauses to look up at me. Unsure how to finish? Or unsure if she should finish in front of me?

"Forget what you dad said," the woman says. "He'll never understand *dubhealaín*. He doesn't have our blood."

Our blood?

"Our and your mother's blood."

The longest pieces of Sloane's bangs have blown in her eyes, but she's making no move to fix them. All she can do is stare at the woman, and all I can do is stare at her. I need to teach the girl how to keep a neutral face because the layers of expression are unreal. Shock, panic, grief, with a healthy side of suspicion and disbelief. But laying it all out in plain view like that? I don't know how she survives around people.

She's gone back to the phone. *My mother?*

"Carries black magic blood and passed it to you. She's lost it, but you're still young enough to learn. I can teach you how to manage it."

Sloane shakes her head like she's just been offered candy by a stranger.

"It'd be wise to shed your father's hatred of our kind and rethink this. My number is in your head once you do." Then the woman looks at me. "Rex Moore, you have something of mine."

Here's where I take my own advice and keep my face blank. Release just a little grin to keep this friendly until I'm ready to not be friendly. "Okay, hmm. Youth? Nope. Superior magic? Help me out because neither of those are yours." Pressure coils around my throat. I subdue a cough but it gets away from me, not easing the pressure but increasing it. Even though I'm taking in air, it feels like it's through a tiny tube that doesn't cut it. The woman has crossed her arms to watch me struggle. And Sloane has a hand against her own throat, her eyes showing the fear mine should be. I decide to shut up.

"Finished?" the woman asks.

My throat finally opens to its full capacity, allowing me to fill my lungs.

"Because we only have a few minutes. Your father stole something of mine I'd like to have back."

"I don't have it." Which is true. It's in my other pants. Along with a blade I'd love to have on me right now.

"You'll need to find it then."

Moths pour out of the trees into a whirlwind above our heads. It's enough of a diversion for me to reach around Sloane for the .45, which slides right into my hand since Sloane is dropping to the ground. I get a violent tug in my stomach that stops me still. Does she think I'm going to shoot her?

I feel a hundred feet tall standing there while she's on her belly smacking at my ankle. The woman and her motor-cycle have disappeared without a sound. Sloane smacks again, the moths circle, and everything else has gone com-pletely silent.

Gunshots explode from all around, bullets popping earth and pavement around us. Sloane is army-crawling to the R5, and I'm covering her, shooting down guys emerg-ing from the woods and behind the house. A sting peels across my shoulder, and I'm out of ammo. I dive toward the R5 where Sloane sits against the wheel, both hands pressed on her leg over a gush of escaping blood.

Everything blurs around me. All sound mutes. What I see instead is my thumb on that crease in her palm. How perfectly it nested there. And how she let me do it.

A man's voice is shouting at me to get down. Someone else has knocked me to my knees. My wrists are being wrenched behind my back. And Sloane is setting fire to the ground around her for a barrier to the three guys stalking up to her. Her leg runs with red. All she can do is sit and hold that wound. If she gets up, she'll bleed out. Now it's not just the crease in her palm I see. It's the way she tilted her face to me when I backed her into that wall. The trust in her eyes. No one's ever looked at me like that.

I slam my head back, making contact with something that feels like a nose. My wrists return to me. I knock away grabbing hands, kick an aimed pistol, and roll to catch it. It's firing in my hand with no work from me because everything's on autopilot and I can't find the controls. Heads blow out, chests go bloody. No more bullets and they're on me again, three at a time. I dodge and counter until I get a good hit on one and then I'm on offense. Elbow to throat, foot to knee, stomp a neck. The snap of a bone, the splatter of blood. A body falls and there are no more.

Space stretches around me instead of the crush of moving bodies. I take in air, assess the scene. Four left. All staying back. They're the final round, and they don't want to fail. I circle two of them to position myself between them and Sloane, who's somehow managed to drag my bag out of the R5 and is wrapping her wound with a T-shirt. If she could hear, I'd tell her to get in the car. Might be hard to understand me though, with these swollen lips and a mouthful of blood. I spit it out and wipe my mouth.

"What are you guys waiting for?"

They exchange eye contact. A silent decision of strategy. Who knows what my family promised them if they bring me back. Is it something that can be split four ways? They may have been trained as a team, but on the battlefield things like that change.

I point to the guy closest to Sloane. "You first."

The guy to my left charges. I take it head-on, let him knock me to the ground and pull him down with me. Then I slide around him and snap his neck. Something must've happened to my shoulder because there's a hot stream running down my back and my arm tingles. Is that where I caught a bullet? I can't even remember. I stay down and point to another guy. "Next."

He's not so eager. I glance at Sloane—it seems like she called my name, but I know that's impossible. She's shoved my bag back in the car and extinguished her fire, but she's standing so still with both eyes closed—that's when I see the guy near the woods with a rifle aimed right at me.

I roll, the bullet catching me somewhere in the arm. The pain is so bad it's good. The rush of fresh adrenaline and endorphins, the raw sensation of open flesh and blood running free, and the knowledge I'll overcome this. I'll get up and fucking win. That's what I need. That's the high no one understands but me.

I'm up and moving. Sloane has met me halfway, but she shouldn't be on that leg. She's loco.

"Get in!" I push her toward the R5.

Instead she hobble-sprints toward the house, and I'm ducking against the car to avoid another shot from the rifle. At least it's keeping those last few guys away. I have no idea if she's staying in there or coming back out. My other guns are inside, though, so it wouldn't be suicide to go back in—more guns, more cover. Is that guy reloading? Hopefully, because I'm already running toward the house.

Sloane and I collide in the doorway, my bloody arm taking most of the blow. It's great, how that feels. If I could bottle the sensation, I could kill people with it. She's dragging a bag—is that what she came in here for? And would it be a bad idea to smack her right now?

She points in the direction of the car and hands me the key. Good thought to grab it so they wouldn't. Okay, genius, but now we have a rifle to dodge for yards instead of inches. I gather my guns while she dumps the box of food into her bag. We meet at the front door. I hold up one finger, then two, then three. And we run.

Because she's slow on that bad leg, I empty my magazine to cover us. Rifle Guy isn't firing, probably because he's waiting for us to stop. If he takes out my new tires I'm going to kill him. But that's not saying much because I'll kill him anyway. At the car I aim into the woods where he last was, hoping to take him out before he ruins my tires and our smooth getaway. I don't see Rifle Guy, though. All I see is a cluster of coyotes.

Then I'm tearing through the gears and wondering how the hell we survived that. Or if there's another team waiting at the main road. Or a helicopter tracking us. My brain is firing faster than that last mag unloading and my heart is choking me it's beating so hard.

Sloane's hip slams into me when I take the turn onto the road. Her upper half is buried in the back, searching through the bags. Another hard turn would conveniently put her hip against me again but there's no turn to make. Plus that would be weird. She's back in the seat then, strapping into the harness with a first aid kit on her lap.

"Where'd you get that?" Not that it even matters. She needs to doctor up that leg and then see to me. My multiple bleeding wounds are trashing the R5's interior.

An hour later we stop because I've bled through my bandages. She wants me out of the car so she can do a better job patching me up. And I'd like to take a look at her leg since there's no way it's fine like she says it is. It was too serious of a bleed back there.

I pull off the road into the empty lot of an old church. Unfolding out of the car is no easy effort, which leads me to believe I'm more wounded than I thought. At the back bumper of the R5, Sloane waits, clothes thoroughly mottled with brown-red dried blood, face and arms smeared, leg covered in it. It's like her warrior paint, only instead of mud, it's blood. The clean white bandage on her thigh blinds me in the hot sun. She holds up three fingers and taps them on her lips. I don't know why she keeps signing to me when she's well aware I don't understand it.

She knocks on the R5's hatch. I open it for her. She hauls the remaining water jug to the edge so we can tilt it into our hands and wash our hands and faces. Leaning causes my heartbeat to gain a terrifying intensity that travels into my head, pounding like death, distorting my vision. I put a hand against the car—Sloane's taken a handful of my shirt to steady me. Too much blood loss. Need to sit down before I pass out.

The impact of my ass against the ground sends a painful throb to several distinct points on my body. Must be the gunshot wounds. I'm trying to remain sitting up so Sloane can remove the bandages she applied in the car, but what I really want to do is lie down and never get up again. She tugs the hem of my T-shirt up; I shift so she can remove it.

Moaning like a baby is completely appropriate right now because there's no way to orient my arms out of the sleeves without dying a few times. If I keep my lips tight, she won't even know I'm making a sound.

I slump against the back wheel, half aware she's cleaning and bandaging me up. She must be doing a thorough job for how long it takes. My shorts and legs are as bloody as she is. Seconds or hours later everything from my waist up is clean thanks to her. It would've been a lot more interesting if I could've kept my eyelids open to watch.

My feet are grilling in the sun. Luckily the shade from the car covers the rest of me. I struggle against my eyes wanting to roll up into my head. But then her clothes drop into a pile in my peripheral vision, water splatters the ground as she washes, and I'm fighting a new fight— the urge to stand up and look.

You're a dirtbag, Rex, but not that kind of dirtbag, so stay the hell down.

The pain reliever she gave me is finally kicking in, just enough to take the edge off. So when she comes back around dressed in clean clothes and starts to wipe my face with a wet cloth, I almost find the strength to get up. But it's too nice, her gentle swipes, the coolness on my summer-seared face, her eyes squinted and intent on the task of scrubbing off blood I missed the first time. No one's ever taken care of me like this. The tenderness of it pokes in deep. It just …

Hurts.

Cuts on my face are bandaged, swelling is examined but left alone since we have no ice. I get up, my brain swirling. Bad, but not too bad. I gulp from the tilted jug, smear water over my head and hair. Sloane hands me a clean shirt and leaves me to struggle into it. Then I'm slamming the hatch and going to the driver's side where she has buckled herself in.

"No way."

She grips the wheel and looks up at me. For once her face is absolutely, infuriatingly neutral. There's no way she's driving my car, not unless I've made the decision first. I don't care how near death I am. It's my call, not hers.

"Get out."

From the way her eyes tighten, I know I'm going to lose this, so I get in the passenger side before the stakes are upped and my loss becomes more brutal. Let her try to engage first gear in this temperamental car. I'll be back in the driver's seat as soon as she gives up trying. I bang on the dash to put more pressure on.

It's as bad as I thought it would be, but she doesn't give up. Her changes in the timing of clutch and gas with each try tell me she's learned how to drive a stick, and with each try she gets closer. The R5 pays, though it's a bit hypocritical of me to care. It's not the first pricey toy of mine I've trashed.

I adjust the seat back and close my eyes so I don't have to visually witness it. Minutes later we lurch forward, and I sit up to see trees rolling by and her shifting into second. Well, good. I can nap. Awareness trickles away with the natural fade into sleep, giving me hope of nice dreams instead of nightmares. This is what I miss when I take those pills. A real sleep cycle. A gentle surrender to sleep. It's a treat I don't deserve.

As soon as I recognize the unique drone of the R5 exhaust, I realize I've crossed from sleep to consciousness. It's a shedding of layers, or a gaining of them. Faraway noise becomes central and distinct. The hard plastic door against my cheek was a simple annoyance but now it just won't fly. So I sit up and rub eyes, blur gaining focus, the strap of the seat harness no longer cutting into my neck.

Then the soreness of my arm and shoulder hits and wow, that's something.

"What'd I miss?"

Of course she doesn't hear. She had to notice me sit up but from the way she's staring ahead at the road, I might think I hadn't moved at all. She's lit by the orange glow of the sun setting through the window beside her. There's a shiny line on her cheek. This girl is even silent when she cries.

I reach into my bag in the back and come out with a sock. It's clean, but it's still a sock. She's already spotted me with it though, so I hand it over. Total stud move. Instead of handing a girl a tissue to dry her tears, hand her a sock. What a reject.

She uses it like she doesn't care it's a stupid sock. The tears keep on coming despite being wiped, hitting harder like they're out to prove. Tension curls her shoulders, her body wanting to bend and really give in, but she's fighting it with deep breaths that have me looking away for how uncontrolled they are.

I tell my phone, "Pull over and I'll drive." Show her the screen.

She puts all her fingers squished together against her mouth. That has to be the sign for eating, and my stomach must know sign language because it's growled before I figure that out.

This time we order food and stay inside to eat. Or, she orders food, and I pretend to be as deaf as her. To speak and show my ignorance of the world outside my house would make me the freak, and I'd rather her keep that title. One problem: watching her interact with people proves how unfit she is for that title and how fit I am for it. Self-loathing is getting worse and getting old the more I hang with her, but the shame? Screw shame. It's never plagued me before, and I'm not letting it in. So what if the deaf girl's adapted to the world like a pro. Has no bearing on me. Only more and more it feels like it does.

I get the tray and Sloane leads me to a table around a half wall so the cashier can't keep staring. Sloane must be used to it, has learned how to head it off. She has a strange tremble going on with her hands, probably due to this place being cooled to deep freeze levels. Her eyes are still red from crying. I'm glad I'm the one whose face has been beat to hell. If it was hers, this would look bad. Might even trigger a 911 call.

I go for a burrito. She goes for my phone. *Don't ever look at me like that again.*

"What—when?"

At the counter.

Whatever she caught, I'd rather her not be clued into any of it—my fanboying, my inadequacy, my shame. "Shut up and eat. I didn't look at you any way."

You did. I don't accept pity.

It takes effort to swallow—not because I inhaled half of my Spicy Beef and Cheese, but because pity is so far off I wonder if it was some other dude she was looking at. "It's not pity."

Stupid response. She's going to ask what it was instead, and I have nothing ready.

"I mean, it's not anything. Shut up. Eat. There's so much salt in this we're about to get high. You're harshing it."

Don't tell me to shut up either.

"Really?"

The cold look in her eye says, *Really.*

The cold look I return says I can say whatever the fuck I want. "Shut up."

She chucks her 7-Layer at me so hard it sprays me in the face. Sour cream, for the taste I get off my lips. And when I see how she's watching me lick my lips, I stand up fast because shit, that brings back memories, and shit, there's something tragically wrong with me. I know this because the move I have prepped as response to someone who does that to me—the jarring upheaval of pain I get when imagining it done to her has flushed the thought far away. So I take my food and drink and move to another table.

Lucky for us the restaurant's empty. The scene we caused ordering food at the counter was nothing compared to this.

I finish before her and go outside. The sun is gone, its orange light draining before my eyes. Cars hiss by on the road, anonymous economical heaps lit up and moving like autonomous beings. The level of noise and activity is both exciting and disturbing. A semi-truck passes, rumbling in the pavement. This tiny pointless town swarms with people who make minimum wage, have probably never left a fifty-mile radius, and have seen more of the world than I have.

Sloane joins me minutes later, pointing a few buildings down to the Budget Motel. I drive us there and park, trying to remember what I've seen people do on TV when it comes to motels. So much of TV is fake though, so I get out my phone and search around on the internet. A much more trustworthy source of information, right? Sloane unbraids and rebraids that long piece of hair, and I keep my screen safely tilted away from her. If she knows what I'm doing, she decides to leave it alone. Maybe she knows nothing about motels either.

Feeling more confident after a five-minute internet search, I head into the office. She trails behind, keeping enough distance so she can shove me toward the wolves and run. Which won't be necessary because I've got something most people don't have: loads of money.

Stepping inside is like walking into a box. The ceiling is so low I feel like I'm about to scrape my head. The clerk takes no time to look us over. "Too young."

"I'll double the rate."

"Still too young."

"Triple it."

He pinches at his chin, considering. "Just the two of you?"

"Yes."

"Pardon for saying, but you look like trouble, son. You gonna be any trouble?"

Should I make up some lie about the condition of my face and knuckles? Nah. Nothing would make it look better. "No trouble. You have my word on that, sir." Southern manners always get them.

CHAPTER 15

SLOANE

Alone in the motel room's bathroom, I completely lose it. He's on the other side of a paper-thin door but let him judge. He doesn't know what's in my head. I can handle one crisis. Even two. But now I have so many I can't see where one ends and the next begins. There's no Winnie here to help me process them. There's no Marcas to distract me. No Mom or Dad to put an arm around my shoulders. No wooded mountainside to lose myself in. No dogs or coyotes to sit and share the breeze.

I blow my nose, knowing it's probably loud, not giving a care. He killed so many people back there. Did they have families? Kids who expect them to come home? Dogs now unattended, cats locked in a house to starve and die? I know they attacked us, but Rex considers nothing else. He shoots off their faces and cuts their throats and waits for more. He doesn't question, he doesn't grieve.

Oh, and news flash: I have black magic blood. And my mom! Does she know? Did she and my dad keep it from me? I'm not just practicing non-native magic co-opted by my family like my dad taught me to do. That messed-up trick I did in the Moore mansion—I'm playing with magic native to me. I'm feeding it and growing it, and I have no idea what to do with its power. That woman, whoever she was, woke a kinship in me, stirring up that new magic so it reached and danced and begged for release. Her presence brought a new order to it, a validation I didn't realize was missing. And oh my gosh, when she put words inside my head? If I could master that power, I could talk to anyone.

Don't forget I'm on the run with Rex Moore. And enjoying it way too much. That alone is a problem so extreme it has no legit outcome.

I let my hair down and finger-comb it out. My reflection in the chipped mirror shows a girl who just cried her eyes out. I use cold water on toilet paper to ease the puffiness but it does no good so I forget it. I let myself out.

Rex is flat out on one of the beds. He's grown butterfly wings. It's nice to imagine even though it's just the print on the bedspread underneath him. He's covering most of the butterfly's body with his own so the wings seem to belong to him. He lifts up, tosses me his phone. *Why are you crying?*

I toss it back and sit on the floor to stretch out my legs. There isn't much floor space, so I angle one leg between the two beds and the other in the walkway between the end of the bed and the TV table. Up close to the bedspread I see it's covered in smaller butterflies too. Pastel green, blue, and lavender wings floating among a backdrop of ivy and wildflowers. Above each bed is a matching framed butterfly print. It all has the look of another decade, and I'm not sure why, but it's oddly comforting.

Rex's phone lands in my lap. *I can't really help being an asshole. It runs in the family.*

I look up at him. That's such a cop-out and he knows it. Anyone can change. Everyone has problems. Some have problems worse than his. But he's directed his attention to the ceiling like it's too hard to look at me and admit that at the same time. He's provided me the perfect segue, though, so I get up and sit on the bed next to him. He startles at the accidental contact against his leg and bolts upright. Gosh, he's such a touch-me-not. I start typing.

I know how to turn your family good, but you have to help me and you can't back out, and it's going to take some time. But when it's done, our families won't be at war anymore and you and I can both go home.

When I'm finished I hand him the phone so he knows I'm not discussing it. This is what we're doing. I consider moving to the other bed but no, I have to be close enough to see his face if he does respond. He guards his expression too well. I've learned some of his tics which are better viewed and harder for him to hide the closer I am.

He's staring at the screen instead of speaking, so long he must be reading it again after the voice finished. And I'm beginning to lose the nerve. My palms tingle, about to turn sweaty. A spotlight has been turned on somewhere, and I'm melting in the light. Please don't let him look at me until

I've gained control of this. I rub my palms and think about the cathedral of pines encircling my house, how resolute their spirit, how eternal. The comfort of their scent in the winter cold. I picture myself there beside the sparkle of the river, coyotes brushing my side. Fresh mountain air finds me in this little motel, and I draw it in, cooling the melt of nerves. Just in time for Rex to speak and return his phone to me, so calmly I have to read it. *I can never go home.*

I type, *You can if we do this.*

He shifts away from me, passing a hand over his hair, back to front, front to back. When he starts in the back like that, it means he's unsettled. His hand pauses at the nape of his neck, gripping hard. I see his lips moving, so I glance at the screen.

Why were you crying?

I wait for him to say more, but he only drops his hand to his lap and side-eyes me. So he's bargaining. His response to my proposal exchanged for my answer to his question. Fair enough.

Because you killed sixteen people back there.

He makes a face. *Not sixteen.*

Yes, sixteen. Plus those other guys on the road before. If you're not counting, it must not bother you. Of course it doesn't bother him. Why even say it?

Whatever. Don't forget they came for us.

We can do so many other things. We don't have to kill people.

He leans closer to me. *No, you can do so many other things. Not me.*

He's enclosed his thumbs inside fists, squeezing tight enough they've probably both popped the knuckle. The bruising around his eye has started changing color so it looks worse, not better. It's strange to see actual healing taking place. My wounds don't go through these stages. Or maybe they do, but it's too fast to notice them.

I've changed my mind. I do deserve an answer from him. *So are you going to help me?*

Eye contact becomes a deadlock. He doesn't want to answer even though he owes it to me, and getting me involved in a staring contest is a way to buy himself some time. I break first and go back to the phone, pretending to collect my thoughts for my next message to him. He gets off the bed and paces at the foot. I don't realize he's speaking until I see it pop up on the screen.

I'll help you if you teach me all your magic. He leans against the dresser, crosses his arms, and waits. I can tell his wounded arm still hurts by the way he's bracing it against his body.

If my plan works out, Bevan magic won't be a hazard in Moore hands. Teaching him will do no harm. But that's a big risk to take if my plan doesn't succeed. Is there really any other way though? Now that this is on the table, he's not going to back down, and he'll never help me unless I agree.

Screw it. What's life without risk? I sign, *OK.*

He says, *Yeah?*

A little at a time.

He sits on the other bed, facing me. Mulling it over while staring straight at my face. He must be trying to read my tics as I'm trying to read his.

So how are we going to turn my family good?

You're going to take me to every Moore household, and I'm going to do to each of them what I did to you.

The slightest widening of his eyes, a quick look away, two skinned knuckles against his lips. He'd forgotten what I did to him, that couldn't be more blatant. And now the brows have lowered, and I get a dark look along with a dose of my own guilt. He was full of hate, but he never asked me to remove it. Neither will any of his family. But if they weren't preying upon my family, I wouldn't have a reason to drain them of it without their permission.

Rex abruptly stands, jerks the door open, and leaves. I wait for the door to close before peeking past the curtain on the window. He's on the sidewalk in a squat, rubbing his head, back to front, front to back. Over and over with such aggression I'm afraid he might wear a hole in his scalp. Half a second later he's back in the room, the door is closing fast behind him, and he's stepped up so he's in my face. I catch nothing on his lips because I'm too consumed by readying a defense.

Since he's not backing off, I give him a blunt shove. Jerk-face needs to get a grip. Then he's raised his phone into my face. Like I'm interested in anything he has to say while he's acting like this. So I stare him down until he raises both hands, clearly finding himself in the wrong. Well that's promising.

I take his phone then and read the screen. He doesn't deserve it, but I'm too curious not to.

I don't care what you do to any of them, but you're going to undo whatever black magic bullshit you did to me.

So he can jump back on the Kill Sloane Bevan train? Right.

I type, *Nope*, into the phone, flop onto the bed, grab the remote, and power on the TV. He leaves through the door, slamming it so hard I feel it in the headboard. Anger issues much? What a baby.

Even after turning on the closed captions, I can't focus on the TV. I wish I could video call my family. I wish I could be home, instead of stuck in a box of a motel room, locked away from the song of the elements. When I catch myself nodding off, I get up and take a shower. After so many days without hot water, it's glorious, like bathing in sunlight. Even though there's an unidentified stain running down the middle of the floor and the water pressure is so weak it takes ten full minutes just to get the shampoo out of my hair. But the shampoo smells like citrus, and to just be clean again brightens my mood.

Rex is still missing when I get out. I use the hair dryer on the wall to dry my hair then dig through Rex's bag in search of toothpaste. Lucky for me he packed some. I brush my teeth with my finger and leave the toothpaste on the sink so he knows why I went through his bag. It would be fun to make him wonder, but I'm not the game-playing type.

I wake at three in the morning and swivel the alarm clock so the light from the numbers casts onto his bed. It's empty and still made. Now I'm worried, but I can't decide if it's my place to be. I slip out of bed and outside, connecting with the night creatures like they were waiting for me. Gravel in the parking lot stabs my heel. Forgetting my shoes—not bright. Forgetting a weapon? I pause and consider going back for one. But then the night animals fill in the scene for me. All is calm. Now to find Rex.

He's in his car, forehead against the steering wheel, jaw loose with sleep. I open the door so I can poke him awake. It works, with the added fun of getting a .45 pointed in my face. I press its aim away and tilt my head toward our room. He makes a quick grab for my shirt, jerking me against him, gun aimed past me into the parking lot. I tap into the animals, confirm once again there's no threat out here.

Breaking away from him, I grab his hand and tug, hoping he'll just be normal and come inside with me. That's when I notice that panicky, hunted look in his eye. The pulse throbbing in his neck. The rapid in-and-out of his chest. Another panic attack, and this time we're not on my dad's secluded property in the woods. There aren't any other people nearby but that could change fast. He asks me something but it's too hard to read in the dark. The desperation in it drives in deep. Whatever he's fighting seems to be winning. I so wish he knew ASL.

I manage to get him back to the room but once the door locks he's rearranging furniture to barricade us in. He seems to have forgotten about that wounded arm. A grab for his shirt leaves me with air. In full-on crazy mode he's impossible to track because right now he's not trying to fight me, he's trying to get away from something else. When I flip on a lamp, he hauls me into the bathroom with him. Struggling against him seems like it would make all this worse. His terror leaks into me. Yeah, whatever he's battling isn't real but it still feels better to be on his side. Wedged between the tub and the toilet, he checks the magazine in the .45, holds up three fingers. Checks the chamber, holds up one more. He can't shoot up this room. There could be people next door, people within range all over. And the shots will draw attention even if they don't accidentally kill someone. I need to figure out how to get him out of this and get the gun away from him.

If he went through that fingerspelling app on his phone, he should know some letters. I fingerspell his name. He shifts his gaze to me then away, back to the doorway. I do it again. He cuts a hand through the air—the universal sign for *quit it*. It's a detached motion though, not coming from this Rex but from the one I know. This Rex props his arms on the toilet lid, aiming through the doorway.

He flinches when I draw a line on his forearm. Luckily his finger wasn't on the trigger. I'm halfway through the R when he grabs my wrist, halting what he knows I'm about to do. It's only then that I realize how close we are, how my knees are jammed against his thigh, how he's turned, putting his arm dangerously close to my chest. He's not looking at me but into me, this Panic Rex, the one I haven't allied with, the one I don't know. His pupils are too big for his eyes and they have a suction—no. I close my eyes and shake it off. His magic is spilling out, shrouding me, drawing out my own. But not just my known magic. The new kind too. The kind I don't know how to control.

His gun hand gives a little, the gun dipping down. I disarm him before I know I'm going to do it. One second it's in his hand, the next it's in mine. He makes an unsuccessful grab, earning a knee in the chest and a leg around his neck, contorting him into a wrestling hold I forgot I knew. I pop out the magazine and toss it though the doorway, empty the chamber and toss that bullet too. He braces his feet and bursts against me, my hands going to the wall to protect my head from the tile.

We end up as a two-person pretzel, way too personal for my comfort especially with the way I'm straddling his upper body. I twist away and lower my legs; he unravels himself and sits up. Takes in me and the room, looking unsure how he got here, probably wondering what he did. With his now empty hand, he rakes his head, back to front. There's the Rex I know. He does it again and I stop his hand because that's just too rough. Why would that ever feel good? The bristles of his buzzed hair brush my wrist. I run my hand against it, fingers gently digging, just to experience it again. I don't know why. It's like the automatic gun grab, it happens before I think it, my reflexes faster than my brain.

His shoulders square and go stiff as his lips part—a quick breath in. Surprise, but not a bad one because now he's waiting like there's more if he just holds still. So I rub his head again, slower this time, against the grain of his hair, starting at the back of his neck where I know it feels so good. He puts a hand against the wall like he needs a brace to prevent himself from collapse. Closes his eyes.

If I do it again he looks like he might faint. I shouldn't do it again. I have to do it again. So I do. Fingers splayed, combing through the soft bristle of his hair.

And this time he opens his eyes and turns to me like he's just come up for air. On his lips I easily read, *What magic is that?*

I hold up my fingers and wiggle them, mouthing, *Not magic. Just fingers.*

He rises fast on his knees, his hands going to my shoulders, gripping hard and giving me a little shake. He's talking, eyes big, words running together too fast to read. But then I see it's just one repeated phrase over and over: *Say it again, Sloane, say it again.*

I'm flattened by a rush of terror. My brain does a complete reverse, and I've gone back a moment, seeing it replayed. I've covered my lips because those last words I didn't just mouth, I spoke them. I swore I'd never let him hear my voice. No, just no.

Now he's gone for my jaw, both hands, his eyes trained on my lips like he's in such disbelief it happened he needs to see it a second time for proof.

Come on, he says. But my lips aren't moving, so he looks into my eyes.

It all changes then. He's forgotten he wants me to speak and so have I. We're back in the cottage against that wall in the middle of the night.

Don't.

Stop.

Don't stop.

Next time will be worse.

One of his thumbs drifts to the corner of my mouth. The contact against my skin in that tiny movement incites every nerve. It's heart-pounding ecstasy, yes, but I'm not kissing Rex Moore again. I'm so not. He said next time would be worse, and by worse he means better. I cover his mouth with both my hands. Since I can't stop myself I have to stop him.

CHAPTER 16

REX

THE WARMTH OF her hands on my mouth registers in my brain as the opposite of what she intended. Not a block but a sample. A skin-on-skin connection. A come-on. I jerk away, knocking my skull against the toilet tank. More bumps aren't what this brain needs after that fight at Trey Bevan's cottage. It'd be pretty dorky to fight sixteen guys only to get a concussion from a toilet hours later.

I don't even know how I got in this bathroom, or why she's in here with me. I search for my phone to ask, but she's now standing in the doorway looking very annoyed. All she has on is a long T-shirt. Her hair is extreme. Past her a lamp glows in between two beds—one rumpled, one untouched. It all comes back then: my demand she return me to normal, her smartass dismissal, my exit of the room. My fatigue in the R5, the pill, the nightmare. Waking up under attack.

Which means she saw me have another freak-out. I could puke with the stupidity of it all.

And now that it's been fully remembered the panic lingers, close enough to start it all again if I don't find control. "What time is it?"

She signs something that looks like "What?" from the expression she makes. My phone could help me if I could find it. Where's my dumb phone? She's looking annoyed again, so I get up and push past her out of the bathroom, catching sight of the digital clock between the beds.

Everything wound in me loosens. Held lungs release. Air is so damn good sometimes. It isn't the hour and minutes that relieve me, which is the stupid part. It's just that time exists at all. That clock could be hours off and it wouldn't matter to me. All that matters is it's there, keeping its own time.

Sloane gets in her bed and switches off the lamp. I strip to my boxers and pull back the covers on my bed, considering a pill, deciding against it. It'd be nice to get actual sleep but one freak-out is enough tonight, and I don't want to take the risk of another. When my head hits the pillow, I remember one more thing: her fingers in my hair and the full-body tingle they caused. Just fingers? My ass. She lies worse than me. That was magic, and it's the first thing I'm going to make her teach me. Just fingers can't create feelings like the one that traveled across skin not even being touched. Just fingers can't make me think she cares. No one cares. It's a damn good trick though because a tiny part of me is still fooled like hell.

I rub my head against the pillow again, hoping to rouse the memory of her fingers against my hair. I fall asleep replaying her voice in my head, plotting ways to get her to speak again.

The banging in my head turns real when I come out of a doze and realize it's someone pounding the door. Where's my .45? There—on the floor. Magazine? I dive for it, pop it in. Sloane sits up a second later, her eyes on me hunkered beside the bed like I'm the one who woke her. I check the clock: noon.

More pounding. "Open up, Rex, or I'm coming in."

Holy oak that's my brother. What to do? Hide? Shoot him? Sloane catches my interest in the door and hops from the bed to scoot along the wall and peer out the peep-hole. Then I'm blinded by the burst of light she's let in, and Aaron's closing the door behind him, cutting it off.

"What—" I don't exactly know what to ask.

"You say you'll meet and don't show, so I come find you. That's what." Aaron brushes Sloane's bangs aside and nudges her chin so he can better see her face. I stop myself from getting up to break his hand. She signs something; he signs something back.

"Dude, since when do you know—"

Aaron points at me. "Shut up." He takes Sloane's hands and looks her arms over before stepping back for a full view. But he doesn't have time to record her good health because she rushes him, clinging on, her face buried against him, and I'm on my feet fast. To save him from her or her from him? Rex, you are so damn confused.

"You're lucky she's okay," he says to me over her head. "I was going to save the Bevans some trouble and kill you myself."

"Uh, okay, traitor."

"Me? I was never loyal to them. But you are, so who's the traitor?"

The nerve he just hit has a direct line into my trigger finger. To my surprise I feel the weight of my .45 in my hand, and I have no idea how it got there—I thought I'd put it down. Sloane turns her face a little so she can tighten her grip on Aaron, a line of tears shiny on her cheek. He's staring me down, just daring me to aim at him. I go into the bathroom and shut the door.

I take a piss, splash my face, gulp some water. Look in the mirror. Rip the bandage off my forehead and wish I hadn't because it's as gory as a shark bite. Rip the one off my cheek—same thing, so I stop there and leave the rest. Shower? Okay.

Then I get out and realize I should shave so I don't look so much like a homeless guy. I end up screwing up that wound on my cheek even worse. That's ten bonus points, Rex, for being a genius. A clean-shaven genius, though, so an improvement.

When I get out I hear two voices: Aaron's, and the phone voice speaking for Sloane. My bag is out there, so I go out with a towel around my waist and unzip my bag. There's no break in the conversation. It's interesting how they're instant best friends. Also interesting how Aaron found us. Nope, not a coincidence at all.

"She tell you we were here?" I interrupt. "That's great."

He cuts his attention to me. "No, she didn't. I saw the charge on the credit card I gave you. Don't be dim." He stands up, gently knocking Sloane on the chin with his knuckles. "Get dressed and meet me outside. We need to chat."

I do it because I don't know what else to do.

"What'd you do to your hair?" he asks when I'm outside with him, pulling the door closed behind me. The sun reflects off the pavement straight into my face. Another day so hot I instantly need another shower.

"I cut it."

"You look like a punkass."

"I am a punkass."

"Good point." He looks at me so long without speaking I'm afraid he's going to hug me. Or punch me. I step back to lean against the wall and save him the trouble. The hot brick threatens to burn a hole through my shirt. I can't believe I'm staying in this dump.

"There's something different about you, Rex."

"Yeah, I cut my hair, remember?"

"No, it's—" He slides on his sunglasses. "It's not that. What're you doing with Sloane Bevan? Be real."

I shrug. I'm not sure what she's told him, and telling the truth has never done me any favors. "Can we find some a/c? My face is melting."

"I need to know what's going on."

Yeah, so do I. "My father's sending teams to kill me, and I'm trying not to die. Or get crabs from skeezy motel rooms."

"You and Sloane Bevan, on the run. Together."

I shrug again. "Pretty much."

"Getting along."

"I wouldn't say that."

He chuckles. "Okay, then, not killing each other."

"That's more like. Well, we were, but not anymore. We probably should get back to it."

"No," he says, turning away to face the sun. "I don't think you should. I think this is …" He turns back, grips my shoulder hard. "This is good. Unexpected, but good."

"She's a fucking black witch, dude. She did this … thing. And the other day another black witch just shows up outta nowhere telling Sloane they share blood and giving her advice and crap." Regret surges over me. I probably shouldn't mention that black witch.

"Who did that to your face?" It's like he didn't even hear what I just said.

"My father's guys. Before I killed them." I feel kind of sick saying it, not because Sloane has made me feel guilty, but more because the punishment my family's going to dream up is casting its shadow on me already. That's how big and shitty it's going to be. My stomach churns and it's gotten hard to swallow.

"We don't need to have the safe sex talk again, do we?"

I choke, turn it into a cough. "Please no."

Aaron takes out his phone and starts texting. "I need to get you to my dad. We need to hide you somewhere until we figure out what to do."

"I'm not going. Sloane and I have a plan."

He looks up, studies me a long time before he says, "You're a minor driving around with no driver's license. You get popped and they'll haul you right home."

"I have Sloane Bevan and her bag of tricks."

"Okay, but Sloane has morals. I don't see her tricking or lying to cops. What makes you think she won't tell them she's been kidnapped? Because that's exactly what this is."

"Stop harshing it."

"Harshing what? Reality?"

"Let her tell them that. You know what our family can do."

"I do, but it takes time to work that kind of thing. In the meantime you'll be taken home, and while your dad is working over the police, your uncle is going to be working over you."

I hate how those words find a way inside me, drilling straight into the fear I keep bound with duct tape and shoved into in a dark corner. I hate how he sees it on me, how he's tightened his lips, how he's gone both sad and angry in the eyes. He reaches to grip my shoulder, and I want to shake it off but I can't because he's the only one who ever grips my shoulder like that and I never fucking see him.

"Here's what I think, Rex. This is all salvageable but not without my dad's help. He's still willing to meet. You and Sloane pack up and get in my car and I'll take you to Roanoake now."

Damn my stupid watering eyes. I scrub them dry with my palm. "I told you, Sloane and I have a plan." I don't expect him to care, though, so I don't know why I say it. No one ever listens to me. I'm just a thing to be ordered around. Well, not anymore.

He takes a few steps away and turns his back to me, his phone forgotten in his hand. When he finally pockets it I know something has changed, some decision has been reached. Well it's not his decision to make. I don't want to fight him but I will.

"What's the plan?"

Without seeing his face I'm sure I heard him wrong. There's no way he's entertaining this, and I hope he's not because I can't exactly admit I never agreed to her plan. She's nuts to ever think it's possible or worth it, and there's no way I'll allow her to break any of them before she fixes me. Once I'm back to normal, I'll kill her and all this will be over.

I make a grab for a finger that's poked into my shoulder and find it attached to Aaron.

"You were zoning out," he says, shaking out his hand and the finger I nearly broke. "What's the plan?"

"Ask her."

"I'd rather hear it from you."

If I explain the plan does that mean I'm committed? Maybe that's what he's doing here. Maybe he and Sloane are working together against me. Well, let them. I call my own shots now. I can go along with the plan today. Doesn't mean I have to go along with it tomorrow. "We're going to visit every Moore household and Sloane is going to carve the evil out of their brains with her tricky magic."

"They'll kill you."

"Not with Sloane Bevan on my side."

The scrutiny comes again, hotter than the sun that has sweat trickling down my back and forehead. He's reading way too much into this Rex and Sloane thing. So I don't appear to be bothered by that look he's giving me, I check my phone. Two new email messages from my online friends and one from my game subscription service saying my pre-order was just delivered. Oh, wait, is that date right? Because if so, Blood Tower 4 came out today and I'm supposed to be logging into multiplayer like right now.

"Did you hear me?"

"Yeah. Hey, any chance you have your laptop on you?"

He grabs me by the neck and steers me back inside the motel room. Sloane is sitting cross-legged in the middle of her bed reading something in her lap. Looks like she got dressed in one of her cute—no, not cute—homemade dresses. She's put her hair in a ponytail, the long braid hanging past all the chaos of bundled hair. I get an elbow in the arm from Aaron, start to ask him what the hell it was for, decide not to when I see what's written on his face: *stop staring before she catches you, assclown.*

"You could just say it, you know. She's deaf."

The look he gives me then has me bracing for a follow-up elbow jab, or some kind of painful death. Instead he says, "I can't decide if this is all great or a horrible disaster."

"I'm hoping horrible disaster. We Moores get off on that shit."

"And why the R5? All those cars to choose from. That's the loudest, flashiest one in the garage. You'll be noticed everywhere you go."

"'Cause it's mine." I shrug, hoping to appear nonchalant. I'm the loser who only knows how to drive a ridiculous rally car.

He takes his car key out of his pocket. "Here, take the Tesla."

"And die of boredom? No thanks, old man."

He pockets his key, looking me over. "Really, what's changed about you? I feel like I can finally get through to you."

Maybe for once he's trying? For once he's not too busy to have a conversation? And something else that's actually not his fault: we're finally out of that house, no longer watched by guards and my uncle and all my stupid cousins. We can speak freely. I'm struck by how those two things go together. What if ignoring me wasn't his fault at all? What if he doesn't hate me?

"Give me your phone so I can put my dad's number in it."

I hand it over.

Sloane does the squished fingers pointing at her mouth sign. It's too much to think about right now while I'm picking through memories to see if they fit my grand revelation. Aaron. Not too busy for me. Not uninterested. Just restricted by our hovering family members. Clamped down.

Aaron says, "Lunch?"

She nods.

Right, that's what that sign means. He must know it too. "How come you never told me you know sign language?"

"You never asked. And I don't, really. Just a little to get by."

He makes me replace the two bandages I removed from my face so we can eat out in public without people fainting. On my way out the door, I hand Sloane my phone for her to keep up with what we're saying. Her thanks is a smile that I look away from fast when that spot on my arm where Aaron jabbed me comes alive with warning. Don't stare, Rex, it's embarrassing.

We walk down the road to a diner because I'm not getting in Aaron's car. It's not that I don't trust him. I just don't want to be forcibly taken to Roanoke, and being strapped into his car is a big step in that direction. After we order, Aaron slides an envelope across the table toward Sloane, telling her, "This way you're not reliant on this twerp for money." She reads the words on my phone then checks inside, finds it's a big stack of money, and tries to give it back.

"You can pay me back when you're finished destroying my whole family," he says to her.

Somehow she picks up on that subtle humor that no one else in my family recognizes in Aaron but me. She can't even hear the tone of his voice and she gets it. How well do they know each other?

While we eat, Aaron explains how to order and pay for food at different types of restaurants, when to tip, how to fuel up a car, and how to drive on public roads while Sloane surfs the internet on my phone. I'm trying to pay attention to Aaron because I need the info but my dipshit brain has a big issue with Sloane sitting in the booth next to Aaron instead of me. Why that matters, I have no idea.

She abruptly straightens her back, eyeing the screen like something has surprised her. She hands my phone across the table to me and starts signing as soon as her hands are free.

"She's sorry," Aaron says. "Accident—something she did with the phone?"

On the screen is an open email message. I check the timestamp—just sent. She probably opened it accidentally when it popped up.

To: DruidKing

Subject: Blood Tower User Forum - Group Chat Transcript

Chat session begin.
lady_mantis: you losers ready for this?
Skulldaddy999: haven't heard from druidking
Skulldaddy999: he's showing offline for days
Demonbutter: dude what? is he dead?
princemagicpants: emailing him now, will email yall when he responds

Chat session has ended.

Another new email message pops in.

Yo Druidking did you get the new IP I sent? Server is set up with BT4. Where are you dude? Our stats suck without you, get the hell back.

I hit reply and type, *Sorry, been dealing with some shit. No access to my gaming machine right now and prob gonna be a while. Tell lady and the guys I suck. Kill some demons for me.*

My finger hovers over the Send because all this will do is make them wonder what's up. Is it better to make them think I'm dead? No, because even though I've never met them in real life they're the only friends I have, and I'll need them when all this is over. So I hit Send and hand the phone back to Sloane, ducking my head because now she has another piece of me, and I don't want to see what she thinks of it.

Regret crashes hard—why didn't I lie and tell them my gaming machine fried? That would've been a perfect out, and would've bought me time needed to build a new one. They don't know how rich I am.

"Everything okay?" Aaron asks.

Not at all. I'm missing some epic stuff right now, and I seriously complicated things when a simple fib would've fixed it. "All good."

His gaze lingers longer than needed. He can see through all my lies. I've always known that yet I keep doing it. My milkshake has turned to paste, and I'd really like to put my fist through something right now.

"So why the hell do you know sign language again? Just a little to get by when you're hanging with Bevan trash? It just amazes me with how busy you are that you have time to learn it, that's all." Too late I catch myself, because Sloane has already opened up that speaking app and she's caught it all due to the big eyes she's giving me. Well, too bad.

"Rex." Aaron's warning voice. Like he's my fucking dad or something.

My whole life is in that house—my gaming machine, my books, my custom-designed stereo. I only know how to exist inside that fence. I can fake it outside but for how long? It's getting old. That motel bed is a torture device, and Sloane Bevan is a pain to be around. I want to sit in the kitchen at home and eat breakfast with Emily. I want to train in the puddle of light surrounded by the dark of the basement. I want to sit by the lake and close my eyes. It's all lost though, as dead as Emily. Even if I grow the balls to go back there it will never be the same.

Aaron slaps a hand on the table to snap me out of it. "*A dhearthái.*"

I need to tell him to stop calling me 'brother.' We're too different to be brothers. But I can't right now. I need to settle my head first. "*Cén t-am é?*"

He frowns like he normally does when I ask for the time. To him it's random and irrelevant, a nuisance question asked too often. I've never had the guts to explain how wildly out of control I feel unless I know. He's always acted like I'm using it to change the subject, just like he is now. "Where's your watch?"

"In the woods somewhere." And needing the time for no real reason pisses me off like it never has. Kind of like the mention of that stupid watch and all the things that go along with it. I snatch my phone away from Sloane and check the screen.

"Okay, Rex, you need to walk it off. I need to talk to her alone anyway, so why don't you head back to the room and we'll meet you there after we're done?"

"Sounds good to me, *a dhearthái.*" With that last word I lean into his face, wishing in the darkest way he'd take it like the affront it is and fight me.

Sloane catches my glass and hers before they topple, and I realize how hard I just shoved the table toward them. Between me and the door are dozens of gawking faces. Most of them look away when I raise my middle finger. The ones who don't I take note of, and they see me taking note, and they look away too.

Outside is a wreck of noise. Cars screech by on the road beside me. Trucks clatter and roar. I stand on the edge of the road and consider walking right out in the middle of it just to stop it all, to get some peace. I fish my earbuds out of my pocket instead and scroll past all the metal and drum and bass for that chillstep album I bought. My earbuds do no justice to the sub-bass hits, but I crank it to brain-melt level and walk toward the Budget Motel where my car and its two twelve-inch subs are parked.

CHAPTER 17

SLOANE

T HE LICENSE PLATE on Rex's car is throwing little beams of reflected sunlight all around. Aaron and I pause in the parking lot to the motel and watch it tremble against the car, its dance synced to the beat I feel in the ground. Rex must have some jams really cranked and maybe that's what he needs. Music and some alone time.

Aaron heads to the driver's window and shades his eyes from the sun to see inside the car. Then he's pulling the door open and leaning in. Past him I see Rex bent at the waist, draped over the passenger seat. Very limp and too still. Aaron checks the pulse in his neck then checks Rex's hand.

I see a *Shit* on his lips as he backs out of the car. He hands me his phone, and I check the screen. *I thought he was dead. It's just those stupid pills.*

What pills? I'd love to know what they are.

Those uppers and downers they give him. They like to control when he sleeps and when he wakes up. Looks like he's taking them whenever he wants to now. He puts a hand over his mouth in the way someone might when facing a decision they'd rather not make.

I type, *Can we confiscate? They're in his pocket and his bag.*

Aaron returns to the door of the car and starts prying Rex from the seat. *Probably not a good idea to cut him off cold turkey, as much as I'd love to.* He gets enough of Rex's upper body upright for me to tug him by the arm toward me, allowing Aaron to get a shoulder underneath him. A fireman's carry all the way back to the room ends with an ungraceful drop onto the bed. It's a humbling kind of shock to see such a fierce creature become so unthreatening.

Screwing with someone's circadian rhythm is a special kind of torture, Aaron says, standing over him. *But at least he's getting sleep right now. I think he needed it.*

Aaron sits on the edge of the bed and bends forward, fingers interlocking behind his head bowed low. I'm not sure what to do so I sit on my own bed. Aaron's interrogation at the diner left me enveloped in a veil of anxiety I can't seem to shed. It's crippling, limiting both thoughts and actions, fogging my head so I can't work myself free. Aaron is no stranger—I've known him my whole life. But as soon as Rex stalked away from the table, all those people around us turned from passive scenery to prying eyes and moving mouths trying to be discreet but ending up more obvious than if they'd just openly discussed us. I can't blame them. Rex caused a real scene. I can blame myself for caring so much. For building simple curiosity into a personal witch hunt. For not allowing Aaron's questions to be the perfect distraction that they were. For feeling unworthy of his concern instead of grateful. And for dwelling on the discomfort from those strangers in the unfamiliar place long after it's passed.

The world outside my mountain land beside the river only stopped being a fright for me a couple years ago. Like anything strong enough to need banishing it often resurfaces just to test. Rex makes it all easier, somehow. When I'm with him it's not the Deaf girl they're looking at. It's the glaring guy in camo and combat boots, the hostile not-a-soldier-but-possibly-a-wacko who speaks whole wordless paragraphs with how straight he holds his shoulders and how tightly he holds your eye. Or maybe it's none of that at all. Maybe he just settles me. Maybe I'm calmed by all that firepower. His presence speaks to me in silence, makes me feel right.

Because I've told Aaron I won't be swayed from my plan, that I promise to keep myself safe and take care of his little brother, and that the only way I'll agree to go home is after I've exhausted all efforts to cure the Moores, he gets up to leave. We take a selfie on his phone—Marcas demanded he send one, he says—and I see him out after a hug that feels way more final than it should.

Rex sleeps a few more hours just like Aaron said he would. His phone vibrates with incoming email, but I don't look after I see the first one's from the same screen name on that other message I saw accidentally. After three more come in back to back, there's a lull, so I take his phone to check my own email.

He wakes up fast, the upward motion of his body kicking in my reflexes so I'm up and braced for a fight before his eyes have fully opened. Somehow he's torn a bandage loose and reopened a wound. Fresh blood trickles from the cut on his forehead.

I get some gauze out of our kit and hand it to him, pointing at the source of the blood he's just noticed and smeared across the back of his hand. He's swung his legs over the side of the bed, so I sit facing him on mine then pick up his phone and tell him what Aaron wanted me to tell him.

Aaron trusts you'll do the right thing.

Holding the gauze against his head, he snorts. That's well-rehearsed indifference, but after that scene in the diner, I recognize more layers: the baggage and history and hurt, and a visible, active killing of hope. His skill at this is unmatched; he's had lots of practice in whittling down hope to keep any future disappointment in check. The bloat of it travels into me—a positive thought converted by him into something negative is now inside me.

I have to sit up straighter to allow room for my breath to expand, so I don't suffocate under the weight of it joining that dark mass I already hold. We've locked eyes. I see the carefully guarded surprise in his, but I can't look away. We won't be this easily overcome. Aaron's trust is something to keep and hold on to, not squash into dust. Even if we disappoint him. Even if he disappoints us. We'll cling to it until either of those things happens because that's what normal people do. The Moores abused Rex but it's not going to take place on my watch.

I sign, *I trust you too*, even though Aaron specifically told me not to, because "Rex is damaged and will never be right."

Rex's face makes no change. Being honest, it's set in an evil glare. It's such a front though. I don't buy it, not a bit. I remember how fast and powerful he is. How muscular and dangerous. And how he looked when Aaron dropped him on the bed—all strength sucked out, just a useless frame with the power cut off. A trained fighter tired of fighting alone.

I sign again, *I trust you*, emphasizing the *I* and the *you*. Then I fingerspell it. *Trust.*

If I could offer him more than trust, I would. I wish I knew a magic powerful enough to fix him for good, to undo all that damage and make him right again. A unified effort might pull it off, but I don't know any of our kind who would help. The only person is me.

Those words he's speaking aren't polite. I couldn't begin to read them because his jaw is too tight and he's talking too fast. So I pick up the phone and check the screen.

Screw your trust. I know what my brother told you. Don't act like you're the shit because you've had a perfect child-hood and I haven't. You're a tool to your family just like I am to mine. Only mine was up front about it. So get over it, and fuck off. Your family sent you here to die.

I type back, *I volunteered to come.*

Then you're stupid and a tool.

I can't dwell on how he's right about that, or how it burns me a little on the inside. *I guess we're two of a kind then.*

The stare-down level ratchets up so high I wonder how I'm ever able to talk to him without sweating through all my clothes. I'm now grateful to him for setting the air conditioner on arctic in here. This has become a game of who'll crack first, and yeah, he's the super bully, but I've had a lifetime of people staring at me. I've built a powerful shield against that heat. So turn it up, jerk. It feels good on my feet.

Even with my eyes locked on the blues of his, I notice the perfect dip in his upper lip. The severe, point-blank slant of eyebrows so fair yet so prominent. That old scar, an off-center chip in his chin now more visible on his clean-shaven face. I sense myself going off the rails, desperate for something to bring it back on track. So I sign again, partially to guide me back to sanity, partially to piss him off. *I trust you to the end.*

He snatches my hands, a strike so fast and unexpected if he'd meant to hurt me I'd be dead. I block the urge to free myself, but why? It's crazy not to. What's also crazy is I'm remembering that kiss, and the racing pulse in his wrist makes me think he is too. One small problem though: his anger is building even more. Because I didn't counter like he expected, he's now stuck holding my arms instead of getting the fight he hoped for. And worse, if he releases me, I've called his bluff. It'll prove he doesn't want to hurt me. That he can't, and that bothers him.

Well, he can hold onto me all day. I'm done fighting with him. We're a team, whether he admits it or not.

I see his breathing change as his grip on me loosens by the slightest, enough for me to get one hand free and pick up the gauze he dropped on the bed. His wound still needs pressure, so I stand to better reach him. He doesn't seem to be paying attention when I apply the gauze. He's swiveled my other hand, all his focus on my palm and his thumb that has slid into it like some forbidden move he's attempting undercover, hoping no one will notice.

Curious where it will lead, I play ignorant. I put all my effort into stopping that leak of blood from his forehead, and now that I'm standing above him he won't notice my line of sight. His thumb slides further into my palm, hot and calloused, its pressure sending a signal up my arm and into my head. The risk of it makes it sweeter, more forbidden, something to put an end to, something to beg to last forever. It makes me want to do something stupid—

Like remove the gauze and kiss his forehead where the blood has finally sealed. When he doesn't stop me, I do it again. His thumb remains hot in my palm, planted and permanent. His fingers encircle my wrist. I peel away one side of the bandage on his cheek and kiss that wound too, the heat of his breath on my own cheek, the corner of his lips perilously close to mine. I pull away, and he tugs my hand. His eyes say he wants more.

I shiver despite the heat coursing through me. He runs his hands up my arms, causing another shiver to scatter up to the crown of my head and down to my toes. Now he's holding onto both my elbows, drawing me in. It'd be a demand if it wasn't so desperate, and I give a little just to experience the strength in his arms, the force he could unleash if he wanted.

Because he wasn't ready for me to yield, it brings my knees knocking against his and sliding between. I release my own force—a twist of both arms to free them, a strong step backward and around the corner of the bed. Physical distance seems like a good thing right now. I've lost my mind and he never had one to begin with.

He looks away but I don't. Again with that rough head rub. There must be some perverted reason why he has to dig in so hard. He must like the discomfort in it. Is that normal to him? Is it why he thinks my gentle method is magic?

Either he feels my continued gaze or senses my questions because he looks up abruptly. First at my eyes, then at my hands. He's remembering, maybe wondering the same thing.

I sign, *I'll do it again if you promise not to touch me.*

He tosses me his phone. I type, *Don't touch me.*

That unchanging expression is his yes. He's too arrogant to agree to a command from me, so if he's not chewing me out, it's a yes. I advance. His hands go to the bed. I press my fingers into his shorn hair and drag front to back, spreading them as I reach his neck. What he doesn't understand is it's the gentleness of it that gives the best results.

Leaning into me, he closes his eyes. I step closer so he doesn't tilt himself onto the floor. It's like he's starving for human touch, like he's gone his whole life without it. With every stroke his head inches closer to my stomach until it's pressing against it. If he notices he makes no move to fix it, and even though he just broke my rule, I have to forgive it.

Don't kiss him again. Don't kiss Rex Moore.

He's an ally but he's still an enemy—the worst one. His family won't stop their war against mine.

He raises his head, takes hold of my wrists, and looks at my hands. A moment later he turns them over to view the palms. He still doesn't believe it's not magic. Then he lifts his eyes to mine and that mantra falls off the edge of the world. Along with my brain. I wish it would take my heart too, because my chest can no longer contain the power of its rhythm. It's beating in the empty hole where my brain used to be, in every extremity, in the air around me. It's affected gravity and oxygen and the color of Rex's eyes. Of his lips.

I'm tasting them again but it's not my fault—the gravity's screwed-up. They're soft and strong and every positive word ever created. They're hungry, and they're not stopping. He should stop this—I've lost my brain. But oh, he never had one. He's released my wrists, his hands now on my face, pulling me closer, fingers slipped into my hair behind my ears.

It's not just gravity—time and space are wonky too. This kiss just started but it's forever and unending and repeating—

And impossibly short. He's shoved me away, his hand up. *You*, he says, panting. He can't finish. He doesn't have the air for it.

I press hot hands against my chest, struggling for my own breath. Okay, maybe I should take the fall for this one because it was my bad, one hundred percent. I need to be on probation. I need counseling and community service, and he needs a restraining order.

He absently wipes a slow hand over his mouth as if he's palming the memory to save for later. I wonder if the Moores have magic for that—freezing memories, stashing them away. I'd love to see the other ones he's stored. I wonder if he'd share them with me.

You—

This time he stops on his own, bunching his eyebrows like he's lost his thought. Whatever it is, it's probably not pleasant. So I save us both and sign, *Sorry.*

All his attention is on my face. I've never done this before. I don't know what I'm doing yet I keep doing it. He pushed me away because he's kissed a million girls and I'm this pathetic amateur who can't control herself. All the thrill drowns in a wave of dread. My brain is back, and it's punishing, and it's right.

He's patting down his pockets, still straight-faced, still staring at me. I catch on too late. The pill is already in his hand aiming for his mouth, and I aim for the throat, and he's coughing it into the air. I snatch it off my bed—a bad move, because now he's snagged me by the waist and spun me toward him. I prep to dodge the raised hand but it never comes down. He chokes again, an aftershock of my jab, or something else. Some emotion finding its own way out. I rummage for his phone and snatch it up to type, *You just woke up from one of those stupid pills you can't take another.*

He makes an unsuccessful grab for the phone. No way is he silencing me.

I'll leave if you want me to. Just no pills. I look up at him. Yes, I'm pleading. No, that doesn't put me below him even though it feels that way. I'm right, and Aaron would back me up.

I fingerspell his name, barely getting out the X before he tries a swipe at my hand. Then he's covered his face. His neck and traps are bulging like he's screaming, or growling, or both. Can a person do both?

I type, *You can't just shut everything down whenever you feel like it.*

Yes I fucking can, appears on the screen.

No you fu—

He gets the phone from me this time, chucking it across the room. Well, that's great. I guess he'll be learning ASL now.

Unfortunately, what he says is easy to lip read. *Shut up.*

I sign, *Don't tell me to shut up.*

He says again, *Shut up.* And gets in my face.

Oh I shouldn't, but I have to. I shove him.

He shoves me back. The force of it rings in my bones because I completely didn't expect it or prepare for it.

Really? I sign. *This is stupid.*

Shut up.

He needs another shove so bad it'd be a crime not to. But it's childish. I shouldn't do it. Especially since I think he's baiting me because he wants it. He loves that negativity, he gobbles it up almost like he's the one made from black magic. Because I know it will piss him off worse, I sit on my bed, cross my arms, and smile up at him.

Above me, he's a stony mountain—rugged, impenetrable, a hazard to many. But not to me. I know too much about him. He's a monster Moore who's escaped his cage and needs a harness, or plastic handcuffs, or a tranq dart. I hold the smile. It's both defense and offense. He kicks his own bed and grabs the lamp off the TV table. I think of the nice old man behind the front desk, the one who Rex bargained with, who looked us over with a suspicious eye that Rex somehow turned to a trusting one.

I can't help it—I say Rex's name aloud.

He freezes in place, the lamp half swung toward the wall. I'm shaking my head, my hands over my mouth because the shock of it drew them there. He glances at the lamp, scrunching his eyes as if registering it as a new thing in his hand. I can't even decide if he heard me. He sets the lamp back on the table, levels the shade, replaces the plug that had ripped loose from the outlet. Stripping off his T-shirt, he goes in the bathroom and shuts the door. Taking a shower, no doubt.

Which must be cover for him to take one of those pills. Well, fine, then he's going to have cold tile for a bed because there's no way I'm trying to move his stupid ass.

CHAPTER 18

REX

I WAKE UP IN the bed, covers thrown onto the floor, pillow wedged between the bed and nightstand. Sloane breathes softly in her bed a few feet away. The room smells like her—her skin, her hair, that floral scent of her sweating off her deodorant. All I can see is the shape of her body under the blanket and her dark hair escaping from the top. If the clock is right it's actually morning, like a normal time of the day to wake up naturally. Which is what I did, I guess. Pretty weird. I shower and put on shorts and a tee, but she's still out, her body now tucked into a ball like a little animal nesting in the covers. She's an animal all right, but not a sweet little one. She bites.

And will probably rip your throat out if she feels like it.

I've been making enough noise to wake someone up, but right … she can't hear it. How strange it must be to be deaf and not have sound to wake you up. No alarm clocks, no assholes yelling your name, kicking you out of bed. Wait, did I say strange? More like golden.

I go into the bathroom to brush my teeth and have to stop everything when I see my reflection and those gory-ass shark bite wounds practically healed. Nope, just nope. It's my imagination, or hallucination from withdrawal. I get my toothbrush. But of course I have to look again, and this time I step the hell back because this mirror is jacked-up, or my eyes are, or—

Wait a second. She kissed me there. What the—

Up close again, I press the skin. Tender but healed, almost scarless. I needed skin glue yesterday. The cuts were reopening, and my whole face was on fire with the rawness of it. Today? Like it almost didn't happen. Like I just got a papercut, two weeks ago.

She has immortal blood, okay, got it. But is she that protected that even her saliva carries that magic? I think I need more wounds, like all over me. That's kind of a sick-ass thought, Rex. Actually, no, it's kind of ace.

Covers shift on the bed so I finish up and leave the bathroom. She's turned over and opened her eyes. She looks at me. I get a charge like nothing else. It's a zing in my feet, lighting me up. This girl, she doesn't just practice magic. She's made of it.

And I think it's gotten to me, taken me over. I think I might be—

She does that sign for eating, her eyebrows raised like a question.

"Okay, I'll get us something." Because get me the hell out of this room.

The door slams too hard and I'm glad she's deaf because it was an accident, and I don't want her thinking I'm mad. I'm not mad. I stand outside the door and let the sun bake me. The need to hurl is legit. I catch myself rubbing my head and it makes me remember her touch.

What she does to me is—

She has to be playing me or I've seriously lost my head—

And that sign she just did, my effortless understanding of it—yeah, any dumbass could figure that out but you'd have to want to understand, and I don't, or I didn't, or I don't fucking know. All I see right now is what I just saw: her propped up on an elbow, the neck of her shirt crooked, shoulder peeking out, epic mess of hair, impossibly bright eyes still a little sleepy. She's so cute it makes my heart go rabid. Rex Moore, heart attack victim just a couple months shy of his sixteenth birthday. Found outside a gross motel in who-the-fuck-cares Virginia. Police are searching for his female companion: Caucasian, brown hair, green eyes, five foot three inches of killer cuteness. Armed with teeth. Do not approach—she will bite.

Hey, idiot, growling stomach means stop obsessing over Sloane Bevan and go find someone who can bring me some food. I walk to the office to ask the old geezer. He's repairing the wall beside the front counter right at kicking height. I'm kind of relieved I didn't throw that lamp.

"Can I help you, son?"

It occurs to me this isn't a place where people bring food to you. Our room is basically a prison cell with a TV.

I should probably ask where the mess hall is. So I don't sound like a dumbass, I simply say, "Breakfast."

"Something quick, or something good?"

"Something quick and good."

He looks up from his wall repair to determine if I'm being real or being a smartass. "Well, you can't beat the golden arches."

Should I know what that means? "Okay, where's that?"

"Quarter mile that way." He points.

Pointing is good. I can manage that. I take off on foot because I love the torture of the threatening heat, not quite on my side of the road yet but probably will be on my way back. And sure enough there's a sign ahead—two golden arches. TV and the internet have failed in educating me on American cuisine.

The cashier has to help me pick something for Sloane. He asks if my picky veggie-loving friend eats eggs, and I have no clue, so I say yes. If she doesn't she will be today. I get coffee for me and a fruit smoothie for her and walk back with the bag of food tucked under my arm, the simple act of picking up food giving me the dorkiest mental high. I shut down all thoughts of Sloane. It ends here. It's all business now. She's not cute; she's playing me. Her saliva heals, pretty much like some freakish alien creature. And here's how it's going to go down: She teaches me magic, I help her disable the power structure in my family, I release the black magic to destroy hers, I take over as king of the Moores. The end.

Back in the room, I unload the food onto our wobbly miniature table. The bathroom door hangs about a foot open, enough for me to see she's dressed and doing something to her hair at the mirror. I make sure she sees it's me so I don't get attacked.

When she joins me her hair looks just like it did the first time I saw her. Crown gathered into a high ponytail, the rest hanging free against her back. Bangs uneven across her forehead. Long braid hanging down her chest. That's not something you need to notice, Rex, so cut it out. I hand her the smoothie. She reaches past me for the coffee and takes a sip.

"I thought you were a health nut."

She doesn't understand but she smiles anyway.

A text dings in so I take out my phone.

Aaron: I just emailed you a list of addresses for every Moore household. Be careful and don't do anything stupid.

I text back, *Define stupid.*

Just listen to Sloane, OK?

Dude, how? She doesn't speak.

That's not entirely accurate though. I wonder if he knows that. I check my email and read the list. Philadelphia, New York, D.C., and Detroit I know. A few I don't recognize but know we have family in those states. Detroit is the farthest west my family strayed. I've often wondered if it's because of the Bevans in Chicago. There must be a war front at some longitude. It would be helpful to know which one so I know when I'm in Bevan territory. Pretty soon it will all be mine.

I have several more unreads from my gaming crew, ranging from curious to frantic. I've never been offline for so many days. I need to email them back, but damn, what to say? If I don't, they'll think I'm ditching them. My friend count will go from pathetic to nonexistent. It's not like I ever deserved them to begin with, though.

When I look up she signs the letters to my name. I hand her my phone and start eating.

It's nice you have such a short name.

"What?"

Easy to fingerspell. Can I give you a name sign?

"I don't know what that means. So no."

She frowns at me. I point to her food. She eyes it like she doesn't want to eat it but also doesn't want to hurt my feelings. My feelings win. The silence while eating is a real plus of my situation. At home, whether eating by myself in the kitchen or in the hell of a family dinner in the dining room there's always some kind of noise. Boring discussions among the staff, my family bickering, people ordering me around. Should I admit this is nice? No, Rex, you shouldn't.

What's your middle name?

"Don't have one."

She tilts her head like I'm lying.

"Really. I don't."

Rex Moore. King of the Moores. That's all you are?

I never thought of it like that, but yes, that's all I am. She won't be alive to see it come true though. And did she pick that phrase out of my head or something? Yeah it's my name, but come on.

"What's yours?" Seems polite to ask since she asked me. No other reason. Not sure why I feel the urge to be polite, but hey, whatever.

She signs the letter C. Then an A. And I look away because nope, not game for that. I don't know why I even looked the sign language alphabet up on my phone. I have no desire to learn that nonsense. Looking away was a mistake, though, because it gets worse. She takes my arm and starts writing it out, and I'm sucked into watching her finger moving along my skin. Even her hands are cute.

No they're not.

"Catherine?" I crack up. "That's twisted. That's my mom's name."

Mine too. Her middle name.

I just about choke. "What, are our mothers related too?"

She shakes her head. *Different spelling.*

I'll have to take her word for it. I'm not exactly sure I know how my mother's full name is spelled.

And what do you mean? No people in our families are related, remember? We settled that.

Right. An important thing to settle because of all the making out. We should probably stop doing that. The image of it—the high of it—comes alive in my head, and she's so close all I'd have to do is reach. Curl an arm around her neck and drag her in. Kind of like a chokehold but without the choking until blackout part.

What is that? She points to the burn scar on my arm.

I stare her down because I'm not going there. Ever.

Did you get the addresses? Aaron said he'd send them.

"I got them."

Then we need to get on the road. And I need some more practical clothes. When she looks up from the phone, she suddenly goes still, a hand over her mouth. She points at my face.

I get a napkin because of course I'm a slob. I wipe down and say, "Better?"

She's shaking her head. Now she's on her feet in front of me, and I recoil because this girl can't be trusted. Too fast she takes hold of my face and tilts it toward her, eyes darting all around. She touches my cheek and I swat at her. There's no way she didn't know she'd heal me. Why else would she have done that?

A poke to my cheek and now I'm up, knocking the chair into the wall because she needs to back off. She's pointing, pointing, pointing. Pumping it for emphasis. I retreat from her reach and point right back at her. "You, you did it. Don't act like you don't know."

She opens her mouth as if to say, *Oh.*

"Yeah. *Oh.*"

I dodge her grab to my arm, the one that had the deadly flesh wound in the woods at home. One second later I put it all together. She kissed all over that gore? And then I kissed her? Oh, holy elements. She must see I'm about to heave because she starts shaking her head like crazy. I back away because this girl is sick, just sick. Made of magic but also sick.

She snaps her fingers at me. It gets my attention but I'm not sure what I'm walking into. Charades, it looks like. Her cutting open her palm, turning it toward the ground, blood dripping. She snatches my hand and holds my arm straight, that pretend bleeding palm right above it.

"You bled into my wound?"

She's looking all around—she wants the phone. I find it and toss it to her. She checks the screen and nods.

"Because that's so much better."

I had some crows clean out the maggots first.

I probably should just hurl right now and get it over with. "Okay, so both your blood and your saliva ..."

Apparently.

"You didn't know?"

Not until now.

"Don't fucking lie."

I swear on every sacred oak. One lip tucked under the other, she looks like she's about to cry.

Well, balls. No way I'm standing here and watching her cry. "I like your new method better."

After reading the screen she squints her eyes—another person working to determine if I'm being real or smarting off. Do I have some kind of reputation or something? Yeah, I'm pretty sure I do.

"You gonna finish that egg sandwich?"

Watching me, she slowly sits down. I try to think about food instead of her new method. She reaches past me for the smoothie—my smoothie, since she took my coffee—and drinks it down two inches. Okay, I guess we're sharing then, because I need either caffeine or sugar and I'm not walking in the heat to get more. Both smoothie and coffee have been tainted by her, but does it matter? I've been thoroughly contaminated at this point.

She picks up my phone. *We need a contract.*

"For what?"

For our plan.

"Not necessary."

Some things I need you to do.

I laugh, because she can't be serious. I think I'm doing enough.

You need to learn to fingerspell.

"No I don't."

It will make things easier. Also, you have to let me bind you to my amulet's protection.

"Nope times a million. That thing would probably kill me the first chance it got."

And I want a blood oath. Spoken allegiance is not good enough.

It shouldn't be such a gouge. She's only being sensible. I'm not sure why she finds it necessary though. There's no way she knows what a liar I am because I've never lied to her.

Wait. I haven't? That can't be right. She can't be the first person I've never lied to. Even Emily got it. Aaron too. Even when I knew they knew I was lying, I did it anyway.

No offense, she adds. *Is there anything you want from me?*

Isn't that a complicated question. I could demand she stop being cute, and stop trying to kiss me, but the part of me that likes to keep my life miserable wants neither of those things to stop. "You teach me your magic."

I already agreed to that.

"You give me back my coffee."

She hands it back to me, all polite and businesslike. But I see a tension in her cheek, the smile she's trying to keep in check. And it's about to get murdered by the next thing I say.

"You undo what you did to me in that bedroom at my house."

The cheek smooths. Instead of sweet-cute, now she's scary-cute. I can't decide which one is more appealing. She's a demon in a candy shell. And I think she might be out for my blood.

I'm not turning you back into that hate-filled monster.

"Hate-filled I'll take. Monster? That's a bit extreme." If she thinks the hate in me has been purged, she's in for a big disappointment.

The first thing you'll do is kill me.

I have to ponder that one. Could she be right? Is it so simple? Just a switch, kill Sloane Bevan mode off versus on? I'd like to think there's a little more to me, that I'd still see the value in keeping her around until we disable the key people in my family so I can take power.

The truth is there probably isn't much more to me than an on-off like that.

Okay, I'll agree to change you back to normal, but only after I've finished with all your family members.

"Deal." I pull my knife and split my palm.

She takes it and splits hers. We clasp hands. I get a little lost in her eyes and have to blink myself out.

She picks up my phone. *Because you're not going to want to change back when we're finished.*

"You think?"

I know.

And I realize in my excitement, I didn't just agree to that final thing she proposed. I sealed an oath for all of them.

CHAPTER 19

SLOANE

WE CHOOSE THE Washington D.C. Moores as our first battlefield. Rex makes a few more friends on the road toward the interstate, and when he's halfway down the entrance ramp, he suddenly pulls to the shoulder and unbuckles his harness.

Dying in a car crash would be kind of a buzzkill right now, he says. *So this is all you.*

I hand him his phone, and we switch spots. The road's decline makes it easier to get the car going, and after I've merged and set my speed, I notice Rex watching me like he's taking mental notes. When we stop for the night, I need to sit him down and teach him all I know about driving. Which isn't much, but it's a lot more than he knows.

Nearing a large town, Rex searches his navigation for shopping, and I tap the big retail chain store that'll have clothes. Inside the store doors, he stops fast, mouth a little dropped open while he stands there and blocks traffic. I have to take his hand and pull him in. At first I think he's going into one of his panics. But then I see it's not panic in his eyes but awe. It's almost like he's never been shopping before. It's almost like—

He's never driven on roads.

Never been to a fast food joint.

Never been to a motel.

I shake his arm until he looks at me. I sign, *Is this the first time you've been in public?*

He absently searches his pockets, his gaze shifting all around us like there's too much to take in around him and he has to keep an eye on all of it. He hands me his phone so I can type my question.

No, he answers once I get it typed in. By the way his chin lifts a little, I can tell there's another answer he's preparing to give but something about it has caused him to forget about the store around us and focus only on me. Instead of watching the screen, I keep my eyes on his face.

On his lips I see, *It was the …* He pauses to run a hand over his head, eyes casting away before they return to me. Then he signs: *Eat.*

Wait, I didn't see that. I imagined it, right? I sign, *What?* Because that's the only word I'm thinking even though I completely understand. The tacos. His first time in public was with me to eat tacos. That's mind-blowing enough on its own. But him explaining it with ASL? Just, *what?!*

He signs again: *Eat.* And since I'm freaking out, he thinks I don't understand, and he's talking now. But no he doesn't need to talk. So I sign, *eat,* and fingerspell, *tacos,* because I know he's looked up the alphabet and has to remember some of them.

Yes, he says, nodding. *Tacos.* It's so plain on his lips. And that smile, peaking higher on one side. With the dimple.

I burst forward and hug him before I can stop myself. He goes rigid, all touch-me-not, arms raised awkwardly away from me, but I hold on, the breath in his chest gaining speed, his conscious act to slow it. And I let go and step back fast because my itchy palms just reminded me we're in the middle of a giant store with oppressive artificial lights, surrounded by all these moving bodies and watching eyes.

His eyes are different though. Not watching, not judging. Just seeing. Understanding. We are both tools to our families, and only he knows what that feels like. And the more I look into his eyes, the less I feel the pressure of people all around me. His presence steadies my nerves so ready to undo me.

He raises a hand to keep me back. I don't want to lose this bridge he just built. I don't want him to see it there and set it on fire. So I reach a hand toward him and he takes a step back—directly into some guy's cart. Rex spins around to glare when he should be excusing himself or saying he's sorry. I'd say it for him if I could. The guy gives him this look that makes Rex say something that's definitely not an apology. The guy says something equally aggressive back. Rex kicks the bottom of the cart, and I grab Rex's arm.

We're sorry, I sign. *Sorry.*

Here comes the look of confusion followed by pity. And … there it is. I let it boil in me a little because if I don't, it'll burn buried and the pressure will take forever to dissipate. Rex jerks away from me, stepping toward that guy, mouthing off. I check his phone: *Don't look at her like that.*

More words from Rex are rolling onto the screen, peppered with insults and expletives, and I look away because now the guy is apologizing, retreating, and everyone around us is gawking and giving Rex a wide berth. No one's looking at me anymore. He's opened a circus tent in front of the Deaf girl, and he's handing out free tickets. He turns, surveying the crowd, and suddenly everyone has somewhere very important to be.

I grab his arm and haul him into the aisles where we can hide. I should be mad. He's such a jerkwad. That behavior—I can't begin to break down the stupidity of it. The Moores breed bad manners, everyone knows this, even the Moores themselves. I shouldn't forgive it. But he *signed.*

So all I can do is look at him. And I know I'm smiling like I've just won life. I need a high five, or a fist bump. No, I need something more. I have so many things to say yet nothing at all. I want a repeat, for him to sign again to prove it wasn't my imagination. I fingerspell his name, hoping to prompt something.

He catches my hand before I finish. These fluorescent lights shouldn't make a person so handsome but somehow they have. Even though he dresses down the pretty-boy Moore genes in athletic shorts and camo, they're still there, roughed-up, rugged, and more appealing because of it.

Don't, he says. A magic word. It takes me back to that night. It takes him back too, but that's not why he's reviving it. He wants to feel the torture of it, the need, the unfulfillment. He wants to relive it to overcome it. To feel it and remember it then overpower it by doing nothing.

Should I admit how fascinating it is to watch him try?

I back into the shelves like I backed to the wall that night. Still holding my hand, he comes with me. With only an inch now separating us, I lift his shirt and slide his phone into his pocket. He's tensed, because that's not at all what he expected. And that's why I did it.

His only reaction is barely a smile. It's amused, telling me he's taken my move as a dare. He's planning something now, a game, maybe, of how much we can get away with doing to each other under the guise of innocence. He releases my hand, trailing his thumb like the lightest tickle across the crease in my palm as he lets go.

Game on.

This flirting with Rex Moore, it's a really bad habit I have no intention of quitting.

I split from him to pick out some jeans and pocketed hiking pants. Shirts are harder because they're either boring or not my style. Rex keeps disappearing and returning with some random stuff we don't need, like five boxes of cream-filled sponge cakes or a stainless steel thermos. I don't care how much money he has. We don't need to spend it, and we don't have room in the car for a load of stuff. I make him put it all back. Then he finds the sporting goods.

They don't sell guns to fifteen-year-olds, I try to explain.

Teach me what you did with that cash we used to buy tacos.

That was the memory trick, needed so the cashier would forget the blood she saw caked all over me. I'm not teaching him that. I don't trust him with it, and it's not the right thing for this anyway.

Or I could just kill everyone nearby and take what I want. Leave the cleanup to you.

No sign of amusement on his face means he's either serious, or he wants me to think he's serious. He's a total jerk either way.

Go ahead, I sign. He points to his phone. I type in, *I'll be in the car.*

As I hand back the phone, I swipe his car key from the pocket I know he put it in. He reaches too late to stop me. I'm already a step away. I stop in cosmetics for a cheap eyeliner and grab some other toiletries and a gallon of drinking water, silently thanking Aaron for his loan as I hand over the cash at the checkout. When I unlock Rex's car and open the door to let the heat out, I remember this is his first—no second—time in public. They kept him locked inside that fence his whole life. No wonder he's so messed-up. No wonder he never learned to control himself in public. I line my eyes in the sunvisor mirror, breathing in the heat that hasn't yet escaped.

In need of air, I get out of the car and glance at the entrance of the store, worried he's really doing what he just said he'd do. It had to be a bluff. Right? In the reflection of the car's window, I see a group of guys approaching from behind me. I'm at once aware of the sun's punishing rays, the heat simmering on the concrete, the rising tempo of my pulse. My palms are instantly sweaty. I duck into the car, but they've already reached me. If I don't look up, it's a snub, it's my fear, it's me beneath them. To some guys that combination is a door marked *PREY*. All they have to do is open it.

So I stand back up and look them all in the eyes, one after the other. One of them is my age, the other two are older. Brothers, maybe. I can breathe a little better when I see they're checking out the car, not me.

One of them says something directly to me, so I shake my head. Trying to figure out the words takes backseat to trying to breathe. They're looking around now, probably for the car's driver since I'm on the passenger side. Two speak at once. One gets an elbow jab from the other. They laugh. I don't catch any of the words. I'm sweating worse now. I feel every trickle down my back, every unloading pore. I could break all their knees right now if they threatened me, but the anxiety is a concrete block tied to my ankle and I'm falling off a bridge.

The tallest one is repeating. Stepping closer. The same sentence again.

I'm Deaf, I sign. I point to my ears. Shake my head.

They look at each other. The one who took a walk around the car joins us again. If I had my phone, this would be a lot easier. Now my fall from the bridge has broken the water's surface. It's a sea of memories of every bad experience in the hearing world—surviving elementary school, getting lost in the grocery store, being picked up from the land behind my house and taken to town by the sheriff. Too young for a phone to help me communicate, too frightened to know what the hell to do. The memories are all around me now, on top of me like a whirling current. I struggle against them.

Hey, are you okay? It's easy to read. They look concerned now.

The closest trees are so far away. All around me is blinding concrete and shining cars and the looming store. I back up, feel the hot surface of Rex's car against my back. Rex—captive in that hate-filled house, a prisoner inside that fence. He's had it bad, not me. There's no reason for me to deconstruct over a simple friendly encounter in a parking lot. It's not even about me. It's about the car. I don't know why the spotlight always feels like it's on me even when it's not. So I straighten my darn shoulders and sign, *I'm fine. It's just super hot today.*

They exchange glances. The youngest one points into the car. They want to see inside. I step back and they crowd forward, leaning to look in my open door. They're all talking at once but not to me, to each other. I open the back to put my bags inside and see Rex crossing the parking lot, his gaze fixed in a way that makes me wish I'd been able to warn him of his car's new fan club.

Rex has sized up the situation by the time he reaches us, and he's not so much interested in the guys. I follow where he's looking—my hands, still shaking from the anxiety. It's so common I don't realize it happening sometimes. I cross my arms and tuck the hands underneath.

When the guys notice him, they stand back a bit, excitement turning wary because Rex has the narrowed eyes in full effect. He seems baffled by their interest as they talk and gesture. He doesn't know his rich guy world is not the real world. Not everyone gets a rare souped-up race car before they're old enough to get a driver's license. I should probably explain this when I teach him it's considered rude to change lanes inches from another car's bumper.

He's changed his mind though. Now the hood's been popped and Rex starts the car. The guys seem to like that. I shade my eyes from the sun and try to catch words but it's all lost to too many people talking and my bad angle. Rex meets them again by the front of the car. Some kind of deal is going down. Cash transfers from Rex to the oldest guy and the three brothers head into the store. Once they're a good distance away I go for Rex's pocket. He calmly lets me do it. Watching, enjoying it. I find his phone and take it out.

Okay, perv, what's going on?

He's buying me some ammo. Guy at the counter inside said I'm too young.

Yeah, like I said.

He scratches his eyebrow, a cover for having just looked straight at my chest. He gets in the car. I get in beside him, careful not to rub my arm against his. He shifts in his seat and does it himself. I look into his eyes, trying to determine if that was intentional or accidental. He looks at my mouth.

I'm not sure if this is a continuation of the game we started in the store aisle or if this is just spoiled Rex Moore struggling to cope with wanting something he might not get. He's been given everything he's ever wanted in life without question. Or is that an unfair judgment?

Nah, it's the truth. But here's another one: I so want to give him what he wants.

I sock him gently in the jaw instead. He turns away, laughing. For once it's not for show. Not to unsettle someone. It's genuine and real, and I know that because of how he's shielding it from me like he doesn't want any witnesses to this side of him.

He hands over more cash when the brothers return with a heavy bag Rex checks before stashing it in the back of the car. After a few handshakes, he's back in the car with me, tapping my chin with his knuckles in a sweet version of what I just did to him. *Who needs magic when you have money?*

Is that the Moore family motto?

He takes a moment to consider this before answering. *Maybe. But pretty soon we'll be rich with both.*

He stops for fuel on our way out of town. I help him get the pump started then take Aaron's money into the shop and buy some candy for the road and some sunglasses: mirrored aviators for him, hot pink plastic frames for me. But when I get back to the car, I decide to let him choose. He picks the pink ones with a smart-ass pretty-boy Moore smile that makes me slide on the aviators so I'm free to stare undercover.

The reprieve from the glare of the sun makes me remember that meeting with the black witch. What did I do with that pouch of mint? I search my bag, finding it at the same moment Rex finds the gas station squeegee and holds it up to me like he's found a prize. I take a leaf of mint and fold it onto my tongue while Rex squeegees the windshield in his pink sunglasses. The daylight around us eases like a cloud has passed overhead, only there's no cloud. I lower my shades. Without them it's still bright, but not pounding in my brain like it was before. Okay, I'll use her mint. Someday I might know the magic in it.

We drive by the D.C. Moores' home as the sun burns mandarin on the horizon behind it. Surrounding that ball of orange is a smear of brilliant purple clouds, their color leaking into the sky itself. I glance at Rex to check if he's seeing this, if his normal eyes can pick up on that color. Or if mine really have been so affected by black magic.

But he's too focused on studying his relatives' house. A monolith of antique brick soars above the cobblestone sidewalk. Several ornate chimneys reach even higher. The third level is shingled like a roof but completely vertical, windows jutting from its face with smaller roofs of their own, the pane of glass in each one twice as tall as me. Or maybe taller. They're so high in the air I think my perception is off. No ladder could reach up there. To wash those windows a person would have to rappel from the top.

I expected another palace surround by acres of land like the Virginia Moores, but this setting is thoroughly urban. The street is packed with three-story historic mansions, giant trees, and stone walls. So many windows all around us. So many possible witnesses. I don't know how we're going to sneak in or escape. I count at least twenty windows on the Moores' house alone. And that's just the front.

Rex has gone stone still. He drives to the end of the street and turns then turns again onto the next one. We cruise the street behind it, finding more mansions with a ton more windows all staring right at us. A white-haired couple walks twin collies on the sidewalk. When the man turns to watch us drive past, I look at Rex. He's mouthing curses I don't need his phone to understand.

We backtrack to the main drag, Rex hitting the gas hard as soon as traffic allows it. I know what he's thinking. We need somewhere to hide, close enough to allow us to trek back here on foot, far enough to allow a safe getaway. I poke around on his nav and find a nearby park. He glances at the screen, nods.

The sign at the entrance tells us the park closes at sunset. Rex turns onto a narrow gravel service road reserved for park vehicles, following it until he spots an opening in the trees just big enough to drive into. We plow into the woods, taking down underbrush and saplings. I grab his arm to object, but it's too late. The damage is done.

And he's reacted to my touch with a sharp flinch like he normally does, but this time he follows with a lightning fast grip on my forearm and another arm ready to swing. It's not personal. His nerves are taut, and he can't overcome that training. He's lucky I understand that. I type into his phone, *You could've parked beside the road. I know how to make this car invisible all night.*

You need to do that anyway. We need all the cover we can get. He leans forward to take in the tree branches above us. *My cousins know how to coerce the trees...* He looks over at me, seeming to decide he'd rather not show too much of his ignorance. For once I see how this weighs on him. Trained in combat, hardened for war, but never taught all the magic our families have passed down for millennia. Because why would he need it? He's expendable. A one-use tool. Our magic is what makes us Bevans and Moores, but not him. He's something different.

Well, so am I. I'm a Bevan and something else. A combination of earth magic and black magic, a weapon built for surprise. Not expendable to my immediate family, but made for one purpose by my ancestors. I know enough about the plan that brought my parents together to understand now why they chose my mom. Without meeting that black witch, I might have never known.

There are bigger holes in my knowledge of the Moores, and I'm starting to see why. This is the same psycho family that raised my dad. As I wonder about all the twisted things they've done to Rex, I also imagine what they did to my dad. Some of those things have been confirmed with Rex. Should I ask him what he knows about my dad? Am I strong enough to stray there before we've even completed one stop in our plan?

Rex has left the car and disappeared into the trees, probably for a bathroom break. I tug my packed bag out of the car then go around back for my new clothes. We pass each other a minute later. I locate a clear spot to make camp and by the time he's joined me, I have removed all the sticks and rocks and have a blanket of leaves started. He starts to sit. I snag the shoulder of his T-shirt and point into the woods, fingerspelling a few easily gathered flora I'll need to make his car invisible. He gives the blankest of looks.

Can you at least build a fire? I sign. I pantomime the act.

He points double index fingers at me, gives a short nod. And that smile again, it's a solar flare, its radiation entering my flesh so I burn, energized and full of gooey heat. He's walking away, stooping to gather a short dry limb. And I'm watching the roll of muscle in his back, the determined set of his bristly jaw, the way his shorts hang on his hips.

This is bad. So bad. Not going away like I hoped it would. In fact, it's getting worse.

Or do I mean better?

CHAPTER 20

REX

After singeing the little flowers she gathered from the underbrush over the fire, she's grinding them against a rock. This is the magic she agreed to teach me but my lesson is completely in sign language, so I don't understand a thing. Either she's spacing on this flaw, or she's a crafty one at making deals. I keep my mouth shut though, because it looks like such tedious work she doesn't seem to mind doing on her own.

As if I could even pay attention if I wanted to work. I'm too distracted by memories of her seeking hands in my pockets. Her arms tight around my torso in that store, the scent of her hair wafting against my face. And that jackass with the cart, his patronizing, pitying face aimed at her, backing away because he felt sorry for her. I still need to kill that guy. I can't let it go.

Then there's her smile after all that. Like nothing else mattered but her and me. Like she's into me for who I am, not for what she wants me to be. No one has ever smiled at me like that. Not even Aaron.

All this, as if I wasn't worked up enough from watching her drive the R5. It's so damn hot seeing a girl drive my car. Not just any girl but Sloane Bevan. I've picked it apart to figure out why it's so hot, and what I've come away with just makes it all worse. Sloane driving my car— it's not that she's taken that control from me. She hasn't, not this time. It's because I've let her have it. It's the easy surrender, the sweet submission. Both are a new thing for me, but I don't think it's the newness of the feeling that's gotten me so wound. I think it's the feeling being associated with everything else: that not-so-innocent gleam in her eye when she's fishing around in my pocket; the warm spot in the center of her palm where my thumb fits, the hint of her pulse; the rainbow of expression on her face, changing by the minute; those newly dark-lined eyes, annoyingly and perfectly goth; how she's not afraid of me, even when I say stupid shit, even when I push, she's unchanged. No fear, no anger, no anything.

My hate for her has undergone some screwed-up chemical reaction. It's retained all power but it's become something else. There's this new problem I have: I can't kill her anymore. Be honest, Rex, you've gone farther than that. Yes, I have. I want to protect her. I hear my breath go ragged and hollow just for the thought spinning up, but this time I breathe through it and let it form.

I think I like Sloane Bevan.

There.

Yes.

An outward breath. Heart beating in my ears, my neck, my wrists, my feet. Crucified by my own pulse.

It's out now, but I feel something behind it, because this wasn't what I planned. This wasn't supposed to happen. It's someone's fault and it's not mine. It's hers. She was nice to me. She should've killed me. I like her, and I hate her for it. That mix—it's the heaviest trip, a nonstop explosion in my head. It's hate fueling like fueling hate, rotating and confined. Centripetal force.

It makes me want to do things to her. Things I know she'd be into. And knowing she'd be into it gives me a path right there.

I smack away a force against my shoulder. Tense for another one. But I see it's only her, withdrawing her fist while making pissed eyes at me because I'm not paying attention. More sign language, more expression all over her face. I need to see the time on my watch. A solid reminder of reality. The constant of time. It's gone now. You're such a dumbass for ditching the watch, Rex.

She's still eyeing me like I'm purposely pissing her off. Why is she so cute? She's a Bevan. No Bevan should be that cute. And in a few hours we're going into that house we just drove by to ambush and disable part of my family. If I'm this distracted, it's not going to go well.

"You know we could die in there tonight." I speak it fast, hoping to make it harder to lip read. "I have to kiss you until the need to kiss you is out of my system. So I can go in there with a clear head."

Her face is lit by the flicker of fire. Dusk has turned these woods dark. Not long ago she went far from the fire to scrounge for tiny plants I can't believe she found with no flashlight. Maybe night vision is part of her black magic blood. No fair on that shit.

She sweeps a hand at me as if to say, *Forget it.*

Bats swoop in from overhead. I stifle the urge to duck because they're too close and getting closer. She sits back on her heels as more bats gather between our heads and the lowest limbs, their flapping and high-pitched squeaks obscuring the night insects and faraway sounds of human civilization. An awareness hums low in my head, like I'm one decryption key away from decoding their noise.

Now they're flapping down to land on her arm, her knee, the stone where she's collected her ground ingredients. They seem to be reacting to her, and she to them. One by one they peel away, disappearing into the dark sky.

She stands. Looks at me.

"I need a translator to learn from you." I pop the pill I've been holding in my hand and swallow. Because I know she hates it. Also because I'm going to need it.

She folds her ingredients into an oak leaf and heads off toward the R5. I lie on the ground and close my eyes for a moment of rest before the chemicals and magic infiltrate my bloodstream. For those few minutes, I regret taking the stupid pill. Rest is sublime. The horizontal release of muscle and bone better than any drug. Her footsteps return before the pill has kicked in and I stay down, relishing her quiet sounds mixed with cicadas under the rising half moon.

Her hand on my head—oh, those fingers. She's weaving them in, back and forth, a perfect death. I tuck my chin to give her better access. A second set of fingers joins the first. She might not notice the full-body tremble. She won't hear the groans. The tingles scatter down my back, my legs. Oh hell, I'm so doomed.

I scramble upward and find her mouth with mine. Kiss her, kiss her, kiss her. My fingers now in her hair, her arms locked against the ground behind her to keep me from laying her down. But she's kissing back. So much. So good. My knees sweeping through leaves, butting against her legs, getting me closer. The lock of her elbows gives. Her arms go around me. She's holding on, and the only thing left to do is lay her down in the leaves, so that's what I do.

Our lips break for a moment of clarity. Moon and fire light her eyes—all black, pupils eclipsing irises. She's a night creature. A black witch. The way I fit against her, though, is like day joining night. Shadowed earth joining starlit sky. A colossal meld of two worlds, making two wrongs right.

And one more thing: rebellion. The way it settles all over me. How I absorb it, make it mine. It's perfect.

She doesn't move as she looks up at me. Flat on the ground, arms straight, palms against the earth as if keeping herself from melting into it. I'm breathing harder than I'd be after the hardest combat. Her chest rises and falls in time with mine. I could stop this now. She could stop it. But I want it. She wants it.

So I lower myself against her and kiss her softly, such a change from what we were doing before. She turns her head—a second thought, maybe, but because I'm an idiot, I put my lips to her ear and whisper, "I think I like you."

Just to hear it voiced, released in the wild. Freed even further beyond forming the thought.

She swivels her hips against mine. Oh—okay. That's—

I can't—

I brace my hands against the ground and lift up before … I don't know. Before something.

Before I lose my mind.

She's scooted out and gotten to her feet a couple yards away. Good. Smart.

It's hard to keep an eye on her with how alive the woods have come around me. The sway of limbs in the breeze like a pull in my core. The breath of every creature joining my own. The moonlight trickles through the canopy like a caress on my skin. And water—the scent of it carving through earth, its shimmer in the thin light I can sense more than see—so present somewhere, nearby, I could close my eyes and walk right to it.

Sloane's hand snaps out, urgent for my phone. I toss it to her.

You're doing it. Do you feel it?

Feel what? Yes, I feel a lot right now. But I can't decide what.

The elements. You're tapping in. First with me, now on your own.

With her? I turn away from her to get a grip on it all. The pill I took is in full effect now, making me jittery and focused on too many things at once. I need to dial it back a notch, get an overall picture. I'm being slaughtered by the details. I glance at my empty wrist, remember my absent watch.

She comes around to face me, going down to her knees, pointing at the ground for me to join her. I do it. I don't know why. Maybe because my lips feel hot and freshly punched from all the making out, and going to my knees gets me closer to her. Maybe because I've been ordered around my whole life, and following orders is my natural position. Maybe because I'm wondering what else she'll let me do to her.

Opening her palm to me, she offers a handful of ash from our fire. It's not for me, it's only to look at. Then it goes to her shoulder, swiping down her arm. Before my eyes a pattern appears on her skin. Her war paint, scribed on her arm in ash. She does her other arm. A few swipes on her chin and cheeks for a coordinating series of lines and curves.

Now she looks at me, part firelight, part shadow. She's the girl from my nightmares, the one leading the army. She's the girl from the woods by my house, killing me, healing me. Fleeing from me, following me. I watch her stand above me. If I'm king of the Moores, she's queen of the Bevans. She's their warrior queen. But with her above me, I feel less like a king and more like a subject. Like a slave.

She walks to the fire and stoops, returns to me with a fistful of ash. She pokes my chest over my heart, points to my arm.

"We don't have a family design," I say. "Or, if we did, we don't anymore."

She scrunches her eyebrows. She doesn't understand. Well, I don't either. We're one side to a forever war that's never stopped. There's no reason why her side would remember its war paint and mine would not. I make a quick, pointless swipe down both arms and shake my head at her. "We don't do this."

Her eyebrows go way up. I shrug and hold it. It's just another thing we've lost from our past, like so much of our magic. Might have come in handy, might not matter. Nothing will save the Bevans from my bottle of black magic I'll unleash as soon as she puts me back to my normal self.

Now she's analyzing my arm though, glancing between it and the handful of ash she was hoping to hand over to me.

"Oh, no you don't." I hop to my feet.

She's back to her knees before me. Warrior queen, making her plea. But no, there's no pleading. It's more like a request, an invitation from the *Máistreás na nDúl* herself. A different kind of blood oath, a deeper form of allegiance. She raises her empty hand, and damn the elements, I take it, allowing her to pull me down. She rolls my T-shirt sleeve to my shoulder. The thud of my heart is a natural disaster; soon the earth will split from its force. I try to imagine my family, what they'd do if they saw me here, what they'd say, and all I come away with is more desire to let this happen. To send them pictures of this scene stamped with my middle finger. This is me calling the shots now. It's me joining forces with the only person who can overthrow them. It's time for them to sit down and shut up. It's a revolution.

So I take her ash-filled hand and join it with my upper arm, holding it there a second while the heat builds between her skin and mine. Her face says so many things all coming to me at once: solace, fear, relief, resolution. I hope mine says nothing. Since she seems to be waiting for my cue, I give her a nod and watch as she drags her hand down my arm, covering it with the same design. Ripe magic swells between us. All those feelings she just expressed fall through me as if they are my own. And there's something else—a current rolling underneath it all, a thick, unsettling grit. Something I've sensed outside of me, never inside like this. It doesn't mix with me like everything else does. There's no fluid movement, no swirl. Instead, it displaces things. It crackles and sparks.

I pull away because I can't get down with that right now. There's too much, too many other things to work out. She scoots forward, marks one cheek and half my chin and stops there.

"Only half a warrior?" I ask, lifting my non-painted arm.

She takes that arm and stretches it out, writing words on it like she's done before.

Moores suck.

And I get up and head toward the fire because I'm laughing too hard.

She naps for three hours. I do push-ups and practice leaps out of trees because the pill's still in my system. I don't want to take a sleeping one because I won't wake in time for battle. Two a.m. is what we decided. I eat all the snacks on me and head to the car for more but can't find it. It's even invisible to the touch—at least I think I remember where we parked. I could be feeling around in the wrong spot.

I unload and reload my .45 a few times, sharpen my knife. I need to email my gaming crew with an update so they know I'm alive. I can't afford to lose the only friends I've ever had. Honesty is where it's at, but I know that's the pill talking. Maybe I should go with it though. I'm not capable of making correct decisions unaided. Before I can talk myself out of it, I fire off a group email: *Sorry, guys. Dealing with some bad stuff right now. Had to leave my house. No worries though. I'm okay, except for not being able to get online. Hopefully you won't hate me too much by the time I get back.*

I hit send, feeling twitchy and exposed and unable to determine how much of that is the pill and how much is the real me.

Finally it's time to wake her up, but the moths have beat me to it. They're flapping against her cheeks and arms and she's stirring, not even swatting them away like most people would be if insects were all over them. I can't figure out where her hair ends and the moths begin.

"Bevans are weird." Yeah, she can't hear me, but maybe the moths will pass it along to her.

She stomps out the dying fire while I pack up the stuff we brought from the car. The half moon is high now, directly overhead. I wonder if that's why she suggested two a.m. We change clothes—pocketed camo pants, boots, and a clean tee for me, dark jeans and black tee for her. Still those soft boots. She leaves her amulet outside her shirt. It catches a beam of moonlight, and I know what she's about to do.

Look at your arm, Rex. Bevan war paint, remember? Being bound to her amulet makes no difference now. You've already joined the wrong side.

Point taken. But it's temporary. Only part of my strategy. I haven't joined them, I'm using them.

I realize I've stiffened against whatever she's going to do with her amulet when she takes my phone from my hand, and I practically pull a muscle from the flinch I have to suppress.

She types into my phone. *I need to ask you something before we go.*

"Okay, shoot." I'm a little terrified though.

What did your family do to my dad when he lived with them?

I doubt she wants to hear they took in Bevan trash and gave him shelter and education and training and put up with all the times he attacked people for no reason. She wants to hear the bad stuff. Probably needs some motivation for what we're about to do. "I can only tell you what I heard."

She signs an O followed by K. I can't believe I recognize it.

"They chained him in those crappy old buildings and didn't feed him. Destroyed his things, tortured his mother. Probably smacked him around a lot. Fun stuff like that." From the way she's put a hand to her mouth, I should stop here, but why end it before the best part? "And you know they tricked him into thinking they killed his wife and new baby, right? And he bought it. For like, fifteen years."

Her eyes have gone watery. She slowly hands my phone back. Rigid shoulders, unfocused stare—she appears to be going into a state of shock. So she didn't know all this? Well she needs to know. I'm not sure why, but it's important.

I show her the screen and say, "After that he executed everyone in the house. Did you know that?"

Tears are running now, but she's not wiping them because she's glued to the screen.

"Tons of people. Thirty? Fifty? I don't know. That was when my great-granduncle and his son were in charge. The two Martins. And they sent guys after him for years and he killed them all. You know how many of our guys he's killed?"

Her eyes flick from the screen to my face. There's a hint of disbelief in all that shock, and I'm afraid I'm dishing out too much. It's starting to sound too hard to believe. Well, it is, if you don't know it's true. I lower the phone because, wow, what if it's not true? My family isn't famous for their honesty. And think about it: how could one dude kill so many Moores? We're impossible to kill. Is it some kind of tall tale to rally the troops?

"You think I'm lying? Ask Aaron." I shove the phone at her. Because no way it's a lie. I've believed that shit my whole life.

She takes it mechanically. Reads my last words on the screen. I step beside her because I want to see his reply come in as she does. She opens a text to Aaron and types, *This is Sloane. How many Moores has my dad killed?*

He's not going to reply in the middle of the night, but we stand and wait anyway. An owl calls from far away, the sound gaining volume until large striped wings soar down, flapping once to land in a low limb. If Sloane notices, she doesn't take her eyes from the screen.

His reply pops in: *A hundred.*

She inhales sharply. He's including their trained guys and he's underestimating. Probably better that way so she doesn't think he's pranking her.

Another text comes in: *But most were self-defense. He's not a bad guy no matter what Rex says.*

Trey Bevan not a bad guy? Fuck Aaron. I take the phone from her, wishing I'd have thought before bringing Aaron into this. Yeah, I needed him to vouch for me, but I forgot what a shit-head traitor he is.

I hold the phone in front of her so she can read my words. "Your father killed Aaron's grandfather and cut off my mother's pinky when I was a baby. Came to the house completely unprovoked. That sound like a fucking bad guy to you?"

She steps back, shaking her head, and I see how close I had that phone in her face. Her tears are big now, puddling under her eyes, running down both cheeks, a glint in the moonlight. And the shuddering gasps coming out of her, the rawness of it—I'm not sure I've ever heard someone cry, or if I have, I've never cared enough to pay attention.

I'm paying attention now, and it's cutting me up inside. So much that I don't need to find some way to release my anger with Aaron, it's just disappeared on its own.

I untuck my shirt and wipe her cheeks with the bottom of it. She just stands there letting me do it. It's pointless though. More tears come. I wipe those too. Her makeup is coming off and I don't know how to wipe without smearing it worse. I could do more, like apologize, but for what? Telling the truth? I need to do more but I don't know what.

Then I remember what she did to me when I was pissed off and in my car about to leave her at Trey Bevan's cottage in the woods. How that hug laid such a heavy calm on me. So I wrap my arms around her and fold her against me. She loses it then, crying hard against my chest, and I know it's because I'm doing something wrong. I've never hugged anyone before. Never been hugged—well, only by her. I don't know what the hell I'm doing. I can't let her go though. My arms won't release. I'm making her cry harder, and I don't know how to stop it. Her arms go around me and she's holding on, tight enough for the shudder in her chest to become a part of me. I'm afraid of what this is doing to me. It just might be irreversible.

CHAPTER 21

SLOANE

IT'S SO OBVIOUS to me now, what my dad carries inside him. All the little things my mom has told me over the years. The walks my dad takes on his own for hours at a time. That bottle of liquor in the cabinet, its level regularly scrutinized by my mom and Aunt Tara, even by Dad himself. They don't know I see them do it. They don't know I've caught on.

How my dad disappears sometimes when Marcas or I really piss him off. The distance he creates when things get tense. How he leaves certain things up to my mom to handle. He doesn't think he can trust himself. He learned from abusers, and he's afraid he's one too.

Okay, I can deal with that. He's not an abuser. He's in a good place now.

But what he's done, I'm not sure how to accept. Holding onto Rex seems like the only answer until I come up with something better. He knows I've stopped crying because I feel his voice rumbling through his chest against my cheek. It might be an apology for the rough delivery of the truth, but I can't even blame him for that. There's hurt on both sides of this, and his is just as valid as my own.

When all this is over, I can't let him go back to those people, even if they're cured. He needs to stay away from them, from the memories, from that house.

Rex is trying to untangle himself, so I finally let him go. His shirt is wet and wrinkled from where I was plastered against him, but he doesn't seem to notice. The two of us, what we're doing together, it's a curse. Nothing good will come of it, and we have to stop. We need to do what we need to do, part ways, and move on with our lives.

I sign, *Ready?*

He hands me his phone. *What's the plan?*

We get inside the house. Find every one of your relatives and do what I did to you.

And?

I shrug. *And we leave.*

That's not a plan.

Unsure what to say, I frown at him. How is that not a plan?

He takes his knife from his boot and tests the blade on his thumb. *Just tell me what I need to do.*

I don't know yet. We'll figure it out when we get there.

That's the stupidest shit I've ever heard.

Oh, he's going to be rude? I'm so done with this. I shoulder my bag and take off for the car, but he's become a roadblock. He points to his phone still in my hand. I'm so sick of reading that stupid screen. I want to see his face and his hands, not words on a screen.

He says my name. Seeing it on his lips like that does something to me. I tighten my jaw against my stinging eyes. He says it again, almost like he knows what a weapon it is, how completely it can disarm me. Then one hand is in the air and he's fingerspelling. S-L-O-A-N-E.

I drop my bag, ready to shove him to the ground. Now isn't the time for him to pretend to care about learning to speak my language. But he's already caught me by the shoulders, and I fear he knows me too well. How could I have let this happen? Rex Moore is the last person who should be predicting my moves.

And no one learns to fingerspell after one casual glance on a phone. He'd have to have been studying it.

He releases my shoulder to point to himself. On his lips: *don't have.* He points to me. Then he fingerspells, *instincts … I need orders.*

I don't have your instincts. I need orders.

It's a pitiful attempt at signing but it's beautiful. And his eyes, locked on mine, so fierce and needy for acceptance—no one has ever made such a desperate attempt to connect with me.

OK, I sign, but I'm not sure what to tell him. This job has been coded into my blood by my ancestors. His role, a last-minute add-on by me. I've never created or given orders to anyone in my life. To save myself from fingerspelling it all, I go back to his phone.

Follow my lead. Be my backup. I need fresh running blood from each Moore and about fifteen seconds with each of them. Forehead to forehead, remember? You'll need to keep the room clear and keep everyone else away. And we need to do everyone in the house. I'm not going back in a second time.

He smiles, bloodthirsty and savage. Raises his fist for a bump. Our knuckles connect, and I wonder what kind of monster I've enlisted for the good I'm about to do.

The house looks even more massive on foot. Rex snaps a picture from the sidewalk before we go around the side and climb the short stone wall. The packed-together urban-ness of it is so unusual to me it's hard to get nervous about what I'm about to do. It's more like a game or an outing in some foreign country.

Rex has morphed into hardcore soldier mode. He even looks the part with his pistol in a shoulder strap and pockets heavy with extra magazines. He swore he'd try not to shoot anyone, but the suppressor he brought along doesn't give much weight to that. I'll just need to be effi-cient enough so he doesn't have to.

We duck behind a holly bush near a door to an all-glass garden room jutting into the rear lawn. He points—that's the door he wants. I keep watch of all the windows facing us as he sneaks away. Three stories high, a million glass panes wide. All dark. Most curtained. I'd know if someone was watching, right? I'm afraid calling upon the animals will create too much commotion or put them in danger. We're on our own.

I take inventory of the yard, the patches of moonlight and shadow, still and reverent in the calm of night. It's easier with no breeze. Movement will stand out to me. A well-tended garden of mixed flowers and herbs sleeps beside me, seasoning the air with a heady mix so much like our garden at home. I lean to identify the plants, hoping to disprove how similar they are but what I see does the opposite.

Rex returns to our hiding spot with a thumbs-up. He breached the door. Time to go in. I raise my eyes to the moon one last time. *Ancestors, guide me.*

He opens the door just enough to allow us to slip inside. I expect darkness, but the shadows are dialed up so they're merely gray instead of black. I get a few steps into the room, concentrating on silent footfalls until they take over as default. That's when I sense the dark cloud of hate. I reach for Rex's hand—I'm not sure why. He comes up beside me. Something inside me is opening, drawing forward to tap into that cloud so similar to the one in Rex's house. I need to cough but I stifle it, holding a fist against my mouth, swallowing it down. That dark lump I took from Rex's head has come alive in my chest. Missing for so long, it's now being revived.

Rex is looking at me hard, all business. Yes, that's how I must be too. So I take a breath and hold it, let it out slowly. Whatever darkness roosts in this house will soon have nothing left to feed it and it will die. That's my job, and I'm not leaving this house until it's finished.

I point to a fancy staircase ahead. Rex leads the way.

We go up and up. The temperature rises with each flight. An insignificant change, probably, but I'm sweating already from nerves and it feels like a hundred degrees of difference. Rex gets ahead of me, almost out of sight down a large hall. I follow the carpeted runner and meet him at a closed ornate wooden door. He puts a hand on the doorknob, a finger to his lips.

In we go. Moonlight casts a dim glow on a figure sleeping in a large canopied bed. Rex has closed the door and is screwing the suppressor on his pistol. I'm trying to control my breathing. Trying not to throw up.

Rex tilts his head toward the sleeper like he wants me to do something. I can't even remember why we're here, what we're doing. I want to go, get out under the trees and start running until I'm safe back in Montana where I'll stay forever. He jerks his head now, impatient.

Okay. Inhale. Exhale. Take a step. Take another. Rex is behind me, aiming that long barrel over my shoulder at the person in the bed—a woman, not old, but not young either. My mom's age maybe. A tap on my shoulder, an offered handle of a knife. Rex's belt knife. I take it, look behind me into his eyes. He gives me a you-got-this nod.

My palms are slick with sweat. I tighten my grip on the knife. Restrain her, then cut her, or cut her then restrain her?

Motion explodes in front of me. She's up, scattering pillows, scrambling away from us. Rex makes a successful grab of her ankle but his other hand is occupied by that off balance pistol that's now in my hands and aiming at the woman. Rex is in her face dishing out tight-lipped words. He has both her wrists now. She stops fighting.

Recognition crosses her face. His name on her lips. His name again, more force.

Rex says something to her that makes her look at the gun I'm pointing and close her mouth. Then he's lifted his arm to expose that discolored patch on his arm in her direction, making sure she sees. Anger boils under the words he's saying to her now. I sense the cloud of hate building in response. She allows a glance at his scar, but her attention moves to his other arm, the one marked as a Bevan warrior. Her expression changes with a new recognition so ripe with disgust I feel struck.

The dark power rises in me. Reaching for the hanging cloud of hate now connecting, drawing down. It's attempting an exchange of power I have no control of. And it's dipping heavy between them, so close to me I can't get away. I have to do what we came here to do. We've gone too far to go back now.

But something has changed in Rex. He's released her and slid back; she's speaking directly into his face, inching closer with each word. She lays a hand on his arm but there's no flinch, no touch-me-not reaction from him. Her other hand is sliding to the edge of the mattress, in perfect line with Rex's knife I dropped in the commotion. She locks eyes with me—she knows I know she wants that knife.

I'm faster. In one swipe it's off the ground and transferred to Rex. The contact of my hand against his snaps him out of his trance. He checks what I've just given him like he just awoke and needs to catch up. Awareness fills back into his eyes like water pouring into a bowl, and now he's turning them on her, newly savage, all patience lost.

He snaps an arm around her shoulders and spins her off the bed, slicing down the length of one arm. The wound wells with ready blood, dark and syrupy in the dim room. Now he's restraining both her arms, her back against him like he's presenting her to me. But that arm, that's way more blood than I need. The gush of it, the quickly accumulating puddle we're standing in—oh elements, he's sliced the brachial artery longwise. I stumble back. He's saying my name. Then again with added demand. He kicks the woman's legs from under her and goes to his knees bringing her weight lower. Her head slumps forward. He drops her, splattering blood outward. She hits the floor like a limp corpse.

Whoops, I see on his lips.

This is my fault. I should've acted before she woke up. He's supposed to follow my lead, not the other way around. She's dying—no ambulance would get here in time. Rex backs away, wipes his knife on the bedsheets. My legs won't move until he's next to me, and then I grab onto his shirt and shake him. We weren't supposed to kill people. This went wrong, so very wrong. He's looking down at me, saying, *It's okay.*

I shake him again—hard. It's not okay. I feel like we're wading through blood. My boots stick to the floor, my feet drag. We back to the door. He takes the pistol away from me, aims across the room and shoots the woman in the head. No.

No, no, no.

Rex starts, perking up like he's heard a sound. I place a hand on the wall and try to isolate my senses all into feeling for vibration. Rex jerks me aside. The door swings into us, slamming his arm which catches me in the mouth.

The heat and tingle of the blow tell me I've got a bloody swollen lip on the way. One man enters, another behind him. They take in the room; we all take in Rex's pistol now lying on the ground. One of the men reaches for it; Rex kicks him in the face. The other man surges toward me. I duck, get behind him. Kick him in the back of the knees, rise and elbow jab him in the spine. He grabs my hair. I twist, feeling a slight rip before my knee makes contact with his jaw. Now he's down, knocked out, and I can do my thing. What I came here to do.

I look up, directly into Rex's eyes. With his guy held at gunpoint, he tosses me his knife. I split my victim's palm. Draw the symbol in blood on his forehead and mine. My eyes are blinking closed on their own—the instinct rears up, impossible to fight since I made it wait so long. The hanging dark energy swirls like a funnel cloud around me, joining me, reaching through me into him, a white-hot light exposing the soot of anger, the char of hate. I gather their pieces like I did that first time with Rex, trembling from the power of it all. I stand above his body, now cured of all of that because it's alive and fat in my chest. I'm choking, gagging, a backwards vomit until it finally spreads and settles around organs, between mindspace.

Rex and the other guy are equally mortified. Rex recovers fast, shoving his victim toward me. But the guy isn't having it. He's turned to confront Rex with ugly words. Gestures between Rex and me. Points to Rex's marked face and arm. Spits on the ground. Rex has a glare leveled at him that would make any normal person shut up, but the guy only gets more vicious. Rex takes a deep breath in, lets it out with a slow, sinister calm. The guy points at me again, and Rex grabs him by the shirt collar and headbutts him in the nose. I see the guy making a slight adjustment of his shoulder but it's too late to warn Rex even if I could— they're grappling, gunfire flashes, Rex falls away, clutching his shoulder. I leap for the pistol—bad move. Hands are on me, and I've been yanked into a bone-crushing body lock.

I don't fight. He's so much bigger and stronger, I'd only waste my energy. He drags me over the dead woman's legs and shoves me onto the bed. I roll; he catches me, slapping a pillow over my face. It's too quick to have held my breath. The weight of his arm squashes the remaining air out of me. The pillow presses with more might. I'm now tasting the blood from my busted lip.

Blind to Rex, I have no idea if he's able to help and no oxygen to consider it. False bright specks scatter in my vision. I reach for the dark power still looming above us. The lump of gathered hate heats in my chest in response. My amulet blazes, scorching my attacker who's jumping up from the invisible ball of fire pancaked between us. I knock the pillow away in time to see Rex lifting the guy's head by the hair, pressing the pistol against his temple, and firing.

I'm quick to shield my eyes but it doesn't matter. I'm already coated in blood—mine and everyone's. Rex offers me a hand, heaving me up despite our slipping sweaty grip. He's holding his other arm tight against him, bent at the elbow as if in a sling.

I point to his shoulder. He shakes his head like it's nothing. There's a darkening spot in his shirt though. I know that's something. I go to the wall beside the open door and flatten against it. He sidles against me. As we catch our breath, I try to peel my charred shirt from the burned skin on my chest underneath. The pain goes into my teeth, my gut. My amulet is still hot to the touch but due to the destroyed skin on my chest, I can't feel it resting there.

He fingerspells, *Lost cause, clean up, get out.*

Any more … I point to the dead woman.

Two fingers. So, two Moores left in the house. Then he looks at the guy who's unconscious but still alive. He raises the pistol. I knock it away. His brows tighten to an angry line. He points two fingers toward his eyes, then at the unconscious guy, then at me. Okay, if he saw me, then I need to steal his memory. Easy. I think I need him awake for that though. Awake and calm and not trying to kill us.

Too late. Rex has fired. I took that hate inside me for nothing.

Now I'm the one with the angry face, and Rex shrugs, wincing from his injury.

Halfway down the hall we notice light flooding up the stairs from below. Rex stops, takes a moment of contemplation. Dark power writhes in my chest, my head. I don't know what to do with it. I've never been so powered by this fuel, firing up black magic that feels so like my own but has no place to stay. I get an upsurge from my stomach, hold a fist to my mouth to keep it quiet.

Rex starts kicking in doors. I lean against the wall, my head heavy, my knees weak. I can't fight people if I'm fighting this energy inside me. I think it wants to come out, but then what? It repowers the hate in this house? Undoing what we've done here? Lives have been taken, and they won't be wasted.

Rex has a hostage now, a woman, older than me but not by too much. He's steering her with the pistol against her back. She's sleepy-eyed, more annoyed than afraid. I trail them down the stairs where we walk into a small crowd of men. Rex said two were left, so this must be their security. This couldn't be going any worse. I grab Rex's arm, trying to convey through my face: *We should go back up the stairs and escape out a window.*

He's undeterred. At the bottom of the stairs, he transfers the pistol and hostage to me. An older man steps forward, appearing concerned for Rex. Helpful, even. Wary eyes travel over me. They think I've lured their prince to the dark side? That he's been compromised? Oh, please.

Now another guy steps up, appearing to negotiate. Rex gives him the finger. Takes out his knife. Raises a hand to me and fingerspells, *Shoot out lights* as men gather around him.

I count lights without changing the direction of my gaze because I don't want anyone clued in. I consider how many rounds should be left. Then I start shooting—chandelier, side lamp, stairwell light, hall. As lights blink out and glass rains down, Rex leaps into action, visible in my sensitive vision even in the dark. Gunfire goes off all around me, but Rex remains in motion. He's a manic blur of death, handing out lethal stabs and blows, unstoppable.

The lump of dark power sends tendrils from my chest, reaching for thoughts now so vivid in my head. Images of my dad chained in that crumbling shack. Of him being struck by people who claimed to be his family. Of how he looked when they told him they killed his wife and baby. The thoughts become my present. They add power to my pulse. And every life Rex takes feels like a wrong made right. A necessary vengeance. A score evened.

This isn't me. The dark power I consumed is trying to validate itself, make itself a home in my head using my own thoughts as its bedding. I need to close it off like I did before. Separate it from me. But not now. There's no time.

I drag my hostage to a rear room and turn her to face me. She's mildly irritated. It's so out of place I wonder if she's gone into shock. I remember Marcas' face when Dillon Moore took me from my home. The grief, the fear, the instantaneous loss of that innocent and boyish twinkle in his eyes. And I drop the pistol and take hold of her face, draining memories with all I have—my known magic powered by black magic. Reaching high to summon the light of the stars, delving into earth for the life it supplies. I mix all that power with the resident dark power and channel it into my fingers to break through a crust of magic over her mind. The memory of this night is the first to go. Her thoughts press against me then. Freed, when they'd been captive for so long.

Gratitude leaks from her into me, and I withdraw, seeing it painted on her face instead. Along with a wide-eyed surprise, finally awake after so long. She's no Moore. She probably married in, and that spell was designed to keep her complacent, to force her eyes to unsee each of their crimes. Well, not anymore.

Taking her hand, I hurry her to another room with a door to the outside and release her like an animal from a cage. She streaks across the night at a frantic pace, disappearing from view.

Then I head back into the house to find Rex, hopefully still alive.

CHAPTER 22

REX

Sloane catches my arms before I crash into her. I don't know how she can see in this pitch-dark hall. I sure can't hear her—my ears are fuzzy from the gunfire, and who knew a deaf girl could move with such stealth?

"Stage clear." I know she can't hear me but it feels better to talk to someone right now. I can't think about the pile of gore back there. All those bodies I'll have to answer for someday. Or maybe not, if I can figure out a way to blame it on the Bevans.

She takes my hand. We both need to be hosed off. My face is dripping and I've sweat through my shirt. But her hand—it's a tether, when a minute ago I was flapping and loose and terrifyingly alone. I won't admit that out loud though, not even to a deaf girl.

From the way she's tugging me out of the house, I wonder if she knows something I don't. Like my father and uncle just pulled up front. My great-granduncle Martin Sr. returned from the dead to remind me of my place. Prince Rex, not yet a king. What doesn't kill you makes you stronger and you're not yet strong enough, so here, this is what we have planned for you today: a European rally car for your birthday, and a two-hundred-fifty-pound heavyweight waiting for you in the ring to batter you around and remind you who you are. Gifts and punishment all at once just to screw with your head.

Sloane shoves me into a grove of tall bushes in the backyard, the pointed glossy leaves clawing my arms. As I'm adjusting my jaw—I think one of those guys repositioned it—she latches onto my shirt. For a second I think she's going to kiss me—scratch that. She's about to unleash hellfire.

Which is kind of the same thing, I guess.

Her war paint has been upgraded by blood streak and splatter. Does that make her cuter? No, Rex, you are seriously messed-up.

My shirt is stretching tight across my back, my wounded shoulder—oh yeah, I should probably see to that. Impossible right now though because of the twisting grip she's not releasing and the eyes as latched onto me as her fists, pleading for me to explain what just went on in there.

"Witnesses. Can't have witnesses. They see us together? That's bad. This is why we needed a fucking plan. Don't look at me like all that was my fault."

She rests her forehead against my chest, still holding onto my shirt like her hands have frozen into fists.

"What do you think would happen if we left any of them alive? They'd contact my father or my uncle. Tell them I'm in Bevan war paint working alongside you. I don't need that getting back to anyone."

Her breath keeps catching on itself. I know she can't hear me but there's no stopping my mouth. It's working without me.

"If we're doing this, we need a better plan, one that works for both of us. Otherwise, I'm out. And I'm not leaving you the R5, so you better—"

My phone's vibrating. I squeeze it past ammo and suppressors and check the screen. Aaron.

"Get out of there, Rex. They know."

"Who—how?"

Sloane has finally let me go. She's lowering to her knees, her head bowed, fingertips going against earth.

"My dad has someone on the inside. They got a message at the house from the D.C. Moores. Said you showed up out of the blue and they were talking to you. And that Sloane ..."

I don't remember seeing anyone with a phone, but I guess I could've missed it. That's a damn shame for me though. This goes on my record. Well, I'll have to play it differently then. Use it as an example. "Okay, okay, I feel you. We're leaving."

"What are you doing there?"

"Killing a ton of people apparently."

"Shit, Rex, is this what you—"

"No, it blew up in our faces. Noob mistake."

"You're giving me a heart attack."

"You're giving yourself a heart attack. Go back to bed."

He mutters something unintelligible and the call ends. Okay. Think, Rex. There's no hiding this. They know I was here. So I have two options:

One, blame the whole thing on Sloane. She made me take her here so she could slaughter them all. Now I've escaped so all's good. They'd never believe I'd be such a victim though. And no way in hell I want them to think I'm that easy to whip.

Option two is full responsibility. This is what you get when you mess with Rex Moore. And by the way, guess who's in charge now?

There's no contest, really.

I fire off a text to my father: *Might want to send a clean-up team to D.C. I made a little mess.*

Them trying to figure out why I've snapped and what I'll do next is bonus material. And here's something weird: Normally we dispatch that crew to houses full of slaughtered Bevans. I'm not sure how I feel about this change to protocol.

When I look down at Sloane, all I see are the tears dripping into the trimmed grass. The image of it creates a drain on my system so tragic I have to lock my knees so I don't collapse beside her. I'm afraid seeing her break now after surviving that shitfest just might break me.

With effort, I unlock my knees and stoop, taking her elbows to draw her up. She spells with her hand, *So much death.*

I hand her my phone. "No choice. They saw us together."

We could've …

Instead of finishing, she looks up at me. I need to find out which one bruised her cheekbone and deface his corpse so it's unfit to return to the elements.

"This is why we need a plan."

She wipes her nose with the back of her hand, turning to look off into the distance. She's never looked so preoccupied. So haunted.

"I mean, a better plan. We mark this as a fail and learn from it." Wow, is that me trying to make her feel better? Making it sound like it's not her fault?

All those people. Your family, Rex.

The use of my name sends a surge through me almost as piercing as when she spells it with her hand. When I usually hear my name, it's such a loaded sound. Except when it comes from Aaron. Sometimes Emily. Emily never again.

Sloane's hands snap to her chest and she bends, shoving the phone at me and staggering away between the bushes. She's coughing, choking. I follow her and find her vomiting tarry viscous liquid that reflects the light from the night sky in a strange, grotesque way. We stare at it together, her more stunned than embarrassed, me suffocating under a blanket of doom.

Nerves. That's all it is. Grief? Who knows. Don't read anything into it, Rex. Vomit is vomit even when it doesn't look like vomit. She just witnessed a mass execution. Of course she's going to react. It would help if she knew more about what kind of people they were.

"Those two guys in the bedroom."

Her attention moves to me. I hand her the phone.

"They just found some Bevans in Nova Scotia. Husband, wife, three kids. Decided they were sick of working around kids, so they blocked the doors and torched the house at night when everyone was sleeping."

Her eyes narrow. Mouth wants to frown but she keeps it tight.

"That first woman? She gave me this." I show her the burn scar on my forearm. "She kept doves to sacrifice in rituals. You'd have loved her."

That's a crime against our magic.

"I'd say you could go in and tell her, but she might not be open to advice right now."

Where are the doves?

Good question. I turn to face the house. Don't be an infant, Rex, you could totally go back in there if you wanted to. "I'm guessing basement."

Whoa. Head rush.

And I'm on the ground.

Sloane's ripping the neck of my shirt. Cool night air swells against the hole that should've clotted but maybe didn't clot and if not, I'm so very screwed. A poke into the open wound—oh god, no, not a poke, a fucking icepick. Wiggling, tugging fingers, her fingers, digging out a bullet she slides into my pocket. The stars swirl behind her. I'm seeing time-lapse photos of the night sky in real time, and she's lowering her face, her lips against my wound like a dream and I drift away.

I open my eyes. Pointy-leaved bushes standing guard around me. Endless universe above. And doves, flapping past, landing on limbs, cooing into the night. I watch them scatter, hundreds of them it seems, until Sloane pops into my view.

She's a perfect mod to this dream. I want it to last forever. She smells like gunpowder and blood. Her mouth is art, her eyes are the payout of a wish I never knew I had. If only she'd stop nudging me I could enjoy this.

Nudging me? Oh god, we have to get out of here. I'm up—too fast, my head spins. She gets her shoulders under my arm, and we hobble down the sleeping street, a gauzy moon lighting our way until we reach the edge of the woods we crossed through. I expect her to slow down because the canopy makes it impossible to see, but she pushes through like it's daylight. I need to ask her about her messed-up night vision. And by messed-up I mean kick-ass and so fucking useful.

We reach the opposite end of the little woods and stumble onto the street where we stashed the R5. She drives. I try not to pass out. The window bangs against my head, and I realize how unsuccessful I'm about to be.

I wake to a citrus colored sunrise spilling a weird mixture of light into the car. The road noise in the R5 is an undying drone, the music of crappy sleep littered with fun memories. It's okay, Rex, you killed her. Yes, but she burned my arm when I was what, six? She gave me a bandana. Told me to wrap it around my arm then she set it on fire. When I asked why, she said, "Because you didn't ask me which arm." And I was the one who got punished, for crying. Thanks, Uncle Jared, you're the best. And thanks, Dear Mother, for watching the whole thing and not doing shit about it.

I unload all the gun paraphernalia from my pockets into my floorboard and find my pills. Is it rude to knock myself out and leave her alone at the wheel for who knows how much longer?

I straighten up. "Hey."

She's a driving robot. Eyes locked in an uncompromising stare ahead, hands firm on the wheel.

I poke her in the arm. "Let me take over."

She points to a billboard. *Budget Motel, 5 miles ahead.*

Five miles later we're outside the office. I'm checking my shoulder wound in the car window, and she's applying the Bevan mind trick to some cash. Because wow, one glance at us, someone needs to cue the horror movie scream.

She must've done something extra to the cash because our age isn't a concern this time. In the room I let her shower first. She blows her hair dry in the tiny box of a bathroom while I shower. Privacy no longer matters after what we just did together. Then I close the heavy curtains against the rising sun, fold the bedspread back, punch the pillow down, and lie down with the bedbugs on a mattress that's more metal than cushion. If this is poverty, or even how most people live, I'm so glad I was born rich.

Sloane stands there looking at her untouched bed, physically present, mentally gone. Exhausted? Traumatized? Rethinking the whole thing? Probably all of the above. Turning onto my side to face the door, I pat the mattress behind me. "Join me?" Totally kidding.

She does.

Don't react, Rex, don't react. The weight of her there, the slightest disturbance of air. Tension has hijacked my backbone, and damn it all, there's the jerk of muscle. All she does is move in tighter as if she didn't just feel my whole body seize.

I don't dare move as she snuggles against my back because punishments and gifts coexist in my world and maybe if I pretend I'm not here, that punishment won't find me this time. I don't dare turn toward her because I'm afraid of what I'll do. And I don't dare take that pill I crave for fear of missing any second of her warm breath against my back, her knees interlocking behind mine, the pads of her toes pressing into my bare calf. Her skin, god, her skin.

"*Oíche mhaith*," I whisper, because no one's ever wished me a good night and I've always wanted to say it.

Falling asleep is a miracle and a crisis and stupidly unavoidable due to how exhausted I am.

Wakeup call: Sloane Bevan is still in my bed. It's worse now. I'm on my back. She's slung a leg over mine and has somehow traveled between my arm and me. In peaceful sleep she doesn't even look like the kind of creature that would bite a man. She used the same shampoo as me but in her hair it's rain in the mountains—fresh air, loamy soil, pine needles, dew. I've never been to the mountains though, so I need to shut up. Sensing the same fragrance on her as me corrupts my brain somehow, tricking me into thinking she's a part of me, or I'm a part of her. And what's in my shorts is completely untrained and should probably be removed from the ring before it hurts itself.

The sun drives in low from the west. I put on my sneakers outside the door and take a good look around. I'm starting to miss the food at home. Fresh fruit in the morning. Multigrain homemade bread. Steak, gourmet soup, wine. All we have out here are meals prepped in two minutes with enough salt and grease to make up for absent taste. My stomach's all about salt and grease right now with how it's started tumbling all over itself, so hey, can't argue there.

A video call comes in when I'm almost back from picking up breakfast—oh, balls. Aaron's dad. Ignore and wait for them to kick in the door or accept and deal with it now?

"Greetings and salutations, Mr. Bevan. I mean, Mr. Moore."

Christian Moore is not smiling. Which is kind of a big deal with that guy. He's always smiling. "Where's my niece?"

She's not his niece. Probably shouldn't correct him though. Everyone acts like they're not afraid of him, but they're not fooling me. He has allies on both sides and not a care in the world. The dude is a walking nightmare. "Sleeping."

"Sleeping where?"

"You don't already know?" I keep the phone close to my face so he can't gather any details from my surroundings.

"Dial down the sass, kid. Your mother's influence is showing." He waits for me to say something, but all it would do is prove him right, and I'm not giving him that. "Don't smirk, you little shit. It's not a compliment."

"Says the guy who banged her."

He laughs, big and loud, and I get the impression my last comment made him like me more, not less. Why does everything keep backfiring in my face?

"Touché. You have about two minutes to get that camera on a very happy and healthy Sloane Bevan, though, so—"

"Chill out, geezer. I'm almost there." I let myself back into our motel room. She's sitting cross-legged on the bed, shielding her eyes from the slant of light I've let in the door.

"Here, it's for you." I hand her the phone, set down the bag of food, and take a seat beside her. As her kidnapper, I have to monitor phone calls with her family. Except technically he's more my family than hers. Kind of depends on definition of family though. Blood relatives who don't give a crap about you versus distant non-blood relatives who do.

She lights up when she sees him, spelling like crazy with her hand, expression off the Sloane Bevan expression charts.

"Slow down, girly. You're gonna have to use the text."

She types, *Where are you? Can you meet us? I miss you, miss everyone so much.*

"No," I say. I go for the phone. She jabs me in the ribs.

We tried that. Didn't work out. Aaron says you're good though, are you good?

She gives a thumbs-up. Types: *Some weird stuff though.*

He looks right at me. *What kind of weird?*

Barfing up gross black liquid. Eyes hurt in any kind of light.

That sounds bad.

She nods.

I'll have to ask around.

She nods again, signs something.

Good call. I'm wondering why you'd say that, though. But we can talk later. So you're okay for sure?

Another thumbs-up.

Your dad's about to hang himself. He'll trust what I'll tell him, but I have to be certain. So answer correctly to this if you're okay. Who's your hero?

She signs something, her smile getting away from her. It breaks up that lasting exhaustion-slash-trauma from earlier, which is a good thing but makes me feel like a worthless moron.

He nods and kisses two fingers, presents them to the phone. She pretends to catch it. It kind of makes me sick. Not because I'm jealous—hell no. Not because Christian Moore is an asshole. Everyone knows that. More because she has all these people—her people—and yeah, I have people too, but no one's checking up on my health. No one would ever.

He texts, *Get back to work destroying my bloodline, then.* He covers his mouth and says, "Rex, you hurt her and it's not the Bevans you'll need to watch out for."

"Yeah, yeah, you and Aaron. I get it."

"Not us. I'll sic a black witch on you. She'll hand you a potato peeler and make you think it was your idea to skin yourself alive."

"Sounds like a party."

"Yep. I'll bring beer."

As the video goes black I'm moving onto something else: none of these people hassle her about what she's doing.

There are no demands, no orders, no questions. It's just pure trust. That's bullshit.

She's gone into the bathroom to stand before the mirror and that's bullshit too because this food I just brought back is getting cold, and I'm not getting her any more. So I get up to tell her that and catch her tugging her shirt collar down to reveal an angry blazing wound across her chest. My brain sends a sadistic throb straight to my own burn scar. "Holy oak, Sloane, when did you get that? That's—"

Bad. Emergency medical assistance bad.

That sadistic throb pulses again, head to toes this time, so hot it's cold. Not from the memory held in that scar but from the shock of understanding something new. One hand has gone to the door frame, nails digging into wood, the other to Sloane's arm to get her to look at me. "Did that woman—"

Breathing takes the controls. If it didn't, I'd be tearing through these walls to take the R5 back to D.C., find her corpse, and destroy it. Tear skin, crush bones. Set it all on fire.

"No," Sloane says, her hand on my chest.

Her voice, like her skin. So perfect it hurts.

She plucks her amulet off the sink and holds it against her chest. Makes her hand open around it, a simulated explosion.

"Fire?"

Scrunched brow, a pensive shake of the head. Almost like she can't remember.

"Heat?"

She nods, removing my hand from the door trim I've almost ripped off the wall. Okay, Rex, calm down. No need to go rabid over some imaginary attack on Sloane that needs to get out of my head because it didn't even happen. What did happen is technically the Bevans' fault. Their amulet, their own stupidity. So we're done here. Stop thinking about her burn, Rex. It has nothing to do with you.

God, what time is it? I check my phone and see a recurring calendar entry I must've missed when I cleared the rest of them. I'm hours overdue for Latin class. I leave her and go into the main room, yanking the curtain aside for some kind of distraction to the sharp lash of homesickness. My R5 waits outside, soaking up the orange glow from the sunset. It's the only piece of home I have. I ache for the return to my pain-in-the-ass schedule. For the regularity of the pills. For the mindlessness of my downtime spent reading, gaming, sitting by the lake and watching the water for hours.

I won't even fit at home until Sloane puts my brain back together. That encounter with my D.C. relatives brought a new weight to my mega load. Until today it never clicked: how much I hate them, how many things they've done to me that I simply dismissed. It's all in my face now, as glaring and present as my burn scar. And I'm not so sure I want to fit at home anymore.

Here's the point though: When I go back, it's not going to be the same. With everyone's power diminished, I'll have no reason to hate. They'll no longer have the power to do anything to me. With zero Bevans remaining, and no drain of constant war, we can all just chill.

I take the bottle of black magic out of my pocket and turn it over in my hand, watching how the magic responds to the late-day light. Slipping and twirling around itself, testing the glass, tendrils pressing against the cork. Soon I can release it. Soon this will all be over.

If I can figure out a way to shield Sloane from its Bevan-aimed beam, everything I want will be mine.

CHAPTER 23

SLOANE

T HE MOMENT THE final slice of the sun sinks below the horizon, I know. It's a strange sensation, knowing something visual when I don't even have it in my sight. My boots are still wet from being rinsed of blood in the sink, but I slide them on anyway and head outside. Rex looks up from his phone but stays slumped in the chair by the window. He must know I need a moment alone.

Because now I have a plan. A really good plan. So good, I'm afraid to tell Rex for more than one reason. He could find an unfixable hole. He could also sabotage it. But holes need to be found and sabotage has to be disregarded. We're a team, and I trust him, and he trusts me. So what's my problem?

Finality, that's it. I finally have a way to the end. The way itself is not so bad. The end? Not so pretty for me, with no options to fix it. And I don't know how to spin it to Rex so he isn't clued in. Maybe I should just straight up ask him. *You cool if I've decided to die a martyr?*

Dying as a martyr is okay if you have no one to mourn you. I have too many hearts to break.

I walk to the edge of the parking lot and step onto the dry ground, brown grass crunching under my boots. A breeze ruffles my shirt against my burned chest, still biting with sensitivity even though it's halfway healed. At least the smell never stuck. Burning flesh is a smell I'll gladly forget and take big steps to avoid forever.

Cars streak by on the road ahead, taillights blinking like a team effort when the light turns red. Street lights come alive all at once, dim at first, growing brighter. Across the road a filling station sits like a spotlight the dusk, its shiny white light contrasting against the darkening sky, making my sensitive eyes water. I'm afraid I'm turning nocturnal, and I'm not sure how to stop it.

Out here in this unfamiliar town filled with artificial light and rushing cars, I'm losing my sense of self. If I went home right now, would my family recognize me? Or have I been too changed by the things I've done? Instead of killing Rex Moore I saved him and joined him. I've hurt people. I've witnessed death and not stopped it. I've gathered hate and darkness and taken it inside my body, and I don't know what to do with it. If my blood were to run, it would swirl red mixed with shiny black. This darkness speaks to me. It justifies the awful things Rex did in that house. It tells me to do awful things.

I cover my face with my hands and think of home. My trees, the straight steeples of their trunks against the clear blue sky, their needled branches bouncing in the breeze. The snowy peaks of faraway mountains on display at Aunt Tara's. The glitter of the river, catching sunlight as it travels through the woods. The coyotes' presence all around, their wise eyes, their bristly coats brushing under my fingertips.

If I quit now, if I went home, I could have all that back. I'd be changed, but not too changed. Maybe this resident darkness inside me would slowly die, be consumed by good, be dissolved. No longer my family's warrior, I'd be their failure. I'd disappoint, but I wouldn't break their hearts.

I take in a shaky breath. Okay then. Okay. A good plan with a bad end makes a bad plan. So I cast it away. There's nothing better. All that's left is surrender, failure, hands in the air, I give.

Moths swarm above me, vying for my attention. Someone coming. I close my eyes. The moths' senses join mine to fill in details I can build into an image: upright, sturdy, focused, unthreatening to the moths because of how his eyes are so keenly set on me. Could be a stranger I suppose, but I know it's not.

Rex comes to stand beside me, eyes aimed tightly ahead like he's trying to figure out what has me so entertained. Although I haven't been crying, I've wanted to and my eyes are wet enough to smudge if I wipe them, so I blink, trying to clear the tears before he sees them. He shoves his hands deep in his pockets almost like he's shackling them so they don't do something else.

I thrill at the thought of bringing Rex home with me. So much that my heart goes a little berserk. He ducks away from the swooping moths, agitated, a carefully hidden swear on his lips. I dare them to swoop harder and they do, and now his hands are out, swatting, and I'm laughing into my hand.

If I give up, I'll have to bring him home. He has nowhere else to go. It sobers me so much a tear escapes, my breath hitching before I can catch it.

He forgets the moths and turns to me. Concern looks different on everyone. On him, it's a forehead with a deep, angry furrow. An initial flash in the eyes that softens, reaching. And crossed arms, ensuring protection from whatever is wrong. Shielding him so something doesn't accidentally seep in.

I'm done, I fingerspell. *I'm going home.*

No, he says, one slight change in his eyes moving his expression from concern to anger.

I can't do this.

He grabs my spelling hand, his eyes so hard on mine I feel a defiance rising, my instinct to fight him waking with the power it had the first night he came into my room. I make a fist with my other hand, prepping to sock him in the ribs.

He's talking now, but I can't make it out. The moths flutter behind him, and I gather the sound through them and hear the words inside me: *Not just you. We. We can do this.*

I open my held hand inside his. He interlocks his fingers with mine, rough like a restraint, not at all sweet. He says again, *We can do this.*

And I know my eyes are smudgy now because why? Why does he want to help me? My ancestors never saw this. We're walking new ground here and it's quivering under my feet. I don't know which step will be solid and which will sink. Each little move either one of us makes could lead to miracle or disaster. It seems safer right now just to stand still.

With a finger he brushes my hair off my cheek. A move he initiated yet he still has to subdue that touch-me-not shudder. Anger lingers in his eyes but they've been touched by something sparking and electric, something ripe to explode.

I should look away. Looking away would discourage his next predicted move: a kiss. My move is to not look away. Where we're headed, miracle or disaster, right now it doesn't really matter. His anger tempered by that spark, my defiance softened by that hot trail left by his finger on my cheek. The mixture coils heavy between us, and that thing sparking in him is arcing toward me.

The thought returns like a rush of storm wind—home, surrender, failure. And him, abandoned with nowhere to go.

I turn away, expelling that kiss. His fingers, still inter-locked with mine, loosen. He ducks his head, rubbing a hand against his hair. Distance cleaves between us as if dropped from the sky.

I want to give up.

I want to take him home with me. For my dad and aunt not to kill him. To show him my everlasting Rockies, my hallowed trees. Introduce him to my dogs, my coyotes, my deer. Prove to him that love exists in families, and it can exist for him. I want him to laugh at Marcas' nonsensical jokes, drink tea with my mom and Grandma Sloane on the back porch while the sun tucks itself behind our mountain. I want him to be loved.

He's squinting at me now, closed off, suspicious. His head tilted like he's gauging my degree of danger or scoping out a way into my thoughts.

My memory of the day my dad explained my place in the world looks completely different in the dusky light of a different day's sun. I now see how his caged anger made his ASL careless. The tightness in his face. And the weight of it all, so visible on him, being transferred to me. And how he held my face and kissed my forehead like he knew I'd survive it anyway, no matter how grim the whole thing sounded. His trust in me backed up by the trust of our ancestors I felt that day and sense now like a hand on my shoulder.

"I have a plan," I say. Not ASL, not fingerspelling, but real words, and I have no idea how they got out.

He's taken a step back. My level of danger must've just reached threatening levels.

He opens his palms as if to say, *Enlighten me.* Part of reading lips is knowing what the person is about to say and if he'd have spoken, that's what he would've said.

Millennia of crimes won't be left unavenged due to my surrender. It's not even vengeance I'm after, but peace. I will see this to the end, even if the darkness takes me over. Even if I break underneath it. Even if I become as hate-filled as the Moores, I'll keep their gathered nastiness inside, let it devour me. I won't let it get away from me, let it become words and deeds, let it make me one of them.

I turn and walk to our motel room door. He follows me inside. I'm momentarily blinded by all the glaring bulbs; I take hold of the door frame to anchor myself as I turn my face away, scrambling for the switch. Rex slides his phone into my hand. I blink at the screen.

Is the light that bad or are you clowning?

I reply, *It's bad. Getting worse.*

He hands me the aviators. I shake my head because it's not that bad—yet. I swipe into his texts to see if Christian replied and find nothing new.

Telling Rex my plan means explaining that dark entity that lives in his house, the house we just cleared, and hopefully every Moore home we'll visit. So I launch right into it, not checking him once while I pound it out on his phone. I don't know what I expect to see when I look up, but it's certainly not that jerkwad mocking grin or his rude disbelief.

Is that some kind of Bevan superstition?

We aren't superstitious. If I glare at him harder, maybe he'll burst into flames.

He laughs. It's bold and obnoxious and jarring in the way it changes his whole face. I can't decide if it's meant to make me feel stupid or if I just do.

We only believe in proven things.

So you've proven there's a cloud of fuel for black magic hanging inside every Moore home?

I've seen it myself. In both of them.

You used it on me.

Yes. And when I used it yesterday, my amulet reacted and burned me. I can't wear it anymore. The next time it might do more than burn me.

He puts both hands on his head and turns away. His fingers grip like they're threading through invisible hair. I can see the movement in his jaw, so I check the screen.

Sounds like you need to install the black witch mod on your amulet.

Would be nice. Perfectly accessible solutions like that only exist in Rex Moore's world, and I guess I should remind him he's been transported out of Spoiled Rich Kid Land. Even if there was a way to adjust it, the magic encased in my amulet is so old I wouldn't dare touch it myself. I lift the amulet over my head and hold it out to him. If I have to draw any more black magic, it will try to protect me not knowing it's protecting me from myself. It'll expend power unnecessarily, hurting me in the process. It's of more use to him now than me.

He's speaking when he faces me again, but I don't check the screen because he's cut himself off at the sight of what I'm offering.

I stand. He lifts a hand to hold me back. I point to the healing gunshot wound in his shoulder and tilt my head toward the amulet. This amulet would've protected him from that and more.

Hell no, he says.

I've backed him to the wall now, and he's just waiting there to see what I'll do. Defy him, or wait for his permission. Well, he's never going to willingly accept a gift of an ancient relic created by Bevan trash. It's a violation to him only because of his ridiculous bias. If he'd get over that, he'd understand our magic is the same as his. It's the Moores who chose to forget their magic and condemn us for doing what's necessary to keep it alive. They thought their money and violence was enough, and they were wrong.

It'd be nice if he'd bow his head so I could put it on easily, but no. He gets off on this running power struggle between us. The resistance, the submission. I see his eyes go lusty, a lick of his bottom lip. So I tilt my face up, rise on my toes to close the distance. All he has to do is lean down—he does. I slide the amulet over his head and press my lips against his as soon as the cord is past his chin. I clasp a hand around it so it warms before settling against him as he tangles his fingers in my hair, dipping down, greedy for more of this fooling around when I said I would stop this. It's a distraction. A curse. Nothing good will come of it. I shove away.

He knows the amulet is there, but the intensity of his eyes on mine proves he's avoiding a glance down to confirm it. He wipes his mouth with the back of his hand. *It was worth it*, is what that motion says. *You win, but so did I.*

I fingerspell, *Pervert.*

He releases a smile, the one with the dimple that goes straight to my head like a blow to the temple. This is why making out with Rex Moore is bad. It creates a drumming of my heart over a cute smile instead of what I should be concerned about: life and death. The end of an ancient war. Stealing all the Moores' hate one person at a time, consuming it, praying to the elements I find a way to partition it from the good in me so it doesn't take over until there's nothing recognizable left.

Hey, he's saying. *Sloane.*

It looks like anger, but I know better. It's concern.

Sorry, I sign. Because I am. Even if he liked the trick, I shouldn't have done it.

He signs it back. *Sorry.*

Does he know what that means? I pick up his phone to tell him, but I can't do it. Can't ruin the magic of this. He's picking up ASL almost like he wants to, and I can't determine if he's playing me in some way or if he truly wants to speak my language. It's another crisis when I have too many to deal with already.

He points to the phone so I'll look at the screen. *This fucking amulet is worse than the Bevan war paint.*

I go to him and tuck it inside his T-shirt. Type a reply: *No one has to see it.*

They'll see it.

Not with the plan I have. So I take his hand and tug him to the bed, pushing him down and taking a seat on the opposite bed to face him. *We'll use that cloud hanging inside every Moore house. It's a part of them all. I'll cast a Bevan sleeping spell and tie it to that cloud.*

He puts both hands on his knees and leans toward me. *You're gonna patch an earth magic sleeping spell into the cloud of black magic fuel and it's supposed to put everyone in the house to sleep?*

Yes. And then we move in. You do the bloodletting, I do the brain sucking.

He laughs so hard he chokes. It's almost contagious, but I hold a breath until it passes. I fear if I give in, I'll go into hysterics. I have too much death on my conscience to let the slightest pebble slip underfoot. That's all it would take to get me sliding down, buried alive by all that we've done. Distance will help me cope, I just need to keep it.

Maybe you should do the bloodletting too, he says when he recovers. *I don't think I can handle surface wounds. All I know is killing.*

It takes effort not to roll my eyes. *Be serious.*

You saw what happened back there.

Okay, maybe he's right. Once again, I see that *whoops* on his lips after dropping that unsalvageable woman in that puddle of blood. If that wasn't genuine, then nothing that comes out of his mouth ever is. And I know that's not the case. It can't be. I've seen him toy with me. I've seen him be real. I know the difference.

I better know the difference, or I'm heading toward a worse disaster than the one I've planned.

CHAPTER 24

REX

SOMEHOW THE GIRL convinces me to drive her back to the house where we just slaughtered my people. She says there's belladonna growing near the house, and she needs it for her sleeping spell. Halfway to the R5 I realize it must've been some evil Bevan mind trick because I have the spotty memory to go along with it. All I remember is her pleading eyes and her cheeks still rosy from having kissed me. Another trick, that kiss, come to think of it.

I'm the biggest sucker virgin piece of shit Bevan slave. How did this happen?

The midnight sky spans above us. Legit stars galore. I take a good look before I unlock the R5 because it could be my final look. Every look could be. My family will have some serious guns on us as soon as they get any hint of us or the R5, and we're about to return to our last known position. My final look could be any second of any day from now until the end.

This motel is so remote I see the clustering of the Milky Way banding across the sky just like it does at home. It's hard to resist staring. To think myself back there, to my before, to my sweet ignorance. That shiny bliss of anticipation, knowing someday I'd kill Sloane Bevan and score all the cred that goes along with it. Sloane's eyes are on me like she's wondering what I'm so interested in.

"*Claí Mór na Réaltaí*." A test to see if she can lip read Irish. What else do we call the Milky Way? Oh, right. "Or how 'bout, *An Láir Bhán*?"

She extends a hand, fingers curling in a *gimme gimme* for my phone. I open the doors to the R5 and we get in. I hand her the phone and say, "You wanna drive?"

Headshake. No indication of knowing I was saying something else. It seems like something I could use against her, but in what context? And why, Rex? Why be such a shitwipe?

I start the car and scroll through the music on my phone. I know I have something goth-girl would like if she could hear, like some dark synthy doom metal or no—psychill. The one with the slowed-down drum and bass and dubstep added in. I find it and raise the volume. She stiffens in her seat when the bass kicks in, lips parted, a hand on the door like she can't decide if she should jump ship or brace herself. She freezes like that, concentrating like she can hear it. There's no way, right? Supposedly she's the deafest you can be, at least that's what I was told. She reaches for the volume, but instead of turning it down like most people would when assaulted with this dope shit, she turns it up, past brain-melting level. Now those thick vibrating synths have turned heart-murdering. I wait for the bass drop. It steamrolls through me, a thorough gutting—I jump like an idiot to her hand snapping onto my forearm.

"You can hear that?" I can't hear my own voice.

She puts a hand against her chest, the other on her abdomen. She can feel it.

And I have to look away. The idea that my music has rolled through her body—it's so hot, so sexual, and fuck it, we have to get out of this parking lot before this noise wakes the entire motel. I turn onto the road to a soundtrack of crunchy, metallic synth and body-blanketing bass that shows off my ten-thousand-dollar audio setup in the sweetest way. As soon as we stop, I'm going to ask her how much of this she's getting, like, only the bass? Some of the mids? Any treble? I'm not lowering the volume to ask now because I'm feeling way too much like a little boy. Get a grip, Rex, you stupid virgin. You slave to Sloane Bevan.

I regret nothing.

I take a cloverleaf fast, feeling the Gs, and she's raised her arms to shoulder-dance to music she might not hear but can definitely feel, completely unselfconscious, as if it's just her and my two twelves thumping away. And this— what is this? Happiness? I must be a virgin to that too, but not anymore as of like two minutes ago because my face is about to explode from smiling, and this girl.

This girl.

I think I might die for this girl.

Because we're stupid, I pull onto the street of the D.C. house full of bodies we murdered and park at the curb. She consulted a swarm of bats two blocks away and according to them, the house is quiet and unburdened by the living. Completely solid coming from bats.

Then she's got my hand, and we're sprinting among shadows and scaling the stone wall into the backyard. She leads me to a garden plot where we pick plants until we can't hold any more, and then we're tearing back to the car, no regard for stealth this time. She snags a small metal pail on our way; water splashes our feet as it swings into her hand. In the car I dump my stash into her lap, jam the gearshift into first, and peel away. The shriek of rubber and whining turbo so loud, so conspicuous. So golden.

I drive into the city. Buildings packed around us, cars whooshing by, a skyline from a movie. We're in a street racing game without all the crashes. The busy life of the city invades the car through the windows; too soon we're driving out the other side. Light pollution turns to inky night. I voice command my audio system to play a favorite song, years old but more relevant now than it's ever been. And I'm not sure I'll be able to take it if she hates it. Its sexy synth groove fills the car. She's nodding along and what it does to me—damn. I open the window for air. There's no relief—the sticky summer moisture charges her scent, swirls it around me. She smells like midnight, like cool air that calms the head and heart. Like the breeze across the lake at home when the house sleeps behind me. Like freedom, like an unwind. I'm glad she can't hear the lyrics because I'm pretty sure this is a love song and it would give away too fucking much.

In this car with her time is on hold. As long as we keep driving we can stay like this forever. And when this song is over I'm going to be as deaf as her.

Another state park somewhere in Maryland, another park vehicle access road. Sloane cloaks the R5, and we hike into the woods, silencing insects and frogs as we pass by. My pills scream louder though. My schedule has been so disrupted I don't know if I need an upper or a downer and the desperation is telling me to take both. I finger the pill case in my pocket while Sloane organizes the plants we swiped into separate piles.

I finger the bottle of black magic.

"So, are we just going to be nocturnal now?" I curb my compulsion to check the time. It doesn't matter, Rex. Settle down.

She doesn't look up from her work.

Reality creeps up behind me, a gross presence, an unwelcome tap on the shoulder. Even if I figure out a way to shield her from death when I break open this bottle, she won't forgive me for killing her entire family. It's never been so exhausting trying to figure out how to get everything I want. Usually I just get it. Sometimes without asking.

She waves me over. Time for a magic lesson. I'm not in the mood, but if I tell her that she's not going to care. She'll win, and I don't feel like being a loser right now, so I drop down beside her and give her my full attention. Or my best exhibit of it. There's so much in my head right now and my pills want me so badly I wouldn't be surprised if they broke out of the pill case and climbed into my mouth themselves.

Belladonna and lavender, ground into fine dust and added to water inside the pail. Three smooth stones dropped in. Then she takes my phone, and when she returns it she's written a long string of Irish, every *fada* painstakingly typed which is no easy feat on a phone. She must think I won't understand it unless it's perfect.

She points to my mouth.

"You want me to read this?" Because she can't speak or because she wants me to do it? Rex Moore, painted with Bevan war paint, wearing their amulet, now reciting their spells. It's a sure way to buy an execution from my family instead of a life sentence of being chained in one of those old shacks. Since I'd rather have the execution, I read it. She points to the screen when I'm finished.

"Read it again?"

The second time isn't so harmless. A pulse unlike mine builds in my ears, an echo of the background forest noise becoming almost musical. I falter; Sloane reaches, her hand on my arm like an amp for the music, a touch that should've triggered a flinch but for the first time, nothing. She gestures for me to read it a third time. Now the music isn't just coming from around us but through us like the bass in my car. And that pulse is no longer unlike mine. It is mine. It's hers. It's the earth, the trees, the sky. All life around us joined.

I look at my hands, fearing my body is converting into magic itself, that I'm turning to soil, decomposing into the forest floor, absorbed. I'm no longer a single being but a part of something huge. A single leaf, a grain of dirt, powerless on my own but connected to so much raw power stretching so wide and vast it's overwhelming. I've lost myself but this space proves what a liability my singular body is—how fragile, how tiny on its own. I was so alone before. I was alone always. I'm no longer alone.

The next breath I take returns me to my own form, my arms and legs, my skin, my pounding heart.

"Fuck." It's like a first word after years of silence. I decide too late I should say something nicer. "Balls." Great, Rex, that's great.

I take in the outline of branches ahead of me, the lighter night sky beyond. The shimmer of stars create so much light I'm not looking into the night sky but a depth of endless purple. "Bunnies, kittens, rainbows—shit." Perception shifts due to a sudden awareness of gravity, bringing attention to the plank of ground under my back, and I sit up, my vision readjusting to accommodate what's really up versus what's really down like I'm waking from a KO. I flex my fingers, relieved they don't crumble into loam. I stretch out my backbone, gulping a lungful of air.

What I can do with my fists and elbows, a knife, a gun— it's nothing. The ready power all around me, sitting idle, waiting to be used … no wonder my family wants all the Bevans dead. No wonder the Bevans think just one of their kind can take down all of us. The big question is why the Bevans don't fully use this. Don't abuse it. They'd have won this war a long time ago. I'd probably have never been born. My parents, grandparents, every Moore snuffed out centuries ago.

It's not something I'll ever ask Sloane, but I turn to her anyway as if I can. It takes a frantic moment to find her. She's on her back like a corpse, eyes closed, palms flat against the forest floor. Ferns curl around her body as if she's been there years not seconds. She's just another piece of debris, a fallen log, a weathered stone.

All at once the spell words make sense. The essence of our sudden sleep, now captured in those stones in the pail, waiting for release on someone new.

The Baltimore house is an alternate reality version of the D.C. one. Same historic neighborhood with boring luxury sedans tucked underneath porches that probably used to hold carriages. I've convinced Sloane to bring a firearm this time. Of everything I brought, she went for the most boring and practical Glock. We had to stop to buy a shoulder holster that would fit her. She's stashed that straight razor in her stretchy silver armband, extra mags in her cargo pockets. I can't decide if working alongside her like this is a dream or a nightmare.

We split up this time because her animal allies reported two armed guards—one at the front, one at the rear. I take the guy at the front by surprise and knock him out. She made me pinky swear not to kill him. And as I'm hog-tying his limbs with the duct tape I brought, I'm laughing that my family could ever think two armed guards would stop us.

I take a pic of the front of the house, part souvenir, part log entry. And it will be nice to have a visual of everything I own once this is all done.

Following our plan, I test the downspout for its ability to hold my weight and climb, spidering over the decorative wood inside the gable and meeting Sloane on the roof over the opposite side. In the wall under the roof overhang she's found a vent she lifts easily out of its frame. A moment of silence, her bowed head. And I'm rewarded with a big smile.

"It's in there?" I mouth, not believing this can be so easy.

A thumbs-up. The cloud of black magic fuel is here. A wind rushes up the side of the roof. She ducks down to gather balance; I readjust my feet. She points to a little window off another peak in the roof and then dives into the vent, sliding in, her boots disappearing before I can stop her. I've unconsciously reached, throwing off my balance which can't be righted until I've slipped a few feet down the roof. The rush is to die for. I stay in position, one leg stretched, the other bent, all my weight reliant on a tiny lip of shingle caught under the edge of my boot's tread. I'm dangling so close to death all it would take is the slightest shift of weight. I let my feet slip a little just to feel it again.

Sloane's face pops into the little window she pointed at earlier. I crawl to it as she slides it open soundlessly. Someday she'll have to tell me how a deaf girl learned to move in such silence. I climb in and hop down, knees absorbing the fall. The room appears unused. A stack of boxes, cobwebs, dust. She leaves the window open and sneaks to a door, turning to look at me over her shoulder. She must sense I haven't followed.

I'm stuck in place. She's confident in that magic. She thinks this is going to be routine, but I'm reliving the gore from last time. I'm watching the bodies fall. I have a fistful of hair, a finger pressing the trigger. I'm slipping in blood, getting the spray on my face, my mouth. I'm wiping it away, feeling the smear across my skin, tasting it. Another killing spree is the only way this can go again. Bevan magic is powerful, yes, but there are ten people in this house. We can't count on them all being plugged into that dark cloud.

Will ten more bodies make a difference to my family after all I've already done? Not a chance. Will they make a difference to me? Depends on whether I'm going to admit what I'm feeling right now is a conscience. If the whisper of chill in my bones is imaginary or real. If the old Rex wants to stomp it out, replace it with the hate I've been taught, the ground-in duty I'd rather die than disown. Or if the new Rex wants to accept it, let that whisper of choice color the things I do.

She's come to me, her pupils so big and glossy I wonder how they see me. If she sees the old Rex or the new one. If she likes either one as much as I like her. I brace myself against her approaching touch. She puts both hands on my chest. Her heat transfers through my shirt. A new heat fires up between them—the amulet. Strange. Not sure if I should be concerned about that. Hopefully this thing never malfunctions. Hopefully it's still not trying to protect her from me. Having it strung around my neck might be a bad idea.

She pats my chest twice, demanding attention. Then she draws an invisible symbol on her forehead, then mine. Two hands, cutting the air horizontally as if to say, *that's it*. Two thumbs up. A smile.

I can't stop myself from tracing the lines of her war paint on her cheeks, her chin. If I die in there, this is the image I want to revive while I bleed out. Her pale face tipped up to me in the dim light, framed by those perfectly screwed-up bangs. The trust in her eyes. Her confidence in me. Her patient acceptance of someone she should hate. And how it's rewired me. If I don't die before this is over, she's going to put me back how I was, severing all the new wires, twisting them onto old ones. This new Rex is temporary no matter which happens first.

She's frowning now. She's captured my hand and placed it over her heart, and I decide working alongside her is in fact a nightmare. I'm so close but I can never have her. I've made a new home inside her beating heart, but I can't stay there, not for much longer. And I could never bring her to the home I plan to reclaim even if she'd let me. She's the first thing in my life I can't have; she's the only thing I've ever needed.

All this—it's just noise. I need to shut up and move.

So I yank my hand from her and head to the door. She slips around me to lead us to a staircase we descend. An old clock stands at the bottom, ticking away. She's stopped to search her pockets, so I stare at the shiny brass hands of the clock, fully knowing I shouldn't but it's like that extra slip on the roof. I have to do it, just to feel what it's like.

Then she's grabbing my hand, and I don't know why I'm fighting her until I'm looking at the pill that just flew from my hand to the floor. She crushes it with the heel of her boot.

I'm not a slave to Sloane Bevan but to my own family. They made me like this. They taught only what I'd need to avenge them while keeping me ignorant of my missing connection to magic. They got me addicted to pills they crafted to control my sleep and wake cycle. I'm a thing to use. To use up.

She has a twisty grip on my shirt, an expression that both asks if I'm okay and demands I get it together. I raise both hands and mouth, "I'm cool."

I'm so not cool.

She takes one of the sleeping stones from her pocket and raises it high, eyes closed. Her breath releases in a whoosh. A shudder runs the length of her. I'm primed to reach and yank her away from whatever seems to be possessing her, but then she lowers that stone to the floor in slow motion and steps away from it like it's a landmine. Her index finger points to the rooms beyond. Time for the fun.

CHAPTER 25

SLOANE

THE FIRST BEDROOM we enter holds a couple sleeping in a bed. Instead of seeing them, I see Rex's burn scar. I see those caged doves. Closing my eyes, I imagine my dad as a kid, chained in that old shack on the Moores' land.

I point at the woman. Rex is ripping a piece of duct tape off the roll with his teeth. He slaps it over her mouth and rips another one for the man. Neither stirs, not even a hitch of breath. The dark cloud of hate is like a conduit between my black magic and my sleeping spell, the cloud fueling my black magic which then fuels my spell. It's such saturated power I worry these people will never be conscious again.

Rex stands back to assess them, laying a hand on the handle of his .45. He must be like me and expects them to leap up because there's no way this is so easy. Then I see the troubled glare, the sideways shift of his jaw. That hate was at one time directed at me, and I remember what he did to try to alleviate it.

So I flip my straight razor open and walk to the bed. Where to cut her? Palm. Her blood oozes onto the sheet. I paint her forehead and mine. As soon as the second symbol is complete there's a rush through me, a rearrangement of atoms. I'm not just harboring a taste of black magic, I'm made of it. I've turned molten and charged. I thought I'd need these people awake to cure them but no, I sense her corruption there. I feel it drawing toward me, magnetic and alive. My forehead against hers and I'm lost in time, just for a moment, and then it's there, in my head, falling down into my chest, taking form around the original lump I stole from Rex.

Next victim. His head lolls off the pillow when I'm drawing the symbol; Rex comes to my side to hold him straight. Again, I'm snatched into new space then back again, returning heavier, lopsided like the balance of my magic has been tipped. Unfit for my own body until I swallow it down, match it to what I've already gathered.

One after the other they go down, room after room. The hate I'm collecting starts to fade, not away, but in. Fleshing me out in a foreign but expected way. Pushing out existing parts of me to make room. And I don't know what Rex's problem is, but if he doesn't clear that glare from his face I'm going to make *him* bleed.

Should that be a shocking thought? It seems it should, but right now it's just admitting the truth.

We finish off a guy who must've fallen asleep on the sofa with the TV on. Either that or my sleeping spell ruined his movie. I'm too bloated on hate to put any thought into seeing Rex screwing on his suppressor. Then he's blowing the guys brains out and I'm blind from the terrible flash. My vision is made of liquid green spots, but I manage to grab Rex by the arm anyway.

He shakes me off. I chase him into the room we just finished, but I'm too slow—he's stuck a knife in the neck of the man we already fixed and now he's twisting it, watching the blood spray onto his forearm like he's not even here. I already cured Rex. What's gotten into him?

I yell his name. He jerks upright, dropping the knife like it's just cut him. I snatch it up—why, I'm not sure. Evidence? We've left plenty of that already. I find his hand and tug and we're running. Down the hall, the stairs, out into the air. If I don't leave now the dark cloud will drink me up. I don't know how to block it, and right now, I'm not sure I want to.

A couple blocks later we're hopping into Rex's car. Five minutes on the road I make him pull over so I can throw up. If someone told me it was demon blood I'm vomiting, I'd believe them. There's no relief this time. My body has become a host for a concentrated mass of hate, and I don't know what to do with it.

It's okay. Sloane, it's okay.

I see the words but I don't believe them. Where are we?

His hands, strong against my jaw, tilting my face up toward him. I sag, but he's holding me up. He seems very interested in my eyes. Am I crying? He smears thumbs against my cheeks. Yes, I must be crying. I close my eyes, feel the tears squeeze out, his arm hooking around my neck, his warmth against me. A connection—so faint, just a trace. The simple act of recognition taxes me, sending it spiraling away.

Rex shifts against me like he's bracing his feet for an oncoming blow, his arms still tight around me. And again, that connection, stronger this time. The forest—it's near. Here. Life, movement. Creatures moving in, curious, helpful. I take in a missing breath. Scented by pines, it cripples me with longing for home. I reach for it, finding a different kind of home. The swirl of breeze chilling my arms. The steady comfort of the earth beneath my feet. Above me, the expanse of limbs and leaves, the stars and sky beyond.

I push away from him. His face is drawn with an angry determination others might mistake for panic. It's the mark of control he's found, not lost. He tapped into the elements and brought them to me so I could locate myself again.

I sign, *Thank you.*

He nods. He knows that one.

Two dead, though. We weren't supposed to kill anyone this time. And he did it for no good reason. I hold up two fingers, certain he'll know exactly what I mean.

Sorry, he says, looking away. He runs two rough swipes over his head then looks back at me. Hands me his phone to say, *No, actually I'm not sorry. I hate those people. I'll kill them all.*

Anger comes so fast and hard I'm overcome by vertigo. I shove the phone back at him. Typing isn't a solution for this moment. The computer voice could never do the words right.

No more killing, I sign. *I don't care what they've done to you. You're too good to have that kind of blood on your hands, and if you think it's going to solve anything, then you're not their king, you're their fool.* I think I imagined it all. He has to be too good for that sick stunt I witnessed, just has to. I can't like a boy who can kill people that mechanically.

He watches me blankly.

I reenact his knife jab and twist into that guy's throat.

Still no reaction.

I point to him and fingerspell, *Fool.*

His response comes from a mouth too tight to read, along with three vicious steps toward me so he's close enough to shove. That's what he wants. Knowing a non-reaction will deprive him, I simply stand my ground.

He points to me and fingerspells, *Naïve.*

I point to him and fingerspell, *Callous.*

He points to himself. *Realistic.*

Coward, I reply. And too weak to face whatever troubles he lives with due to those people. Killing them is the easy way to overcome it. Well, that's the coward's way, and he knows it.

Both his hands go to fists, and I've already squashed my reflex to dodge. Let him hit me. It'll prove what I need to learn the hard way: Rex Moore is an unsalvageable monster

I need to run far away from once we're finished curing his family. I obviously can't figure it out on my own. He's tearing me up with that glare though, and I'm giving it right back. What I'm holding inside me is more toxic than anything he could summon. It's releasing like a slow drip, a terrifying promise of something so unlike me it makes my teeth chatter.

He turns and stalks away. I let him get ahead but have no choice but to follow. I have no clue how we got into these woods or where his car is. I'm missing time. I think I'd gotten lost in it, or out of it, and Rex brought me back. Thanking him doesn't seem to cover it, but there's nothing more to do, and definitely nothing I want to do now.

He passes motel after motel before I realize he's following the interstate signs to Philadelphia. That's our next address on the list. The exit ramp we take is too far outside of Philadelphia to see the city skyline. We cruise past 24-hour quick shops and drugstores lit like night will never end before taking a road protected by two elegant white oaks, thick trunks forking into several V's, exposed roots twisting from the ground. When I see a tall iron fence sprout beside the road, I know we're in for another palace on acres of land like Rex's house.

He notices the fence not long after I do, slowing to the side of the road to give it a full analysis. The sun is due up soon—the eastern sky has already begun to lighten. This is a bad idea. He knows as well as I do. He's going to power ahead though, to prove some stupid point I doubt I'd understand even if he explained it to me. And I'm going to go along with it so I can see this stupidity fail and prove my own point: We're only successful as a team. One that agrees on strategy. One that communicates. One without egos.

Without a look at me, he kills the engine and gets out. We gear up like we did hours ago. I cloak the car. He climbs a nearby ash, swings off a high limb onto the top of a brick fence pillar then slides down the iron bar on the inside. Of course the filthy rotten jerk doesn't wait for me. He disappears into the woods on the other side of the fence as I scope out trees I can climb. The one he used won't work for me. The branches are too far apart for my shorter height. Once I got up in it, I wouldn't be able to reach the one that will get me high enough to land on the brick pillar.

I walk the fence and find a low spot under one section where an animal must've dug underneath. The earth is still loose from its powerful claws. I find a tree branch and dig more. After squeezing under the iron bars and popping out on the other side I feel a breeze down my ribs and see I've ripped a hole in the back of my shirt. Rex'll be paying for that. I'll have to start a tab because this house is going to cost him.

The crows are restless in the trees, ready for their morning meals. They swoop down, teasing me. I ask for aid: one to find and lead me to Rex, another to check out the house ahead. Help finding Rex isn't necessary though. His tracks are bold and uncovered, either left that way so I could easily follow or left carelessly and irresponsibly because he's on a mission of stupidity. I guess it could also be both.

I don't catch up until the forest edge where he's stopped in the shadows to watch the house. Across a dewy clipped field sits a modern mansion, built outward instead of upward, a sprawl of clean white brick and walls of pristine glass, darkened by the house's sleeping innards. It won't be for long though. Even if rich people can sleep in, their staff won't. And if they live on the grounds like they do at Rex's house, then someone's bound to be starting breakfast right now.

This is stupid on steroids. As if reading my mind, Rex pops a pill and swallows it dry. Because that's going to make this go so much better. The only person on this land I want to kill right now is him. I'll take his phone, his car key, and finish off the list myself.

He takes off across the field. I brace myself for flying bullets, for his prone bloodied corpse. Once he steps under the closest eave, I follow in a sprint, not taking my chances against no cover and the rising sun and those black windows that could light up at any moment. We find a side door unlocked. Which probably means someone is up and about, but Rex moves ahead like he owns the place. In an inner hallway he looks straight at me for the first time since I called him a coward. It dawns on me then, what this is. He's out to prove he's not a coward. To me and to himself. And he's totally missed the point.

Inner coward. That's what I should've said. *Emotional coward.* I'm tempted to grab him and write it on his arm in the warrior markings right now, but I notice how faded they are. I check mine. Also faded. I don't know how much a problem that is, if it's a breach in our protection, or if it's just a missed formality. My family just told me to do it. They never told me why.

Too much hesitation earns me a jab in the shoulder from Rex. I restrain myself from jabbing his jerk ass back. He motions above us, asking if the cloud of hate is here. I nod. I don't even need to search for it this time. It's already extending toward me, hungry for me, anxious for a path to affect more minds and spread like a disease. It thinks I'm here to enable it, not capture and cage it.

I draw a sleeping stone from my pocket and hook it into the cloud, black magic rooting me into wooden floorboard and concrete foundation and into soil like a toxin. Once it's filled me to the brim, I give a nod to Rex. Go, genius, and pray to the elements your people are in their rooms and not sitting down for breakfast. I can't be sure how this would work on people not already asleep or drowsy. It seems there'd be a bit more fuss.

He leads me to a first door—empty of people. Another— also empty, but the bed is unmade and the lamp on the side table is on so we cross the threshold. He closes the door and ducks into the bathroom. Out he drags a limp man with shaving cream on half his face and a wicked cut on the other side probably created when my spell took hold. Convenient for me, though. I use the blood to draw the symbol on his forehead and mine. Pure liquid hate and anger cascades into me; I can't breathe until I've gathered it, squashed it onto the mass I already carry. Rex binds the man's wrists and ankles and leaves him on the bathroom floor, turning off the bedside lamp as we leave the room.

After the third victim, I stumble under the weight of the darkness I'm gathering. Finished with the fourth, I actually fall to my knees. Rex's face is close to mine when he lifts me, and I can't admit the new degree of my anger toward him. It's combined with the rest of it, been corrupted, powered beyond possibility, too strong to stomach. So I close my eyes and think about that first time he signed. His shy smile, the real one, turning toward the cover of the unseeing car door. How he shivers when I pet his head. His dimple.

My eyes focus on his. He asks, *You good?*

I nod.

He locates more unconscious bodies, and I pack more hate onto the mass I already own. We've finished the final person when Rex lays a quick hand on my shoulder to hold me still, one ear tilted toward the window. He walks against the wall to peek out onto the yard two stories below us. *Shit*, he says, counting on his fingers, raising the final number of seven to me.

The clump of hate inside me pulses, both hot and cold, liquid but hardening, turning me inside out. I'm swollen with it, nausea spooling up so fast I'm afraid if I give in to it I'll vomit out my life itself. And thinking about it makes it worse. The act of holding back the nausea is too much—a tendril of the hateful mass escapes, leaking from its container. Contaminant spreads, numbing my chest, lighting a new thought in my brain: why not just kill all seven? It would be easy. They deserve it.

No—that's not me. It's that mass of hate speaking. And yes it would be easy, but Rex and I don't do easy. We do right.

I point out the window, needing confirmation. Seven people outside? All awake?

He's too busy checking the ammo in his .45 to answer. And if seven of them are coming from the front lawn, how many are coming from the rear? It's growing harder to keep my balance and not give in to the disaster I've accepted inside my body with no idea how to handle it. I can't rest until we get out of here though, so I take off, sensing him follow. Out a rear window the morning sun has woken the eastern lawn with a slant of light. Four—no, five—long lean shadows gather near the back door.

Moores? I fingerspell to Rex, hoping he'll see it as a question.

He shakes his head. Points out the window, then to the front of the house, holds up his hand formed like an O. Okay, so zero Moores left. All we need to do is escape.

CHAPTER 26

REX

THREE GO DOWN before Sloane makes me stop shooting. She's not doing the saint act anymore. She looks more like she's about to jerk the .45 out of my hand and use it on me. "Okay, how else do you plan on getting out of here?"

Perfectly accurate shots that disable but don't kill, that's how, and I didn't even see her unholster that Glock. A knee here, a butt cheek there, overcoming distance with a handgun like she's enabled some cheats. Then I spot a familiar face.

I was wrong about there being no Moores left.

She's caught me looking at the guy. I'm trying to remember where he fits into my family tree and how many extra years I'll add to my sentence if I kill him. He's older than my father by a generation or more, probably has some sick amount of power he's spent a lifetime gathering. He's not from this household though, so he was either here for a visit or he's come just for us. Well, Rex, decision time. Kill him, blame it on Sloane. Disable him so Sloane can do her thing and run. Or just shoot myself in the head right now and never have to think about anything ever again.

She elbows me. By now the ones we haven't taken down will have entered the house, made it up the stairs. I do some quick math: three left, plus the Moore. I hold up three fingers which she shakes her head to, holding up four of her own to correct me. I hold up one more. In the moment it takes to register on her face, I know I could just pretend I counted wrong, that yeah, he's just another guy, and oops, headshot, totally didn't mean that, but what's done is done so let's beat it outta here. But I can't lie to her, not now, not ever. So I fingerspell, *Moore*.

An emotion I've never seen on her fills her eyes: defeat. Along with exhaustion that slumps her head and shoulders, sends her swaying toward the wall. I grab her arm, stick the .45 in my waistband and get hold of her other arm. Give her a shake so she looks into my eyes. She's nearly limp, fading under the consumption of the dark matter—it's evident in her pupils, now even more impossibly massive, and the heat of the amulet against my skin shielding me from the walking mass of radioactive hate she's drawn inside herself.

"I'll just kill him, then."

She shakes her head so weakly I fear I've just caused her to use up the last bit of her real human strength.

"Okay, then one more. You can do one more." I release her.

She pops out her mag for a reload, but her hands are shaking so much she drops it and the Glock on the floor. I catch her before she goes down with it. She's coughing as I get her upright; she pushes me away to puke against the wall. I'm not going to look. I know what it is. And I think I'm on my own here because she'll be a liability more than a help until I can get her out of here so she can figure out how to cope with this or get rid of it.

One of the stairs creaks from down the hall. I take a spot next to the doorway and take out the first guy with an elbow to the face. As he falls I clasp his head and twist—whoops, shouldn't do that. Too late though. I look at Sloane—she's reloaded, sitting with the Glock rested on an upright knee, aiming at the doorway.

"Rex, I'm willing to talk." It comes from the hall outside. "Off the record. Your household doesn't have to know."

I laugh—not sure why. Nothing's funny here. "There is no record, fucker. But send the rest in, because we aren't done yet."

"*We?*" It's not a word but an assault. Proof of his ill intent. An offer of truce followed by shots fired. Is every single member of my family this two-faced?

"I wasn't planning to kill you, but I'm kind of thinking I'd love to feed your face to the wolves."

"You're under Bevan control, Rex. Those aren't even your words."

"Don't be butthurt because I've broken my shackles. I do have a mind of my own. Maybe if you'd seen that sooner, I wouldn't need to kill so many of you."

The plaster creaks behind me, his weight transferred from the floorboard into the wall.

"I'm trying to help you."

"*Póg mo thóin.*"

He sighs deeply, almost resigned. Without knowing how many of the remaining guys are standing out there, I can't exactly round the door frame and grab him. But I need to get him to Sloane so she can do her work. I need to get Sloane out of here.

I look at her and shrug. Mentally, I'm spent. There's no brain power left for anything. Physically, we should've slept a long time ago. There was a reason I brought us straight here, but I don't remember it anymore. A moth flutters through the door—in my jacked-up state I've aimed for it. Sloane gasps. She hits the floor on her belly, and I follow just as the wall explodes with gunfire.

I army-crawl toward her, drag her behind a sofa. When the shooting ends, I raise my head. Dust fills the slant of morning light coming through the window, but no one has entered. I inhale plaster particulate and something metallic. She's latched her arm onto mine. I pry her free. The action is hot, slippery. My brain connects that metallic smell to the warmth running down her arm and her other hand pressing against her side where a stain of darkness spreads in her shirt.

She makes a grab for me as I stand, ripping my shirt. I don't stop. I can't stop. I unload into the wall they shot up. Eject. Reload. Go through the door. Unload again. None of the bodies are the one I'm looking for. I check the stairs, catch him rounding the corner one flight down. I hop the banister and jump. If she's dying, I didn't say goodbye. I didn't kiss her one last time. Didn't hold her while she left me.

His hands are up when he spins to face me. "Rex, be sensible. The power you're throwing away—"

I shoot him in the chest, the head. Why the shithead isn't armed is beyond me. So used to having servants do his dirty work has left him stupidly vulnerable. And now dead.

Two flights up. One long hall. I skid to a stop on my knees beside her. She's not a girl but a limp thing in a puddle. I turn her face toward me but find nothing there but closed eyes and skin too pale. She's rolled up her shirt, bunched it against the seeping wound but there's been no pressure against it since she passed out.

I take off my shirt and ball it, hold it against the wound. Five minutes. Is that enough? No fucking idea.

"Sloane?" Don't be stupid, Rex. She can't hear you, dead or alive.

We have to get out of here. I start to haul her up but stop fast when I see blood bubble from the wound. Above it, the stretchy fabric of her bra. Well that's perfect. So I wad my shirt again and shove it underneath. Cutting the shoulder strap with my knife allows me to shift it directly over the wound. I get my shoulders underneath her and fireman-carry her down the stairs and out into the hot sun. If they see us and shoot us dead, there will be nothing I can do about it.

Another stage clear. This one though? Not worth it.

We get out via the main driveway and front gate left unlocked for whatever stupid reason. The R5 is a dream when I see it on the side of the road. So jacked with endorphins, I'm nearly floating. I'm sure they're making me hallucinate too. The door is solid in my hand when I open it. The seat catches Sloane's body like I expect. I stand beside the car and glance around at the vacant road, the forest imprisoned by the signature Moore iron fence. My vision shimmers with sun flares—probably not a good thing. Now what's more important, escape or first aid? Escape won't matter if she dies, so I dig out the kit she brought. Flush the wound, bandage it tight. I tuck floppy arms into the seat harness, adjust lifeless legs in the floorboard, try to position a useless neck against the seat so she doesn't get whiplash from this stupid car. She's a breathing lifeless body, and I don't know what else to do so I get behind the wheel and hit the gas.

Fifty miles later she blinks awake and covers her eyes with her arm. My relief nearly swerves us off the road. I grope for her sunglasses and hand them over. She gropes for my hand and holds on tight. The constriction in my throat that's been slowly cutting off airflow since I strapped her into the car returns muscle control to me, and I swallow down the scream I've been trying to contain for miles.

She twists, lifting her arm to check her wound. I hate how she whimpers. If I had something sharp, I'd stab it right in my throat so I'd have my own pain to deal with and not have to think about hers.

"Don't—" I jerk my hand from hers to stop her. "I wouldn't mess with it. Wait until we stop."

I've passed three motels. The farther we get, the safer we'll be. But the next one is ours. A double dose of my upper has gotten me this far, but it won't last much longer.

I'm afraid to see what kind of exhaustion will assault me when it wears off.

Since I'm not going to ask Sloane to affect some money to get two gored-up teenagers a motel room, I find a hose on the back of a gas station and spray myself off. The cutting cold water is both a refresher and a penance. By the time some guy tells me to get lost, I'm clean enough.

In the motel room she showers first, with the light off, the door open just a crack to allow a sliver of light in. I sit on the foot of the bed because I don't know what else to do. I keep my phone out of her reach because I don't want to talk about what just happened and how it was all my fault. We both already know that, and I'd rather not go there any more than I already am in my own head. I couldn't handle any more.

And when I swallow a downer and she snuggles against my back, I put it far, far away. This lesson could've been learned a much harder way. Her wound is now thoroughly cleaned and bandaged, but a couple inches to the left would've turned it fatal. I need to remember to keep an extra bullet on hand for myself in case that lesson ever pays out.

We sleep twelve hours then get back on the road. Her wound has become a scratch. I don't hate her for it, I admire her. Okay, maybe I hate her a little. She's now wearing the pink sunglasses *and* forming her hands into blinders beside her face. I'm too busy trying to figure out how to kill the sun for her to notice the car behind us until it's become so desperate for attention it's glued itself to my bumper. The same car that has been following us for a long time. A really long time.

I check the hood emblem: Tesla. The driver: that's my brother. But there's something off about his face.

I drift to the shoulder. Before I get out, I check my phone to see how many calls and texts I missed. It's dead. Ah, this is going to be fun.

When we meet between the cars, I forget how to form words. One black eye, a cheek bruised purple, a split lip crusted with a bloody scab. Not Aaron, my studious, thesis-writing, doesn't-want-to-get-too-involved brother but a mirror of my own post-fight face. He leans to check the inside of the car. "Where's Sloane?"

I point in there, since I still can't find my voice.

"She okay?"

I nod, aware I'm staring, mouth open like a reject. I snap it closed.

"There's a kill order on you, Rex."

Because it's too hard to figure the reason for the state of his face and keep up with the conversation I say, "What?"

"It's not just her anymore. They've ordered everyone to kill you both on sight."

He and I turn to Sloane's door popping open, her stumbling out to puke in the weeds. I need to stop feeding her fried fast food. Find an organic market somewhere. Maybe that's all this is. She's a mountain-raised, veggie-loving farm girl who just quit clean food cold turkey and is now being force-fed meals sold on the interstate.

"Did you hear me?"

I turn to face him again, see the black eye, the bruise, the lip, like I didn't just see it all a second ago. "Holy oak, Aaron, what—?"

"Your uncle Jared and some friends paid me a little visit. I fed him a few lies and got off easy. Listen, Rex, this is getting serious. I don't know what your timeline is, but you need to cut it in half or more. You can't take all summer to finish this. I'm not even sure you have weeks."

Sloane pulls one of my black T-shirts out of the car and lays it over her head to block the sun. She's cramming mint leaves into her mouth as she hikes into the woods beside us, weaving between the tree trunks.

"It takes as long as it takes."

"They're pulling guys from all over. They expect you at every house. They're flying people in from Europe as we speak."

I turn toward the spot in the woods where Sloane disappeared, rubbing my head, trying to determine if this pile-on of bodies is an issue for us. If it's added Moores, it just means more work for Sloane, more danger to her in the long term, and a reach into a part of the family we never expected to break down. If they're just hired soldiers, it's going to make each household harder to breach, harder to keep people away as Sloane does her work, harder for me not to up the body count.

"And I can't help you anymore. I need to disappear. My dad sent Bethany and Jess on a long cruise—"

"Who's Jess?" I keep my face turned away. I don't want him to read anything from me when he answers.

"My girlfriend."

Of course he has a girl I don't know about.

"My dad's heading to Montana to help protect Sloane's family. I need to stay on the move, until this is all over. Rex—"

I still don't look at him. The sucker punch of withheld info so key to his life carries the same jarring power it always has, even though now I have Sloane, and I'm not such a loser with nothing but online friends. Sloane is real but temporary. Aaron will never think I'm good enough to be his real brother. To be anyone worth telling anything about his life.

"Hey," he says. "I was going to introduce you to Jess."

"*Imeacht gan teacht ort.*" Because simply telling him to fuck off just isn't strong enough considering how much I overuse that word.

He chuckles. "I took a real beating for you, man."

I finally look at him. "You don't have a clue."

Whatever shred of joy or irony that hatched the chuckle dies hard. A shadow crosses his face, almost like he knows the shit I've been through. Almost like he cares. "I guess I don't."

Before it gets any weirder, I say, "Okay, Bro. Message received. I'll charge my phone so you don't have to play private investigator anymore."

"You were stuck in that house. I'm not going to bring my girlfriend there for any reason. You see that, right?"

"Yeah, I get it." But not really. Because he could've still told me. Video called me with her. Sent a dumb picture or something.

"Our mother would put her on the menu for dinner."

"I said I get it."

The shadow hasn't passed though, and the way he's looking at me … it almost looks like—I step back but not quick enough. He's got me, arms restricting shoulders, voice so close it's vibrating against me. "I'm really proud of you, Rex, you know that?"

I've escaped, but he's got a look on him like he's going to do it again. Sloane can hug me. I haven't made the call about anyone else though, so he needs to back off. "Okay, Aaron, I get it. Stop being weird."

"I'm serious."

Don't smile, Rex. It would only encourage him. "Whatever."

"Yeah, whatever." He socks me in the shoulder. "Don't die."

"If I do, it'll be my doing. Not theirs."

He takes a moment to roll that around, and to my surprise, decides not to say a damn thing. Instead, he squeezes my shoulder, gets in his car, and tears away. Okay, what? My overbearing brother recognizing my autonomy? Just like that? I need to find Sloane so she can bring me back to the ground.

I find her in the woods, huddled in the deep shadow of giant oak. She's working on something in her a lap, a pile of half-dead leaves clusters beside her. She raises her face, her eyes still shielded by sunglasses, and signs, *I'm sorry*, then spells Aaron's name.

"He's okay. He understands. He'll catch you next time."

I'm not sure how much of that she caught, but she goes back to her work as if satisfied. This shade has sure taken the edge off the heat. Because I need to re-chew what just happened between Aaron and me, I sit down, feeling grounded again just by having her in my sight. Aaron's full blessing to do whatever I want seems entirely terrifying now. The old me would question his motive and find it obvious: they beat the shit out of him and he wants to sic me on them for revenge. The new me says no, that's not Aaron. It's really just what he said. He's proud. Which means he backs the decisions I've made to get here. And he wants me to make him prouder.

Sloane leans toward me to place her creation on my head. An oak leaf crown, just like the one she's now putting on her own head. Magic revs high all around, raining down, bridging us. The oak rising beside us like a beacon, our knees against earth magnetic. She takes my hands and I feel the otherness of her second half. She's dual-powered, hybrid, a new technology built to advance beyond the others. A secret weapon built to overpower me. I was never supposed to win this. My whole family was duped. Or maybe they knew I'd fail and promised me the opposite, hoping I'd believe it and run with it, a lie turned self-fulfilling prophecy.

She stretches out my arm and writes, *Maybe I should call that black witch.*

Learning to harness that other power would be sweet. It might make our work easier. It might keep Sloane from caving in under the burden of that darkness she's not trained to carry. The bad news? That black witch knows about the bottle and she'd expose me. Once Sloane finds out, she'll know what I plan to do. She'll never trust me again.

She shouldn't trust me now, but she does, and I'm keeping my hold on that as long as I can because I'm a

Moore and I'm selfish. I'd feel shitty about denying her the help she needs if I didn't know she could handle it without help, because she totally can. So I take her arm and write back, *No, you can do this.*

She readjusts the crown on my head before answering. *She could help me.*

She'll use you. And turn me in. Which is not a lie. So I don't understand why I feel like such an asshole when I write it.

It's changing me and I don't know what to do. The pressure she uses on my arm is a bit intense, and when she's finished she holds on, fingers encircling my wrist.

I should probably ask her to explain what she means by "it" before I respond, but the area on my arm probably isn't big enough. Her eyes under that oak crown tell me more than a thousand words. I write, *You're The Catalyst. Nothing about you should change.*

She blinks at me like she's surprised at how much I understand. When she takes my arm to respond, she sits there holding it a moment as if sharpening her thoughts. *Then I'm doing something wrong, I just don't know what.*

It's too late to tell her trying to salvage my family is wrong. It's wrong to spare them. If she knew all I know, she'd be killing them in their beds and torching every house. None of this matters though, because in the end she'll have the peace she's worked so hard for. But what she's gained from this, that thing inside her that's changing her—I'm starting to think it's not her problem to take on, but mine. My family's sewage. Our constructed hate, generations old, its origin not even known to the two kids tasked to end the war it's mutated into.

She's not the one doing something wrong. I am.

We don't even discuss our new strategy: teamwork or die. It's a truth so real we don't need to say it. Our next stop is New York, a trendy neighborhood packed so tight we ditch the R5 miles away. The house lights up the night like a party. Sloane sends a team of city-dwelling bats on recon, and we find it's just as Aaron warned: hired soldiers crawling every square inch. We don't have a choice though, so we move in, skirting into the house undetected.

It's just as stupid inside. As we know, the sleeping stone works on my people but not the patrolling security now too numerous to work around. Sloane won't let me kill them. The two KOs I manage are too noisy and just bring more people to KO. If I could get them to queue up, I could do them assembly line, but without each of them knowing and starting a mass attack …? Good luck. So we hole up in a closet. She goes into my pocket for my phone. Should I admit what that still does to me? No, Rex, please don't. Not now.

With the volume muted, she types out: *I have an idea.*

I roll my hand at her to get her to spit it out. I'm not claustrophobic but this closet is making me sweat. We've parted the hanging coats, but they're still draping all over me, returning like pests every time I shove them away. Losing it right now would be bad timing, so I hit snooze on the freak-out and hope we get out of here before it goes off. Breathe, Rex. You're fine.

Water effect. Child's play, remember? In the phone's light, she's grinning at me for the first time in days. *You did it to your car when we first escaped.*

Yeah, and I had gallons of water on hand. Not so awesomely prepared now. She slips the phone back in my pocket and pulls me up, peeks out the cracked closet door before slipping out. We move in the shadow along the wall, into a hall bathroom where she closes the door and locks it. A porthole window glows with light pollution from the city. She unloads her pockets. Unloads mine. I wish I could load them up again and make her do it all over.

Then she's turning on the shower and beckoning me inside as her hair and clothes flatten under the stream of water. Deaf girl must not be aware that a running faucet makes sound. I put an ear against the door and listen to the hall. Then I realize something. At home, there'd be no threat in the sound of a running faucet at night. Also true for a house this size. Someone could be getting up for a drink. An appliance could be kicking on. No one's going to think running water means Rex and Sloane are here.

I get in with her, keeping my distance until she takes my arms and spins us so I'm under the stream. The spell words evade me—she's too close, and I can't get my head there. So I close my eyes and think myself back to that night, those jugs in the back of the R5, my fresh escape. And I whisper them under the water, my hands on Sloane's hips, feeling the magic drench us, cloak us, make us one.

Every house we hit from then on starts with me and Sloane under a shower head. Bangs hanging wet in her eyes, clothes clinging. It's all business until the time I steal a kiss. After that, it's every house me and Sloane making out under a shower head. Then she cuts people and steals their hate while I try hard not to kill them with the hate I carry. She purged my hate of Bevans. My hate of Moores roots too deep to be purged by any magic, and it's revived by each one of them I see.

We work our way up the coast. It gets cooler and wetter. The photos in my phone prove how many houses we hit because I've lost track. Then we move inland and work our way south. Sloane seems to have found a way to cope with her dark burden. It involves ignoring me, ignoring everything, really. Except for my hair. It's started growing out, and she can't keep her fingers out of it. I'm pretty sure I've learned how to purr. The only other thing that eases her burden is lots of deafening psychill. Every time I fire up the audio, I'm afraid the speakers will be blown but they hold up just as Sloane does. Maybe they're powered by magic too. We need to finish this soon. I don't know how much longer she can last.

CHAPTER 27

SLOANE

W**E'VE BECOME NOCTURNAL.** I'm so punished by sunlight it's a necessity now to do all the driving and work at night and sleep, eat, and plan during the day in motel rooms with the curtains drawn tight. I can't think too much about it. Panic looms over my shoulder. I've turned so much mental space over to the hate I've collected I don't know if any of the real me still exists or where to find her if she does. The more of me I give it, the less of a burden it feels like. And for this dark mass of hate to not feel like a burden—that's like candy to the panic. Rex has already called dibs on panic attacks. I need to pick something else, like fainting or insomnia or serial murder. But I think Rex has dibs on that last one too. He finds some reason to execute at least one person per house, and he never tells me why. I feel like the reasons travel into me from the hate I remove from them, and I'd rather not have the gory details to apply to the roiling monster that has made a home inside me.

And if I decided to use this monster of hate I've collected as fuel to the black magic I know, I could tear apart the world.

Rex is the only thing keeping me from doing that. The elements sing through him. When I plant my fingers in his hair or snuggle against him to sleep, it awakes the elements in me, and I remember the life I used to have that feels more like a distant memory with each house we hit. I remember bare feet against pine needles. My dad's strong arm around my shoulders. My mom's bright morning smile. Coyotes pranking my dogs while Marcas and I walk the woods at dusk, Marcas bending over with laughter. The elements remind me to be homesick. Without them, I'd forget. I'd stop caring. I'd lie down and give up, just let the Moores take me.

I'm like a wildcat now. Short bursts of energy followed by days of rest. Rex has bought an expensive gaming laptop so he can have something to do while I sleep. This lethargy should concern me, but I'm too lethargic to be concerned.

There's a new language building inside me. Not Irish, English, or ASL. Nothing with concrete words I can see but in bursts of thoughts, hazy at first but becoming clearer with each house we hit. It's providing a new understanding of this war we're fighting, of justice and consequences. It's knocking away dreamy ideals that used to matter to me but don't anymore. I'm not becoming hardened. I'm waking up.

I need to have a talk with Rex about what needs to happen when we finish. What I've collected can't ever get loose in the world again. It has to be destroyed. And since I don't have a way to remove it from me, I might have to be destroyed along with it. Sloane Bevan the martyr. I was right all along.

We arrive at another house. Rex knows which one. It's stopped mattering to me. We find a shower for Rex's spell. He kisses me like usual but for the first time I can't kiss him back. He pulls away, water washing down his face, drips dropping of his eyelashes. *What's wrong?*

Nothing. Everything. I don't know myself anymore. I should sign it—he's picked up so much ASL I wonder if he's taking lessons online while I sleep. But it's too much effort to raise my hands.

I close my eyes and drench myself under the showerhead. When I'm finished, he's still watching me. Not just a casual glance but a full analysis. Well, screw him. It's none of his business. I slip around him, forcing him to trade sides. He takes his turn under the water, and I close my eyes as he seals the spell. Then we get out, grab our gear, and go to work.

In the first room, the bed is rumpled but empty of people. There's an upright dark stain in the shadow near the door. Rex sees it a split second after I do, a heartbeat before it lunges, throwing an arm around Rex's neck, the pointed end of a knife firm against his side.

They're both spitting words. If Rex's spell failed, then the whole house will wake and see us. We need to call this off and run. Rex sends a headbutt backward; the guy dodges, giving Rex the tip of the knife as warning or punishment or both.

I chamber a round and shoot him in the head.

Suddenly relieved of weight, Rex stumbles forward. He cups his bloody side and looks at me. Looks at the dead guy on the floor. Looks at me again.

I chamber another round and aim it at the door because I probably just woke up the whole street.

Rex raises an S—shorthand for my name. We can't talk right now. What is he thinking? I jerk my head toward the door. He gives it a quick glance before heading over to me. *You ...*

I, what? Soldier boy better get on his game or this is going to end fast. I kick him in the leg for his attention because he's staring at the dead guy on the floor. When he turns back he says, *You just killed ...*

And that's it. Because the rest comes through his eyes, locked on mine with so much shock and concern I want to kick him again. Harder. How many people has he killed? He has no right being all judgy about me taking down one.

Bodies come through the door. I'm about to squeeze the trigger when Rex reaches, shoving my pistol's aim toward the ceiling. That shake of his head is a stunned, desperate no and there's no way this level of conscience has suddenly sprouted in Rex Moore. A dream, that's what this is, that's why everything feels upside down, why my body is just a disconnected shell I'm traveling around in, why it doesn't make sense that Rex would be so troubled by me killing a guy when he's popping people now like they're soda cans lined up on a fence.

His face is inches from mine then. His hands cradling my jaw, tilting my eyes so I'm forced to look directly in his. His bloody hand slips against my skin, ripe, fragrant, and alive. *Sloane*, he says. *You're okay. You can do this. Just once more.*

Do what? I want to ask. This is a stupid dream so I get to choose. I want to swim in the ocean. I want to jump, feel the plunge under its choppy surface, the surge of the current tugging my limbs. I want to kick to the top, take a breath of sea air as a blue whale surfaces beside me. I'll swim to the beach where Rex is waiting for me to lie with him in a bed of sand under the stars until I wake up.

He tugs me through the door, down the hall, into a new room where a woman sleeps. He tosses the blanket aside at her feet, slices her foot deep.

Sloane, he says. *Go.*

I watch the blood seep into the sheet. Sprinkle on the floor.

Rex comes to me, pulling me forward. *Go.*

So I go. A dip of blood on my finger, a symbol on my forehead and hers. Darkness drifts to her body's edge, tentative for a new host until it latches onto me. I draw it in like an inhale of smoke, a poison I've grown accustomed to. Once inside it pushes against me, too confined. I release one of the last remaining parts of the old me, let it fill the space, overwrite what's there. With more room to expand, the compacted mass shifts into its new position. I don't think about what I've lost to accommodate its expanding power. My family—I don't think of them. My life—irrelevant. What I am is what I am now, not what I've been or what I've done. The return to normal seems far off, unlikely, impossible. I wonder if this is what it feels like to be a Moore. To just give in, let the darkness fill in, the hate rule.

Rex drags me from room to room, person to person. Outside, I throw up three times on the way to his car. Inside it, he beats the steering wheel while I buckle up. After a few minutes on the road he pulls to the shoulder and gets out to scream, hands over his face, bent at the waist, falling to his knees out of sight.

My new language has gained vocabulary tonight. I was misguided before. I should've listened to Rex. Sometimes killing people isn't just easy but necessary. Warranted. If that's what has him so angered, then maybe I need to explain it to him again, either in his own words, or in the new ones that live inside me now.

I go for my harness release to get out and help him, but my fingers feel slow and unattached, my eyelids heavy. Sleep is a thundering tidal wave, and I drop to the ground so it can roll over me.

Swaying light above me. The pesky tickle of a breeze. I rub my eyes, feel the gritty soil against my skin. Lifting on my elbows, I blink awake, my watering eyes turning the dusky light sparkling and prism-like. The canopy of a giant oak drapes above me. I breathe in mint and look down, finding my pouch lying on my chest. I take two leaves and put them in my mouth.

Peach sky peeks through the trees to my left. To my right, deep cobalt. I suppose it could be dawn instead, so I sit up and check the tree trunks for moss to figure out which is east and which is west. Yep—it's dawn. I scoot toward the trunk of the oak and find a resting spot in the deepest shadow against its curling exposed roots.

Rex has laid out a blanket. A small campfire burns several yards away. I take off my boots and let the air weave through my toes, trying to remember how we got here and where we're going next. How long I slept. When I last ate. None of it seems to matter though.

A butterfly drifts into a shaft of sunlight. Beyond it, Rex, coming toward me in his underwear, his hair spiky and wet. When he gets close, I see that knife wound in his side has scabbed over, dark against his skin. He tosses me his phone.

There's a great little creek through there. Highly recommend.

The body language is all wrong. Almost like we're strangers.

It will make you feel better.

I type, *I feel fine.*

Really?

Fine enough. I get up and stretch.

He watches me until it gets creepy. Then he goes to his bag for shorts and a tee. I stoke the fire while he unloads grocery bags on the blanket. *All this shit is organic. I found this grocery store with a food bar. It's probably cold now, but we can heat it on the fire.*

I'm not hungry, but he seems to have gone to a lot of trouble here. Fresh fruit, stir-fry veggies, flatbread, bean salad. Fancy carbonated fruit juice and that same brand of mineral water Aaron sent via drone a lifetime ago. I see he's put place settings on the blanket with paper plates and plastic utensils, so I sit.

He holds out a take-out box. *Chicken? Organic and humanely raised and fed with rainbows.*

I shake my head, feeling like I should laugh but it never surfaces.

Okay more for me, then. He catches my eye, tentative, almost shy. Again like we're strangers. He speaks again. It takes effort to break his gaze to check the screen. *You have to eat though.*

I load a plate and nibble, wishing I'd gone for a dip in the creek instead. Maybe by the time I was finished, I'd be ready to eat. But my stomach is twisting and growly so it doesn't make much sense why I'd wait.

We're taking a few days off to rest up, he says. *We have one last house to do.*

When I raise my eyes from the screen the expectation on his face is hard to miss. I'm supposed to guess something, but how? He's been keeping track of all the households on Aaron's list. I haven't seen it or cared to see it for a long time.

And I wonder what he's planning. Why his body language is so off. Did he drag me all over the country only to walk me straight into a trap at the end?

My house, he says, deadpan. Seeing him so withdrawn has me second-guessing every promise we've made. Every hard-earned understanding. Every kiss.

I set down my plate to type back to him, but there's nothing to say. He's right. We can't skip the most important house in the family. Aaron had no need to put it on the list—Rex and I know where it is, and we should've included it. It feels like a betrayal, though, not knowing we'd have to go back there this whole time. Not expecting it or planning for it. He could've at least mentioned it once. But can I blame him for not mentioning something I should've been prepping for myself?

He reaches for my shoulder. *Sloane.*

I sign, *What?* Because why is he being so weird? Or maybe I should ask, why am I?

His spoken response looks like an unfinished sentence; he withdraws his fingers, looking aside like he's just remembered something. We both reach for the phone, but I get it faster.

On the screen: *You can trus—*

He attempts a grab but I hold the phone out of his reach. He needs to finish because that sentence cut off like that is a damning contradiction of itself. This time he holds out his hand. I place the phone in it. He checks the screen. Sees how much of the sentence I got. Looks up at me. *You can.*

I fingerspell, *I can what?* That's a challenge and he knows it. Because I have a hunch that there's evil in him I never removed. It's too integrated, too untouchable. If I removed it all, there would be no Rex Moore left. All this talk of trust and allegiance and teamwork has been one big lie to get us through what we needed to do. I've lost too much of myself to know if the lie was on both sides or just his. If he was this much of a liar the whole time and I'm finally clued in to it. Or if all the faking it has finally gotten to him, made him think there's something here that isn't.

He sets his phone on the blanket. Then he's tugging me up by the arms, towing me behind him into the trees. I stumble along, my legs too short to match his strides, my bare feet no match against his boot-covered ones. Distantly I wonder if my old self would've fought him because right now I'm too tired to even try. He must realize that too; he squats, heaving me onto his back.

Water twinkles through the underbrush ahead. Seeing it before sensing it convinces me how far gone my old self is, how dulled my earth magic, and how apathetic I've become. I smell the freshness of the water still in his hair against my cheek. It takes me straight home to the bank of my river, the river I love, the river I forgot.

Rex lets me down beside the creek. I turn away, blinded by its collection of dazzling sunlight. Its image remains in my head—clear water, swift current, tiny fish darting all around. The opposite bank is a swim away, at least forty feet. This isn't a creek but a small river. Rex pulls me forward. I feel the shade cover me like a blanket on my skin, a refuge. I open my eyes. He's raising his eyebrows, *Better?* I take in the bliss of thick canopy above, blocking the sun's rays.

He grips my shirt, lifting it over my head and off without warning. The waistband of my shorts, tugged down to the ground. His own shirt over his head. Shorts, down, kicked off. He turns, waving me toward the water, and I see what an innocent thing that was. How platonic. Well good, that's good—I think? But he's caught on to my hesitation because now he's looking deeper, taking a step back to look me over in my stretchy bra and undies. Which causes me to check him out in his tight boxers. His eyes return to mine, asking, *Keep going?*

I shrug. A dare. He wants to be bold; well, I'd like to see how bold he can be.

He rubs a hand over his smiling mouth as he glances away. An act of cover that reminds me so much of the shy Rex I know that I can't stop my own smile from creeping up. I don't wipe it away though. I let him see it. It isn't a swim in the creek that's going to make me feel better, it's him. It's already him.

He's fighting the same fight I am: to keep my eyes on his and not let them travel to body parts wrapped only in underwear. To end the torture, I offer him my hand. He takes it so cautiously I'm tempted to promise him I won't bite. Not anymore, anyway.

We wade in and dunk down. Summer-warmed water churns with the colder current, swirling around me. With his chin dipping into the water, he watches me, curious and attentive. Light reflecting from the water highlights the golden hue in the shadow of stubble on his jaw. I send a splash toward him. He splashes back, harder. A giggle bubbles up into my throat as I wipe my eyes; he snags my arms, hauling me against him. His lips move against my ear, out of sight and impossible to read, and that's how he wants it. A tender kiss on the cheek seals his voiced secret, then he pulls back, his face turned away like he's just become embarrassed by that impulse and afraid of my reaction.

To avoid having to explain what he just said, he pushes away into faster current and submerges. I'm filled with lead. If I go under I'll never be able to overcome its weight and I'll drown. Elements that used to comfort and revive me are now a danger. I'm so out of tune I don't know how to preserve what's me while harboring this mass I've collected. It's a power source for black magic, not earth magic. And if I draw upon it for the little black magic I know, I'm afraid it will be too much for me to handle.

Rex pops up downstream in deeper, stiller water, beckoning me with a hand. I imagine deep sea creatures and sharp-toothed piranhas awaiting my flesh. For the first time in my life, nature sends a shiver down my spine, and the black magic roars inside me in combat. I'm made of two kinds of magic. There's no reason they'd be in opposition. But I'll never be able to join them with this mass of hate filling every space inside me, damming the flow between them.

Forget this crap. I refuse to be afraid of a creek. I kick off toward the faster current, riding it until the water flattens out and I lose the bed of rock below my feet. Rex swims to meet me. He goes upright, feet planted, but water laps at his mouth which means it's too deep for me. I aim for the shore, but he catches my foot and hauls me back, against him.

My skin finds the slippery warmth of his. It's sinfully perfect how our bodies align. In his arms my lead-filled body becomes weightless. I hug him, bury my face against his neck. We become the water. We sway with subtle current, our warm blood mixing with its cool depths. His heartbeat joins mine, bringing with it the rhythm of the elements so present I can't believe I'd missed them before. I sense a faraway rain trickling in on the breeze, the pull of the sun reigning in the eastern sky. The mighty trees, roots dipping into the water on the bank. The animals basking in the morning all around. I reach with all I have, drawing it all together and in, crushing and compacting that dark hate down into itself, into a more manageable size.

Rex shudders in my arms. Our connected heartbeats falter; I lose the rhythm that was guiding me. I lift my head to look at him. He's saying my name, apologizing. One arm has stretched into the water to stabilize us, the other goes around my waist to keep me from drifting away.

I take a breath and go under. The distance to the shore doubles and triples as I imagine how condensed and heavy that mass of hate must be. I break the surface, gasping for air. That mass isn't a tangible thing though. It has no weight. It can't hurt me here. So I take another breath and swim until I hit the slope of the bank and drag myself out of the water.

He's still in the middle of the creek watching me. He should come; I want him to come. I don't want to sit here alone. And my eye contact must be the invitation he needs because he crosses the water and bursts out beside me. *Feel better?*

I guess he's choosing to ignore that strange discord that overcame us. Or maybe he didn't feel it? And from the way he's looking at me, I can tell he doesn't need an answer. He already knows. He leans in to wipe a drip of water off my chin, a move designed to get him in kiss vicinity. It would be the perfect way to thank him for what he just did. So I don't understand why I stand up instead.

He rubs a hard hand over his head. That old habit—too rough, painful to watch. Almost as painful as what it feels like to see him rejected. I see him shutting down, walling up—an expert reaction produced by much practice. Rejection must be a common thing for him, something he knows well. That new language is speaking to me though, saying it's okay, it's what he deserves. He's a Moore. He's not worth it.

CHAPTER 28

REX

NIGHT MOVES IN like an army. The day's heat retreats. Sloane teaches me how to warm the earth, a skill that comes so naturally I wonder if Aaron taught me long ago and I forgot. We line up together on our heated pad of earth under the only break in the trees, a high-def vid of stars versus wispy clouds and a random flapping, dipping bat on its way to somewhere important.

Every inch of my skin burns with the urge to kiss her, but she's been so distant I'm pretty sure she's come to her senses and started hating me like everyone eventually does. What we've been doing isn't rebellion. It's a mistake.

I use that thought to extinguish the fire all over me. Infatuation with each other will only ruin what we need to achieve. Power for me, death for her. My family under new rule, her family obliterated. Expected and easy, the natural end to this war. There will never be peace between our families no matter how much hate she steals. If it's removed from my side, it will survive on her side. Hate breeds hate. Which is why her side must die once we're finished with mine. One more house to hit and we're there.

My heart punches me awake. The creeping footsteps in my dream have slipped into the waking world around me. I stiffen, blending with the shadow, trying to separate one footfall from the next and count how many surround us. Five? No—ten. Completely doable. It'd be much slicker with my .45, but I'm pretty sure I left it in the car. I slide a hand on the ground toward Sloane and find bare ground. I'm on my feet then, unable to stop myself.

The embers of our fire glow orange a short distance away. On the ground beside it a person—a girl—hugging her knees. Of course she hasn't heard what I heard. They've stopped moving in because I got up. They want to see what I'll do before they attack.

I grab her, haul her up. A red sunburst pulses in my eyes—she's clocked me so hard I've eaten my own lip. Don't hit back, Rex. I halt the retaliation before it reaches her even though she's dodged and grabbed me by the shirt. I turn my head to spit blood. Then I grab her back, yanking her into my face to whisper, "They're here."

She pushes against me for space, but she's not strong enough. A rapid succession of kicks to my knee, my ankle—I avoid them all. It's work though, making my heart pound harder, my blood soak my chin and shirt. Her regretful gaze lands on the mess she's made of my mouth, but god we have no time. We have to get out of here.

"Sloane, we have to go!" The blood and saliva are so thick in my mouth I can barely get the words out. She ducks and twists—one moment my death grip on her solid, the next, all I have is air. She's walking in a small circle, eyes leveled and wide like a cat hunting at night. Those black magic eyes will see what I can hear, and then we can infiltrate the woods and take them down one by one.

When she turns to me she's relaxed. She does the sign for *all good*.

No, not all good. I spin her body to face the last set of footsteps I heard. Poke a finger in their direction. Too late I realize what a bad move it is to show them we know where they are while I'm being pricked by ten sets of eyes. I haul her behind a tree trunk, push her down against it and block her in.

She presses her finger against my forehead until I look at her. When I do, she taps my skin in the same spot, her expression so dull it gives no clues to what she's trying to tell me. All at once I'm reminded of the vivid thoughts that used to display so clearly on her face, and their new absence. Missing temporarily? Or zapped forever?

Because I'm not reacting, she's taken my arm, writing, *It's all in your head.*

The sky falls. Shadows crumble around us. I turn around and take in the scene with enlightened eyes and fresh ears. A sleeping forest. A soft breeze creaking through the underbrush like footfalls on a path. My own panicked gasps now slowing because of Sloane's hand on my back.

I'm sorry, she signs when I look at her. She brings fingers to my lips, admires the blood she comes away with. The idea must spring into her mind as it does in mine, and I could stop her but I don't. She kisses me, her clean lips against my swollen bloody ones, seeking the cuts she caused, healing them. This girl is twisted, a queen of gore. She's as messed-up as me. The thought is so sweet it hurts my teeth. I can't help but love her. It's like she was made just for me.

I wake a second time to a scream. Grope for Sloane's body beside me—gone again. It's a dream, a nightmare. Another freak-out. I dig in my pockets for my pills. Find a car key, bottle of black magic, a random bullet. Move down a set and find gum, a pocketknife, more bullets. Damn it all, I need my pills—there, in the left cargo. I shake one into my hand. A shriek unloads above me; I duck, cover my head. Not fast enough to avoid a set of razors tearing through the shirt on my back which feels too real to be a nightmare. The itchy sting of torn skin. The weep of blood. I reach, see the blood on my hand.

Not real, Rex. Figure your shit out.

I bend until my forehead hits earth. Press palms hard and reach for the elements like Sloane taught me. My view pulls up, spins around, circling like a bird above, flapping wings in my periphery. I look up, directly into the yellow eyes of an owl in flight above me. It shrieks and swoops. Not an attack. An alarm.

This is real.

Again I hear the scream that woke me. A sound unlike any I've ever heard, it's so guttural and completely unaware of itself. Not a cry for help but a warning to run. I know whose it is, and I'm running between the trees toward it. Upright bodies of men move in the shadows ahead, shoulder to shoulder, a united front, separating me from her. I grab the low branch of a nearby tree and climb, trying to determine if it's real strength or dream strength to decide if any of this is real. I ease out on a branch and leap before it breaks, swinging into a new tree. Below me I can now see Sloane's fighting frame, restrained by several men. Behind her, a dozen more. There's a hood over her head, covering her face so she's not only deaf but also blind. One of her arms is held behind her while some guy positions a steel bucket filled to the brim with a dark liquid that shines in the night. Because of what I've been dealing with lately, I think blood. But no, it's worse. It's what we use to block magic in our rivals. To torture them.

Tar.

Anger broils in my head. I lose my foothold, slide a few inches before jamming boots into a wedge of trunk and limb. My .45 could blow holes in some brains right now and end this fast. I could drop right into the center of the gang, but unarmed? Against what, twenty guys? Possibly more in the surrounding trees?

Sloane slips out and they snag her again. More guys pile on. Brutish hands all over her arms and legs. I don't care how skilled she is, this is death. Her body disappears under an onslaught of black tactical wear and muscles. My head's about to explode from helpless rage. I can't stay here and watch this. If it's her death, it's mine too. I unwedge my feet, calculate the best place to land.

A flurry of black bursts forth from the gang of bodies. All faces turn up toward me. Wings, feathers, talons, beak are silhouetted against the moon-flooded sky. I look down at the spot Sloane last was, see her rumpled shirt and shorts alone on the ground, shiny black feathers drifting to rest on top.

Voices shout orders. Scoped rifles raise toward the sky. And the trees around me explode into a cackling madness of wings and wind. Birds in the hundreds diving toward the men, creating chaos and a perfect diversion for escape. I'm not sure how they got here, if they were here the whole time, or if this dream has just turned bizarre, but good, I'll take it. Whether Sloane's disappeared into thin air or has shapeshifted into one of those dive-bombing crows, I'll leave it to her to find me. I'm so out of my league.

I monkey through trees. Bullets split wood all around me. I duck behind a trunk, wishing I was on the ground to disarm the shithead and blow his face off. Risking a peek rewards me with a scorch across my shoulder. I tug the neck of my shirt down, find it's just a graze. There's a weaker limb beside me that branches far out, heavy on the end and right over the guy's head. So I jump onto it, feel the wood splinter. I get a grip on the limb above and kick; it snaps and crashes down. Time to go.

When I no longer hear men trampling through the underbrush, I drop from the trees and race for our camp. I hop a log I don't remember hopping before. I've lost my way. Stopping to find the moon gets me tackled. I didn't even see him coming. The barrel of a pistol jams into my gut. I knock it away, seeing the flash that would've been my death. His sick weight piles on, but I'm contorting around him, his gun arm in my grip, twisted—snapped. He grunts, pissed. But I have that gun now. A pop to my ribs so brutal I taste blood. I press the barrel into flesh that isn't mine and fire, his weight falling away. I get up and shoot him in the head. Survey the woods around me for more. Then run.

At our camp I snatch as much of our stuff as I can and sprint to the R5. Wheels spin under my impatient foot; my neck snaps as the tires find their grip. I struggle into my harness while I steer and shift, trying to get latched before I brain myself on the window or roof. Once I reach the pavement, it's smoother driving but I slam the brakes anyway, unsure what the hell to do. Night insects float into my beam of headlights as I catch my breath and cough blood into my hand. It sure feels like I'm leaving Sloane back there. Like I'm all alone. I can't—just can't—

Shoving out of the car only makes it worse. The empty road stretches far in both directions. The world is huge and I'm nothing. She's been abandoned and so have I.

I turn and glance down the road in the direction I came from. How ridiculous would it be to go back? If it's a dream, I'll do it. Even if I go back and die, I'll wake up safe. If it's real, though, it could be the last bad decision I make. I take my phone out and check the time: fifteen past four. I count sixty seconds and check again: now sixteen past. Okay, so not a dream, right? I get back in the car and hit the gas.

A dark thing swoops in front of me, the gibbous moon bright behind it. I lean forward and look up. A crow is circling, drifting down beside the car. Maybe I should slow down but the shock I've entered has hijacked my nervous system. We're neck and neck in this drag race, bird versus car, but she's drifting further down, nearing the ground, and oh shit, it's not really a bird but Sloane as a bird, unskilled in flight, about to crash into the pavement.

Between one breath and the next I no longer see a crow but a deer springing beside me in long leaps. When she pulls ahead, I realize I've let my foot off the gas and I'm slowing down. The R5 shudders; I stomp the clutch before it dies and come to a stop. I look through the glass at the deer. She looks back.

I get out. She comes forward, takes a gentle bite of my shirt and yanks. I'm not prepared for the power in it, and I have to stumble to keep from falling forward. "You want clothes?"

That's good news, I guess, that she knows how to shift back. I shed my shirt and drop it at her feet—hooves? She nudges my arm. I turn my back to her, too anxious to get her into my car in her human body to pretend I don't know what a deer wants.

A tingle of magic plays down my back as I hear a thump on the ground behind me. A shuffle of fabric, then a tap on the shoulder. I spin around and find a human girl, messy hair, sheepish grin. That stunt was so damn sick I think I might have to get on my knees and worship her, like right now, broken ribs and bullet graze and all.

"Witch," I say.

She gives me the finger. Wearing only my shirt. It's so fucking hot.

Sloane opens the R5's hatch and digs through her bag. On the other side of the car she gets dressed, tossing my shirt back to me over the roof. As I tug it on, I think I hear crows—no, I know I hear crows. I walk a few steps backward on the road. She comes to stand beside me.

They emerge from the darkness like a fast-moving fog, and for a moment I wonder if they're after her. If she stole one of their bodies and they want it back, but too bad, it's been turned into a deer then back into a girl so sorry, guys, you're out of luck.

Sloane shows no fear though, so I take the cue from her and stand my ground. The flock swoops in, filling the sky with noise and wings.

"What do they want?"

She lays a hand on my arm that says, *Shut up, I'm trying to figure that out.*

Then she's yanking me back to the car. We strap in and take off, and I'm looking at her because I need to know what's going on. She goes for my pockets—shit, that bottle. I shift, pushing her away and find my phone myself. I check the time before I hand it to her. It's incrementing normally. Real life. Not a nightmare. Not a freak-out.

Those guys are coming.

"Say the crows?"

Yes.

"They're not mad you stole their body?"

She shoots a sharp look my way. *No, because I didn't.*

In the rearview mirror, headlights blink over a hill behind us, so noticeable on this dark road she turns in her seat to watch them through the back window. I don't like how quickly they seem to be gaining on us, or how they've been joined by two more vehicles behind them. I check my fuel level—all good. So I downshift and we both get whiplash. I flip off my lights and stay off the brakes until we've done enough curves to lose them. She points at an upcoming intersection on the nav. Once I've made the turn she finds my phone.

Go to your house.

"What—why?"

It's time.

I look over at her. Yes, I'm ready for this to be over, but after all that shit back there, I'd like to rest up a bit, maybe get some food, heal the broken ribs, or at least have some time to load my guns.

Their army is back there. And they won't expect us. How fast can you get us there?

Pretty damn fast, that's how fast. By the time we roll up to the iron border fence on the north, I'm shaking from the adrenaline of the drive. She's as cool as a coma.

"Would this be a bad time to mention my ribs are broken?"

She pokes me *right there.* After my vision returns, I'm surprised I'm not dead.

You'll just have to deal. She gets out of the car and knocks on the hatch.

Miss Sympathetic, huh? I wonder if part of her brain disappeared with the crow body, or deer body, or both. How can I even be sure this is the real Sloane? I get out and grab her arm, force her to look at me. The tightness in her face is so new I hardly recognize her. It's morphing before my eyes though—falling, losing structure. And her breathing has changed to match the wet eyes and new frown. It hurts so bad I forget the broken ribs. "What happened?"

She places a hand over her chest and spells, *Had to let it go. It's all over me now.*

"That shit you've been collecting?"

Her lip quivers. She nods, wiping her eyes.

"Okay, so now what?"

She shrugs. *Now I'm like you.*

Wait a sec. Like me? First of all no, she hasn't put me back to my normal self yet like she promised. Second, she didn't grow up like I did. Third, she doesn't fucking know what it feels like to be me.

She goes for the hatch release, and I put my hand on the glass to keep it down. "You're fixing me before we go in there."

It doesn't register on her face so I hand her my phone and repeat it.

I'll never fix you.

"You promised. Swore a blood oath, actually."

I lied. She hands back my phone like she's done. The queen has spoken. I slam a hand against the hatch window so hard I brace for broken glass but it miraculously stays intact.

Next thing I know I'm on the ground supporting my broken ribs with both hands and she's loading guns inside the open hatch. I kick her in the ankle. She leans, her signing hand in my face. *I said I'd do it after finishing your family so back off.*

And she actually looks like she might kick me in the ribs again, so I push away to gain some amount of space for defense. To think I ever thought she was crazy before this moment. To believe she was trash like the rest of her family. I was so wrong then; I had nothing to compare to. *This* is crazy. *This* is Bevan trash. This is why we hate them, why we fight them, why we have to destroy them.

All good for me. I pat my pockets and find the outline of the bottle. She's made it so much easier.

I pick my ass up and load guns beside her. Strap on holsters, fill my pockets with ammo. She tosses me a pressure wrap; I take off my shirt and wrap my torso. The support against my ribs gives instant relief. I swallow some pain reliever and slap a bandage over my grazed shoulder. She applies a butterfly bandage to my temple and a bandage to my chin. She doesn't kiss it, and I take fucking note of that.

Her amulet is the last thing. I kind of hate it right now, and all it stands for. Our allegiance—a formality, a joke. Our friendship—no, forget that. Our hardcore connection, whether love or infatuation or just shallow making out … maybe it was a game to her but it was something to me, and I'm not going to deny that. I have honor now. Maybe it's a new thing, but it's here. So I string the Bevan family amulet around my neck and tuck it in my shirt and ignore her lingering gaze and the open door it is. I'm just not in the mood right now.

We find the break in the fence and go in. I also take note she's skipping the Bevan war paint, and hell yeah, I'm too stubborn to mention what a mistake that could be because that mistake is on her. The walk through the north woods is more silent than a walk with a deaf girl. She's not just deaf now, she's encased in ice. If I chiseled it away, I'd probably destroy her too, and that would be premature because I need her to disable my family first.

She pokes me in the .45 and points through the underwood. I catch reflective eyes and a set of ears. "Coyotes?"

Her face says, *Yes, and don't shoot them, dumbass.*

Okay but can I shoot her? I'm about done with this shit.

As we advance, more coyotes gather, sneaking along with us like government surveillance. Above, bats have gone from random to all over, and it's kind of nice to have so much activity so I don't think about how I'm about to attack my own family with our sworn enemy. So I don't imagine who I might kill. I must have a dope amount of adrenaline today because it's filling me up again. I'm trying to breathe. Sloane's presence used to help me with this, but today it's making it worse. I power ahead, following her because I can't see the path on my own.

We reach the edge of the woods. The lawn spans ahead like a waiting battleground. I look at her, some tiny piece of me begging for the camaraderie we used to have when facing a new house to take down. Being together made each one easier than the last. It never felt like some unsurmountable task. It never felt like walking into a battle with questionable outcome. We could only win together. Divided? Who the hell knows.

Now there's a thick buzz building in my head, which is great. Probably a side effect from marching through the woods with broken ribs or a concussion. Did I get punched in the head recently? Probably.

I step onto trimmed grass in a growing pack of coyotes—so many of them I can't believe they've all come off our land. Since I've lost sight of Sloane, I follow the pack, amazed they aren't ripping me apart. Gunshots echo across the property. We pick up the pace, coyote trot turning to hard run, head low, tails like arrows behind them. For the briefest moment I wish I had Sloane's power to shapeshift and blend with this unified pack. My family would never know it was me until the end.

Ahead, coyotes slow and circle. Sloane stands above them, aiming two-handed at the windows on the north side of the house, taking them out one by one. Bats swoop into the new openings so hard and fast it's like the house is sucking them in. Sloane turns around then and cuts the coyote pack down the middle with a straight hand. They part—half with her, half with me. She looks at me, points at the front of the house then turns and marches up the rear steps to the back patio and rear entrance.

Dividing up shouldn't be such a blow. It makes sense. We've always worked together, though, so it's a change—a change that I don't agree with.

I can't get myself to move right away because three armed guards have leaked from the house, and I'm dying to be at Sloane's side. They're holding fire, knowing if they hurt Sloane those coyotes will attack, and they won't be able to take them all out at once. Sloane shoots all three guys mechanically, non-lethal hits that take them down and out of the game without killing. Not right away, anyway. Not if they find first aid. She steps over their bodies and disappears into the house.

Coyotes nudge me. I turn to face the pack. One raises its muzzle to yip-yip-howl. It catches on across the group and gets my legs moving to the front of the house. We encounter a whole group of guards who hesitate just like the others, and I'm not so humane. I stare at the open front door. This is my last time entering this house as Rex the soldier. When I leave through this door, I'll be Rex the king.

CHAPTER 29

SLOANE

Inside a vacant kitchen I withdraw my last sleeping stone from my pocket and raise it high, beckoning the dark cloud of hate, the first one I ever encountered. It swirls down like it remembers me, like it's been waiting. The darkness inside me pulses hot in my head, its echo traveling all the way to my toes.

I can't use this sleeping spell. I've given myself over to the hate. I'm made of it now. It's not a concentrated mass anymore; it's uncoiled and spread through my whole body and being. And the black magic in me has latched on like a starved thing I can no longer deny. If I connect this stone, it won't just knock out every resident Moore, it will take me down too.

Coyotes mill around me. One sidles close enough to brush against my leg. They're not just here to help me their friend, they've been summoned by me the black witch. They're working out of both loyalty and fear. I've been bred to draw two magics together, and they clash inside me just as I clash in the world. I'm a freak. I'm unstoppable. I'm being ripped in half.

I stumble to the kitchen sink and barf into the drain. My earth magic is still fighting to reclaim its space. The black magic is winning. And I'm about to give in too.

A bat lands on my shirt and climbs to my neck, tangling its claws in my long braid. I'm helpless without the sleeping spell. We didn't predict this problem and had no backup plan. Without Rex I don't know who's a Moore and who's hired help. We shouldn't have split up on this mission. I need him to identify which people I should bleed and cure and which need to be disarmed and left alone.

Coyotes push against me. They've found a small staircase leading up. I take it to the second floor and recognize the hall outside the room where I was held captive. The room Grandma Sloane lived in for decades. Bats stream along the ceiling, doing the work I've demanded. Find people. Bring them to their knees.

Men rush from the opposite end of the hall. Coyotes attack as bullets fly. I raise a hand to alter their direction away from my army. They burst light bulbs and pit walls. A pull of black magic will drag more hate from that cloud and add to the poison inside me, but I do it anyway, offering a thought to the men: *Drop your weapons and go to your knees.*

They do at once.

Now lead me to Rex's mother.

They stand in unison. I follow them up a luxurious staircase to a room at the corner of the house. The door pops open at my command, and the men fearfully step back, as if this little trick is more shocking than straight-up mind control.

Leave this house and don't come back.

I go through the door into a wide room with a sofa and chairs but no people. A second set of doors opens as I will it. Coyotes trot through before me, surrounding a woman as she stands at the end of the bed as if prepared to meet me. She's an older version of the woman in the photos at my dad's cottage.

A voice inside me says, *Kill her.*

I'm not sure if it's my real voice or something else's. I'm not sure if I agree with it. But I'm looking down the sight of my pistol aimed straight at her heart.

Another voice says, *Rex's mother.*

A second bat has landed on my shoulder to join the first. I see my name on the woman's lips but my attention has been stolen by the coyotes beside her. By the trust in their eyes. They still see Sloane Bevan even though she's been taken over by black magic. They see the good in me, the part of me that's here to cure, not execute.

I holster my gun and flip out my straight razor. Stolen from this house, it's been beside me through this whole journey, like Rex himself. I can't kill his mother. Even though she's smiling at me like she's just gained some insight to hold over me.

You look like your daddy.

The words are only readable because it's exactly what goes with that look. I don't know why that would give her such creepy pleasure but whatever. I raise my pinky finger and wiggle it in the air. She loses the smile so fast I get a wave of secondhand fear. It's sympathy and it needs to be squashed; it has no place here. Taunting people must come with being a black witch, and I don't like it at all.

I love it.

Snatching the sash on her robe, I slip around her and cinch it tight around her wrists. She aims an elbow; a coyote lunges, teeth bared, and she rethinks that move. I kick the backs of her knees so she's on my level. For what she's done to my dad, she deserves pain. For her obvious neglect and abuse of Rex, she needs something worse.

Do it, the black magic says.

"No," I say aloud. Because that's not the girl my dad raised. The girl my mom nurtured. The girl they love. I won't become that no matter how right it's starting to feel.

She remains still when I slash her arm with my razor. I'm impressed by her level of chill. I draw the symbol on my forehead first so she can see what she's getting. When it's her turn she takes it stoically, a fearless mistress of evil. I'm sure she's dished out worse. Her hate swarms hard into me, knocking her to her back, sending me stumbling into the coyotes. They nip at each other, riled by the static exchange of power in the room. And I leave her there, splayed on the floor, unconscious, carrying the mark of a black witch.

Outside her room I stagger again, my knees cracking against the floor, my hand bracing against coyote shoulder blades that remain solid and strong. My stomach crumples with the bloat of what I've taken. For once I'm too sick to vomit, too overcome to fight it. When my palms hit the floor, I think of Rex, of what encouragement he'd give if he saw me succumbing when the end of our work is so near. I convert sickness into stubborn will and push myself up, my head spinning, my vision going glittery.

Another room houses an old guy sleeping through it all. I take him easily and leave him on the floor. The next, a teenage girl. She begs. I'm gentle. My army finds a perfect method: bats seek victims, coyotes rush the room, I come in and do my work. We clear one hall and then the other, go down a flight and do the same. It can't be this easy. I start to wonder why we haven't met up with Rex. This house is big, but we've cleared about half. So where is he?

Down to the main level. The bats move ahead but return with bad news: a commotion ahead. Lots of people. Some kind of fighting. I command the coyotes to wait. I need a minute. My hands are shaking, and I can't catch my breath. We've stopped in some kind of library, surrounded by another century's furniture, floor-to-ceiling bookshelves, and tall windows displaying a wide expanse of grass lit by the dawn.

A huge oak stands alone, catching morning light in its deep green leaves. It's the same oak I viewed through my window when I was captive here. The song of its magic weaves across the lawn, through the stone walls of the house, and along the floorboards. I place my cheek against the polished wood floor, drinking in the hum of its power. It's a much-needed recharge, a thirst so desper-ately quenched. I feel my old self settle back in my bones like a ghost returning to its body. Exhaustion comes alive, along with a days-old hunger for a real meal—how long has it been since I've had appetite for more than a nibble?

I have to contain this hate again, have to get its venom out of my blood. Black witches use darkness and negativity as fuel but it doesn't come from the inside. It's culled from the world, from the people around them. What I'm housing in me shouldn't be contained. I don't know how to neutralize it. It's like a swollen, infected appendix. Only a matter of time before it bursts and kills me. I've let it grow and spread and take me over. If I add any more to it, my earth magic will be poisoned and so will I.

I reach for the oak. Its power is ready and pure. I let it pour in over the darkness, forcing it back. My fist against my chest where it first settled, I draw it there, piling it together, compacting it down.

There. I breathe. Yes, let it stay there. Just for a while. Just until I can figure out what to do. Just until I finish my work, until I can die.

I turn my other cheek against the cool floor. I imagine Marcas here with me, that I'll sit up and find him. Jack-o'-lantern boy, missing both his canines. He signs in his sleep. I'm wrecked from missing him. I can't bring what's inside me back to him. If I can't leave it here and walk away, I'll leave it here safe inside my fallen body.

The sun has filled the oak now. It glows with orange morning light. I stand and breathe in the waxy wood of the room, the smell of old books. Grandma Sloane survived this house so I could return and end this war. I need to finish this now while I'm ready to die. Tomorrow I might not be.

My animals and I push ahead, into the main entrance I remember with the rounded double-tall ceilings painted like a church and a staircase from a Disney palace. Halfway through, the bats turn as one in the air, returning overhead. The coyotes halt, clustering around me. I back up when I spot people through the doorway at the opposite end of the room. One of them is Rex. He's arguing with a muscular guy twice his size.

Their argument is so heated they don't notice me at first. When they do, it only seems to add accelerant to their chemical fire. The big guy gestures toward me, and Rex meets my eyes across the wide room. This moment of distraction offers the guy a chance to pull a gun and aim at Rex's face. What follows is a command, spat out, and a chin jerked my way. Rex laughs—half a second later that big guy's gun arm is being twisted behind his back.

My coyote pack seeps into the room. Rex's half of the pack must've joined mine from the rear. He unloads the other guy's pistol into the ceiling and chucks it back at him, empty. Plaster snows down, dusting Rex's shoulders and hair. My eyes don't seem able to focus on the falling dust. I close them, pressing my knuckles against them. The reprieve of closed eyes is a moment I wish could last forever. They burn in the light when I open them. It draws my stomach upward; I hold a fist against my mouth to contain it. I can't vomit here. It would show a weakness I'd like to stay secret.

Two men stroll down the stairs, one with hair combed fresh from the shower, straightening the collar of a polo shirt. The other on his phone, crisply dressed in oxford and slacks. I recognize them at once. This "just another day" act is a show of power, of fearlessness. Their house—their whole family, centuries of their brand of power—nearly dismantled and they're still at ease. I don't buy it. My eyes are on Rex to witness his reaction. He catches something tossed from the stairs to him, takes a long moment to study it before strapping it on his wrist. Crippling doom falls hard upon me. If that's the watch he chucked into the woods he's just become more lost to me. I fingerspell his name. He looks at me blankly, uninterested.

Now the three of them stand together in the middle of the room. My memories of their faces prod a very dark, uncontrollable nerve. Dillon Moore, kidnapping me from my home. Jared Moore, dragging me up the stairs, grabbing my hair, locking me in that room. And Rex, attacking me in that bedroom in the middle of the night. He's morphed back into that Rex in my memory. The cruel, sadistic soldier. Hateful because of the lies he's been told. Ready and eager to use all his training to act on that hate, to hunt and kill what he believes is owed to him.

I can't let them talk to him. If he's not fully compromised, there's a chance to bring him back. Coyotes shift around me, restless. I call the bats from their roost on the ceiling above. They come down like a curtain as Rex nods at his father and takes a step away from the two men to glance up at the descending bats. Fear strikes low and cold. I brought my friends into this place so carelessly. No animal can be as vicious as these people surrounding me. Rex has stopped under the fluttering bats. I come forward—too late. He's already spoken a command to them I can't hear. I brace myself for mass murder but they soar up the staircase instead, a black cloud headed to the broken windows and out into the night sky.

Rex sways, bends to brace hands on knees. Appealing to animals is something I taught him, something he's not used to doing. He looks up at me. The sadist is gone. His eyes are haunted, lonely. He fingerspells, *Leave, S. I can't—*

Jared claps a hand on Rex's back, yanking him upright by a fistful of T-shirt.

I get a rush like I did when I killed that man who knifed Rex in the ribs. I hear the voice that's not mine, feel the burden of hate trembling inside me. I close my eyes and find the oak, reaching, drawing its magic over me like a warm quilt. When I see the room again, I've lost a moment. I'm on my knees being held upright by coyotes. Rex has gone dead in the eyes, and the whole room has filled with Moores and their men aiming every kind of firearm at me and my coyotes.

The Moores won't hurt the creatures of the forest. They're afraid of the consequences; they can't afford taking any hits to the little magic they still know. But they're notorious for hiring people to do their dirty work. I can affect some approaching bullets but not this many at once. The coyotes and I should've stayed in the hallways, clearing one room at a time. They can't help me against dozens of armed men who are under orders to shoot all threats.

I bid the double front doors to open. The dark carved panels burst inward, banging against the wall, knocking identical antique mirrors to the floor on each side. Broken glass floods the room. The coyotes know what I ask, but they won't leave me. They skitter around, nipping at my clothes, nudging me with annoyance at the promised fight they'll miss. But this isn't their fight. So I take a deep pull of power from the condensed mass of darkness inside me and command them as a black witch.

As they flow out the door, I turn to face the Moores. It's just me now. One against the rest; one against them all. This final battle was supposed to happen with Rex by my side. In my choice to split from my ally, I've lost him. They've sucked him back in, slapped their chains and their control back on.

I don't just need him on my side. I want him. I can't finish this without him. He's my stepping stone in the river separating life from death. I'm afraid to cross over without him. No matter which side of the river he stays on, I don't want to do it alone.

We swore in blood. That's an oath of the heart. It trumps any magic assigned to that watch. It's truer than the years of abuse and conditioning that molded him. How do I make him see that?

I focus on Rex, taking a tiny sip of magic to help me into his mind. Blueish-white electricity scatters up the walls around us, leaving ashy jagged lines in its wake. That's my work, but not my plan or consent. It wasn't at all what I wanted to do. What's cycling down inside me isn't me. I'm made of both black magic and its fuel. The ideal eco-system for unguided sentient black magic is caged inside me, and it's become powerful enough to no longer need a human practitioner. Any pull of magic will open a door to let it through. I need to lower a wedge against that door, and ready myself to shove it into place.

The muscular guy Rex disarmed earlier has more to say. He's stabbing a finger in Rex's chest, and Rex is just taking it. A woman lays a hand on the big guy's arm; he flings it away, now mouthing off at her. While they argue I shuffle toward a fireplace and try to contain my joy to see a nice bed of ash lining the bottom. When I rise I've gained the attention of more loaded weapons. I lower the neck of my shirt, smear the ash on my skin where my amulet normally hangs, and draw my family's symbol, identical to the one on my amulet. The connection rings across the room. Rex shoves the big guy away to gape at me, his hand against his shirt where my amulet hangs hidden.

Soldiers surround me. I refuse to raise my hands. This is not surrender.

Rex shakes his head as if to clear it, taking in the room like he just woke from a dream.

They're shouting commands at him, but he's locked eyes with me and won't look away. When he steps toward me, I expect someone to stop him, but perhaps they're as curious as I am. He's under their control. He's still on their side. This interest in me is nothing but an act. It can't be this easy to awaken a blood oath.

We're face to face now, his eyes on mine. I want to sign but I'm afraid it will break the world. He holds up a hand to silence someone who must've spoken, and it stays in the air, hanging, forgotten.

It's a perfect act. His eyes say nothing, when I've learned to read every thought from the million Rex Moore expressions I've catalogued. His mouth is a fixed, indistinct line, incapable of the shy grins, the smirks, the tight anger, the temptation drawing my lips in. His breath, controlled and even. The song of his magic has been muted, clamped off, unreachable. He could join me right now. He could kill me.

There are no other options, no in-betweens, and not a thing about the Rex I've learned to love exists here anymore. He's a statue, a shell. He's not my Rex.

He grabs me—I don't even counter because I have to know how far he'll take this. An arm around my shoulders, his unsheathed knife flings a glint of light. A slight jerk in the base of my scalp, and then I'm released, going into a squat with the force, fingers against the floor. No blood. Nothing hurts. Shock may have kicked in first. I'm so exhausted maybe I won't feel the pain, I'll just lie down here and bleed out.

I reach for my long braid. It's missing.

Not missing but unattached. In Rex's hand, now being tossed to Jared who tucks it into his pocket.

I've been growing that braid since my dad told me who I am. It's been cut away just like the girl I used to be. I'm a killer now—I killed that man who stabbed Rex, and right now I have a building terrible urge to kill more. To kill them all. I can pop this mass of collected hate. I can let it empower the black witch in me. Let it spin around and around in an endless cycle of centripetal force of hate powering black magic creating hate to power more black magic. No matter how much I control it or condense it or pack it into that spot in my chest, it will always be there, pushing against me, driving me to do terrible things. I should let it go. Let it spread again. Let it take me over.

Rex offers a hand to help me up. All the spells to set a person on fire evade me. The room has turned blood red. I can't just kill him. I need to torture him first.

Since I haven't accepted his hand, he lifts me by the shoulders. If I strike him now I'll break his every bone.

My teeth chatter with the effort to hold back. He's digging around in his pocket. He's leaning into my face. *Do you trust me?*

I sign, *No.* Shrieking, boiling anger keeps the tears away. Betrayal is a paralysis that keeps me still when he draws even nearer, now only inches away. His lips are so close I want him to close the distance, want him to kiss me one last time as I jam the knife I've slid from my pocket into his stomach. If I have to die, so does he. Without their next leader, the Moores will fade away. This war ends here. The Bevans will have their martyr, and the Moores will have their murdered king.

He raises his hand in the tight space between us, fingers the band of the Moores' watch. Hidden from eyes, he unlatches it, slips it off. My knife hand tingles, adrenaline reminding me of my purpose even though I've become unsure. Rex presses the watch against my chest, and I take it with my free hand, its overpowered magic hot in my palm. Rex takes a breath so huge his chest presses against mine. He snapped his chains. He broke his conditioning. His free will has been secured, from his own choice, his own power.

And in front of his family, he leans in and kisses me.

Calling a shield against bullets seems unnecessary. This is how I want to die. The sweetness of his kiss both softens and empowers me. The lurch between murderous anger and truest love sends an earthquake up my spine. I slip; he catches me by the elbows. Our lips have broken, but he kisses me again, passing me something on his tongue. In my mouth it's small, hard, slippery. One of his pills, but I'm not sure which one.

The chaos around us spills into our moment. It seems some Moores want their hands on us and others want to keep us safe for drawn-out torture later. And this is a fight about to divide them. Rex still has me by the shoulders, but he's pulled away to say, *You should trust me.*

I do now. Now and forever. I swallow the pill because I do trust him so much it hurts. I have to get him out of here. Even if I can't be saved, he needs to be free of this place so no one can ever chain him down again.

Someone's on the ground. Rex turns to watch, one of the many catalogued expressions tweaking a corner of his mouth up, sending sinister joy into his eyes. Jared has fallen to the ground. Hornets pour out of his pants pocket, filling the air, scattering the crowd. Rex tugs my hair where my braid used to be. Smiles big.

My braid—into hornets? I never agreed to that. I never taught him that either.

I can't dwell on it, though, because the magic from his pill is spreading like a flash flood. Each muscle wakes with new life, stimulated with impossible power. All fatigue and exhaustion gone. Hunger eliminated. There's a prickling in my blood; if I don't run a marathon right now, I just might explode. I'm a burst of lightning, a hurricane. The fiercest elements thrum in my blood, in muscle and bone and synapse. I'm earth magic and black magic, power half pure, half illegal, multiplied.

Shots flash around us. Rex and I duck, scooting against the wall. We unholster our guns, both chamber a round. The air contains more hornets than oxygen now, but they aren't after us. Rex ducks a flyby, curses, and ducks again. He takes my hand and starts into the room, losing the nerve at the last second. I'm not able to tell him what I'm thinking: *Your own summoned hornets won't hurt you*. But maybe he has a phobia or something. So I stand and walk into the room, dragging him behind me.

Two women are trying to escape up the stairs. Rex holds them while I bleed them and draw the symbol. Two at once is tricky, but we get it done. Rex's pill has made me so high I can't tell where I'm stashing the hate. It's an assembly line of blood, symbols, and harvested darkness. Rex supplies victims and I perform the cure. The hornets keep the guns away. Then we're running down hallways, escorted by our swarm. New rooms, new people. Men and women, young and old. A stash of children locked in an upper-floor room, compliant and less afraid of Rex than the adults. My steps are losing bounce and gaining drag.

One more, Rex says. But it's not just one more. It's a hundred.

I fall, Rex picks me up.

I watch Rex grab Jared, cut his throat. I can't figure out where we are. The room is blinding white but dark at the edges. Did I try to cure Jared already? Did it fail? Rex drops him on the floor, watches the blood puddle against his boots. He spits. Wipes a hand against his mouth. Blood on his hands, smeared up his forearms. Blood everywhere.

He comes to me. I can't. No more.

A new room. Rex's dad? Yes, Dillon Moore. His mouth is bloodied. It's all I can see. Rex walks around him. Stops. Hesitates. I can't let him kill his own father. I push away from the wall that's keeping me up. Rex's hand on my arm. I shrug him away. One more. I can do one more. I see my finger draw the symbol. I feel the hate fill me, the last space, the last bit of me, gone.

CHAPTER 30

REX

Sloane collapses in the middle of the foyer. I lift her shoulders up, cradle her head against my arm. Her eyelids haven't closed completely but her eyes have rolled all the way into her head. Like a dead person.

It's not supposed to end like this. I didn't sanction it. This house is mine now, and I say no to this.

Five minutes ago she was tearing through the house like the hornets I called, not a single girl but a swarm, in several places at once. Disabling one body, latching onto a new one a second later. Terrifying in her efficiency. Now I can't fucking find her pulse. Can't see any evidence of breathing. She's crumpled in my arms, a wadded, discarded paper. All used up.

She took on too much, and I let her. I shouldn't have let her and I don't know what to do.

I drag her onto the rug and lay her on her back. My ear against her chest, I beg to hear a heartbeat. All I hear is my own screaming, my mouth muffled against her chest. A finger against her wrist, her throat, nothing.

I take the bottle of black magic out of my pocket. This is how it was supposed to end. She can't die without my permission, not in my own house, the one I now rule, the one she helped me overthrow. I test the cork. An almost insignificant creak loosens it by a hair. The black magic swirls inside, ready, anxious. There was a time I questioned this end because I wanted to spare her. Well she hasn't been spared. Decision made. Easy.

Her skin is still warm. How long does it take for a corpse to cool? I put my ear to her chest again and really fucking listen this time. Miracles happen or we'd have no word for it.

Miracles don't happen to me.

I stand, wrap my fist around the bottle. I'm not going to uncork it. I'm going to crush it to pieces.

"Rex."

I spin. In the doorway stands my father. Ripped collar stained bloody. Swollen torn cheek, soon to be very black eye. I don't remember roughing him up so much. He raises his hands. I lower the gun I've unconsciously drawn. His eyes go to Sloane. I step in front of her, ready to blow his head off.

"Get her out of here. She's—all this…" he gestures above us, all around "…it's killing her."

"She's already dead."

He shakes his head. "But she will be if you don't get her out of here. That oak on the west lawn—can't you feel it calling?"

I notice then the pulse, the one I hoped to find in Sloane, riding toward me. It's hers but not of her. It's been stolen, preserved. I reach and trace it through the wood of the house, the earth and stone outside.

"It's…" he turns in that direction, squinting as if viewing through the walls "…I don't even know. This is all new to me."

I'm already heaving her up. New strength bursts through me. I pound down the front steps and out in the grass with her limp frame draped over my shoulders. The exiled bats dip and cry. Coyotes race across the lawn to meet me and run ahead like they're my guide, like they know what a screwup I am, that I might miss the obvious.

I lay her under the shelter of the oak. Wind gusts from nowhere. Falling leaves blanket us. I don't know any magic for this. I'm stupid and lost, and she's too dead to help me. I take her hand, flatten it against my heart, wish I could transfer my own heart to her. Wind hits me again; I prop an arm against the oak's trunk to avoid being knocked over.

Moths flutter down from the branches—a hundred, a thousand. They cloud around us, keeping their distance from the bats above. It's so much commotion, so many bodies. I need to make them leave so I can focus on Sloane, but I don't know how.

Sounds dial down and away like I've ducked underwater. There is one thing left: my heartbeat. And another sound far away, but gaining volume. A second heartbeat slowed beyond comprehension but gaining, syncing to mine. When the beats join, I feel the rough bark of the oak's trunk on my palm and pull it away. The day's sound returns: the rustle of wind, the cries of a crow above us.

Wetness shines on Sloane's cheeks. I touch it. Rain? Dew? It's smeared the makeup on her eyes. Tears. She's corpse-still but those tears are new and corpses can't cry. I breathe in, calling the elements to unite around me for the first time in my life. Please, *le do thoil*, help me. I'm not a king but a servant, and I'm begging. Restore her; make her right. Take my life in place of hers.

I lower my ear to her chest and listen. It's not real, the pulse I hear. I'm mistaken. It's mine. It's the earth's. I find her wrist, press my fingers against it. An unmistakable surge of blood. Slow, but there. So very there.

If my dad was right about this, he's right about something else: I have to get her out of here.

I don't think about where I need to take her, I just find the interstate and drive. She's strapped in and reclined in the seat next to me, but I've stretched her arm into my lap so I can check her pulse often. And by often I mean every thirty seconds. It's obsessive, but I can't help it.

Hours later I stop to hydrate because my lips have gone chapped I'm so thirsty, and she must be too. The gas station has too much activity for me, though, so I get back on the road for a few miles then pull to the shoulder. Leaning in on her side I give her a sip of water. She chokes it back up in her sleep. I hold her and scream every curse I know. She can't hear me. No one can.

It's uppers, scarfed food, and fuel stops for I don't know how many miles. I exit the interstate for nothing else. Somewhere in the Midwestern nothingness, I start hallucinating. Dusk invites ghosts into the car, their icy fingers in my hair, on my neck. Demons land on the roof, the thump of their weight nearly sending us into a spin I hit the brakes so hard. When I've swerved for the third murky pedestrian and see once more in my mirror there was nothing there, I pull to the shoulder and down the embankment, pop a downer, and crash hard into sleep.

Waking up wet with sweat next to a three-quarters dead Sloane sends me out of the car to scream again. Her pulse is barely there. An offered drink is more successful now because it just runs down her throat, her choking mechanism broken, unconsciousness plummeting deeper by the hour. With the bottom of my shirt, I dab the water that leaks from her lips. Where's that superhuman Bevan healing?

I get out of the car and holler at the sky. Me calling the shots wasn't supposed to be like this. I need someone to tell me what to do. My decisions are crap. They only lead to failure. I text Aaron: *Help.*

He calls immediately. My end is a frantic, hysterical stuttering of words, and I'm instantly ashamed.

"Go, Rex. You're doing the right thing. Hang up and drive. Go!" The line goes dead.

The right thing. Then what's the wrong thing? I take the bottle of black magic out of my pocket and watch it fold around itself in the daylight. Cracking it open at this point would be a mercy kill. Plus the end that I wanted. I look at Sloane, at her limp arm hanging out of the car, the one she slides around my stomach when she snuggles me in bed. The mega bruise on her chin she earned curing my family. Her blood-caked fingernails. And the short piece of hair on her shoulder where I severed her braid.

So I don't chuck this bottle so hard at the ground it explodes on impact, I tuck it away. I get behind the wheel, and I drive.

The land in this country never ends. The R5 is nothing but a speck blowing across it. I've covered so many miles I can't believe I haven't hit an ocean. I must've gone through a wormhole at some point, probably when I was hallucinating. Any minute I'm going to hit the eastern edge of Richmond and be right back where I started.

Sloane's pulse is bordering on pitiful. I need to sleep. I pop another upper instead. The road is razor straight, flat featureless land flanking us. We might be on another planet now. Either that, or I'm hallucinating again.

We've reached mountains but they're fake. Not just CGI, but bad CGI. They annoy me, but I can't stop looking at them.

Sloane's arm slips off my lap, and I reach for it, panicking when her wrist gives me nothing. I screech to a halt on the shoulder and check her neck, my ear against her chest, listening. I find it, but it's too weak to be a comfort.

I steer onto the road and hit the gas. Eighty feels like sixty. A hundred feels like eighty. It's just not enough. And the silence in the car has been painful for so long I'm afraid I might off myself just to end it.

There's a mailbox on the road next to a gravel driveway leading into the forest. The pines at the opening look more like guards than trees. I take the turn anyway. Time is running out.

The R5's nose dives as the road pitches down. It's a severe descent straight into premature night. I flip on my headlights because the shadows are deep and we've lost the light from the sky.

A black car heads toward us. Camaro versus R5—it's a game of chicken at gravel-road pace which means plenty of time to decide who's going to yield and who isn't. We end up stopped nose to nose. I put it together. Black Camaro ZL1—it's him. It's gotta be him. I am so about to die.

He gets out, all twenty feet of him. He's as massive and angry as I imagined. I try to forget how many people he's killed. He's an old man, Rex. Yeah, the kind of old man who's seen so much brutal shit he's no longer human.

I climb out with my hands up because I'm not stupid. I wish I had a shotgun trained on him. No, two. That'd be bad, though, because right now my prey-animal pulse would be coercing my trigger finger to squeeze and I need his help.

He's closer now. I can clearly see his eyes. Behind them lay the ruins of a decade's long, hard-fought war, and he's the last man standing. Is he the war hero or the criminal? Unconfirmed. He wears crazy like it's normal, unnoticeable, like *move along, nothing to see here*. Only you can't.

And I finally understand why my family hates him. Why he's untouchable. Unstoppable. It's not just who he is but what he is. That thing that sparks our hate matches a fear buried a million miles deep in my subconscious that I never felt until now. What he's made of has been encoded into my blood, a genetic memory passed down. He's both enemy and victor. Indestructible because it's true, because no one's tried, we're all too afraid, and our ancestors passed all that down to us. Fear creates hate creates war.

He ducks, checking the inside of my car.

"She's..." I want to say dying but figure that would be bad to say right now. "I need help."

He rips open the door and lifts her out. He takes off down the driveway past his car, and I stay put, unsure what the hell to do.

Over his shoulder, he says, "In front of me where I can see you."

Orders. Good. I'm used to that. I lead the way, my pace fast enough for my boots to scatter gravel, but he keeps up fine even with Sloane's weight.

No longer alone in my screaming worry for her, I take the first actual lung-filling breath in days. The air is cool, unweighted. Stories-high pine trees create a gauntlet around us. I'm too fascinated at seeing Sloane's place of origin to think about how stupid it is I'm not in my car right now getting out of this. He's occupied. He won't drop her to pursue me. I could totally get away.

A cabin comes into view, dwarfed and mobbed by all the pines. Everything my family said is true. They do live in the woods with the animals. They are common, content with their crude lives and savage ways. And right now I'm wondering why any of that's a bad thing. Sloane's spirit is here. I sense it all around me. Her confidence. Her defiance. Her clear sense of right and wrong. Her connection to the elements so present here it's like the magic itself is being fed.

The porch is as far as I'm going. I take a seat on the wood pile and get out my phone, pretending I have people to contact. At the door he pauses for my attention. Some power makes me look up even though I don't want to. His face promises death if I try any shit. I don't want to see the rest of the scene: Sloane's dead limbs, her knotty neglected hair, her eyelids only half closed even though she's unconscious. He takes a long, stalkerish look at the burn scar on my arm. As he turns to go in, I get this weird vibe that he totally understands. More than Emily and Aaron. More than Sloane.

I text Aaron, *Made it. And he hasn't killed me yet.*

How is she?

Not good. Alive though. And in much better hands than my own.

Keep me posted.

Two dogs tear across the front yard and cut around the house. I get up, go to the edge of the porch, and look up past the eave at the trees towering over us. I can't get over these trees. From the road it's one thing. Standing underneath them? Completely sick. Fantasyland, and I wonder for a second if I'm hallucinating. My last nap and meal happened a billion miles ago.

I take the bottle of black magic out of my pocket and wrap my fingers around it.

The door opens. It's him again. "Why."

Is that a question? And how do I figure out the rest of it? Somehow I think it needs some kind of answer from me—fast—so I'm going to go with *Why did you come here?* "Had nowhere else to go."

"You're not fucking welcome in my house."

I extend my arm like a bridge between us. In my sleep deprived vision it happens in severe slow motion. Or maybe that's my brain trying to slow down the insanity displayed in front of it: my open palm, the offered bottle.

This wasn't planned. I don't even know what I'm doing. A peace offering? Maybe. Proof of my goodwill? No one would believe it even with the bottle. Reality is I just don't want the thing anymore. It's a knife in the back every time I think of it. I want it away from me.

He looks at the bottle for so long I'm afraid there's something wrong with me. The pills, hunger, and sleep deprivation have finally caught up and this is the first symptom: slow-mo vision. I wonder how I'll ever drive the R5 again.

Staring. So much staring. He finally takes it but won't stop looking at me, intense as all get-out. I need those two shotguns. Or maybe it would be better just to run. No way this guy raised Sloane. She's much too sane.

"I'm good with the wood pile." I say it to get us back to before that exchange so I no longer have to think about the power I just surrendered. I'd return to my comfy-as-hell seat to drive it in, but I don't really want to lose my balanced stance right now. And keeping my ground and my eyes on his is proof of something, I'm just not sure what. I'm not about to lose this contest, though, that's for sure.

He goes back in the house. I wish I'd asked him to tell me when she's better, because I have a hunch he wouldn't mind leaving me out here forever. I sit on the edge of the porch. And whoa, those trees. The breeze crinkles through them. They sway, just enough to flaunt their deadly might should one of them decide to come down.

Two women walk into view on the road. I'm tempted to hide before they see me because at this distance one of them looks frighteningly like my mother. They don't appear to be dressed for a hike, but oh yeah, the driveway's blocked. They had to park and walk. Neither say anything as they pass by and go into the house. The granny gives me a thoughtful look-over. The other one isn't so much like my mother close up. And from the hostile look she gives me, I gather she hates me more than my mother, which is a pretty major thing.

Alone again, I rest my head on my knees and close my eyes, breathing this damn perfect air, wishing I could get in the R5 and shoot out of here. Impossible without knowing she's okay first. Impossible without saying goodbye.

He comes out again about an hour later. "I need details."

No, he really doesn't. Not the details I'm thinking about right now. Like that absent way she'd sneakily slide her hand in mine, almost like she didn't think I'd notice, or was afraid of what I'd do if I did. Or how she'd lean forward a little when I'd try to sign. How she'd just go with it, not correcting me, not criticizing. She'd figure it out and respond and not say a damn thing about how stupid I am. Or how I'm wondering if it's possible for a fifteen-year-old to have a heart attack because I can't sit here anymore and guess at whether she's improving or not. My heart is fit to explode.

"I need to know what got her into this state."

So he doesn't know what's wrong? Not comforting at all. I thought Bevans were supposed to know everything.

"She cured my family—all of them. Stole their hate. So it's stuck inside her now, and—"

"She stole their what?"

"Hate. It's some kind of black magic thing. I don't really know."

He turns away from me, stares across the yard. Coyotes slip from the forest as if summoned, awaiting orders. "You're saying she's full of Moore evil?"

"Yeah." And it needs to come out now. Doesn't he know how to get it out of her? "It's used by black magic, but I don't think she knows how to use it, or—"

"She didn't want to release it back into the world."

I nod at him. I don't even think I realized that. He goes back inside.

And something occurs to me. All that hate was contained in a whole bunch of people. Now it's in her. It needs a new carrier. A new host. It's only fair that Moore evil go back into a Moore. And just like that, my purpose is laid before me. It's meant to be. It's written into prophesy. One of us destroys the other. I—my family—tried to destroy her and failed. That's proof it should be me. I'm the one to be destroyed.

I bang on the door. A different woman, with Sloane's thick dark hair, her long bangs—only cut even, not rebellious. Holy oak, Sloane's mother. I'm momentarily speechless, too fascinated to have Sloane's home life so easily revealed. I used to dream about coming here. Not like this, though, as a peon waiting on the porch. Something more along the lines of home invasion slash mass murder.

"I'm sorry, Rex, I wish I could—" She turns to glance inside the house as if checking to see if she can get away with something.

"I need to talk to him again."

She disappears. He returns in her place.

"Put it in me," I say.

He comes outside with me, closes the door.

"It belongs to my family. It should be mine. Put it in me." I hate how desperate I sound. Be a man, Rex. Don't screw this up.

His eyes turn to slits and he leans into me, just enough to make me want to step back. "What is this?"

I stay put. Try to appear at ease. "I'm not who you think I am. Not anymore, anyway."

He starts to say something, rubs a hand over his mouth instead. It shouldn't be so unsettling.

"It's too much for one kid to handle," he says finally.

"But not for your daughter?"

Scrutiny comes again, so intense I wonder if those five words gave away more than I wanted to. Controlling the gritty desperation in my voice has defeated me. I'm too exhausted, too sober. I need both an upper and a downer.

I need a year of sleep. And yeah, I'm desperate. Desperate beyond words.

He reaches. I flinch against the shoulder squeeze I only ever get from Aaron, too shocked to move away. He's probably altered it just enough to pinch some hidden nerve that'll cause my brain to slowly swell and kill me in my sleep. I'm tragically in love with his daughter. He probably should kill me.

The door opens. Is that Christian Moore? My luck can eat shit.

"Everything okay out here?" he asks, glancing between me and him.

I'm not going to answer such a complicated question. Apparently no one is.

"Why don't you two bring it inside? You're making the ladies nervous. They seem to think you need supervision."

We say nothing. Christian goes back in the house, watching me as he closes the door like I'm a victim he can't save. I don't need saving. It's Sloane who needs help. I drove her here because this is her last hope. Someone needs to do something. *I* need to do something, if only he'll let me.

"If you want to take this on, I won't stop you," he says.

"You have to tell me how."

He turns away, knocking a fist against his leg. The coyotes are back, nearly invisible in the thick grounded darkness that's overtaken all I can see. If not for the white light of a waxing gibbous moon, I'd have no idea I was being stalked by so many eyes. They left for a while, but they're here now like they need a briefing. Yes, I'm still here. Yes, I'm still not welcome. No, your queen is not awake yet.

He pushes into the house, holding the door open for me. I don't move because c'mon, I'd rather spare myself from that bucket of awkward. Then he jerks his head and I'm marching in as if that motion was a crack of a whip. The warmth inside is bliss. I'm suddenly aware of how hunched and stiff I've become against the chill out there. He takes me into a microscopic kitchen and makes me sit in a chair at the table. The woman who walked down the driveway comes in to replace him, taking up a position against the countertop. Arms crossed, hostile look even more serious than before.

"Are you my keeper?"

She says nothing. In the reflection of the sliding glass door, I see him and the granny go into a door. Their feet creak on stairs, moving down and away. I pretend I'm not under sadistic surveillance and allow my shoulders to slump, my arms to settle on the table, and my head to crash on top.

I wake up jumping from the chair. It's just me and him again. Someone's killed all the lights, leaving only a dim bulb on over the stove. He sets something on the table. I blink and rub my eyes so it comes into focus: two small cubes wrapped in brown paper and tied with a string.

He offers a folded piece of paper to me. I take it. Open it. Spell words in Irish.

"Do you want to get some sleep before you do this?"

"I just did."

I pick up the two wrapped cubes. He leads me out of the room, down a narrow hall, and stops at a closed door. It's only about ten paces, the house is so small.

With his hand on the knob, he turns to me. "I know Sloane trusts you. She gave you that." He points at the lump under my shirt made by the amulet. No idea how he knew that was there. It's been hidden the whole time. "Don't let her down."

It's the extended pause afterward that gives the statement so much threat. I say nothing because I don't trust my stupid mouth.

We enter a room of flickering candlelight and rippling shadow. Sloane lies flat on her back on a tiny bed against the wall. A little kid sleeps curled next to her legs like a dog. Her mother sits in a chair at the bedside, her hand resting on Sloane's limp one.

"We took a shortcut with the magic. Her grandmother seems to think your minds are already bound."

Since I'm sure both confirming and denying that would get me in trouble somehow, I stay quiet. And I'm also not sure Sloane would want him to know she drew a black magic symbol on my forehead and hers, or how many times she's done that on others.

He goes to her. Brushes her bangs aside, kisses her forehead. Then he picks up the sleeping boy and follows Sloane's mother out of the room.

I unwrap both cubes. Part her lips, tuck one inside on her tongue. Take one on mine. Then I read the words from the paper, and I'm drawn in and away so fast I'm not sure if I've finished them or not.

My limbs dissolve. I have no sense of up or down. But there's a familiar sensation all around, burying me. I push and kick and dig and—there. There. I think her name but I can't sound it out. My tongue doesn't work right in this world.

The familiar blanket of hate hits me hard. Instead of struggling against it, I make a blind grab, pulling it in like tug-of-war with an imaginary force. It spills in, familiar yet foreign. An old part of me I've learned to live without, returning like an old friend. I yank and gather and tug and there, back there, it's her. She's there, she's behind all this. I need to suck it in and away and free her, make her right again.

Resistance. No, Sloane, quit that. I dig in my heels and take more, more, more. It's clearing up what I see ahead. I'm weighted and buried, but I keep fighting until it's all mine, gathered into me, stolen from her.

I'm on all fours, gagging, choking, gripped by a savage, invisible creature. My body's trying to throw it off like an opponent in the ring but it's a no-go. I've lost this one. I need to just let it have me.

I get to my feet, still bent, crippled under the toxic mass swarming in my guts, my blood. I reach for a dresser to stabilize myself but my arm slips, bringing objects crashing to the floor.

She's sitting up in bed.

My vision doesn't last long enough to enjoy it. I'm on all fours again, feeling the floor but not seeing it. I need to see her, to get some kind of payoff for this mess I'm in. I crawl to where I think the bed is and hit something soft. Then I feel hands on my arms, her hair brushing my cheek. She's helping me up. It's just enough to get my feet under me. She pulls me toward her. I drop onto the bed.

Her arms around my neck. The tip of her nose pressing in. Her smell, her smell.

Inside, the mass presses in, crowding my chest, my heart. Expanding down both arms that are now shoving her. I try to control the level of shove but it gets away from me.

"Away," I choke out. "You have to get away."

It's taking over again. Replacing that bright ecstasy that lights up with her smell with things I've been taught. Stories I've been told. My training. Our hate.

She reaches. I stand, stumble away. Get my hand on the doorknob, twist it open, fall into the hall.

I'm in their house. Here to save their daughter but majorly unwelcome. I drove across a fucking country for them and this is the hospitality I get? My boots can't get any traction on this floor, and I need to get up, get out. I crawl out the end of the hall then use a nearby armchair to help me stand.

He materializes in the doorway to the kitchen, Sloane's mother behind him. Not even a thanks from Bevan trash for what I've done for them. I make a break for the front door, falling against it, twisting the knob. I miss the step and I'm down again, rolling off the edge of the porch.

I just need to stop fighting. Embrace it. This isn't just hate but power. It's what drives us, what fuels our survival.

Without it we'd be as pathetic as the Bevans, living like savage animals, content in our inferiority.

It spreads through me, a cool perfection. The comfort of an easier time. A favorite jacket found at the back of a closet, shrugged on, zipped up, fitting even better than before. I'm upright now. I feel righteous. I'm glowing. The trees are bending at the tops but fuck them. They won't come down. Not on me. I'll set them on fire.

Feet pound gravel behind me. I spin, annoyed I left every weapon in the car. It's only her, though, one hand raised, spelling my name. If only the return to normalcy could've purged all that knowledge too. Recognizing the letters is a complication I don't need right now.

She reaches. I take a step back. I'm surprised I don't need to kill her anymore. The return to normalcy didn't fix that either. I'll have to work on that. She tightens her mouth like she's clamping down on tears. I'm washed through with some kind of stomach-gushing panic. It might change something if she does any more of that. I need to go.

Too late though. She's surged forward, her arms around my torso, her face against my chest. My new stable ground shifts, crumbles beneath me. She's eroding it. I can't return to that crippled mess I was inside that house. I peel her arms, pry her loose. Shove her back. "I have to go."

Big tears now. Her eyes are endless wells. I turn away and walk off the panic, ignore the gush that floods me with each pound of my heart. It's an illusion. She's done this to me, and it will only get worse until I get far away.

The R5 is waiting, boxed in by those two cars. I inch out and around, floor it up the hill to the road. Think about home. Don't think about her. Drive, Rex. Drive.

SLOANE

T HE SUMMER SOLSTICE arrives too fast for what I'm about to do. Five years of crafting magic will finally be put to the test, and I'm not ready. Nervous stalling would've gone on forever, though, so yes, today's the day. No more excuses, no more waiting.

I pack my supplies into the trunk of my hand-me-down Camaro. These last couple years spent living so far from my family would've been more lonely without such a familiar piece of my dad here, even though I'm living in his cottage. The version of him who lived in this house has been purged with every room I've painted and each light fixture I've replaced. Cottage chic has replaced dated and depressing. Instead of hauling away the old abandoned furniture, I updated knobs and colors and polished with new life. Hand-sewn gossamer curtains now hang in every room along with Marcas' framed artwork, surprising me in the mail one piece at a time. On every wall is a view of home. Pencil-sketched coyotes, their expressions captured with precision. Dappled sunlight sparkling through the pines in full color. Each time I start feeling lonely, he sends a new one.

Aaron hired a crew to rehab the cottage's exterior with new white siding, mint green shutters, and a copper roof. He tried to hire landscapers too, but I wanted to clean up the yard myself. The overhaul of my dad's rose garden took the two full years I've lived here to return to health, and it wouldn't please me so much if someone else had done the work. And new last year: a vegetable garden to rival my dad's. We trade pictures of our harvests, a contest he always lets me win. I think he's only showcasing his runts.

I slam the trunk lid and go back inside for my family's texts, now packed full of bookmarks and sticky notes. On top I lay my notebook filled with the handwriting of four different Bevans: mine, Dad's, Aunt Tara's, and Grandma Sloane's. Once we arrived at a breakthrough, I took the group effort over as my own, perfecting the magic until it couldn't fail. I have only one chance. I don't think I'll get another.

Sitting beside the stack of my notebook and family's texts, I start the Camaro's engine and lower the windows to release the buildup of steamy Virginia heat. Someday I'll return to my cool mountain air. But first, I have a job to do.

I drive with the windows down, allowing the wind to tangle my hair. Heat from the engine seeps through the vents. The killer temperature and beating wind keep me distracted from where I'm going and what I'm about to do.

The drive is much too short. And also a million years long.

Ivy has consumed the wrought-iron gate at the entrance of the estate, the Moore nameplate overtaken, choked out. I pull next to the access keypad and tap in Aaron's code. The gates swing open. Ahead, the driveway is nearly overgrown with underbrush spilling from the forest. No longer the landscaped perfection in my memory, this place has become a forgotten ruin.

At the end of the driveway the house sits proudly, even though it's stained with disrepair. Weeds cling to stone walls, climbing so high into the heat they've gone dry and brown. Dirt and grime dull the window panes. It's as sad and uncared for as my cottage when I first moved in. It looks like I might have another house to rehabilitate here too, on a much larger scale.

I park the Camaro out front and gather my stack of texts. Up close, I see some maintenance has been going on. The front steps are clean and the doors have a shiny coat of polish. That could be Aaron's doing. But some of the tiles have broken out of the porch floor, and the wooden ceiling panels hang loose. Clearly he's not here enough to make a dent in what needs to be done. And since all but one person have moved out, there aren't any others to demand the lawn be mowed or the mold be washed off the house. Rex released most of the staff without consulting Aaron. He's a king over no one, with self-prescribed captivity and seclusion as his only friends.

Which is why I'm surprised when a man opens the door and relieves me of my stack of texts. He speaks; I point to my ears and shake my head. On my phone's screen I see, *It's nice to have a visitor. Is Mr. Moore expecting you?*

If I didn't already know how lonely this place has become, I'd easily gather it from the surprise he's unable to smooth from his face. I shake my head and type my name into my phone, wondering if I should use a fake one. Rex will probably tell the man to make me leave. But no, I'm not playing games. I'm here to see him, and if I have to fight my way to him, I will.

Anything in the car to be brought in?

A few boxes in the trunk. I hand him my car key.

Mr. Moore won't come down for visitors, so we must go to him.

I nod. It's perfect really. He won't be warned. I wonder if this man knows Rex'll turn me away, so he's conveniently removed that option. He leads me up the stairs to the third floor, one story higher than the one that held me captive five years ago. I remember little from this house, perhaps because I never saw it in daylight with an unburdened mind. The man drops me at a set of doors at the farthest corner of the house. Carved into the door is a wreath encircling the letter M, vines twisting all around. He knocks, opening the door to call inside. A moment later he gestures for me to enter.

It's this simple? I was prepared to fight dragons in moats.

I pocket my phone and take my stack from the man before he leaves. I cross a large room, its furniture covered in ghostly sheets. A second set of doors waits, slightly open, darkness painting the crack between them. I've been ignoring my pounding heart until now. Its spasm moves front and center, makes my palms sweat, steals all my attention. I shift my stack, nearly dropping it.

Today is the summer solstice. Today is the day I do this.

I shoulder open the door. It's so dark my first glance goes to the bed to check for a sleeper. Covers pulled tight, it's empty. A figure moves in the corner. I set my texts on a nearby table in order to free my hands. Even though my eyes are adjusting to the dark, I'm dying to flip on a light, to yank those heavy curtains back and let in the sunlight. It's not healthy to spend a summer day in a room like this.

The figure rises from a chair, and I'm jolted by the shock of my own mistake. It's not him. This man doesn't match the Rex I know. He's too tall, too thin. I feel up the base of a lamp and switch it on to witness my mistake in the light and yes, it's not him. His hair is too shaggy, his face too drawn.

But I see my name on his lips like he recognizes me. I see him take an uncontrolled step forward. I see him stop himself from taking another as if jolted by his own mistake. So I sign his name, my heart ready to choke me, my tears way too close. I'm drowning in the density of air in this room, unable to get a full breath.

He raises a hand, signs the letter S.

I go to the windows then, yanking back the heavy fabric so we're both bathed in sunlight. He turns quickly away; I close my eyes, allowing the light seeping through my eyelids to help them readjust. And when I reopen them he's facing me, the rise and fall of his chest as rapid as mine.

He runs a hand through his hair, combing it back. Long pieces fall back into his face but he doesn't bother fixing them. With the haunted eyes and undisciplined hair in this sorrowful old room, he appears to have traveled from a different time. He's a medieval knight. A ruined king. Imprisoned, starved. In mourning.

I'm here, I sign. *I'm going to help you.*

He signs, *Why?*

My breath catches. That was ASL, not fingerspelling. Okay, maybe he remembers the sign. But he also understood me, which is a bit harder to accept. Especially after five years.

Because I swore a blood oath to return you to normal. And I finally figured out how.

He signs, *I am normal.*

ASL again. The unexpectedness of it throws a rock in the gears of my head, of my carefully rehearsed plan. He's waiting for a response from me, and I can't screw this up. So I gather myself up and remember why I'm here. He's *not* normal. I know the normal Rex; I also know the one who's buried under a mountain of hate.

I unpocket the small apothecary bottle, the only part of my work provided by my black witch consultant. Inis said the only way my magic would succeed was if she provided a *dubhealaín*-blessed container sanctioned by a full-blooded black witch. That wasn't the surprise. The surprise was she actually came through. And both my dad and Tara owe me money.

Unlike the bottle Rex remembers, this one is empty, waiting. Ready to be filled with what now fills him. As the idea dawns on his face, a dusky shadow crosses over him.

He points to the door, anger settling hard like it was always there. Like the shock and relief that greeted me a moment ago was only an altered version of the dream I've repeated for years in my own head.

Since I don't obey, he closes the distance. One rude clutch on my arm, I'm spun toward the door, dragged a step forward before I jerk free. He tries again; I knock his arm away.

There is no 'no,' I sign. *Only yes.*

No, he signs.

I just look at him because that's not an option.

He fingerspells, *Don't.*

Don't stop? It's an unfair play, but I've lost control here, and I've rushed forward to wrap arms around him faster than I can stop myself. My capacity for missing him has been so brutally reached. My tank is full. In front of him now, in flesh, not in dreams, I can't live without him anymore, no matter how ruined he is.

Instead of resisting he grabs my head, tilts it to face him. The catalyst of our mingled breath ignites the connection we once shared, bottled for so many years. I lift to my toes and he leans down. Never has a kiss been so hateful and anguished, so vengeful, so punishing. He's out to prove how far gone he is, how cruel, how unfixable. And I kiss him back, my love to match his hate, my hope to conquer his despair.

When he draws away, he places a finger against my lips as if to quiet them. He notices my braid then, not yet as long as the one he severed but soon it will be. His finger runs down its length with such reverence I have to stop him. And I press the empty bottle against his chest where

I know the mass of hate aches cold. That hate was once mine, and I'm here to take it back. This war between our families will not reach its end until our mutual enemy is imprisoned in its glass forever.

Rex Moore, I sign. *Will you end this war with me?*

He kisses me again, so tenderly it nearly breaks my heart.

He raises an S and signs, *Yes.*

DEAR READER,

THANK YOU FOR reading *The Alignment Series*! I hope you enjoyed reading it as much as I enjoyed writing it. It's been an eight-year journey of many, many hours and I wouldn't change a thing. I don't think these characters will ever fade from my head, so I have no idea what the future holds. I do have plans for new worlds and new characters, so be sure to subscribe to kaycamden.com to receive updates on my writing progress and other news.

If you liked this book—or even if you didn't—please consider leaving a review. All reviews help, and indie readers count on them because we don't have big publishers promoting our work. And please tell your friends! All my ebooks are lendable, so pass them along!

Are you on Goodreads? Send me a friend request!

I love to hear from readers! Email me at kay@kaycamden.com

Again, thank you for reading. Our time is valuable and finite and there are far too many good books to read. Thank you for choosing mine!

—*Kay*

ACKNOWLEDGMENTS

My thanks go to—

Debra, who's supported this series from the pathetic first draft of book one and helped guide me into being the writer I am today.

Clara, for providing the soundtrack and musical inspiration for this book, future books, and life in general. \m/ forever!

Dr. Bill and his website lifeprint.com and ASL University.

Authors of books that helped in my research of Deafness: Thomas Spradley, Brandi Rarus, Marc Marschark, Peter Hauser, Oliver Sacks.

Elsa S. Henry and K. Tempest Bradford and the *Writing the Other* class series.

Countless online resources for Deafness that I wasn't diligent enough to make note of.

The ILF. *Go raibh míle maith agaibh.*

My readers, who took a chance on an unknown author and followed me this far. Thank you for turning pages until the end, and for believing in these characters as much as I do. Thank you for your support, your reviews, your email messages, and most of all for giving this story life in your heads.

the
ALIGNMENT SERIES

The Alignment
The Two
The Oak and the Moon
The Catalyst
The Warrior

www.ingramcontent.com/pod-product-compliance
Lightning Source LLC
Chambersburg PA
CBHW031928110726
47902CB00001B/82